PENGUIN CANADA

THE SILENCES OF HOME

CAITLIN SWEET is the author of *A Telling of Stars*. She lives in Toronto with her husband and their two daughters. *The Silences of Home* is the prequel to *A Telling of Stars*.

ALSO BY CAITLIN SWEET

A Telling of Stars

The Silences of Home

CAITLIN SWEET

PENGUIN
CANADA

PENGUIN CANADA

Published by the Penguin Group

Penguin Group (Canada), 10 Alcorn Avenue, Toronto, Ontario, Canada M4V 3B2
(a division of Pearson Penguin Canada Inc.)

Penguin Group (USA) Inc., 375 Hudson Street, New York, New York 10014, U.S.A.
Penguin Books Ltd, 80 Strand, London WC2R 0RL, England
Penguin Ireland, 25 St Stephen's Green, Dublin 2, Ireland (a division of Penguin Books Ltd)
Penguin Group (Australia), 250 Camberwell Road, Camberwell, Victoria 3124, Australia
(a division of Pearson Australia Group Pty Ltd)
Penguin Books India Pvt Ltd, 11 Community Centre, Panchsheel Park,
New Delhi – 110 017, India
Penguin Group (NZ), cnr Airborne and Rosedale Roads, Albany, Auckland 1310,
New Zealand (a division of Pearson New Zealand Ltd)
Penguin Books (South Africa) (Pty) Ltd, 24 Sturdee Avenue, Rosebank, Johannesburg 2196,
South Africa

Penguin Books Ltd, Registered Offices: 80 Strand, London WC2R 0RL, England

First published 2005

1 2 3 4 5 6 7 8 9 10 (RRD)

Publisher's note: This book is a work of fiction. Names, characters, places and incidents either are the product of the author's imagination or are used fictitiously, and any resemblance to actual persons living or dead, events, or locales is entirely coincidental.

Manufactured in the U.S.A.

LIBRARY AND ARCHIVES CANADA CATALOGUING IN PUBLICATION

Sweet, Caitlin, 1970–
The silences of home / Caitlin Sweet.

ISBN 0-14-301681-4

I. Title.

PS8587.W387S54 2005 C813'.6 C2004-905384-1

Visit the Penguin Group (Canada) website at **www.penguin.ca**

For my grandfather, Lew E. Oakley, with love

The Silences of Home

Prologue

It is only now, as I begin my chapter about Queen Galha, that the immensity of my task has become clear. "Choose among the deeds of every queen," my own Queen commanded me, "and craft for me one tome in which these will be documented. Do not linger overlong on any single queen, for the greatness of the line must be seen to have been shared equally."

I have read consort-scribe Malhan's scrolls in the vast library that echoes with silence. I have watched children launching parchment ships in fountains and listened to their chatter. All of these words, written and spoken, are of one queen only: Queen Galha, who led her fleet across the Eastern Sea in pursuit of vengeance; Queen Galha, only inheritor of Sarhenna the First's mindpowers; Queen Galha, whose reign saw the expansion of the Queensrealm to the very edges of the world. I do not know how I will be able to choose among these achievements. I have filled pages with writing, effortlessly, until now. Now I sit in the darkness of this empty library with an empty page before me and cannot make a beginning. She was too great, and I am too small, and my only desire is to read of her exploits again and again, until the morning finds me.

Book One

ONE

Leish was very young when he first heard the land beyond the sea. He was swimming with his brother Mallesh, darting and drifting among the bones of the abandoned city by the shore. Leish heard the familiar singing of this shallow water, and of the land of earth and green above—a singing he had known from the time his body had slipped free of his mother's. He heard the thread of the river that twined inland; he heard the distant hills and forests he had never seen. These farther places were more difficult to find and hold, and some selkesh were well past childhood before they could do so. Leish had heard them before he spoke his first words—and he had heard other places, as well, that no one else could. But none of the singing of his life prepared him for what he heard that day in the Old City, in the sky-clear water at the edge of the great sea.

He was not trying to listen. He was stirring the water to froth behind him so that Mallesh would not be able to grip an ankle or foot. He was also giggling, sending bubbles dizzily up to break in the sunlight. And then, as he twisted around the porous pink of an ancient tower, he heard it and was still. Mallesh lunged up toward him, grinning and reaching, but he stopped when he saw his brother's face. "What?" he motioned. A few moments later, when they lay panting on the moss-patched sand, he said again, "Leish—what? What is wrong?"

Leish gazed up at the sky, *his* sky, brushed with leaves and blossoms and a wind that was always cool, and knew that he would not be able to explain. "I heard …" he said, and swallowed. He felt his limbs trembling, as if he had been swimming for days or had dived too deep. "I heard a new place. A very … faraway place."

Mallesh sat up. "Really? Farther than the peaks, or the lakes old Radcian hears when it's storming?"

Leish looked up into Mallesh's face, which was dark because the sky behind it was so bright, nearly white with sun. "No, not that way. The other way. Across—*there*." He was sitting now as well, pointing at the ocean that rolled gently and forever away. Or not always gently, but forever, yes, this was known and told, this was a truth.

Mallesh blinked at Leish's finger. "But—" he said—only that, for suddenly Leish was filled with words, none of them exactly right but all of them urgent.

"I heard sand—but not like this—and stone—but not like ours—and a place so dry that there is no green and hardly any water at all above the ground, except somewhere that is white and so tall ..." He could not hear it now. Even as he spoke, he felt sand and stone and white-blue dazzle blurring, roar dwindling to trickle.

"We must tell this to everyone."

"No," Leish said, for although the song was silence, he could still feel its power—coiled or crouching—and was afraid.

"Don't you realize what you've heard?" Mallesh demanded, standing up, gesturing at the water. "This is the song Nasran foretold, when she first led our people out of the sea. She said there would be another far-song someday, and another leader who would bring our people to glory."

Leish said "No" again, but Mallesh did not seem to hear him.

"Imagine what would have happened if Nasran had not told our people about the singing *she* heard! Where would we be?" He was waiting for Leish to speak now.

Leish rose to stand beside his brother, licking his lips to moisten them even though the salt taste made his tongue sting. "We'd still be down there, swimming all the time like the yllosh."

Mallesh nodded. "We would never have ventured from water to land. We would never have heard all the songs of above and below. We would never have replaced yllosh-scales with this skin that is so soft and yet so strong." Mallesh did not look at Leish as he spoke, but Leish looked at him. At his flushed cheeks, his lips that seemed to curl around words the way fingers curled around a stone. At his eyes. "Nasran heard the land and spoke of it, and a brave band followed her to it. She said there'd be another song of change someday—and now you've heard it. You must speak too."

"I'm not Nasran," Leish said as another fear began to hum beneath all the songs he knew.

In the end, Mallesh spoke for him. He stood on the green stone that rose from the gathering pool. Leish sat on the moss at the pool's edge. The tiers of half-circle benches were scattered with people, mostly other children but some parents as well, including Mallesh and Leish's. They had not allowed Mallesh to invite anyone else. "If everyone came to each of your speeches," their mother, Danna, had said, "no one would ever leave the gathering pool. I am amazed that your father and I get anything done." She and Noral were sitting on the bench closest to Leish. He did not look at them. He stared at the carvings in the wood beneath them—scenes of Nasran and her descendants, images of near places and far ones, heard and carved by generations of selkesh.

Mallesh looked quite small atop the great stone, but his words were loud and firm, and the children stopped their whispering to listen. (*Like they always do when he talks,* Leish thought, with envy and admiration that were already old.) He spoke for much longer than he had earlier that day. Of Nasran, of course, who had heard the song of earth and trees and rivers, and inflamed her followers with a desire for change and greatness. She had led these brave followers out of the sea depths. They breathed the air and still breathed the water, still heard the singing that none of the drylanders could hear. They fought battles with these drylanders, who had been on the hard earth before them, and despite their lesser numbers and their newness to the air, the selkesh won these battles. They had lived well ever since, along the seacoast and the rivers that branched inland. Never since Nasran, though, had there been one who could hear songs of great distance.

Leish shifted as his own name was spoken once, twice, over and over. He wanted to slip into the pool and circle quietly beneath until Mallesh had finished. He wanted to leap to his feet and cry out that he had heard nothing really, that the strange noises of his mind had only *seemed* like singing. He also wanted to stand beside Mallesh on the stone and nod and look wise and perhaps describe a snippet of the song in order to amaze the children and his parents. Instead, he listened only, and gazed at the bench carvings, and tried to silence his fear.

"It could be," Mallesh said, so slowly and precisely that those assembled knew his speech was drawing to a close, "that this song will lead the selkesh to a new place—somewhere exciting and strange, where our lives will change. Leish will be our guide to this place. He *will* hear the song again. We must be ready when he does."

The children clapped, then began to drift away. A few of them lingered, muttering and glancing at Leish, but no one approached him. Some of Mallesh's friends leapt onto the stone and declaimed loudly about nothing, until Mallesh threw pebbles at them. Then they all disappeared into the nearby river.

"Leish." He looked up at his father. His mother, he suddenly saw, was kneeling on the moss beside him. "I sometimes fear that Mallesh loves the sound of his own voice more than he loves the truth. So tell us—was there much truth in his words today?"

Leish had no voice at all now. He swallowed hard and nodded, and as his mother laid her palm against his cheek, he began to cry.

~

The wind is hot, the sand is hot—hot as flame, or ocean roaring with volcanic steam. The stone too must be hot, though it sounds cool: white-blue or clear, ringing and chiming and sighing where the water touches it. Water, bubbling from so far below that its song has no beginning, only a gentle faint murmur where it winds in sand, and then a slow blooming, a faster rush like birds' wings, and it bursts into the basins and troughs that lie in the sun beneath the towers.

The towers are too tall, rising up and up to the thin keening of sky and cloud. And there are so many of them, clustered thick as anemones, as the houses are below. Too many, too tall, too hot ...

Leish woke in dawn stillness and lay shaking, sweating, as if he had been spread out upon the sun-beaten stone of that other place. He heard it frequently now, but although many years had passed since that first hearing, he still could not control or anticipate it. It surprised him, left him weak and wrung with fear, and desire that led to more fear. He mostly heard it while he slept, when his attempts to twist away were slower. He often woke like this, in deep or paling darkness, and lay trembling.

There were starmoths clustered around the hearth pool. Leish sat with his legs in the water and watched the green, gold, scarlet, blue flickering of their wings. He breathed deeply and listened to the pool and its soft, familiar path to the river's mud and rock. He sank into the old singing and almost believed it was enough.

"You heard it again." Mallesh was beside him. The starmoths' colours looked like embers in the darks of his eyes. When Leish did not reply, Mallesh said, "You *know* that you will have no peace until you see it, Leish. We must go."

"I ..." Leish said, and was silent.

Mallesh stood very tall atop the gathering pool stone the next day. The tiers of benches rippled with people. He still spoke of Nasran and her hearings and the first glorious change of the selkesh, as he had when he and Leish were boys. Now he also spoke of boats and weapons of metal and wood. "We have not had need of weapons since first we emerged from the sea and confronted the land-dwellers, and we have never had need of boats. But this sea journey may be longer and harsher than we can imagine. Perhaps our bodies will tire and collapse. We will need to build boats. And I will ask the mountain selkesh to forge new weapons—for we will need them. Leish has heard the people of the land across, and they are hard and fierce."

Leish stood by the gathering pool and shook his head once, quickly. He *had* heard them: their pride and strength and will. He had also heard, humming like blood beneath, their joy. Or beauty. He was not sure; these notes were as strange and confusing as those of the land and towers. And they were not creatures of water as well as earth, as the selkesh were—so there was a warping to the song, an extra strangeness he could not understand. But he understood enough to know that they were not one thing only; and he looked up and wondered again at the ways in which his brother's words changed the song, bit by bit, until it was more a shaping of his than Leish's.

"And why," one of the oldest selkesh asked, her voice tremulous as a breaking wave, "should we do all this—build boats and weapons and risk our lives for this far land? Why? Do not," she went on more firmly, holding up a knobbled hand to stop Mallesh from speaking, "tell us again about Nasran's triumphant journey and her prophecy of another to come. Those are merely tales. Talk to us of what is real."

Leish saw Mallesh clench his jaw and his fists, and for a moment he held his breath, waiting for the rush of his brother's anger. But when Mallesh spoke, his words were slow and quiet.

"The song is real. Leish's torment is real. Young selkesh are told to follow the songs that draw them, and this is what Leish must do. I do not think that he should do it alone." He paused. "And there are many others like me," he continued, and the youths in the front rows stirred, "who see this journey as an opportunity for all selkesh, as well as a necessity for Leish. Though you have commanded me not to speak in such terms," he said, smiling slightly at the old woman, "I must say that I feel a new age approaching, a second era of change and advancement. We have lived here in Nasranesh for a long, contented time, and now we must seek out other shores, other places to inhabit and hear and know. We must follow this song."

Leish could hear the waves in the silence that fell. The sea was high today, with swells that climbed and broke like thunder on the moss-lined shore. Even the gathering pool was ridged and hissing.

"And Leish?" asked an old man who had taught Leish and Mallesh how to harvest long-necked snails from the coral. "What does *he* say? What do *you* say?" he repeated.

Leish looked back at him, then away at nothing—at the clouds and treetops, the creepers, the wind-stripped blossoms. "I must follow this song," he said, his words too soft, not at all like Mallesh's hard, grinding stones. "Others must choose for themselves."

He could sense his brother looking down at him and knew he would be frowning, just a little, so no one else would see it. *You are too timid,* Mallesh had cried when they were boys. *You have no determination, no dreams. You could be happy sunk in the mud at the bottom of the river.* Leish saw his parents on the lowest bench: his father gazing up at Mallesh, his mother sitting very straight, her hands clasped in her lap, looking at Leish. He wanted to smile at her, or shrug—something helpless and gentle. His eyes slid away instead, back to the trees and the sky that was heavy with rain.

~

The river is bleeding. He hears it: deep, pulsing red, cries like torn flesh and sawing bone. The trees as well, and all the pools, all the places beneath the sky and water. Bleeding, rending, gaping—not even a song, just a confusion, as if hundreds, thousands of people are screaming together in their separate voices. Like a current beneath are the drum-hollow sounds of sand and white stone. And another, higher, twisting: words, a voice calling the blood …

"Leish—quiet, quiet, be still …" Someone was curled around the knot of his body, her skin and breath warm against him, easing him back. She smoothed sweat and hair from his eyes, and he looked at her in the light of the starmoths above the pool.

"Dallia," he said, his voice a rasp, as if all the screaming had been his own.

She smiled. "Yes, my dear. Welcome home." He saw her lips form the words but could not hear her: his ears still echoed with blood. "This one was very bad?" she said, frowning now, and he nodded.

"It was … here," he said, when he knew his voice would be strong enough. "Here, and everything was bleeding and dying, and the song of the land across was here as well, and someone was *speaking,* such terrible words. Everything was dying." He felt her arms wind and tighten around his ribs, but they were not enough to keep him still, to keep him from dissolving into the silence where the song waited.

"Dallia," he whispered, "this is what will come. This is what will come of Mallesh's boats and weapons. And it is my doing. If I had never spoken of this song—"

"If you had never spoken of this song," she interrupted, "Mallesh would be mounting an expedition inland with boats and weapons and you would be mad. Do not talk of meaningless ifs. Do not talk at all"—and she kissed him until he smiled and wove his own arms around her.

"Now follow me," she said suddenly, drawing away as he moaned and reached for her. She slipped into the pool and he did follow, swimming down into darkness beyond starlight. She led him from pool to river and from river to sea, where the bones of the Old City glowed with opening night-plants and ancient, breathing coral. Leish and Dallia spun slowly, trailing fingers, long strokes of skin that almost felt again like scales. He watched her breathing and yearned to hear her, only her—but singing, hearing, were deeper and broader than one person. He saw her dappled silver and blue, saw her hair and felt it wrapping around him before they moved apart. Then he closed his eyes and listened to the songs of his land, above and below, and he ached for the sea distance in his heart.

TWO

"*Finally* she is sending me away," Lanara said. "But to the shonyn. The *shonyn!*"

The Princess Ladhra smiled widely at her friend. "I know—she just told me. Not the most … tantalizing of postings, it's true—but don't you dare complain. At least you get to *go* somewhere. You must write me something every day, as you will for my mother. That is, unless you're too busy sleeping, as I've heard the shonyn do from sun-up to sunset …"

Lanara groaned and leaned her forehead against the balcony railing. She and Ladhra were sitting in the highest of the palace's terrace gardens. Their legs dangled among trails of ivy. They were so high that they could not hear the sounds of Luhr's marketplace, only the wind, and the water that fell against the stone of the fountains.

"I had hoped," Lanara said, "for the northern lands—Bektha or Gammuz, or places even further away. The ones with no names. She's known me since I was born—she *knows* I want to explore. But no, she will send me to watch sleeping shonyn."

Ladhra brushed a long strand of black hair away from her mouth. "Remember, though, Nara: when they're not sleeping, they gather fruit. And their skin, apparently, is blue. So." She was smiling again.

Lanara turned to her with narrowed eyes and growled, "I'd pitch you off this balcony if I could." She shook her head and looked back down at the blur of golden stone that was the city. She knew where her house was: somewhere directly below and to the right of this tallest tower. Her house, nestled against the back of the palace, surrounded by countless other houses like a bee's honeycomb, all joined by stairways that arched across hot, windy spaces.

"Your father will be relieved," Ladhra said. "I'm sure he would have worried endlessly about you if you'd been sent to Gammuz."

"Yes, well, as long as my father's happy," Lanara said—but as she spoke, she felt fear and sadness twisting through her eagerness. She would leave him alone in their little house. She would ride without him through the great gates of Luhr, into the desert.

"You *will* come with me?" she asked him a week later, as they stood by the table. "For the leave-taking?" She had not asked him this until now, when her bag lay packed and ready by the door—and he had not told her. Both of them stepping, as ever, around the memory of her mother's last leaving.

"Of course I will," Creont said, with his frown that she knew was really a smile. "Why else should I be wearing my best tunic?"

Lanara nodded and looked away from him. The table was littered with maps and mugs and practice arrows, as it had been since she was a girl (they had always cleared away plate-sized places at meals, or eaten outside, sitting on the sun-warmed stairs). The doors to the bedrooms were closed. Her bag—new, pungent leather, a gift from Ladhra—was sitting buckled and bulging beside the door that was open, a bit, to the wind. She swallowed over a sudden dryness and turned again to her father.

"Well then," she said, smiling up at him, "let's go. The Queen hates waiting."

She did not look back from their stairs, or from the maze of steps that tangled down to the palace's western doors. She felt her feet falling on old, familiar stones and sand, saw the palace doors swing open for her as they had for years—and again she was eager, quick, alight with what would come. Her own, smaller shadow ran like water among the great trees of the Queenswood—her shadow and Ladhra's, laughing and hiding among the wide trunks, beneath whispering green that almost held back the sun. Their shadows were in the corridors as well: behind statues and hanging vines, streaking past motionless guards. Lanara saw these small shapes and she felt her strong, present edges in the forest and hallways, and she smiled.

Gellior, the old Queensguard who seemed to have stood forever before the Throne Chambers' doors, winked at Lanara and bowed his head briefly to Creont. "I suppose you want in, girl?" he said in his low, rumbling voice, and she replied, high and childish, "Please, oh great Gellior—may we?" As she passed through the doorway, he said more quietly, "Nara—I wish you well on this day."

"Thank you," she said, also quietly, and went past him into the first antechamber.

Creont, beside her, drew in his breath, and she remembered that he had not been here in a long, long time. She and Ladhra had played here as well, despite the grumblings of some of the Queen's advisers and guards. This room was large and round and filled with reeds, both real and painted; also a painted sky, blue and cloud-gauzed and speckled with faraway birds in flight. Real birds stretched and flapped around the wide pool in the centre of the room; others swam, drifting lazily, sometimes raising their wings as if to fly. They were water birds, white, with long black beaks and slender, knobble-kneed legs. Lanara touched one on its loop of neck as she passed. It twisted and blinked and clacked its beak at her. She and Ladhra had named them all once, making careful note of the size and shape of beaks, webbed feet, outstretched wings. Lanara thought briefly that these must be the nameless descendants of those other birds.

She glanced at Creont and saw that he was frowning. "Extravagance," he had declared one day after Lanara had tried to explain, breathlessly, what she had seen in the Throne Chambers.

"But," she had protested, "it is all to show how the queens have given us life in the desert. The First Queen used her mindpowers to unearth the first springs and make the great pool, and she said that there must always be growing things in the palace, and after she—"

"I know the histories," Creont had interrupted in his voice of silencing. "And I still say that such displays are more for the glorification of the Queen than of life in the desert. Spend your days at the palace if you must, Lanara, but do not share news of its wonders with me." She had bristled and sulked then. Now she saw the frown on his lips and in his eyes, and felt too far away already for impatience or understanding.

They walked from the bright, rustling room into a hallway that sloped sharply down, into darkness. "The bird room," Ladhra had told her the first time they had played there, "shows the beauty of the air and land.

Then there's the other place—because the First Queen also had power over what's *below* the land." This other place was a tunnel, bending far beneath windows and ground, lit only by a faint glow somewhere ahead—near or far, it was impossible to tell. Lanara and Ladhra had held hands and run down this tunnel, their laughter muffled and a bit wild, scattering up the hill behind them. Now Lanara walked in long, even strides toward the blue-violet glow. She could hear Creont behind her. Once, he stumbled and she half turned, holding out her hand, but he continued past her, a tall, stooped shadow against the darkness.

The tunnel levelled out and opened suddenly into a space that rippled with the light of countless water creatures. Lanara knew that the walls of this circular chamber were glass, not stone. She knew that the fish and eels and other things she could not name were bound, that the water flowed around and away. But she halted as always, and for a breath thought that the water would sweep over her, that she would feel tentacles and scales sliding over her skin. Her father had closed his eyes. When he opened them, he walked forward, toward the barely visible arched doorway across the chamber. She followed, her own steps slower now, until her palm lay against the smooth wood of the door.

"Are you ready?" Creont said, and she looked up at him, at the colours that washed his eyes and cheeks like breathing paint.

"Yes," she said, and pushed the door open.

~

"Close your eyes—don't look until I tell you to," Ladhra had commanded the first time she had led Lanara into the last of the Throne Chambers. As if Lanara could have kept her eyes open in the sudden dazzle of sun, glass, water, blossoms, polished stone and crystal and gems. This time she closed her eyes before the door had swung inward completely. She stood with her face angled up as the light turned her eyelids to gold.

"Lanara." Queen Galha's voice, solemn but smiling, rich beneath the singing of fountains. "And Creont. Welcome."

Lanara opened her eyes. She saw the Queen standing in front of her painted wooden throne, by the rim of the enormous fountain that lay like a lake in the middle of the chamber. Channels ran here as well, rivers that flowed fresh and almost silently into the larger pool. Above the spray of this fountain soared a tower of glass and gold. Galha's dark hair and the jewels in her long blue tunic flashed in the sunlight. Lanara saw the Queen's consort-scribe, Malhan, on his own plain throne, beside and slightly behind hers. He was always behind her, the brown of his tunic vanishing in the dazzle of her gowns and jewels. He nodded at Lanara, which was more acknowledgment than she had expected from him.

She walked forward over flower-strewn stone and across a bridge. Other water creatures stirred below her, some so large that their backs and tails made arcing waves when they surfaced. These creatures were mostly gifts from traders and Queensfolk who had travelled back from distant lands. "Do the animals here ever die?" Lanara had asked Ladhra once.

The Princess had shrugged. "I suppose so. My mother probably has servants check for the dead ones."

"It must be difficult for them, in our water," Lanara had said, looking down at the shapes that darted or glided below the bridge.

Ladhra had shrugged again and dropped a handful of petals into the pool.

"My Queen," Lanara said now, holding her hands up before her. Fingers and thumbs pressed together, palms apart: the shape of an arrowhead.

"Nara," Galha said. "This is such a wonderful day for me. I have taken such pleasure watching you grow up beside my own daughter, as your mother grew up with me."

Lanara did not look back at her father, but she knew he would be glowering, every muscle rigid. This was another story Lanara had been forbidden to talk about. Her grandmother had served Galha's mother; Lanara's mother had been a favourite of both the Queen and the Princess, and had remained so until years into Galha's own reign. Lanara had been another royal favourite, companion of another princess. Creont had never spoken of this history. Lanara had heard some of it from Queen Galha, and more from Ladhra. When she had asked Creont for details, he had said only, "A queen deigned to befriend your mother, and another has deigned to befriend you. Do not be too proud of this, Lanara."

"And now," Queen Galha continued, her eyes and smile shadowed with melancholy, "suddenly you and my Ladhra are both women, and the time has come for me to give you your first posting in the realm. I hope this is as wonderful for you as it is for me—even though I am sending you to the shonyn and not to some fierce barbarian tribe in the north." Lanara blinked and shifted on the stone, and Galha smiled. "I have known you for a very long time, my dear. I realize this is not a posting you would have chosen. But the shonyn are important to me: I do not understand their ways, even after years of trading, and I need to send someone of intelligence and sensitivity to them. You must write every day of what you see and hear and learn, just as Malhan does. His words and yours will make this land strong when we are all gone."

Lanara watched as Malhan rose and disappeared behind Galha's throne. He emerged carrying a bow: tall, made of dark wood that curved and string that glowed. A quiver also, bristling with ten arrows. He handed these to the Queen, who set the bow before her. Lanara looked up past its tip, into Galha's eyes.

"Your bow and quiver, Lanara," she said in a deeper voice without laughter in it. "May you do the Queen's work with strength and wisdom."

Lanara curled her fingers around wood and soft leather. The arrowheads sang. "My Queen, I will."

Galha turned to Creont then. Lanara had not noticed that he had come up beside her. She gripped her bow as the Queen spoke to him. "Salanne would be so proud of her, Creont. And of you." He did not speak. Their eyes were level and still. "I miss her," Galha said, "every day."

The corners of his lips moved, and the tendons in his neck. Lanara heard the sound of her own blood above the fountain and the swimming creatures.

"As do I," Creont said evenly. "My Queen."

"Lanara." The word was quiet, but everyone turned to Malhan. He watched always, and listened, so that all his Queen did could be turned to writing and kept, unchanging—but he so rarely spoke. "Go safely," he said now. Creont's breathing was very loud; Lanara leaned forward so that she would hear Malhan more clearly. "Return to us, so that I may write of your discoveries." And she was there again, in his words that had perhaps been intended to distract: Salanne, a young mother, a Queenswoman who had gone and never returned.

"I will," Lanara said, her fingernails pressing, digging into the wood of her bow.

~

Today, during the morning hours, the sun shone strongly through thin clouds. Queen Galha rode out from the palace and into the wide main street of Luhr, accompanying the three Queensfolk who had just received their bows and arrows from her hand. The three were Nant, son of Lenon, daughter of Pelha; Lanara, daughter of Salanne, daughter of Bralhon; and Dendhon, daughter of Carre, daughter of Nanhen. The Princess Ladhra rode beside her mother. Both wore their royal cloaks of blue and green. The three with them wore short blue tunics belted with green, and their arms were wound round with green silk. They will bear the Queen's colours into the farthest lands.

Luhr's citizens lined the street and balconies and the rims of the many fountains leading down to the gates. The morning was loud with cheers and well wishes. The Queen herself opened the great double doors that lead the road into the desert. The three young people leaned from their horses to clasp hands with their parents. Then, one by one, they rode past Queen Galha and her daughter, who smiled and spoke private words of encouragement to them.

Nant will go north to the gold miners of Lornuz.

Lanara will go east to the shonyn people, whose lynanyn fruit is prized by Queensfolk.

Dendhon will go south to continue the mapping of the vast Mersid Jungle.

These three passed through Luhr's gates and departed, each by a different road.

THREE

My Queen, this is indeed a strange place, and the shonyn already seem beyond my understanding.

The ship anchored today, at dusk. The shonyn were all gathered on the bank, the old ones sitting on flat red stones, the young ones sitting on the ground at their feet. Even in the dim light I saw that Ladhra was right: their skin is dark and quite blue. Some of them spoke to each other as the captain and I disembarked, but they did not seem to be speaking of us. Their language sounds very smooth and slow. No one rose to greet us as we stepped onto their shore and walked among them, toward the Queensfolk tents that stand behind their village. They have the strangest little houses! Just balls of river mud baked in the sun, with pieces of blue cloth instead of doors. They are small, slight people, but they must have to crawl into their houses like animals. I was so relieved to reach the tents and relax in the company of other Queensfolk, surrounded by Queensfolk things!

As we walked, the captain whispered, "Do not be offended by their lack of interest. I have never seen any of them react to my ship or me or indeed anything at all." So we made our way among them, and only some of them looked at us. Their eyes, though, were empty. I have never encountered such flatness of regard. How could they look on me, a stranger, and not show any reaction in their eyes or faces? But that is why you have sent me here: to learn and understand.

Just as we were leaving the cluster of their houses, I saw a young male shonyn. He was standing, which surprised me, since none of the others had been. And it seemed for a moment as if he were looking at me. Truly at me: I saw him blink and move his head. I smiled at him. Even as I did so, his gaze left me. I cannot be sure now that he was seeing me as I imagined he was. I shall be very careful from now on to watch their eyes. I will smile at all of them as well, since I want them to think me friendly and speak to me.

I am glad you have sent me here. I will understand these shonyn, so that you also may understand them.

~

Nellyn does not expect to understand. He sits on the carpeted sand inside the Queensfolk teaching tent and listens exactly as the others do: politely, in stillness, blue-tinged hands folded while the Queensman and woman gesture with their brown ones. He listens to their words, which he does understand, mostly, although they are not shonyn words. "Repeat: bench, sun, river, sky, man, woman. Small ones"—this word he is not certain of—"repeat now." He repeats; they all do, the sounds emerging strange but whole. After these, though, come the other words, which none of the small shonyn comprehend. They continue to repeat, but unlike "river" or "sky," they cannot use these words.

"The past is time that is gone." The tall Queensman is speaking, very slowly, his hands sketching lines behind him. "You *were* all born, *were* all babies, and that is now the past."

"And there is future," says the Queenswoman, whose words are quicker than the man's. "You *will grow* old and die, and your bodies *will be taken* by the flatboats to the other shore, where you *will be laid* beneath the lynanyn trees. This is future time. *Will be.* Repeat." And the small blue shonyn do, carefully, politely.

Nellyn does not expect to understand, but he wants to. He knows he should not, and he does not speak of his desire to anyone. At night, after his lessons, he sits at the feet of the wise ones, shonyn whose skin is creased and darker than his own. He peels lynanyn as they do, and listens as the blue juice branches down his arms. "These Queensfolk are here," the dark shonyn say. "They come in their ships and speak to us. They take our lynanyn and give us metal and shining stones and think we understand them. They teach you, because you are small and lively—but you do not feel their words. You are shonyn, like the river that flows, always. Now still always, small ones."

Nellyn listens, but his eyes stray to the shadows of the tents on the sand ridge above them. The Queensfolk are all asleep, just as the shonyn are waking. Flatboats are gliding to the other shore, where lynanyn are harvested from the water. Every night the same: the dip and rise of the paddles, the swish and thud of the gathered fruit, the slow return in dawn cloud, the sleeping. Shonyn grow into their skin and crease and sleep more, even through the night—and there is no change.

And yet Nellyn gazes at the Queensfolk tents as his elders speak, and he wonders. It is a slow wonder that blooms even in his sleep and wakes him shaking with fear and confusion. He often lies within the red curving walls of his hut and knows without looking that they are bright with sun. Awake in sunlight, as shonyn never are: the fear blossoms.

At first he lies very still, keeping his eyes closed against the light. He clings to the sounds of sleep around him: soft breathing, a whisper of shifting limbs. But he can still see the sun, a golden-red glow in black, and one day he opens his eyes and sees shadows on the walls. He sits up and looks at his sleeping companions, whom he has never seen before in any but the blurred air of dusk or dawn. They seem harder, their skin more solid in the light that streams into the hut when the curtain blows.

Nellyn thinks, *I must lie down. I must sleep*. He does not. Instead, he creeps out of his hut and into the sunlight.

He stands up, blinking. The river, he soon sees, is blue—bright, dazzling blue—and he has to look away from it. The black flatboats are drawn up on the shore, dry and still. Beside them, the wise ones' stones are empty. He trembles beneath the searing blue sky. Fat white clouds pattern the ground, which is a painful gold. There are sparkles in it as well, like Queensfolk jewels. Nellyn sees his own small feet on the sand with a sudden shivering clarity.

He cannot immediately focus on the lynanyn trees that line the opposite bank of the river; their silver leaves burn and the black bark beneath is melting. He has seen sunrise and sunset on the leaves and thought them bright. Now he rubs tears away with the palms of his hands and strains to find the shapes of branches and trunks and dangling fruit.

He hears sounds then, the hum of heat and the insects that hover above the water or skitter over the sand. Muffled voices from the tents: the Queensfolk awake, talking, laughing, as all the shonyn sleep. Nellyn hears a few words he understands; the others seem warped or broken. He stands looking from his feet to the three tents, which are bright green and blue. His eyes and skin hurt.

Go back inside. Go back.

He walks slowly among the round red huts, watching the lynanyn-dyed cloth doors billowing. He knows the path up to the tents, but it is different now—new and terribly bright, like everything else. The teaching tent's door flap is closed, but another's, beside it, is open. Nellyn draws close, until the voices are quite loud and he can smell food. He does not look behind him at the river and the village; he does not even think to do so. He edges his head around the tent's opening and peers inside.

Soral, his Queensman teacher, is bending over a table. A lynanyn trader sits across from him. They are tossing wooden blocks and laughing and eating something—not lynanyn—from a silver platter. A raised bed stands in one corner, and a small table beside it, covered in scrolls that Nellyn sees are dark with the odd marks Queensfolk make with slender sticks and call "writing." A carpet like the one in the teaching tent covers the sand. It is red, green, blue, woven into shapes he cannot quite see. The sunlight shining through the tent walls shifts in the air like water.

Nellyn does not make a sound, and he moves only slightly in the doorway, but suddenly both faces turn to him. "Nellyn?" Soral says, his voice and brows rising together. The trader—a large woman, older than Soral—frowns. "Nellyn, what are you doing awake at this hour?"

Nellyn cannot answer. His throat feels thick, filled with sand.

Soral smiles, says, "Come in," and Nellyn does.

Soral sets him on a tall stool at the table and introduces him to the trader, who is smiling now as well, but Nellyn scarcely hears him. He is alone with Queensfolk, in their tent. None of his friends are beside him. The sun is high, not slipping below the horizon. He swallows and clenches his fists under the tabletop.

They show him how to play their game, speaking slowly so that he will understand—but he does not. He tosses the wooden blocks several times, then sits and simply watches. When Soral offers him food from the tray, he shakes his head, he tries not to even look at it. The smell makes him dizzy. Once or twice the two Queensfolk speak quickly and glance at each other over his head, and Nellyn knows they are talking about him. At last Soral says, "Nellyn, you should go back and try to sleep. You mustn't be tired at sundown." Nellyn nods and slips off the stool to the carpet, with its images (he now sees) of flowers and rivers and sky. He hesitates by the door flap. Soral says, gently, "Go on, small one."

Nellyn goes, his feet carrying him quickly, as they never have before. He slithers down the slope. Near the bottom he falls, and his breath rasps as he struggles to rise. He does not sleep when he lies again beneath his own red walls.

That night he listens to the wise ones' voices as if they can take his fear away, and they do, a bit, then a bit more as the nights pass. He does not go again to the tents, except for his lessons. Soral smiles at him sometimes and looks as if he wants to speak to him alone, but Nellyn stays with the other small shonyn and does not meet his eyes. Then Soral goes away on a Queensship and another teacher comes, and this one never smiles.

Nellyn sits at the wise ones' feet and listens to their stories: shonyn stories, looping and changeless. It is the same again. Sleep and stirring and sleep, words and paddles lulling him away from wonder, to safety. The same, until another Queensship drops its anchor in the river, and a woman smiles at him.

FOUR

"Nellyn, we are here." The words are far away, like wind in the leaves of the lynanyn trees. "Nellyn. Put the pole down. We are here."

Nellyn lifts his head and blinks at the trees and the dark water beneath his flatboat. It is deep night. Leaves and river are speckled with stars. The shore behind is a shadow. He sets his pole down carefully and turns to Maarenn, his gathering companion, who is looking steadily at him.

"You are strange now," she says. "You are hardly here."

"Yes, I am … thinking. But I am ready to gather." He kneels on the wet wood and leans out, skimming his hands over the river's skin, before she can say anything else. He feels a lynanyn, scoops it up in one expertly cupped hand, lays it on the flatboat. Maarenn begins to do the same thing on the other side. He turns and sees star- and water-light rippling on her bent back. Her curls, also, are shining.

Thinking. The wrong word, and he knows it—but he has spoken this word to Maarenn, and it has to be truth now.

The Queensship looked like all the others: enormous, formed of red-brown wood that curved, topped with a sail of green and blue. The sounds of creaking timbers and splashing oars reached the village long before the ship itself was in sight. Nellyn stood at the foot of the Queensfolk ridge and watched until he could see it clearly against the reddening sky. He had just woken up. Other shonyn were emerging from their own huts, rubbing their eyes, stretching, calling to each other.

The anchor screamed and even the wise ones fell briefly silent. Queensfolk lined the side. Nellyn looked at them from his distance and saw only one clearly. She was standing with the others, but while they gestured and shifted, she was still. Still enough to be a shonyn, though her skin was red-brown like the boat's wood and her hair curled so closely to her head that he could see the lines of her neck. She gazed down at the shore and the shonyn sitting there. Then a man took her arm and they both climbed down a rope ladder into a smaller boat. She picked up oars and rowed, and Nellyn thought that she was still even now, as her arms and back stretched beneath green-wound cloth.

When she drew closer, walking toward him with the man at her side, Nellyn saw that he had been wrong: there was nothing of the shonyn about her bearing or her face. The lines of her body were hard and tight, as if she walked with aching muscles. Her eyes were wide and nearly unblinking. They darted and leapt, barely resting. *She is amazed,* Nellyn thought suddenly. "Amazement is the seed of change," the wise ones would say after the children had returned from their studies on the sand ridge. "They wish for you to be amazed, surprised, excited by what they tell you. These are words we hardly use, because they are so strange to us. We shonyn are not amazed. We look and speak and live our days as always." Nellyn had nodded with the rest—but now he looked at her and saw her, wondering and new, and he remembered Soral's tent, the eddying daylight, the colours of the carpet. He swallowed and felt his fingers pressing into his palms. She walked toward him and her flickering eyes found his, and he too wondered.

An unripe lynanyn brushes his hand. His fingertips press hard, unpuckered skin and open again. *Do not look for her,* he thinks. *Turn away from her when she comes down to the village.* He avoided Soral's eyes and Soral went away. The wise ones' stories soothed: Nellyn's own language, smooth and gentle, with its words of endless river and cycles of lynanyn and night. *Do not.*

"Nellyn," Maarenn says. He looks up and finds her eyes on him. "Nellyn, where are your thoughts?"

He shakes his head and tries to smile. Across the river, a Queensfolk banner snaps in wind that still smells of daylight.

~

Lanara stood in the teaching tent, watching small shonyn file out into the dusk.

"You see?" Queensman Cannin demanded. "You see how impossible this is?" He stacked writing trays on the table with a clatter that made her blink. "They imitate—they do not understand. Apparently it has been this way since we found them. I cannot imagine why the Queen keeps sending us here. It's all far too much effort for some blue fruit."

Lanara said, "It's not just the fruit. She wants to understand them—she has always desired knowledge of other people and places."

Cannin snorted and wiped his fingers across his brow. "When queens say they want to understand people, it means they want something from them: support, allegiance, trade goods. But she'll get no such things from these shonyn. The sooner she recognizes this, the sooner she can stop wasting our time." He saw the expression on Lanara's face and cleared his throat roughly. "I suppose you'll write the Queen about my insubordination now. I've been here too long, girl, far too long—but my time is done in a few days. That boat will take me home to Fane, thank the First." He stood at the door flap, holding it open with one hand. "I leave it to you, this supposed task of understanding."

And so he did. He also left the trays with their wet sand and sharpened stones for writing. He left scrolls of his own observations ("All too few, I'm sorry to say") and lists of desert plants and animals. Lanara had watched him give his brief, sharp lessons. On the fourth day, at noon, she watched him board the boat. "Thank the First," she muttered as anchor and timbers shrieked. She lifted her arm as the ship crawled downstream. No one waved back at her.

Several days later she went down to the river at dusk. The old shonyn on their stones and the young ones at their feet were not looking at her. She smiled at them anyway. "Good evening," she said slowly, in their language. She had found a brief list of words among Cannin's scrolls: *Shonyn words, approximate,* he had written across the top.

One of the old shonyn nodded ponderously at her. "Good evening," he replied, and she heard that it was a bit different from what she had said, though she did not know how. The others stirred and nodded and said good evening, and she felt her smile widen.

She had forgotten the other words. Good sleep? River? Fine lynanyn? She said, "Good evening" one more time, trying to catch their eyes and failing, then walked among them to the houses. She did not look back. She knew that none of them would be looking at her.

The young shonyn man was standing where he had been on the day she arrived. He was staring at his feet, she saw, and she turned her own feet from the path and went toward him. "Good evening," she said when she was in front of him. The words sounded ridiculous now. She said carefully, in her own language, "You must have studied with us—you must understand the Queenstongue." He did not move. "I am Lanara."

There was a long silence. She noticed that his black hair had a sheen of blue, which matched his skin. He looked as if he had been soaked in lynanyn juice. He was a bit shorter than she was—especially, she thought with a brief stab of annoyance, with his head lowered.

"I am not like Cannin," she said in a rush. "He was old and did not want to understand you. I do. Want to understand you." She watched the wind shift his hair and felt suddenly desperate, her chest tight and hot. "Speak to me. *Please.*"

He looked up, so slowly that she nearly did not realize he was doing so. His eyes were very dark, and this time they were quite steady. *Shonyn eyes,* she thought. *I can't tell what he's thinking, or even what he's seeing.* She could not smile now, and she forgot words. When he turned and began to walk away, she did not call after him.

Lanara returned to the teaching tent and waited, straightening the stack of writing trays in front of her. The shonyn children filed in slowly. Slowly they arranged themselves in their four straight rows on the carpet. They looked at Lanara, but not *at* her. They had sat in these rows and repeated her words for days—blurry days she could count only by the number of letters she had written to the Queen. Six letters; six days of awkward speaking that she knew was not the same as teaching.

"Children," she said now, "I want you to talk to me." She had not known that the words were coming until they did. She set down her writing tray with a firmness that might make them sound confident. "Yes—*you* talk to *me*. I want to hear about your lives. What you like to do every day. Or night." She closed her eyes for a moment. *Slow down, Lanara,* she could hear her father saying. *You have always been too hasty.* Or Ladhra: *Don't worry, Nara, you are actually* helping *them learn the Queenstongue when you speak so incoherently.*

"Messannell," Lanara said, and a boy in the front row lifted his eyes. His gaze, like the man's earlier, was unwavering. "Tell me what you do after you wake up every evening."

The silence was very long. She tried not to shift impatiently.

"I go to the river," the boy said at last in a high, clear voice. "I listen to stories. I watch flatboats get lynanyn."

"What are the stories about?"

"Shonyn life," he said after another pause.

She smiled encouragingly at him. "Yes?" she said when he did not continue. "Tell me about this."

"Shonyn life," he said again. "The river. Flatboats and lynanyn."

"The river," Lanara said, "yes—let's talk more about this. It is low now, not a lot of water. Soon it will rain. Then the river will get high again. Do you like rain?"

This time no one spoke. The shonyn children looked at the carpet and hardly seemed to breathe. "What is wrong?" she asked. "What did I say? Serran?"

The girl whispered one word, a shonyn word, rolling and strange.

"What does this mean?" Lanara asked, though she knew there would be no answer. "One of you, please tell me …"

"Fear," said a new voice, and Lanara turned to the open door flap. The young man was standing there, half inside, half out. "The word means fear in your language," he said, and she felt herself nodding. He spoke to the children then, his words like wind-blown sand. They looked up at him, blue-black heads angled away from her.

She cleared her throat. "It is late. You may go. Except," she added as they rose and began to leave, "for you."

The young man watched them until they had all walked down the hill. She leaned against the table and watched him.

"As I have already told you," she said when he looked back at her, "I am Lanara. What is your name?"

"Nellyn," he said. Her brows arched when he continued, "That is my Queensfolk name. My teacher Soral thinks it sounds like my shonyn name."

"And does it?" she asked. *Good,* she thought, *keep talking, Nellyn.*

"Not very much," he said, and stepped out of the tent.

"Nellyn!" she cried as she strode after him. "Nellyn—wait!" He was walking away from her, his feet falling silently on the sand of the ridge. "You will not walk away from me again!" she called at his retreating back. "It's ridiculous—it's *rude!*"

He disappeared down the hill. She saw him a few minutes later, by a flatboat. She watched him push it into the river, a woman beside him.

"Shonyn life," Lanara mimicked in a wavering falsetto. "River and flatboats and lynanyn." She made an inarticulate sound and went back inside.

~

My Queen, I was encouraged today by an interaction with the young shonyn man I wrote about on my first day here. He came to the teaching tent and helped to translate something one of the children had said. After they had left, he remained behind and we spoke, mostly about his own Queensfolk teacher, Soral. It was a brief conversation, but I am certain that we will speak at more length soon. He is aloof and inscrutable, as all shonyn are, but I feel I will be able to change this. His name is Nellyn.

~

Nellyn's footsteps sound too loud on the ridge. He tries to be quiet, to be calm. He does not run as he did from Soral, on the day the sun drew jewels from the sand.

Fear, Nellyn thinks, the Queenstongue and shonyn words both, as he walks away from her.

FIVE

Lanara sat on her bed with a thin stack of parchment in front of her. "Trees," she read, squinting at Cannin's spidery scrawl. "Food … Pottery … Climate." She rested her fingertip beside the last word.

Climate:
Hot and dry. Rains once a year, lasting about seven days. Winds high during rains, moderate at other times. No lynanyn gathering during rains.

Lanara glared down at the page. "That's *all?*" she said, then glanced up to see if anyone had heard her. *As if shonyn would be up here now*, she thought. *Still, I'm talking to myself. I must alert Ladhra that I'm already going mad.*

She set the parchment down on the carpet beside her bed and went to open the door flap. There were long shadows on the sand: dark, distorted tents and listless banners. The shonyn would soon crawl out of their mud houses to sit by the river. Nellyn would be among the first, Lanara knew; she had watched the village every day, though she had not gone down to it. *Patience,* she had told herself, attempting Creont's sternness. *Be as slow as they are. Watch and learn.* But she could not, today—not with Cannin's infuriatingly brief document behind her, and the shadows lengthening into yet another gentle twilight. Lanara offered silent apologies to her father as she descended the ridge and sat down to wait in the shade of Nellyn's house.

He ducked out minutes later—the first to do so, as she had anticipated. He had stood and was starting to stretch when he saw her. She quelled a triumphant smile at his surprise. His arms and fingers froze and his eyes widened until she could see white around their darkness.

"Walk with me, Nellyn," she said as she rose. "To the riverbank, past the sitting stones. And do not try to leap in and swim away from me."

"I do not swim," he said, and she sighed.

"Ah. Of course you don't."

They walked slowly among houses that were still quiet and sat where the bank was thick with plants. "They do grow crops," Cannin had told her, "after a fashion. A little plot of herbs and vegetables which has apparently been there since the village began, whenever that was." Lanara saw that some of these plants were brittle, their fronds brown-tipped and shrivelled. She looked from them to the shallow river and said, "Tell me why the shonyn are afraid of the rains."

After a predictable pause Nellyn said, "The Queensman Cannin does not record this with his writing stick?"

She peered at him, wondering whether shonyn were capable of sarcasm and finding no answer in his face. "No," she replied. "And anyway, I want to find these things out from a shonyn. You. So—the rains."

He turned to look upstream. The stones where the old ones sat were hidden behind the plants. "The rains bring change. We fear this."

She frowned. "Only that? And do these rains not come every year? Are they not a part of your … pattern?"

"Yes, they do come, always—but they are never the same. And we cannot leave our houses or gather lynanyn. Lynanyn fall without being ready. It is very dark, even during our sleeping. It is a very …" For the first time she saw him hesitate. "… strange time. So we fear it."

"I see," Lanara said. She put her elbows on her drawn-up knees and stared at the lynanyn trees across the river. The leaves glinted violet as the sun slipped westward.

"No," he said, surprising her again, "you do not see. You do not understand what change is to shonyn. It is not so terrible for you. And you do not live by patterns. You hardly seem to have stories."

Lanara arched her brows at him. "Apparently, while Cannin was learning nothing about shonyn, you were coming to a full understanding of Queensfolk."

They looked at each other until he looked away.

~

She is angry. He sees it in the set of her jaw and shoulders. He wants to say he is sorry, to tell her that he actually knows nothing at all of Queensfolk, but he does not, since his words might anger or confuse her again. He waits in silence, looking across the river but still seeing her beside him, her blue and green tunic and the brown of her long, slender hands.

He understands shonyn women. He has touched one or two, lying in houses dim before dawn. Smooth blue skin and curls that cling to his fingers; voices that murmur with the river. He has felt desire as a slow, steady warmth, ebbing and flowing in the circle of his nights. He does not recognize what he feels now. It is pain without a place on his skin.

"I am sorry," she says into their long silence. "I should not have spoken to you that way. We obviously have much to learn from each other." She smiles at him as if she is tired. "I would like to talk with you again. Perhaps we could meet here every day at this time, before the children come for their lessons. Would you agree to this?"

Nellyn hears shonyn voices, though the words are indistinct. They are gathering now, to tell their tales and to listen. And he does not want to join them; he acknowledges this with a rush of terror and relief. "Yes," he says to Lanara, and feels the pain prickling in his bones and blood. "I agree to this."

She tries, from that day on, like Soral, to teach him time. "There is a beginning, middle and end to all things. Lives, experiences—this river," she adds, tracing a long, sinuous line in the sand with her finger. "We call it the Sarhenna, after the queen who discovered it. See—this is its shape. Its source is here, deep in the desert. Here is your village. And here is the river's end, at the town of Fane, on the Eastern Sea."

Nellyn looks at the line, and at her finger. There is sand beneath its nail. "The river is," he says. "It flows here, always."

She nods. "Yes, of course—but 'here' is only one part of the river."

"I do not understand. The river here is all," he says, thinking she might frown—but instead she smiles.

"You should come with me. We'll get on a boat and sail to the sea and I'll make you understand *end*."

He feels blood rushing to his cheeks and looks away from her abruptly.

"I am joking," she says. "Being ... light-hearted with you." After a moment she says, "Smile at me, Nellyn."

He gazes at the drawn-up flatboats until they blur into one black stain on the riverbank.

"I apologize," she says at last. "Again. I feel so clumsy sometimes, talking to you."

"I also am sorry for this."

She says briskly, "Well then, if we're done apologizing to each other, let's continue."

When it becomes apparent that she will not be able to explain time to Nellyn, they talk of other things: Luhr's spires and fountains and the marketplace where people from all over the land gather. "But no shonyn," he says, and she shakes her head although it is not really a question.

"Not that I have seen, no. Though there are fruit vendors there who sell lynanyn. Some say it is their most prized and beautiful fruit. And there are breads and sweets, plants from beneath the sea, berries from the mountains. Such a wonderful variety of everything: people, food, music, clothing."

He sees her eyes sweeping over the empty river and the heat-curled plants and the red huts. He says, "This place is too quiet for you. Too small. But for me it is enough."

She narrows her eyes at him. "Is it?"

He cannot say the word that should be spoken. Her head is tilted to one side, as if she is listening to his silence.

"So tell me about this place, then," she says, and his voice returns. He tells her about the richness of uses to which lynanyn is put: food, yes, but also dye for clothing and pottery, materials for cloth and threads and rope, medicine for fevers and wounds. He tells her one of the wise ones' tales, of shonyn who cut lynanyn trees and watch them die, of shonyn who cross the river to settle on this bank so that the trees can grow again.

"When was this?" she asks, her writing stick poised above the parchment she brings with her every day.

He looks at the black marks she has already made on the page. "It is always," he says, "and now, in these words."

She opens her mouth, then closes it again. "Mmm," she says, and does not write anything.

She is a part of his pattern now, but this does not comfort him. The wise ones speak and he hears her voice, talking of mountains and spires and breads—strange words for things he cannot imagine, but they are her words, and they come to him even when he is not with her. He watches her walk up to the tents. When he pulls himself onto his flatboat, he sees that she watches him from her ridge, though he does not know why.

"You talk to her," Maarenn says one night as Nellyn is trying not to look back at the shore.

"Who?" he asks, and she sighs.

"Nellyn. You know who I mean. What do you talk about?"

He listens to the laughter of the small ones who are clustered on the bank, sailing flatboats made of lynanyn-tree twigs. They laugh and splash and he aches to be there with them, ankle-deep in warm river water. "She asks questions about our life and I answer them. She writes what I say."

"Ah," Maarenn says. "She is very friendly. She tries to speak to us in our language. And she is lovely. In a strange way, but still lovely."

He says, "Yes," and feels his pain loosen, just a bit, as if he has shared it.

The night after that, Lanara walks back down to the bank as the flatboats are setting off. He starts when he turns and sees her there instead of on the ridge. She waves at him. He thinks, *She looks sad.* Then, *She comes to see me off*—and he smiles at her across the water, as Maarenn's pole dips and soars. Lanara's mouth opens in a surprised circle and he smiles more broadly, so easily now that he has begun. She clutches her hands to her heart in what he knows is mock alarm, since she too is smiling now. He wants to wade back to where she is standing, to let the flatboats go on without him.

Suddenly he is dizzy. There is a humming in his head that feels like the fear and pain he knows but also something else, something he cannot name or grasp. He closes his eyes and breathes deeply, carefully, and the humming subsides. When he looks again at the shore, Lanara is kneeling on the ground, talking to a wise one.

The next day he wakes early and waits for her by his hut. She does not come. On that day and others that follow, he sits alone on the sun-crumbled bank beside the shrivelled plants. He hears thunder, so far away that it is more pulse than sound. The sky is dry and blue, except in the west, where there is a smudge of low, angry purple. The night wind smells of rain.

SIX

At first the hoofbeats sounded like thunder. Lanara looked up from the letter she was writing and squinted at the desert to the south of her tent. She saw heat shimmer, broken by dark cacti with branches like beseeching arms—and another dark shape, this one moving. She rose as it drew closer, its trembling lines hardening into a rider on a white horse. Even from a distance she could see his tunic's green and blue. She raised her arms, though he was riding directly toward her.

"Queenswoman," he gasped when he had reined his horse to a rearing halt, "thank the First I have found you." His face and hands were crusted with sand and sweat. Beneath this grime, his skin was a peeling red. "I fled a battle," he said as they tethered his horse in the shade of the provisions tent. "And then I got lost. My food and water ran out yesterday. But how rude I am," he said, turning to her with a smile. His teeth were even and white in his tangle of beard. "I am Gwinent of Sordinna, a tiny hamlet you've probably never heard of, to the west of Luhr."

"And I am Lanara of Luhr."

He arched one eyebrow and gave a low whistle. "A real Luhran. I had no idea they could be so attractive."

Lanara laughed. "High praise from a man who's been lost in the desert. Come and have a drink. And a wash."

"Why not a swim," he said, "to take care of both?"

They walked upstream, away from the shonyn village. When they went down to the river, he drank first, in deep, silent gulps. Then he waded slowly in, wincing as the water touched his raw skin and the cuts that crisscrossed his arms and legs.

"How did you get those?" she asked.

He surveyed his arms as he bobbed, chest-deep. "A sandstorm. Bits of cactus and stone everywhere. Not a very dramatic reason. Would you be impressed if I said something about the battle? Or predatory birds?"

Lanara laughed again, then fell silent. She watched her tunic darkening in the water.

"What's wrong?" he said, his legs slicing him in one long glide toward her.

"Wrong? Oh, just that you *know* something's wrong. And you can understand me when I talk at a normal speed. And you're awake in the middle of the day. All of which makes me realize how homesick I've been."

"For Luhr?" he demanded. "Stodgy, stuck-up, smelly Luhr?" He dodged her splash with ease.

"For a man who's been lost in the desert," she said, "you're entirely too energetic."

She told him about the shonyn as they lay drying on the bank and later, eating slices of lynanyn and hard bread soaked in lynanyn juice.

"These shonyn have good taste," Gwinent said as he chewed. "And I'm not just saying that as a man who's been lost in the desert."

She chuckled. "Mmm. But I miss *fresh* bread. And sweets. And vegetable soup. I know I shouldn't. I'm here at the Queen's command, after all, doing important work."

He made a sour face. "And when has doing important work ever been a cure for loneliness?"

She curled her fingers around bread crust and did not look at him. She had called it homesickness, but he had named it truly. Loneliness: the spreading chill in her gut that she had not expected. She wrote to Ladhra and her hand shook with the need to see her, to walk with her among the trees of the Queenswood and laugh at nothing. She wrote to her father—though not as often—and tried desperately to see their small, sunlit house. Just as desperately, she tried not to see it. *I am failing Queen Galha,* she thought. *And myself.*

"Thank you," she said to Gwinent. "I suppose I've been foolish. It sounds so simple and sensible, the way you phrase it."

"Hardly. But you're welcome." He touched the back of her hand lightly. She watched his fingers, with their blunt nails and their cuts.

"Tell me about the battle you fled," she said. She did not move her hand.

"Don't you have to teach soon?" he asked, and she saw that the sky was pink and the sun was low.

"Yes," she replied. "But not for a while. Talk to me until the children arrive. Please."

His forefinger drew lazy circles around each of her knuckles. "I'll be happy to. As long as I'm not keeping you from your important work."

She could not see the houses or the river or the lengthening shadows. She could not see if there was anyone waiting for her by the plants. "Talk to me," she said again, and smiled at him.

~

"Serran." The child looks up at Nellyn as he puts his hand on her shoulder. "Tell me—your teacher is here? Not … gone away?"

Serran shakes her head. "She is here."

He nods and looks again at the tents on the ridge. Already they are difficult to see: the sky is blotted with clouds. Not rain clouds; those are behind, advancing with the thunder.

"May I play?" the girl asks, and he turns back to her and smiles.

"Yes, small one. Thank you." He watches her walk to where the other small shonyn are, gathered by the dry bank below the wise ones' stones. The river is very low; the flatboat poles are hardly wet when he and the others raise them up. Lynanyn they do not pick from the water lie on the opposite bank, their skins split and oozing into the dust.

Nellyn has not seen Lanara from the bank or the village, and he has not gone up to the tents. He wonders whether a Queensship has come during the day and taken her away again—but he knows that this cannot have happened so quickly and silently. *Because she does not come to me, I think she must be gone,* he thinks, and sighs at his own foolishness.

"A man is here," Maarenn says later as the flatboat rocks beneath them. Nellyn kneels facing her and does not speak. "A Queensman," she continues, "with Lanara Queenswoman. I hear his voice at sundown and there is a small tent with an animal inside." He feels her eyes on him in the cloud-thickened darkness. "She does not speak to you now?"

"No," Nellyn says, and tries to smile. "You are curious about these things, even though 'their doings are of no interest to you.'" His voice deepens and slows. She laughs at his imitation of a wise one.

"Even though," she agrees. "And you too are curious, gathering companion, though you do not speak of it and only stare at her tent with large eyes." She rolls a lynanyn toward him. It bumps his knee gently. "Take care," she says quietly. "Remember who you are."

He does not sleep at all that day. The sunlight on his walls is muted, almost grey. When he ducks outside, he sees that the bank of cloud in the west is crackling with white light. The sand beneath his feet is warm, not hot as it was on the day he went up to Soral's tent. But as on that day, Nellyn hears voices. Hers and a man's, low and laughing—and with them another sound, like someone striking a flatboat pole repeatedly into the sand.

They are standing beyond the third tent. Nellyn stays behind it and watches them. Lanara is holding her bow, pulling back a string and an arrow very slowly. When she opens her right hand, the arrow sings, then sinks into a tall cactus. The cactus tips slightly. It is supported by several rocks, not by roots, and Nellyn thinks, *That man tears it from the earth and brings it here.*

The man is beside Lanara. He too wears blue and green, though the colours are more faded than hers. He grins down at her, his teeth glinting suddenly from the hair around his mouth. "Not bad," Nellyn hears him say, "for a Luhran female." She pretends to shove him and he pretends to stumble. Nellyn sees her smile and turns away.

He still does not sleep. He lies with his eyes closed, he lies with them open. "Our sleep is our strength," the wise ones say—and he realizes the truth of this as he bends to gather lynanyn with fumbling hands. His limbs feel heavy and clumsy. His eyes ache until he rubs them, and then they burn. When he speaks, his tongue drags over his teeth.

He listens to the breathing of his sleeping companions and thinks of the Queensman. He imagines he can hear his voice rumbling beneath the hammering of his own heart and the boom of approaching thunder. The dizziness that struck him on the flatboat when he smiled at Lanara returns. Sometimes he feels as if he is falling, and his fingers claw at the sand or at the wood of the flatboat.

He is awake when the rain begins. At first he thinks the sound is in his head, and he sits up carefully, waiting for it to abate. It does not, and thunder cracks, very close. *It is here,* he thinks, rubbing his hands across his forehead and over his cheeks. Lightning, thunder, the hard patter of rain. His vision blurs and darkens. He sees the Queensman's grin and Lanara's fingernail, crusted with sand. Soral's wooden blocks falling in sunlight that eddies like water. The Queensman looking down at her—looking, smiling, reaching. These things are not real, but he sees them anyway, so clearly that he groans and grinds his fists against his eyes. *What is this?* he thinks as he scrambles to his feet. *I am not the same. Something is new.*

He runs over rain-blotched sand. Bile rises in his throat and everything around him spins, but his feet pound up the path to the ridge. He sees Lanara and the Queensman standing in the door flap of her sleeping tent. He hears the man's voice and watches his lips: "So your little blue people are afraid of a bit of rain, are they?" Words and skin swim in the muddy light. Nellyn tries to keep the man still, just for a few more steps, just until he can reach him with all the force of his running and his need.

"Nellyn!" Lanara cries. The Queensman turns to him. Nellyn sees his lips part in surprise, scorn, pain. Nellyn's body holds the Queensman on the ground for a moment. He sees his own hands gripping the man's tunic. "Nellyn!" Lanara cries again, and he sees her reaching for him. He wants to touch her hair and the skin of her neck and the hollow of her throat. He shouts as he raises his arm and twists back to the man. The man's fist rises—and then pain blazed and the world changed its shape, and Nellyn understood.

SEVEN

My Queen, it seems what Nellyn told me about the strange and difficult nature of the rains is true. Today, after weeks of thunder, the rain began to fall. As soon as we heard it, Queensman Gwinent and I went to watch from the door flap of my tent. We had not been there very long when Nellyn came running toward us. At first I did not recognize him: he was moving so quickly, and his face was full of rage. It was the first time I had ever been able to identify an emotion, a real expression. Before I could intervene, he ran at Gwinent and they both fell to the floor of my tent. Nellyn had taken him entirely by surprise and was able to hold him down for a moment, despite Gwinent's greater strength and bulk. But then Gwinent hit him in the face with his fist several times and Nellyn rolled off him, unconscious.

Gwinent was extremely angry. He demanded to know who Nellyn was and why he would have attacked him in such an unprovoked manner. I attempted to explain again about the rains, and ventured the opinion that Nellyn had been affected by them. I too became rather agitated. Gwinent is a seasoned Queensman: he should have seen instantly that his attacker was much smaller and weaker than himself. He could have halted the attack with far less force than he employed. As I spoke, I was staunching the blood flowing from Nellyn's nose (which appears to have been broken).

Gwinent knew nothing of the shonyn. He should have fended Nellyn off and deferred to my own understanding of these people for a solution to the situation. Perhaps his time in the desert has affected his judgment?

When I laid a damp cloth on Nellyn's brow, Gwinent's anger overcame him. He accused me of misplaced loyalty and stormed out of the tent. A short time later he rode away. I watched him make off westward with his few bags strapped to his horse. It seems he does not intend to return here to wait for the next Queensship. I cannot say that I am disappointed, though I do regret the nature of our final exchange.

A far more important thing happened then. Nellyn opened his eyes and looked into my face, and he said, very clearly despite his broken nose, "That was the first time." For several minutes I could not speak. He had referred to something in the past. He had finally grasped the knowledge so many other Queensfolk had tried to convey.

"The first time for what?" I finally asked.

He turned his head to the door flap and seemed to listen to the rain. "Anger and pain. And then knowing."

I was not sure that I understood him, but I said, "And what will happen now?"

He looked at me again. His eyes were very bright, but I do not think with happiness. "Change," he said. "I ... will change. I have changed."

I laughed and hugged him and congratulated him on his success, and he smiled, though his eyes were still strange.

He said he wanted to go home, and declined my offer to accompany him. I offered again when he stood and nearly fell—but once more he declined. For a moment he braced himself with one hand on the back of my chair; with the other hand he held the blood-soaked cloth to his nose. Then, without another word to me, he left the tent and went slowly back to his house. I watched him to make sure that he reached it—and he did, just as the rain that had only been spattering turned into a downpour. (I can no longer see the river, or even the village.) I trust he will endure these rains, and his new knowledge.

I hope I will not sound immodest when I write that his accomplishment is also mine. Patience has been difficult to maintain in my dealings with him—but it has been rewarded. I have this thought to keep me company now, as I wait for the rains to pass.

~

Nellyn stared at the blood. His blood on Lanara's cloth—it was black now, dried and stiff, made darker by the gloom of the hut. The thunder had passed; there was only the rain, which pounded the hardened clay until he thought it would dissolve around him. He heard the muttering of his sleeping companions above the rain. They sat together by the lynanyn pile and murmured, and Nellyn did not look at them.

"What is this?" one of them had said, sometime earlier pointing at the cloth and Nellyn's face. He had not replied. He had turned his back on all of them and squatted by the door, where the curtain hung heavy and the earth was soaked with rain.

He stared at his blood and saw other images as well, too many, all at once, burning and throbbing until he thought he would slip again into darkness, as he had when the Queensman had hit him. He saw himself in the river, splashing with the other small ones, gazing at the flatboats as they set off at dusk. His small self; his young self, before Soral. Everything quiet circles until that day in Soral's tent. *A line,* Nellyn thought. *My life became a line then, just as Lanara told me. My life in the sand, straight, marked with changes from that day, though I did not understand it until now.* Now: aching, stiff, spinning with past and future so that "now" did not exist. *I used to. I have never. I will.* Circles opened into lines and he felt broken and grieving and new.

He looked out of the hut, barely hearing his companions' gasps. The rain was hard and warm, and he was blind for a moment as it coursed over his face. Then he blinked and blinked again and he could see, though not clearly. Everything was flowing and strange: the other huts, the sand. The sky was tiny, crushed by cloud. He saw the river when the wind tore spaces in the rain. It was brown and foaming.

Nellyn crawled outside. "No!" someone cried after him, but he did not turn back. He stood up slowly, stretching his arms, wriggling his toes deep into the sand that was now mud. The falling water made his nose sting. He touched it and winced at the pain that lanced behind his eyes and up into his skull.

He took a careful step and fell. There suddenly seemed to be another river here, gushing among the houses. It plucked him and spun him, and he scrabbled for a bit before he let it take him. He slithered and bumped—and then he heard the roaring foam of the real river approaching, and he dug his heels and hands into the mud. He came to a skidding halt on the bank and rolled out of the small torrent that had carried him. His legs dangled into nothing. He waved them weakly a few times but could not crawl fully onto the bank.

A fish was lying an arm's span away from him, flopping and gasping, its reddish gills opening on air it could not breathe. Nellyn touched it lightly with his fingertips, then swept his arm out so that it sailed back into the river. He lay with his cheek in the mud and his legs in the air and started to laugh. He laughed until he shook. He heaved himself onto his back and thought he might also be crying, though the difference between the two would not matter. Circles and lines, his blood and his stinging nose, a red wheezing fish—and her, the only clear, sensible thing somehow, the only image that did not flow away from him. He laughed, and the rain swallowed his tears.

~

Eight folded, thread-bound letters were lying by Lanara's bed when the rains ended. The first few were quite short, the last few extremely long. She wondered, on the day the sun came out, about the wisdom of sending the long ones, which reflected her increasingly desperate state of mind a bit too clearly. *I will read them again in a few days,* she decided. She thought this almost idly. The sun was turning the remaining drifts of cloud to gold, and she could feel its warmth on her outstretched legs. She sighed and wriggled her toes and listened to the silence where the rain had been.

Green shoots were uncurling around her tent and down the slopes of the ridge. She thought she could see them growing. Some were already very tall, with delicate pink or yellow flowers. The distant cacti were also covered in blossoms. Birds clung to the spines and dipped their beaks in, and she almost went to them, to look more closely at their whirring iridescent wings and tiny feet. But she stayed by her tent, with her back against a support pole, until the sun was directly overhead and hot. Then she rose and walked toward the village, her feet bare on the damp sand.

The shonyn would be sleeping, she guessed, as relieved to see the sunlight as she had been. She would come down again at dusk to greet them and watch them greet each other, all of them hungry for voices and space and the comfort of light before darkness.

She hesitated beside Nellyn's house. The curtain hung motionless, still splotched with wet. She heard nothing from behind it. She thought of his face, bloodied and changed, as she had so often while the rain pelted her sleeping tent. *Patience,* she reminded herself. *You will see him soon enough.* She turned away from his house and went down to the river, which was high and clear and dappled with birds, fish, fallen lynanyn.

The silver leaves were blindingly bright; even their reflections dazzled her eyes to tears. She dipped her foot in the water, which was cool. With a quick glance behind her, she dove in. Five long strokes took her to where the river bottom dropped away. She floated there, feeling the brush of plants and fish against her legs. For a moment she remembered the Queenspool in the Throne Chamber, and the glass-walled room outside it. A bird skimmed the river's surface near her and plucked up a fish. Another bird bobbed among a cluster of lynanyn, slicing them open one by one until the surrounding water was blue. She smiled and swam slowly downstream.

The shonyn crops were thick and tall. Lanara rolled onto her back as she approached them. She saw their green against the blue of the sky and thought, *I must write Ladhra and tell her how beautiful this is*—and then she saw Nellyn. He was sitting where they had sat together, before Gwinent and the rains. He was looking down at a lynanyn, peeling it in one unbroken, winding strip. She felt weak with relief as she watched him: he was here, he looked the same as he always had.

"Nellyn," she called at last, wanting to see his face, and when he lifted his head she saw that he was not the same.

He smiled at her as she swam to the bank. "Lanara," he said when she was sitting beside him, wringing out her tunic. She dropped the folds of cloth and stared at him. "What is it?" he asked.

"My name," she said. "I've never heard a shonyn pronounce it."

"Lanara," he repeated, drawing out each syllable. "Do I say it well? Did I?"

She smiled. "You did, yes." He held out a dripping piece of lynanyn to her. She took it from his fingers, which were warm and dry and steady. "How are you?" she said, her eyes slipping away from his. "How were the rains, after your … experience with Gwinent?"

"Gwinent. So that is his name. I am well, now. I was perhaps a bit mad at first, and my sleeping companions were afraid for me. But now I am well. I stayed alone in an empty hut just there. I needed this loneliness." He picked three seeds from the lynanyn and put them in his mouth. "You still stare at me."

"Yes," Lanara said, her own piece of fruit forgotten and slowly staining her palm. "It's just that you're so different. And you speak almost perfectly, as if you've always used our words for time. I'm amazed that you're so calm, I suppose."

He shook his head. "Not calm—but I thank you for this thought. And my speaking is smooth because I always heard these words as a small one. A child. They were in my mind all this time, without understanding—but now I understand, and they are ready. It is strange, yes. I wish to tell my teacher Soral."

"I could write to him," Lanara said. "I'm sure he'd be very proud."

Nellyn nodded. He threw a seed into the water and it disappeared immediately beneath. The rings that bloomed after it widened to the shore. "And you," he said, "how were your rains? And Gwinent's?"

Lanara cleared her throat. "Gwinent is gone. He left while you were still unconscious and he didn't come back. Which was a good thing. The rains were difficult, but I wouldn't have wanted his company after what he did to you."

Nellyn smiled again. She thought suddenly that he seemed drunk, or younger, or not shonyn. "Tell me about your difficult rains," he said.

She ate the piece of lynanyn before she answered. The stain on her palm was crescent-shaped. She traced it lightly with a finger. "I thought I was lonely here before this. That seems silly now. Each day of rain was a bit harder, a bit emptier. At first the sound of it on my tent was soothing, but very quickly it grated on me. There was no quiet and no escape and no one to talk to or laugh about it with." She sighed. "I was so excited when Queen Galha told me I'd be alone here. Such responsibility! Such a perfect way to prove myself to her! But I'd have begged her for companions, those last few days. Even Cannin."

"But not Gwinent."

She glanced sidelong at him. "No, not him. But since you've mentioned him again, and since you're obviously quite comfortable with talking now, tell me why you ran at him that day. And don't tell me it was only the rains."

He did not answer for a long time. *The old Nellyn,* she thought. She wished she had her parchment and writing stick, and hoped she would remember if he told her something useful.

"It was only the rains," he finally said, very solemnly.

~

My Queen, you will notice that there are several days not accounted for in this batch of correspondence. This is because the fabled shonyn rains kept me secluded in my tent with no one—not even the children—to speak to. Without such contact I found I had little of any importance to relate to you. Now, though, the sun is shining once more and my daily letters will resume.

I am happy to inform you that Nellyn seems to be adjusting painlessly to his new concept of time and language. He has been far more talkative than he was before and has already told me several fascinating things. For example, the shonyn only eat fish after the rains, when they can be scooped out of the water like lynanyn. He said, "Shonyn are finders, not seekers." I thought this very strange, but of course did not let him see this. I am more excited than ever to relate to you what I learn from him.

~

He almost could not look at her. "Will you come again tomorrow?" he asked, each word an echo but each one new. He was dizzy again; he heard his voice as if someone else were speaking. He could not feel the lynanyn half he was holding, though he knew it would be cool. His skin too was a stranger's.

"Yes," she said, "I will."

EIGHT

Lanara woke with a start. The light in her tent was grey and thick—a cloudy dawn, too early to be waking. At first she heard only the hammering of her own heart. As it calmed, she heard the river and the quiet hum of shonyn voices, carried on wind. Then another sound, much closer. She sat up and called, "Who's there?" to the shadow in her half-open door flap.

"Maarenn," said a voice, and a young shonyn woman ducked inside. She hesitated, looking down at her feet.

Lanara said, "Please come closer. I can't see you very well."

Maarenn took three steps toward the bed and stopped. "I am sorry. I know this is your sleeping time, but I can only come now. I …" She finally looked up. Lanara saw dark eyes, curly hair tied back but falling over one shoulder. "I need to speak to you. Of Nellyn."

Lanara wrapped her blanket around her and sat on the edge of the bed. She motioned Maarenn to the chair. After a long moment the young shonyn women sat, very stiffly. Lanara said, "What about Nellyn?"

In the silence, she heard someone laugh in the village below. Maarenn turned to the door flap. Lanara thought she saw her smile before she looked back at the room. She spoke then, quite quickly, as if she had practised the words.

"Nellyn stays alone in an empty hut, far away from his sleeping companions. He does not join me on our flatboat, even though we are gathering companions. He takes a different one and gathers alone. He speaks to no one."

Lanara ran a hand over her hair and down her neck, and closed her eyes, which felt gritty from too little sleep. "And you have come to me," she said, opening her eyes, "because you think this is my fault?"

"Fault?" Maarenn repeated. "I do not understand this. I come to you to say he is dear to me and many others. He suffers with change. Perhaps you do not see this. So I speak to you."

Lanara shook her head. "No—he is happy. I know he is. Confused maybe, because he *is* changing—but this confusion will pass."

"Pass? No. There is no return for him, with you here."

Lanara stared at Maarenn. "You *are* blaming me," she said, her voice rising. "And you're telling me to leave him alone, yes? As if it's any of your business. It's his choice—all of it. Not yours."

Maarenn shook her head again. She rose from the chair and stood with her hands upturned. "I am sorry—I do not know … He tells me you want to understand us, so I try to help you do this. And I try to help him. He cannot give you understanding of shonyn, you must talk to someone else for this. And you must let him find us again."

Lanara rose as well, still holding her blanket close around her. She was taller than Maarenn, and this was her tent, but she felt awkward as her anger dissipated. "I appreciate your concern for Nellyn and for me. But please be reassured: I won't hurt him. I am his friend, as you are."

"No," Maarenn said, "no." She turned and left the tent, as silent as all shonyn were on the sand.

Lanara did not watch her go. She lay on her bed as the grey light turned to gold, and longed once more for home.

~

Nellyn pushed his flatboat but it did not move. He pushed again, grunting with the effort, and it edged down the bank.

"There are reasons why we do not take our flatboats out alone."

Nellyn straightened and turned. "Wise one," he said to the woman behind him. The shonyn words felt strange on his tongue. "Please—do not stand here. Return to your stone and sit with the others."

She said, "No, tall one. I talk to you now."

Water slapped against flatboat wood. Across the river, a lynanyn fell with a muffled splash. Nellyn heard other flatboats, other shonyn pushing them and talking and picking up their poles.

"Tell me why," the wise one said.

He looked at the river, dappled with low sun and growing shadows. "Why …?"

"Why we do not take our flatboats out alone. Tell me this."

Nellyn shifted on the sand. He should be sitting at the wise one's feet; he should be listening and nodding, wrapped in words. For a moment he yearned for this so keenly that he sucked in his breath, but then he saw his own hut and remembered Lanara's laughter, and the yearning became a different ache. "We do not take them out alone because they are heavy. It is easier with two." He answered as he had when he was a child sitting in the Queensfolk teaching tent.

"Yes, that is one reason. But there is a larger one beneath it. You know this one also. Remember, Nellyn. Remember that we cannot be strong or good alone."

The flatboats had all been launched. He could see them upstream, glistening with spray and the last of the daylight. The full moon was already high in the sky. Nellyn looked at it and did not speak. *We are all alone,* he thought. *Beneath the stories is our own breathing. One breathing only.* He turned back to her to say this, or something else—but she was gone.

He was still gazing down at her footprints when Lanara touched him lightly on the shoulder.

"Thinking, I see," she said as he blinked at her. "You were still here, so I came back down. Is anything wrong?"

He shook his head. "No. My flatboat is heavy—that is all. That was all. I go—I will go. Now."

"Let me help you," she said, and they bent together with their hands on the wood.

He looked at her when he was crouched on the flatboat. She was standing up to her shins in water, smiling. "Come with me," he said, and felt suddenly breathless, as if he had fallen.

She said, "Really? Do you …?"

"Come," he said, and held out his hand.

~

Lanara had never seen such darkness. Luhr's streets were lit with lanterns at night, and the palace's tower windows were always bright. On her journey to the Sarhenna River she had set torches outside her tent to frighten away curious desert creatures. And on the Queensship she had slept through the deepest part of the night. Now, sitting cross-legged on Nellyn's flatboat, she could almost feel the blackness around her. The stars still flickered in the sky and on the river, but the moon had set. River, flatboat, Nellyn, lynanyn, herself: all edges were water, in this darkness. Her eyelids were heavy, but she did not sleep.

They had not spoken since he had started gathering lynanyn. She listened to his hand brushing the water and the gentle thud of the fruit as he set them on the wood, then his pole scattering drops as it rose and fell, pulling them slowly back to the shadows of the village.

The darkness had thinned to dawn when the flatboat ground to a halt on the bank. Neither of them moved. "Lanara," he said, and she looked up at him through the mist that was rising from the river. "Let us do what you said before. Let us go down the river."

She shook her head. "I was joking. Not being serious. Remember?"

"We do not have to go to the end. Just a small distance. I get you a pole and you can help me—" And he was gone, slipping away along the bank.

Moments later he returned with another pole. As she lifted it from his hands, she said, "Are you sure?"

He bent and pushed the flatboat out again into the current.

At first neither of them used the poles. The river grasped the flatboat and turned it slowly around. As it drifted downstream, the mist burned away and Lanara saw the banks on either side of them and the red houses of the village shrinking behind. The lynanyn trees too were dwindling, replaced by leafless bushes whose thorn-covered branches arched over the water.

The river bent and the flatboat began to angle toward the far bank. Before Nellyn could reach for his pole, Lanara stood up. She balanced at the front, holding her arms out. "Let me steer," she said, and laughed as the river rocked her off her feet. "Really," she added, picking up a pole and leaning on it, "I want to try. And I want you to be able to look around."

She swiftly found the rhythm of pole and water. It was almost like riding a horse: the clenching and easing of muscles, the motion of something wild and living. Dip, raise, turn, dip, raise, turn. She laughed again and shook the spray from her hair and face.

She set her pole down when the river calmed, in a place between rock walls. Nellyn was staring at the rock, his eyes wide and nearly black. "I do not know this," he said as she sat down facing him. "This kind of bank. This water."

"No, of course you don't. But you must have expected it to be strange, away from your village."

He swallowed and turned his dark eyes on her. "How can I expect? This is another first time. I have never seen banks like this, that are not sand. And the lines in them—they sparkle, maybe like your towers in Luhr? And this water is dark green and still. How can it be that this is the river I know?"

"It is part of your river. There are many parts to know. But it is all the same river, as you have said to me."

"I said this, yes, but I did not see. I had not seen." His one hand was clenched white around his pole. The other was twitching, fingers opening and closing on nothing.

"Nellyn." She leaned forward and put her hands over his. "Don't be afraid. You will become accustomed to these new things. And you are not alone—I am here to help."

He pressed her fingers until they were numb. *He needs me,* she thought, and felt a rush of warmth.

He drew his hands away and held them to his cheeks. "Not alone? But I am not all shonyn now. And I never will be a Queensman. How can you say I am not alone?"

She looked over his head at the red rock. There *were* bands in it: crystal, white and clear and light green. "Your shonyn friends are worried about you," she said. "They want you to return to them."

"I do not know. Maybe I cannot return." He rolled his pole over. The wood beneath it was wet. "Help me, since you say you can. Tell me what I will do."

Lanara did not speak for a long time. *I am a Queenswoman,* she thought. *I have brought about this situation, and I must resolve it wisely. The Queen sent me here for this.* She drew a deep breath. "You must make a choice. Sometime you will have to choose how to live, and with whom."

"Choose," he repeated, as if he had never heard the word before. He lay slowly down on his side, facing away from her, and drew his legs up to his chest.

When he did not move, she eased herself down behind him. She stared at the smooth place at the base of his skull and wondered suddenly what blue skin would feel like. She raised her fingers but did not touch him, though she was warm again with her own need. She fell asleep, curled in the shadow of the rock.

When she woke, the shade was gone and the flatboat bobbed in blinding sun. Nellyn had turned toward her. His sleeping face swam into focus as she blinked herself fully awake. She moved her head and arm and leg, and groaned. Her skin was burned, stretched too tightly over her bones. She sat up carefully and groaned again, and his eyes opened.

"Don't move," she said between her teeth. "We've done a foolish thing and we can never move again."

"What is wrong?" he asked, and she snorted.

"Isn't it obvious? Look at my skin. I'm sunburned." As soon as the words were spoken, she thought, *Lanara, you fool.*

Nellyn said, "I do not know about this, since shonyn do not go out in day sun." He smiled. "But your skin is very red on that side. Like a kind of fish."

She gave an incredulous laugh. "Indeed?"

He nodded and reached for one of the lynanyn he had piled on the flatboat during the night. "Yes. But I will help you."

"Ah, yes—the miraculous lynanyn," she said as he made a hole in one end with his thumbnail.

"Put your arm like this," he told her, and squeezed the fruit until juice dribbled, then flowed.

She gasped. It was very cool, and stung a bit before it numbed. "You aren't burned," she said as he held the lynanyn over her leg. "Maybe because you're darker-skinned than I am. Quite unfair." She wriggled as juice fell on her neck. "Wait, Nellyn, that tickles …"

Her voice died when she saw his face. He was very still. The green river lifted them once, twice, before she said, "Let's go back now." He smiled, and she looked away from its gentleness and its pain. She thought, *Don't touch him. Don't make things more difficult.* She rose and took up her pole. She knew his eyes were on her, and she felt light with strength and the certainty of desire.

~

Nellyn felt as if he had been shaking since dawn, from too much strangeness and too much sun, and a light sleep riddled with dreams he could not remember. Her skin also, streaked with blue and sweat. And then the effort of their journey back to the village, both of them straining against the current.

"I'd like to lie down here," Lanara said when they were standing on the bank he knew, near the red huts. "But I probably wouldn't be able to get up again. And I don't want to burn any more than I already have."

"Yes," he said, the word forced from a jaw that was locked and sore. He saw that his pole was trembling and tried to hold it more tightly.

"See you this evening," she said, "if we manage to wake up."

He watched her make her slow way up the ridge and remembered when he had first seen her. *She looks shonyn again,* he thought, and was amazed that he had ever truly thought this.

He groaned as he crawled into his hut. He drank cold water from a jug and ate five lynanyn seeds. Then he slept, and dreamed the sounds of sails and oars and anchor. He dreamed her voice as well, and her fingertips on the nape of his neck.

"Nellyn. Nellyn—please wake up."

He struggled to lean on his elbows. She was above him, dark against the amber light outside. "What?" he mumbled, dragging himself out of sleep as if he were walking through water.

"There is a Queensboat here. I must go now, and I had to come to you to tell you. To say goodbye."

He could see her now. She was crying, or perhaps she had been. He lifted his hand to her face. He could do this, somehow, now that she had said these words to him. She turned her head briefly so that her cheek rested on his hand, then she backed out beneath the curtain.

"Come with me. Please—walk with me to the boat."

"Explain," he said when they were both standing by the hut.

She slung her bow over her shoulder and picked up a brown leather bag. "While we walk," she replied, and he followed her toward the wise ones' stones and the boat that waited in the river. It was not as large as the Queensships he had seen before. It had only two sails and three pairs of oars, and it was lower in the water.

"This boat brought me messages from Luhr," Lanara said. "From the Queen, and Ladhra. There's a Queensman on board who'll take my place here until I come back. If I come back."

"Lanara, *explain*. The Queen sends for you?"

They were already on the bank. He saw wise ones and small ones, and Maarenn, standing nearby, but he did not *see* them. Lanara waded toward the rowboat that would take her to the middle of the river. An older woman waited in this smaller boat, her hands ready on the oars.

"No, she didn't send for me," Lanara said. "Not really. It's my choice. But she told me about something … and now I must go, right away. We need every hour."

He reached for her hand and she stopped walking for a moment. She raised her other hand and drew it gently down, through his hair and along his cheekbone. "I'm so sorry to leave you," she said. "In this way, and now. But I have no choice."

He grasped at words and felt them tumbling away from him, into a deep space that waited. "And my choice?"

She smiled, though her eyes did not. "You'll make it, I'm sure of this. And I hope it will make you happy, whatever it is." She leaned her forehead against his. "Goodbye, Nellyn."

Shonyn do not have a word for goodbye, he wanted to say. He wanted to hold her, to pelt the boat with lynanyn, to shake himself awake. Instead he stood still and silent in the river. He watched Lanara row and climb and wave. He watched the Queensboat until it vanished into the fire of the western sky.

~

Dearest Lanara, this is not a happy message. Your father is ill: a fever which will not break, and sores that grow and burst on his skin. The Queen's messenger who delivers your letters to him informed me of his illness. I am not certain how long he has been sick, and he will not tell me.

He refused my invitation to be tended to in the palace. I am therefore sending my most skilled physicians to him each day. He also expressed displeasure when I spoke to him of contacting you. He insists that the sickness will pass, and he does not wish you to be concerned for him. I, however, believe that you must know. He is not aware that I have sent you this message.

The Queensman who brings you this letter will stay in the shonyn village, should you decide to return to Luhr. Please be reassured that your father is receiving the best care possible, and do not feel that you must *return. It is your decision to make. I tell you this with greatest care and affection.*

~

Nara. He misses you so much, and he is too proud to say so. Please come home.

NINE

"Ladhra, Dearest Princess, you are the only dream in my heart. You are, to me, a thousand thousand fountains in the desert of my soul; a season of rains where before there was only scalding wind. I beseech you: choose me, when your time comes to pick among the scribes. I am passionate and loyal, and my skills of memory and writing are considerable after all my years of study. I love Luhr and all the growing Queensrealm, but above all, O water of my heart, I love you."

The paper fluttered from Ladhra's fingers to the ground. "Ugh," she said.

"I thought it was sweet," said Lanara. "Ridiculous, but sweet. What's his name? What's he like?" Ladhra pursed her lips and peered up into the leaves, and Lanara laughed. "That bad?"

"He's always squinting. And he's covered in pimples and scars that used to be pimples. His name is Baldhron. He follows me around the palace sometimes. And Malhan sees him writing these letters when he's supposed to be reading dispatches or transcribing the Days of the Fourteenth Queen, or the Eighteenth, or whoever." Lanara laughed again and Ladhra smiled at her. "It's so good to see you happy, even just for a moment. Which is why I force you to leave your house every afternoon."

Lanara nodded and leaned back against the enormous tree trunk behind them. "I know," she said. "You're surprisingly sensitive. And," she added over Ladhra's chuckle, "I'm glad of it. If I didn't have you ..." She took a deep breath and smelled wood, ferns, wet sand. Not pus and blood, though these other smells remained, beneath her fingernails and buried in her skin.

"I wish you would let me help you. My mother could send more doctors so that you wouldn't need to be there all the time. You're going to collapse soon, Nara. Or get sick yourself."

Even with her eyes closed, Lanara could see the movement of leaves in sunlight. The wind was almost cool. "You know he doesn't like doctors. And I don't like people to see him. Especially people like you, who knew him before." She opened her eyes and watched the leaves shift against the sky. Grey-green leaves, so high up, so dense that the sky seemed small. "Anyway, it won't be much longer. It can't be."

"It has already been far too long, my dear. You came back ages ago, and he was sick well before that. He's being too strong. And so are you."

Lanara stood up and stretched. Fingers leaves, arms branches, toes roots, blood sap, ancient and slow. She thought, *If only I could have such peace—be here always, firm in the earth.* She looked down at Ladhra. "Perhaps. Though we may be more stubborn than strong. And now I must go back to him."

~

Baldhron watched from behind an enormous dusky ash. He dug his fingers into the bark as he listened to Ladhra's voice, reading his words aloud to her friend Lanara. He tore a purple leaf to pieces as they laughed. He wanted to stride out from the tree's shadow and make them gasp at the power of his voice and fists—but he stayed still. His desires—all of them—would only be fulfilled with patient vigilance.

He knew, as soon as Ladhra had returned alone to the palace, that he would have to write to her again, right away. Part of his plan—but also a need whose force still surprised him. He never composed his letters to her in the palace, though he often reflected that there would be a symmetry to this: lies composed in a place of lies. Instead he walked through the corridors that would take him out the palace's main doors and into the marketplace.

He remembered now, as always, that the palace had once awed him. He had first seen it at eight years old, his small right hand clasped in the large left one of the Queensman who had taken him away from his home. A squalid, stinking home: a cave in a cliff, always thick with smoke from the cookfire, everything in it coated with ash and salt from the water so far below. His mother had promised him a better place. "Not much longer, Borwold," she would say, bending over him so that he would hear her above the booming of waves. He had had a different name then. "Be patient, my strong boy. We'll soon be away, in a fine house with a roof and walls. We'll never have to dive for them again then."

Not that he had minded the diving. She had; he knew this because she told him so, over and over, and because her face, when she launched herself out and down, was always grim. "We're just animals to them," he heard her say to the other silvershell-divers. "We court death day after day so that they can gasp and clap and feast on the crabmeat we bring them. They feast! They grow rich off selling meat and shells, while we huddle in filthy holes and eat the scraps they let us keep. Surely they could train birds or clever sea creatures to do this work?"

Baldhron tried to hate the Queensfolk because his mother did, but it was difficult. She had known life before the Queensfolk traders came to take control of the city's council; he had not. They praised him when he piled the glinting crabs at their feet. And when he threw himself into the air and heard their shouts of amazement above the wind-shriek in his ears, he felt nothing but joy. He somersaulted and twisted so that they would clap for him, and maybe give him a coin or a crab to keep for himself. As he grew, he dove from higher and higher points on the cliff, too excited to be afraid. "Their applause is not worth dying for," his mother would cry in her voice that sounded like the screech of a nesting forkbill. "You'll go in headfirst someday, or lose your mark and land on a rock, and then what would I do?"

But it was she who had died. She had been feverish the night before, and only seemed to worsen when Baldhron helped her drink more of the watered wine a kind Queensman had given him after a particularly spectacular dive. "And this is for the mother of such a gifted boy," the man had said, smiling, and Baldhron had borne the bulging skin back to her with pride he could not, this time, conceal. She had drunk a bit, then some more. By midnight she was groaning, burning with fever and a thirst that the rest of the drink, and even fresh water, could not slake. She had lurched to her feet at mid-morning, when the first dive horn sounded, had shaken off Baldhron's hand. "If I don't," she had rasped, "we won't eat tonight." She stood, swayed, steadied herself. He leaned out to watch her dive, after the third horn rang from docks to cliff. For a moment it seemed that she would turn and turn again, as always—but she did not. He saw her buck in the air below him, saw her limbs flail and slacken. He went in after her, too quickly for precision, and lost consciousness when the sea closed over his head.

Queensfolk pulled them both out. Baldhron woke lying on the longest dock, where Queensfolk silk fluttered. His mother was breathing on the wood beside him. She breathed for two days after, in the room they had given her—but at the end of that second day she vomited blood, red gouts that quickly became black, and died. The kind Queensman who had given Baldhron the wine put a hand on his shoulder after her body had been removed. "Let me take you away from here," he had said. "Let me take you to the Queenscity."

And so Baldhron had come to the city and its palace, all that time ago, clutching Queensman Senlhan's hand. His eight-year-old eyes had blinked and stared, almost unable to take in the glow of fountains and jewels. He had been installed in the Scribestower; he soon forgot his cave. As he learned to put writing stick to parchment and make words, he forgot the burn of wind and water on his skin. He was given a new name by the Queen herself, as proof of his new life; he forgot Borwold, the way it had sounded when his mother had laughed or shouted it. He was a Queensboy who served the wise and noble Queen Galha in her great realm; he forgot his mother.

He shuddered now, walking the halls that had once dazzled him. It was as if he had two sets of eyes, and saw two layers: one luminous with hope, the other dull and ugly with knowledge. *I was such a fool,* he thought again, and again this thought led to another: *But no more. One day they'll suffer for their lies.* An old vow, but it still made his stomach tighten with desire. He seemed made of desire, these days—many desires, with only one conclusion. "Princess," he breathed as he walked toward the well that would lead him away from the palace's stink.

It was a long, wet, echoing climb, as always. He took the route he had taken as a boy, the one laid out for him in the first of the anonymous notes that had been pressed into his hand in the marketplace. "Read this," the woman who had given it to him hissed. "Then destroy it." By the time he had looked up from the folded parchment, the old woman was gone.

You are Borwold, son of Yednanya, he had read. He was eleven, wandering about the marketplace looking for a coloured writing stick (forbidden in lessons). *You are a victim of deceit and should know it. Go to the well in the eastern marketplace. Make sure you are not seen.* The words flowed on—tiny, square words, very carefully made. He read the directions they gave. When he refolded the parchment, his hands were slippery with sweat.

He was very quick now, sliding over the well's rim and down into the shaft. He had been clumsier at eleven, had had to wait until the area was deserted before he tried it. But that had been part of the allure, even before he had known what awaited him below: the possibility of discovery, the mad, breathless scramble into the earth.

He had carried a torch the first time, which was unwieldy, and which he had to douse when he reached the bottom. He had since made the downward climb in total darkness. He lingered on the lowest foothold for long enough to ensure that there was a sack of clothes hanging where it should be, flat against the stone, away from the trajectory of the well's bucket. (On several occasions he had had to fumble for excuses for his dripping clothing, standing in the dazzling sunlight of the marketplace.) Then he filled his lungs and dove.

You will have to dive, the note had told him. *But you, a child of Xelnarzan cliffs, will have no trouble with this*—and he had not. His full-grown limbs still exulted in the dive and the brief swim that followed. He liked to imagine, as he kicked away from the shaft's wall, that he was an arrow. This amused and excited him: an arrow beneath the Queenscity, speeding toward a mark that would someday ruin the Queen. He stroked so powerfully beneath the water that his lungs were hardly aching by the time he touched the rounded entrance to the southern tunnel and thrust his way into the air. He hauled himself up onto the narrow ledge that jutted from the wall and took a few deep breaths before he began to walk.

You will see torches, his eleven-year-old self had read. *Follow them.* Lanterns lined the walls now; his followers kept them clean and lit. He glanced up occasionally, though not as often as he once had. The walls that curved beside and above him were inlaid with crystal and other liquid, shining stones, sprays of them, stretching from waterline to ceiling as if thrown by a powerful hand. The hand, in fact, of the Third Queen;

Baldhron had discovered this after combing the early Luhran histories for mention of the water system.

> *And so the Third Queen sent workmen beneath the city, and they hacked at layers of stone until they had fashioned a network of passages for the water the First had discovered beneath the sand. And when the passages were dug and the water channelled, the Third sent artisans beneath the city, and they fused glass and clear stones into the rock walls, in the shapes of spouts and waves, fish and other wetland beasts. All this was crafted in thanks to the water that gives life to Luhr, and to the great Queen who tapped its power.*

Baldhron had found a scientific mention of the tunnels on a clay tablet dated to the time of the Tenth Queen, and one other, very brief reference:

> *Today the Thirteenth Queen determined to visit the underground water chambers built by her ancestor; but there was no easy way to access them, as the Third Queen had not thought to make their wonders public, so it was decided that the visit would not take place.*

It is a secret place, the third, and last, anonymous note had told him. *It has been forgotten. Our cause depends on this.*

Baldhron looked at the walls now only to see where he was. The long silver eel … the white-tipped wave … the school of flatskimmers … When he found the towering braid of fern, he turned left into a smaller tunnel. He was very close. He imagined the houses above him, thinning a bit toward the city wall, and his steps quickened. This tunnel was unadorned. Its walls were red, the hard clay beneath the desert. He touched the wall as he walked. It was bumpy and beaded with damp.

"Who's there?" called a voice from the end of the tunnel.

There had been no voices on that first trip. The only sound had been the rasping of Baldhron's breath and the crackling of the parchment clutched in his hand. Now the centre of his realm was guarded by fellow students. They took shifts, standing in the narrow tunnel with water flowing at their feet, holding daggers they were willing to use but had never been required to. Baldhron had not stood guard for two years. This was the Scribesrealm, and he was its ruler.

"Baldhron!" he called back. Part of him still flinched when he heard or spoke this name of which he had been so proud as an ignorant boy. He had considered changing it, here below the city—but its Queensfolk syllables revolted him, and revulsion made him strong.

"I didn't expect—" the guard, Pentaran, stammered. "That is, you don't customarily visit at this time of day ..."

Fool, Baldhron thought, and walked quickly to the tunnel's end as Pentaran hastened after him.

Baldhron always sucked in his breath when he entered this vast, round chamber, even so many years after he had first seen it. Then he had gasped in awe; now the awe was twinned with pride. His chamber: a reservoir whose water lay still and smooth, whose walls arched up beyond sight or lantern light, rippling with cut glass that looked like emeralds and rubies and sapphires. Many of these glass pieces were obscured, smothered by rows and rows of hanging sacks. There had been seventeen of these, suspended from hooks an arm's reach above his head. He had discovered that each sack contained parchment (some crumbled beyond legibility) and small, cracked stone tablets. The ones furthest from the entry tunnel held pages bound with twine and glue. The note had directed him to the second-furthest sack, but he had opened the closest one first, impatient with excitement.

I am scribe Drenhan, he had read, peering close to the first scroll he had unrolled very gently, *and I betray my Queen as I write—but write I must, for there are lies in this city and this land, and someone must tell truth.*

Baldhron had set the scroll down on the ledge. It had been so limp with damp and age that, once laid flat, its ends barely curled. *No,* he had thought even as he rose to walk to the second-furthest sack, *don't do this. Leave now. This is a place of lies, and it is treason even to read them ...*

He saw the piece of parchment as soon as he opened the sack. One corner torn, some of the red writing-stick markings smudged: the note had told him it would look like this. He had felt nothing but dread as he plucked it free.

Yednanya, silvershell-diver of Xelnars, has been poisoned. I was approached with this news by a servant in the Queenshouse here. The servant had overheard a conversation and then glimpsed a written order from Luhr. Queen Galha commanded Yednanya's murder, for the woman had been attempting to convince the other divers (all desperately poor) to revolt against the city's Queensfolk council of trade. It was one of these divers who warned the Queensfolk. The diver was rewarded with silver—and Yednanya was poisoned, as Galha instructed, with watered wine given as a gift to her son. The divers have since been quiet and agreeable to the Queensfolk who exploit them. As for the son: his name is Borwold, and he is to be brought to Luhr by Senlhan, the same Queensman who delivered the poison to him. Another grateful, pliant child to do the Queen's "good work." Watch him closely.

Baldhron had read this letter innumerable times since that first one, and the sickness never failed to return to his gut and heart—bile of rage and hurt and fear that had very soon been rage only. He had scrambled back to the well shaft and up; he had run through the marketplace looking for the old woman who had given him the note. He never saw her again. The next note had been delivered by a half-giant who did not understand the Queenstongue, the third by a boy younger than himself who had torn himself from Baldhron's grip and disappeared into the crowd. *My fellow renegade-scribes have dwindled away*, this third note said, *murdered or afraid or simply old, as I am. But I am not the last of the truth-keepers. You will take our truth and make it yours.*

Thirty-seven sacks lined the Scribesrealm library's walls now. They stretched along the left-hand walkway nearly to the opposite tunnel entrance. Fresh parchment and writing sticks were stored on a recessed ledge by the bridge that spanned the widest part of the pool. Baldhron's people used them, people whose names he had found in the sacks, and others—student scribes—whom he had watched and then spoken to, testing them before he revealed his realm to them. Some of them completed their lessons and were made full scribes and dispatched elsewhere in the Queensrealm; they sent messages back, which were labelled and placed in the appropriate bags. (One of these messages read: *Queensman Senlhan was stabbed to death at the Queenshouse in Xelnars by a "thief" who will never be found …*) None of Baldhron's people had ever betrayed him. He liked to think that this was simply because of the strength of his knowledge, and his charisma, but it was also thanks to the care he had taken in selecting them. When he had discovered people in Luhr whose families were mentioned in the sacks of the Scribesrealm, he watched them, spoke to them frequently, casually, before he revealed his purpose. Some of these people proved unworthy of the Scribesrealm, or unready for it. Some, like Ladhra's friend Lanara.

A palace serving girl has confirmed that Salanne, Galha's dearest friend, has met several times with consort-scribe Malhan, late at night when the Queen has been sleeping. It will not be long before Galha discovers this deception.

Galha had discovered it, of course, and Salanne had been sent away and dispatched. The details were here, curled within a bag. Baldhron had imagined drawing Lanara slowly, carefully into his realm, away from Ladhra, but he never had. She was too close to the Queen's family, too devoted. She would run to Galha with the information he gave her, whether or not she believed it. So he watched her with Ladhra, and he contented himself with the certainty that someday he would ruin them both.

"We will change history," he had said once before a gathering of fifty. "Our numbers and our knowledge will soon be too great to contain. For now, we will simply record history as it should be recorded, and wait." They had cheered until the walls and water seemed to quiver.

"No need to accompany me," he said to Pentaran now. The man fell back and lowered his eyes.

Baldhron walked past him to the recess in the wall that held the parchment and writing sticks. He parted the cloth curtain and opened the wooden box behind it. He lifted its lid, which did not close tightly any more; the air here had warped it and corroded the metal that had once been a latch. He drew out a clean, nearly flat page and laid it on a slanted board he had had fixed to the wall. He twirled the writing stick between his thumb and forefinger.

My darling Ladhra, he wrote at last, *I feel that I am going mad …*

TEN

Lanara walked alone through the marketplace. She had asked Ladhra to come with her, but the Princess had said, "The marketplace?" and wrinkled her nose. "No, thank you. My mother's been telling me for years that there are exotic diseases there, and I'm starting to believe her." As soon as she had spoken, she put a hand to her mouth. "Oh, Nara—I'm so sorry. What a terrible thing to say to you!"

Lanara had smiled, though it had felt like a shadow on her face. Her exhaustion was so great that she thought she could sometimes hear it, like another heartbeat beneath her own. "Don't worry," she had said. "Never worry about what you say to me."

She remembered coming here as a child, hanging on to Creont's hand, straining to see everything at once. She even remembered the three of them there: her father's hand and her mother's, and her in between, swinging her legs off the ground with every other step. *"Concentrate, Lanara,"* he had said sternly. *"We must look only for what we need or we will never leave."*

It was still difficult to concentrate, even now that she was so much older—but she found the fruit vendor's stall quite quickly, between an acrobats' stage and a mound of iben stones. The stage was empty, though Lanara could hear voices in a tent behind it, raised in an argument. An iben woman crouched on the rock, her cloven hoofs hidden beneath the russet folds of her dress. Her taloned fingers and the long horns on her head caught the sunlight. Her eyes were narrow and slanted, heavily lidded against mountain wind and snow and sunlight that was very bright above the clouds. Lanara's teachers had told her of the iben and their mountains. And there was a story: The iben had come to the First Queen when she was young and very ill, drained by the mindpowers with which she had created the Queenspool. They had spoken to her of the greatness of the city she had founded, and of her own legacy. They told her that she would be the only queen for countless generations to possess such mindpowers—but they added that another queen would be born of her line someday who would also use great powers for the benefit of the realm. They had sung her to sleep then, soothed and reassured. All these generations later, young people brought them silver just before their weddings, and old ones gave them coins to hear the manner of their death, though often they did not understand what they were told.

"You would hear words of future?" the iben woman said as Lanara hesitated below her.

"No," Lanara replied after a long silence. "Thank you, but no."

"You are certain?"

Lanara thought of the dark house she had left and the fever-damp skin of her father. She thought of Nellyn, knee-deep in the river, silent and still. *"If I come back."*

"Yes," she said, "I'm certain."

The fruit vendor nodded at her when she turned to him. "A wise choice," he said in a low voice, glancing at the iben woman. "Half of what they say is nonsense. A waste of good coins and better time, is my opinion." When Lanara did not respond, he cleared his throat. "Now then, what'll you have? Some bitter mang? Speckled sourfruit from the hidden groves of Fane? Some sunfruit, perhaps? All these are perfectly ripe now."

The piles of fruit glistened. Flies clustered above, scattering when a boy waved at them with a long spoon, then gathering again. She looked for blue among the reds and oranges and unripe greens.

"I need some lynanyn," she said.

The vendor shook his head. "The only fruit I cannot sell you today. The ones I have are past their time. I'm expecting a new batch in a few weeks, after the next Queensship reaches my supplyman. In the meantime, though, why not try some silverbells? Succulently sweet."

"Show me the lynanyn you have, even though you won't sell them to me."

He frowned. "Very well. I can't imagine why you … but here."

She held out her hand for the lynanyn he drew out from under the counter. It was not blue, not round; brownish-black instead, sunken and small in her palm. It was so light that she knew there would be no juice within. Perhaps even the seeds would be withered.

"So why?" he asked after a moment. "Why are you interested?"

She curled her fingers around the lynanyn. "Someone told me once that lynanyn had healing properties. And its juice is so sweet—I wanted to give it to someone, just to try, once. He always said it was too expensive." She bit her lip and passed the fruit back to the man. *I could have brought back a bagful,* she thought. *Or an entire* tree. *Too hasty.*

The iben woman stood up as Lanara walked past. She quickened her pace until she was almost running, but she still felt the narrow eyes on her, steady and knowing beneath the horns.

When she reached her home, she pulled open the door and stepped without flinching into the darkness and the stench.

"Lanara?" Creont's voice was still his. In the darkness it was almost possible to see him again as he had been, except that it had never been dark here before, with the door open to sun and starlight.

"Lanara?" said another voice, and she answered, "Yes, Dornent, it's me. You can go."

The doctor stood with her for a moment, holding a bag of vials and pipes and herbs to his chest. "A little worse," he whispered. "Send for me tonight if you need to."

"'A little worse,'" her father growled as she sat down beside his bed. "The man says the same thing every day. Promise me …" He paused, and she heard the breath whistling deep in his throat. "Promise me you will *not* send for him, this night or any other."

She smiled as she dipped a cloth into the bowl by his head. She did not need light now to find these things; she knew this room by touch. He winced when she drew the cloth along his forehead, and she held it there, lightly, before she continued down his face. She could feel his fever. "I promise," she said.

He muttered something she did not understand, and moaned and then was silent except for the whistling breath. She sat and thought of the darkness of the Sarhenna River. *"Ages ago,"* Ladhra had said. Lanara felt the rolling of the flatboat, and she heard the water and the gentle sound of the lynanyn on the wood. *If only,* she thought again, and dipped the cloth back into the bowl.

~

Lanara opened the windows and the door. She stood in the sunlight, blinking at the table and its clutter, the sandy tracks on the floor from her feet and the doctors'. She swept the sand over the stoop slowly and meticulously. The air from outside was almost unbearably fresh. She took shallow, fearful breaths. When there was nothing left to sweep, she set the broom against the wall and leaned her head beside it. The clay was already warm.

"Nara." She lifted her head. Queen Galha was standing in the doorway, with no one but Malhan behind her. He remained by the door when the Queen stepped into the room. She was wearing no jewels, only a plain bronze cloak pin. There was a scarlet ribbon in her hair. *Mourning scarlet,* Lanara thought, and began to tremble.

"I came as quickly as I could," Galha said. "I have told Ladhra that she must wait to see you. The Devotees will be here soon enough, and then you will have no quiet." She held out her hand and Lanara took it lightly.

"Thank you," she said in a voice that was not hers. "I know how busy you are, and I am honoured ..."

"Lanara." The Queen's other hand was beneath her chin, raising it so that Lanara was looking into her face and her golden-brown eyes. "You are like another daughter to me. You *are* my daughter, now that your own parents are gone." Lanara began to cry, though she made no sound. Galha brushed at the tears with her thumb, very gently. "I have ordered your father to be placed in one of the tombs set aside for palace folk. We will go there together when the Devotees have finished preparing his body. And I will choose his tomb fountain from my own palace stock." She paused. "I longed to do this for your mother, but it was not possible since we did not have her body. It pleases me that I can offer these things to you now."

"Thank you," Lanara tried to say again, and Galha squeezed her hand.

"Take me to him," the Queen said.

Lanara shook her head. "Please do not feel you must. He is ... it is not ..."

The Queen walked with her to Creont's bedroom door. Lanara opened it, and they looked together at the man on the bed. Galha said, "Oh, my dear," and drew Lanara in, to flower-scented silk and warmth and the steady murmur of her heart.

~

"My darling Ladhra, I feel that I am going mad. You show me no special favour, though I have done nothing but praise and entreat you. Why? Why do you ignore my pleas and my devotion?"

Lanara laughed, her face turned up to the sky, so close atop this highest tower. The stone was warm against her back. Beside her, Ladhra blew out her breath. "You sound like a horse," Lanara said. "I wonder if Baldhron would still love you if you were a horse."

"No doubt," Ladhra said, holding the letter under the spray of a fountain until the writing bled away. "He seems fairly single-minded. *Devoted,* I believe was his word."

Lanara lay and Ladhra sat, and the ivy whispered into their silence.

"It's strange," Lanara said at last, "that I often feel so normal. As I do now. But then I'm so sad, or restless. I thought time would change this, make me feel the same always—steady."

Ladhra angled her head into Lanara's vision. "Foolishness. You've had a fairly remarkable year. It will probably take several more years to recover. Years which," she added, "I hope you'll spend here. Though you say you're restless and I fear we'll lose you again."

"No, not yet. I'm not ready to go anywhere."

There were footsteps on the stairs then and Lanara saw Ladhra look up. "Seront, what is it? Does my mother need me?"

Lanara rolled over and leaned on her elbow. The Queensguard was red-faced and sweating. She thought he might be trying not to lean against the door frame. "No, Princess," he said. "I have brought someone to see Queenswoman Lanara."

~

He was nearly blind with sunlight and exhaustion. Colours blurred as the Queensman led him from a gate into the palace. Colours, shapes that somehow had no form, noises so loud that he could not hear them. Steps, on and on, to a place even brighter than the others. Brighter, but quieter. He raised his head and rubbed his eyes and saw falling water, trailing plants, clouds that he could touch. And her face, lifting to look at him.

"He asked for you at the gate," he heard the Queensman say. "He claims to know you. I was ordered to bring him here and to escort him away if he lied."

She rose and said his name like a question. She took two small steps and then she ran, and her arms wound around his ribs and held him.

"My choice," he said as he dropped to his knees on the stone.

ELEVEN

She is standing on the deck of the ship, looking west toward her home. Her bow is slung over her shoulder and her brown bag is beside her, its buckle winking daylight at him. He calls her name, but his voice is lost in thunder. He tries to walk to her, but the boards of the deck are slick with lynanyn juice. The blue pours over his feet and spatters his legs, and he trips and begins to slide, past snakes of rope and rolled-up carpets and writing trays full of wooden blocks. He slides until he can no longer see her. Then he falls.

Nellyn lay with his arms and legs spread wide, feeling his heartbeats and the firmness of the bed. A soft bed, with cushions and a light sheet. He turned his head and saw a low table beside him with a candle on it. He had never seen a candle; it was her word, and he stared at the colours of its flame as the images of his sleep faded.

When his eyes had adjusted to the candlelit darkness, he saw a shape he knew on the table. He reached for it slowly, his fingers trembling until they touched it. It was nearly ripe, its skin barely yielding. Not one he would have scooped out of the river, one that should have been on a branch still. One he would have left to water and birds and fish. He cupped it on his chest and watched the flame turn it from blue to black.

"Would you like me to help you peel it?" She rose from the floor beside the table. He felt the sheet and cushions shift as she sat on the bed. She was wearing white, not blue and green. Her face and arms looked very dark.

"Yes," he said—a whisper, because he could not imagine his voice yet in this room. He watched her fingertips, her nails, the skin bending and breaking away from the fruit. Juice droplets fell onto the sheet. Her head was lowered and she was smiling. Shonyn time would hold her here, her skin and the wavering candlelight and the night blue of the lynanyn. But he watched her and knew he could not keep this moment; it was slipping like the peel, curling away from him.

She took his hand in her own and they slid a bit, slick with juice. The lynanyn piece was firm—too firm, but he raised it to his mouth and bit. For just a breath the river sang and voices hummed around him.

"Thank you," he said when he had eaten. "I did not take much lynanyn with me, only what I carried in both hands. But the journey was very long."

"And you didn't eat for most of it, by the looks of you." She touched his hair, said, "Tell me about this journey, Nellyn."

He spoke until his throat was dry. She gave him lynanyn juice in a cup and he spoke again. The words of past were echoes, shadows of what had been, and he was amazed at their distance and their strength. The wise ones' faces turned away from the rail of the ship where he stood and could not move. Maarenn's face, shining with tears, and her hand raised to him in a farewell for which she had no word. The village huts disappearing, the last flashes of silver from the lynanyn trees. Sleeplessness and fear. A kind Queenswoman who had led him from the boat to a caravan of merchants bound for Luhr. A desert with no river. Spires that looked like cacti from a distance he could not guess at; closer, closer still, and they were impossibly tall, their tips lost in cloud. Voices speaking languages he did not know; noises, creatures, stones he did not know. The palace, and her name, and an endless flight of stairs. Falling and darkness.

"And now you're here," she said when he fell silent. "With me."

"With you," he said, and felt a sudden, different fear. He had not thought of arrival. He had thought of her as she had been by his river, but not of her as she might be in her own place. The chill of a future that could not be known swept through him, and he looked away from her.

He heard a rustling of cloth and the bed moved beneath him. She said his name. Her fingers brushed his cheek, his neck, the line of his shoulder, under his tunic. He shivered and closed his eyes, and she stroked his eyelids with her thumbs until he opened them again. She was on her side next to him, leaning on one elbow. The candlelight swam over her skin.

He raised his own fingers to her lips, and she smiled a new smile. Moments stilled and passed and stilled again, and he was dizzy but not afraid when she drew him up to her.

~

For a time Nellyn was giddy with strength. Lanara led him through the marketplace and he looked about in wonder, and laughed, and squeezed her hand when she took his. Tents, flags, baskets, food, sleeping mats, ribbons, fur, scales, gems, wood, water: colours burned his eyes, but he blinked until he could see them and did not look away. He cried out questions to her above the din of music and voices, and when she answered him, her lips brushed his ear and then his neck.

She took him into the streets of the city, where Queensfolk gathered around wells and in doorways, and children sailed tiny wooden boats in fountains. Nellyn watched the children and for a moment he felt a quiet settling upon him—but then they called to each other, and their strange names and voices shook him back to the cobbled square and Lanara's fingers laced with his.

They ate in shaded courtyards with many tables, on cushions in the marketplace, on the top step of the staircase outside her door. "Now try this," she would say, leaning forward to watch his face as he chewed or drank. At first he needed lynanyn as well, before and after the rest. Very soon he did not. He ate her food only and felt his flesh stretching away from his bones, taking a shape that was larger.

He hardly slept. Once, she woke and turned to him and murmured, "Nellyn, you must sleep sometime—at night when I do, or during the day if that's what you need still. But you must."

"Why? I am not tired. See?" And he covered her waking, laughing mouth with his.

He lay beside her while she slept, or he sat at the table looking at the maps and cups and arrows and scrolls, all familiar now, in candlelight. He did not go outside until she did, when the sun was bright on stone.

"I can't believe you aren't exhausted," she said one morning, almost frowning.

"I'm not," he said, touching a finger to the skin between her eyes. "Not any more."

~

"Nara?"

Lanara groaned and rolled away from Nellyn but did not wake. He slipped out of bed and drew one of his new tunics over his head. As he fumbled with the belt, the voice called out again.

She was standing inside the door, dark against the daylight. Nellyn blinked and began to see her: black hair pulled away from her face, wide eyes that looked green, mouth still open a bit on the name that had also been a question.

"I am Nellyn," he said after a long silence.

"I know. I was there when the guard brought you to the garden."

"I do not …" He strained to find the word he needed, another new one, another sound that fractured time. "… remember. I do not remember you." Only the water, and Lanara.

"Where is she?"

He was about to gesture to the bedchamber behind him when Lanara emerged, smiling, rubbing her hands over cheeks and hair and down her neck.

"Ladhra," she said. "It's so good to see you."

"Ah." Such a small word, but Lanara stopped walking, stopped smiling. "The Queen my mother wishes to see you. And him." Ladhra did not glance at Nellyn. "Shouldn't he be the one sleeping?"

"His name is Nellyn." He recognized anger in the flatness of Lanara's voice.

Ladhra turned and walked out of the house. "Come with me," she said from the steps. "Now."

Lanara's fingers dug into the skin between his knuckles, but she did not look at him as they walked. *"I'll take you to the Queen,"* she had said, *"when you're rested and ready. She'll be eager to meet you. And so will Ladhra."* But now the woman Ladhra strode ahead of them and Lanara too was angry, and the palace was closer, looming so far above that he could not lift his eyes to it. He felt weak, as he had not since his arrival. Lanara was bending away from him even as he clutched her hand.

When they entered the grove of trees, his dizziness passed in wonder. There were trees in the city, near fountains and lining the road into the marketplace, but not this many or this tall. The sky was leaves and branches, thicker than stars or even cloud. He stopped walking when the trunks had drawn around them, blocking out the walls behind and ahead. For a moment he felt the same stillness he had felt by the city fountain—but before he could breathe it in or push it away, Lanara tugged at his hand and drew him on.

The palace corridors were cool and dim, and lined with guards who raised their hands as Ladhra passed and sometimes spoke to her. She nodded at them but did not reply. Lanara and Nellyn followed her to a staircase that wound up and up, ringing with their footsteps. Soon Nellyn heard only his breath, which twisted his insides until he could hardly stand up straight. Lanara was a step ahead of him, holding his fingers. He could not lift his head to look at her. The walls pressed in toward him and the air darkened, and he tried to say her name.

"Ladhra!" Lanara's voice was faint, emerging from beneath his own breathing. "Wait for us! *Wait!*"

He was sitting, though he did not remember doing this. Lanara was standing beside him; he felt her hand resting on his hair. As his breathing calmed, he heard footsteps coming slowly down to them.

"Ladhra." Lanara spoke quietly now. "He isn't accustomed to going so fast. Please wait for us." Ladhra nodded and turned her head away, pressing her lips together so tightly that they whitened. "Don't be angry with me," Lanara said.

Ladhra let out a long slow breath. "I haven't seen you for so long, and I knew you wouldn't notice how long it was." She glared at the tower wall. "I wanted to be angry for much longer than this." Lanara laughed, and Ladhra looked down at her and smiled.

"We've never been very good at sustained anger," Lanara said, "thankfully. I'm sorry I disappeared."

Nellyn stood up and Lanara asked, "Better?"

There was still a darkness at the edge of his vision and his legs still trembled a bit—but he said yes because he did not want her to worry about him now that she was happy again.

They climbed the rest of the stairs very slowly. "Here," Ladhra said at last as the tower ended in another hallway, much wider and brighter than the one below.

Nellyn stood gasping in the sunlight that fell onto the flagstones and turned them pink. "In here," Lanara said, and drew him to a door flanked by guards.

Nellyn took a step back when the door opened. He blinked against even more brilliant sunlight and a breaking wave of voices. He saw more guards, and women sitting at small round tables eating grapes and bread. He heard music, maybe a stringed instrument he had seen in the market-place, whose name he had forgotten. The marketplace, where no one turned to look at him.

The voices and music fell silent as he and Lanara followed Ladhra into the chamber. He tried to stare only ahead, but could not. He saw lengths of silk against the floor, and brown hands plucking grapes from stems. Glass goblets full of sparkling crimson. Eyes and lips, blurred with the speed of his gaze, but still there, clustered and close.

A woman was standing beneath an arched doorway. "Welcome, Lanara," she said, and for a moment he thought he heard a wise one; her voice was slow and rich, and there was water flowing somewhere nearby, almost river.

"And welcome also to you, Nellyn," she went on, and he was closer and saw her clearly. She was smiling at him, though Lanara and Ladhra were raising their hands to her, their fingers pressed together. He did not speak. *"She is so beautiful,"* Lanara had told him. *"And so strong. I love her as I would love my mother if she were living—and you will love her too."* Nellyn followed Queen Galha out beneath the doorway.

At first he was relieved to have left the crowded room, but then he glanced around and felt his breath leave him again. They were suspended in sky, fastened to the stone of the palace only by a slender metal railing. "Come and look," he heard Lanara say as she guided him around fountains and blossoming plants. "Ladhra and I would come here and sit ..." They reached the rail and her words vanished in wind.

For a moment he saw the city, flat and heat-blistered beneath them, and a gleaming snake of wall. Beyond that was a haze of sand that did not end. Lanara's hands were resting on the silver metal. He looked at them as if they could soothe the rising sickness of his fear.

"Sit here by me," the Queen called from behind him, and he did. The chair was soft and faced the railing. Ladhra and Lanara sat, and there were others as well: a man dressed in brown, who sat beside but a bit behind the Queen, and a woman holding the stringed instrument whose name Nellyn could not remember.

"Nellyn," Galha said, "we are honoured that you have chosen to be here with us. Let me name those here, so that you can begin to know them."

There was a goblet in his hand. He took a sip as the Queen spoke on, and coughed as the crimson liquid seared his throat.

~

Lanara watched water falling in the fountain. She could not yet watch Galha or Nellyn. "You are the first of your kind to come within the circle of my friends," Galha was saying. She was pitching her voice higher so that her words would be clear to him. "Speak to me, Nellyn. I want to hear your voice."

The wind scattered the water like rain. Wind so strong, this high, that if you leaned out over the balcony railing you felt tugged, hands slipping, cries torn away. Lanara turned to Nellyn as the silence continued.

"But I am being so vague," the Queen said more slowly, with a gentle laugh. "Please forgive me. Let me ask you, so that you will be able to talk more easily … What do you think of our city?"

Nellyn was staring at the blue jewel in the Queen's hair. The goblet in his hand began to tip. Lanara reached over and righted it. He did not look at her.

"Your city has no river," he said at last, "but the fountains are beautiful."

Well done, Nellyn, Lanara thought. She rested her fingertips on his hand—such a slight gesture, when what she really wanted was to put her arms around him and hold him, strengthen him as she knew she could. Tenderness had ached in her ever since he had come, so weak and beautiful, to find her.

The Queen was nodding. "The river here is beneath the ground, and we tap it for our fountains. These fountains are the queens' gift to their people—a sign of life power and hope, homage to our First, greatest Queen, who drew the water up above the sand with only the powers of her mind." She leaned forward, and Lanara saw the silk of her tunic tighten against her shoulders. "Lanara has told me of your river. She wrote me so many letters, I feel as if I have seen your town and your silver trees." Galha was smiling at Lanara now.

"I wrote to you as I was expected to," Lanara said, feeling warmth in her chest and on her cheeks. "I am happy that my letters entertained you."

"Entertained," the Queen said, "and educated. You have a gift, Nara. You are lucky, Nellyn, that—"

There was a sudden clatter. Lanara looked down and saw the goblet Nellyn had been holding spinning slowly on the stone. The musician put her instrument down with a jangle of strings. Ladhra raised her eyebrows at Lanara, who bent to pick up the goblet. She saw that Galha's sandals were speckled with wine. "I am sorry," Lanara stammered, "he is not usually so ..." and then she turned to Nellyn and did not speak.

He was looking past her, past all of them, out into the sky. His eyes were so wide that she followed his gaze, but she saw only drifts of thin cloud and sun-bright blue. "Nellyn?" she said, kneading his limp hands, digging her fingers into the fleshy part of his palms. Galha was standing beside them. She too said his name, but his gaze did not waver. A steady shonyn gaze, distant, not present.

"Nellyn!" Lanara said again, more loudly. *Come back,* she thought, *quickly. Everything was going so smoothly* ... She felt the Queen's shadow over them both. "I'm sorry," Lanara said, tilting her head, "he seemed well until now." When she looked back at him, she saw that his eyes were closed, and she saw tears on his lashes, melting and slow.

~

The marketplace was quiet in darkness. Light shone from within some of the tents and wagons—red cloth, golden cloth, spaces bright between wooden slats. Nellyn heard laughter and singing, also within, and blurred. The palace towers broke cloud and stars; he knew this, even though he did not look up. He could not: he felt himself shaking, still weak from the height and strangeness of the balcony where he had wept that afternoon.

He held his wrists up one after the other and traced the flesh where his veins were, hidden by blue. He drew breath from his belly to his chest to his throat to his mouth and let it out in a silent stream. "*The river is within you."* He heard the words: wise ones' words, sounding above water. Water against the bank like breath against the air. Water threading sand like veins in skin. Life moving through places of stillness—all life together, all breath one. He remembered these sounds and these words, but he could no longer feel them.

He stood among the tents and wagons and unrolled sleeping mats, and opened his eyes wide on a night he did not know. The lights winked out as he watched, and the voices died. He began to walk through the silence, listening for wind or waves. He heard only the tearing of his own breath.

"Tall one." He did not turn because it could not be a real voice. It had to be from before, from that other place. Not real. Just as the small red huts were not real, on the balcony that saw so much desert. "Tall one—I see you." He felt hands on his arm, and stopped and looked down into a shonyn face.

She did not waver and disappear as he looked at her. She was solid. He saw the deep creases of her blue skin, and his own skin was pressed almost to bruising beneath her fingertips. "Wise one," he said in his own language, and the woman smiled.

"Wise one—no, not I," she answered, and her words fell like lynanyn into the river that had found him. "Not I, no—I am a nothing, a small, lost shonyn—but not. Though I am, yes, old," she continued, the last word in the Queenstongue. Nellyn eased his arm away from her gripping fingers.

"I was young but now am old. I was foolish, they said, and I will know this sometimes, but not all." Queenstongue and shonyn language mixed—words not lynanyn, and no river after all. He looked away from her shining, darting eyes.

"Our shonyn do not say they remember me, but they will. I left them on foot, when I was strong. I followed the Queensman's footsteps here and we live together, but he has cast me off. And you," she said, her nails digging again, "you also followed?"

He shook his head and his arm and tried to step back. "Yes," he heard himself say.

"Then you and I will walk together. I find lynanyn on the ground at night, or I steal it in their day. I take you to get some."

"No," Nellyn said, and his feet finally carried him backward. Something tripped him up, but he righted himself. He stepped and stepped again and did not look away from her.

"Tall one," she called, "we are both forgotten. Walk with me."

He wrenched himself around and ran.

TWELVE

Every time Nellyn moved his head on the pillow, Lanara expected to see blue—a blot or a smudge in the shape of his skull or the strands of his hair. This was a strange thought, and it made her feel as if she were the feverish one. She had been attempting to cool his fever ever since he had crawled into bed beside her three nights ago, whimpering, his flesh already burning. His episode on the Queen's balcony, and now his sickness. Lanara lay beside him and murmured to him, hoping that her voice would bring him back.

On the morning of the fourth day, she woke to Ladhra's voice. Lanara slipped out of her sleeping shift and into a tunic. She hesitated for a moment by the bed. Nellyn's lips were moving, though she could hear no words. *They're probably shonyn words,* she thought, and went quickly into the main room so that she could imagine she was shaking off her fear.

"Nara," Queen Galha said. She was standing where she had stood on that other morning, though there was no scarlet mourning ribbon in her hair today. Malhan was behind her and Ladhra beside him. Lanara looked out the open door and saw two Queensguards on the top step, their backs turned to the house. She saw the shining lengths of their bows, and the tips of the arrows that filled their green-and-blue-stitched quivers.

"Your father's tomb is ready at last," the Queen said. "It took longer than I wished it to, but the artisans have more than rewarded my patience."

"Oh," Lanara said, the word thick and rough. She felt three days of sweat and sleeplessness upon her, and knew her tunic was wrinkled and threadbare—but Galha smiled at her as if she saw none of this.

"Come with me. I will show it to you, and Ladhra will stay here with Nellyn. One of my Queensguards will stay as well, in case she needs to send for you."

"Yes," Lanara said. "Good." She followed the Queen past Ladhra, who was already at the table, sorting clean cloths from soiled with one hand and reaching for a bowl with the other. "Thank you," Lanara said to all of them—and then she went out into the daylight.

The palace tombs lay beneath the northernmost ring of towers. Lanara and Ladhra had often stood at the low doorways and stared at the ladders that angled away into shadow, but they had never gone any further than that. Now Lanara followed Galha and Malhan down, while the Queensguard who had accompanied them stood at the bottom, awaiting them with a lantern held high.

They did not need the lantern when they stepped beneath an arched entryway and into Creont's tomb. Its slanted roof was cut with long, thin openings. Morning sun lay on the stone walls and floor, washing the crimson paint with gold. The cut glass set in the walls flickered and burned. Lanara stood still. She stared at the glass pieces and saw shapes: blooming flowers strung with arrowheads, drops of water falling from slender hands. Real water sang atop the stone sarcophagus in the centre of the chamber. Creont's tomb fountain was crystal, fashioned somehow into a copy of the palace. Lanara forced herself to walk to the sarcophagus. She leaned in close to the fountain. She saw that there were tiny fountains within it, cascading down towers and pooling in courtyards and open rooms. She drew quickly back, brushing the Queen, who had come up behind her.

"It does not please you?" Galha said.

"Oh yes," Lanara replied, "it does—it's beautiful ..." As beautiful as the painted, glass-encrusted stone and the ivy that was already beginning to unspool up the walls. As beautiful as the sarcophagus, also red, inlaid with rubies and emeralds and sapphires in patterns that made her vision blur.

"Gaudy. Self-indulgent." Creont would have growled the words. He would have been turning away as he spoke. *"More queenly show—and for whom?"*

The city's dead were set in tombs outside the city walls, caves that were not painted or adorned and were filled only with blown sand. The bodies were buried, not placed in stone boxes, and there were many bodies in each cave. Lanara had known this since she was a child, but she had never thought of it until now. *He should be there,* she thought, guilt threading through her misery. *There's nothing of him here—nothing to call him back or give him peace. Nothing he would appreciate*—except, perhaps, for the large sand snail that was tugging slime along the sarcophagus lid. Its heavy brown shell tipped to the side and she thought it would fall, but it righted itself and continued ponderously on.

"Nara." Galha's voice sounded very loud. Her long tunic hissed across the stone as she stepped to Lanara's side. "Tell me what's troubling you."

Lanara's breath felt thin; too little air underground, or a weight of tears in her chest. "I miss him," she said. So few words for the feeling, but there were more. "And I can't stop thinking about how he died, now that I'm tending Nellyn. The fevers and the words that I can't hear or understand—it's death again, and I can't do anything to stop it. It's my fault, too: I wasn't here when my father fell ill, and I was the one who took Nellyn away from his people." She closed her eyes, but the mourning crimson was still there before her like a stain.

Galha touched her hand. "I should not have brought you here. Forgive me, my dear—and let me help you. Let me help you and Nellyn."

Lanara opened her eyes as the Queen was going out into the dim corridor. When Lanara did not move, Malhan said, "Follow her, Lanara." She did, hastily, while he walked steadily behind her. Her breath came more smoothly as soon as the tomb's glow had faded.

This time Galha led her deep into the palace. They passed many tower doors and guards whom Lanara knew, but soon they reached the innermost ring, with its two towers that she had never seen before. One of these was the Queen's sleeping tower; the other was her study. Queensguards Lanara did not recognize made the sign of the arrowhead and tugged open two thick wooden doors, and she began to climb, dizzy with confusion and weariness.

"My mother's study isn't at all like the Scribeslibrary," Ladhra had told her many times when Lanara had demanded a description. Lanara had been to the library often. It was huge and sunlit, and filled with the sounds of writing sticks and unfolding parchment. *"The study is silent,"* Ladhra had said, *"and dim"*—but these words were not enough, Lanara realized as she stepped into the room. It was round, the entire top of the tower, which was ringed by other, taller towers. No sunlight fell through the high,

arrowhead-shaped windows. Lanterns and candles lit rich red wood: table, chairs, floor, and the rows of drawers that stretched from floor to domed ceiling. The open cabinets in the library contained the scribes' transcriptions, rough and final, of documents provided by the Queen; public documents, many of them transparent with age and handling. The drawers in the Queensstudy held all the records of all the days of the queens since Sarhenna the First; private, closed, kept for the eyes of future queens. Lanara stared at these drawers, shifting her feet on the smooth, strange wood.

"Sit with me," Galha said, gesturing to a chair by the enormous triangular table. Lanara sat. "Drink," the Queen said, and Lanara saw that there was a goblet by her right hand. She took one sip, and another. The wine stung, made her feel dry and stronger. "Why is Nellyn sick?"

Lanara licked wine from her lips and set the goblet down on the table. "Because," she said slowly, "he's overwhelmed. There are so many people here, so many buildings, and his own town is tiny."

Galha shook her head. "But for many weeks after his arrival he was well. Why has his sickness struck him only now?"

Lanara took another swallow of wine, waited for it to sear its way down her throat before she answered. "When he arrived, he was content only to be with me. I was so excited by this. I dragged him into the city and I made him try all kinds of different foods. At first he didn't seem bothered by any of this. But he hasn't been eating recently—not even lynanyn. And he won't go outside without me. He's frightened here. He chose to come after me, and now he's discovered that he can't live where I do." Another gulp of wine. She would be too drunk to stand when this conversation ended.

"So," the Queen said, tracing the stones inlaid on a box of writing sticks, "he may simply need to be in a smaller, quieter place. Somewhere that will not frighten him."

"Maybe. Yes."

Galha stood and walked over to one of the drawers. She reached up and pulled it open, lifted out a stack of parchment. "Let's see," she said, spreading the sheets out in front of Lanara, "if we can find somewhere that will serve you both. A place where you can do my work and he can feel more secure."

Lanara watched the Queen bend over the parchment, moving fingers and eyes across the shapes there. "Why?" Lanara asked after a moment. "Why do this for me? For us?"

Galha looked up at her. "Any wise ruler knows that an unhappy subject is an unproductive one." She smiled. "Also, it is what any mother would do for a beloved child. Now, see—there is a posting about to become available somewhere here. Malhan, come and tell me if I am right about this …"

When Lanara returned to her house, hours after she had left it, she found Ladhra hunched over a pile of parchment. "You look like your mother," Lanara said from the doorway.

Ladhra grimaced. "No, thank you," she said, letting go of the parchment's ends.

Lanara ignored her friend's bitterness. "More love letters?" she said as she picked up a lynanyn from a bowl on the table. She skinned it with her fingers and squeezed it. Blue juice poured over her hands into a small bowl.

"No," Ladhra said, and sighed. "Though I almost wish they were. My mother, wisest of all the queens, has decided that I should familiarize myself with the writings of my great-great-great-grandmother. Or, more accurately, my great-great-great-grandmother's consort-scribe." She drew her palms across the parchments and they curled away from her.

"No change?" Lanara asked, glancing at the bedchamber door, and Ladhra shook her head. They went together into the other room, where Ladhra stood and Lanara sat, the bowl balanced on the bed beside her.

"Nara."

Lanara eased her hand behind Nellyn's head and held it up. The juice dribbled into his mouth and she saw him swallow. His eyes were moving beneath their lids.

"Nara, he needs to go home."

She laid his head back down and wiped his lips and chin with a cloth. "Your mother doesn't think so," she said, and continued quickly, before Ladhra could reply. "And anyway, he can't. He isn't one of them any more. He told me they wouldn't have him and he wouldn't want them to."

Ladhra knelt beside her. Lanara felt her gaze, though she looked only at Nellyn. "He said that before he got sick. And he isn't one of us either—you know that."

Lanara turned away from him. "Does it matter? I love him."

"It does matter. You're too different. Let him go back to his people and recover his strength. You'll soon find another love here, among your own people."

"Ah, yes," Lanara said, rising, striding around the bed to the windows and back again. "A Queensman—like Baldhron? Is that the kind of love you'd have me find?"

"No. Perhaps! I don't know—you're angry, you're confusing me—let's go outside and—"

"Baldhron?" Nellyn's voice was soft and very deep, but both women started. "Who is … Baldhron?" He was smiling at Lanara, and his eyes were clear and steady.

"Oh, Nellyn," she said, and knelt by him as Ladhra's footsteps faded on the stones outside.

~

Today, as darkness came to the city and the air grew cool, Queen Galha met Lanara, daughter of Salanne, before the royal stables. The Princess Ladhra was also in attendance, to wish her dearest friend well. The Queen made Lanara a gift of a wagon and a brown mare, so that the shonyn Nellyn would not be further weakened by riding.

Lanara was also given her royal orders, sealed with the Queen's mark: she is to travel east to Fane, where she will assume responsibility of the signal tower there. Her journey too will be of importance, for she will record details of the places through which she travels and the peoples with whom she has contact. Although these eastern lands are part of the Queensrealm, many of them remain little known and are manned by only a few Queensfolk. Lanara's writings will deepen our understanding and thereby strengthen our place in history. For this reason, Queen Galha has commanded Lanara to journey slowly and linger wherever she wishes.

The Queen kissed Lanara upon both cheeks. Princess Ladhra spoke briefly to Lanara and embraced her. Lanara took up the reins and the wagon left the palace grounds. The Queen climbed to her tallest balcony and from there, many minutes later, witnessed the quenching of the gatekeepers' lanterns. Only then, when she was certain Lanara's wagon had left the city, did Queen Galha turn to other matters.

~

They rode down through the Queenscity as darkness fell. The wagon lurched and jolted; Nellyn clenched his teeth and clutched the seat until his nails bent. He glanced at the brown horse in front of them, then slowly upward, past lantern-lit windows and the shadows of fountains and courtyard walls. The sky was filling with stars, though the moon had not yet risen. He wondered whether there would be a moon at all. He had been inside too long, beneath sheets and ceiling, so far from the night.

"Tell me again," he said, hoping Lanara would smile. She had been silent and grave since they had left the stables. He supposed this was because Ladhra had not spoken to her, or even looked at her. He was not entirely certain that this was the reason, however; Queensfolk emotions continued to confuse him. "Tell me again about where we are going."

Lanara did smile, and he kissed the skin below her ear so that she would laugh. "Fane," she said, twisting to catch his lips with hers. "A much smaller place than this," she went on, straightening to look ahead, still smiling, "but we won't be living in the city itself. We'll live in a signal tower, and it'll be perfect: high above the city but only a short walk away if we need something. It'll be so quiet."

"We'll see the end of the river together after all," she had said after he had woken from his long fever-sleep, eight days ago. *"We'll see the ocean. If you wish it."* He had thought of her by her Sarhenna River that had had no name for him, as the lynanyn trees swam with sinking light and the wise ones gathered on their stones. Maarenn would be waiting for him, her feet already in the water. Blue curtains would be stirring, and blue-black hair, and the fruit in the river.

"I do," he had said. *"I do wish it."* He knew the constancy of fear and sorrow now. Better to feel them far away from this city of towers and voices and water that was bound.

Spirals of bats darkened the sky above Luhr's walls. Nellyn heard the blurring of their wings and cries, and he felt Lanara touch his knee. The double doors swung open before them and Queensguards raised their hands as the brown horse drew the wagon out into the silence of the desert.

Leish could not look at the land.

He had been listening to it, though, for days, weeks, even longer. Its song had swelled like the sea, buffeting him as he lay at the bottom of the boat. "Imagine, Leish," he had heard Mallesh say once, the words nearly lost beneath the song, "if these boats had not been built. Where, then, would you have cowered?"

Leish had wanted to cry, "I would not have come. I *should* not have come"—but he had no voice. And if he had spoken those words to Mallesh, he would have shrunk more deeply into the darkness at the bottom of the boat. For the singing of that far place was in him, and he would have followed it alone, swimming, if Mallesh had not ordered these boats and this journey.

Leish did not know how many boats there were. When he had looked out of his own, early in the voyage, he had seen a shifting mass of them, dark as birds on the waves. Selkesh swam as well, skimming beneath the ocean surface, surging ahead of the boats and circling back to rest as others swam. Leish had swum once, so deep that the light had vanished and huge eyeless fish drifted past him. He had heard underwater shelves, molten fissures, plants whose roots echoed into the rock below the water. But even then he had heard sun on stone and towers that pierced the sky.

He knew, dimly, that the moon had waxed and waned. He heard islands, and saw them days later, raucous with trees and beasts. Other selkesh heard these places, but as the boats travelled on, Leish was the only one who heard the other land. "How far?" Mallesh would demand, leaning so close to Leish that he could feel breath on his neck. Once, when Leish answered him, Mallesh had rested his hand on Leish's back. A warm, lingering pressure—but when Leish rolled over to look at him, Mallesh had drawn away.

They were not alone on the water. One day sea serpents lifted their heads and tails from the water, and the selkesh cried out in fear as sunlight leapt from golden scales—but the great beasts looked, only, and sank back beneath in silence. Fish leapt and darted, and porpoises, and other creatures the selkesh had never seen before, whose songs were new.

And then one day Mallesh said, "Do you hear them?"

Leish was sitting up, his eyes closed against the midday sun. Cloth-draped planks provided some shade, but he felt sunlight on his legs, burning them dry.

"Yes," he said. The song of the yllosh was like that of the selkesh, but twisted, with sounds he did not recognize. He opened his eyes. Mallesh was leaning over the side, staring down.

"They're getting closer. What will we do?" Leish thought, *I should enjoy his fear, or at least share it.* He was far away from the boat and the sea and his brother.

"Listen to them," he said, and then they were there, rows and rows emerging from the water, stirring it into waves. Leish dragged himself up beside Mallesh and looked at their blue and green scales, their white eyes, their web-joined fingers. He tried to hear beneath the scales and bone, to listen to the blood that would be like his despite the centuries between them; but he saw and heard only strangers.

"Stop there!" Mallesh called as the yllosh drew closer to the boats. All of them stopped, except for one. She swam slowly on until she was directly below Mallesh and Leish.

"Why do you enter our waters?" Her voice was thick, threaded with hissing, and the words themselves were odd. *Older,* thought Leish, as Mallesh's fingers clawed at the wood.

"We are journeying across the sea," Mallesh said. "We seek to fulfill our destiny in a new land. Do not hinder us."

Her white eyes were unblinking even when they slid from Mallesh's face to Leish's. "You will not enter our deep places," she said, and Mallesh snorted.

"Those stifling underwater lands? We would not want to. We left those behind long ago." He paused. Leish felt him straighten. "Do you know who we are?"

"Of course," she replied, bubbling, hissing. "Why else forbid you entry to our places? Nasran-slaves."

Leish saw the blur of Mallesh's arm and lunged for it. "No," Leish said quietly, and Mallesh's hand shook so that the knife fell with a clatter. "Do not hurt them. They would surround us, overturn our boats. Think only of our goal." He did not recognize his own voice.

"You are fortunate, yllosh-woman," Mallesh said at last. "We will do you no harm now. But when we are established in our new land, I will return to these waters and find you."

"Your new land," she repeated, and began to turn away. "You were fools to leave the golden waters of our ancestors, and you are fools still. Will you hunt for land until no land is yours?"

She did not wait for an answer. Scales flashed as the yllosh disappeared silently, leaving only the gentlest of ripples. The selkesh boats bobbed beneath the sun.

"On!" Mallesh shouted, standing. "Faster! On to the western land that awaits us!"

A great cry rose from the other boats—and they did go faster, they sped into the setting sun, day after day, until all of them could hear the land's song and Leish was nearly deaf with it.

"There!" he heard Mallesh call one morning, and for the last time Leish shrank against the boards so that he too was salt-rimed wood. "Leish—there it is! Stand with me …"

Leish lay still. When the boat ground onto pebbled shore, he cried out his own song, beginning and lost.

Book Two

THIRTEEN

Alea met Aldron when they were children, on the great plain bordered to the west by autumn-coloured woods. Alilan caravans had been gathering for days, and the tall grass had already been flattened by wagons and horses and the fires of countless families. Children shrieked and ran among the wagons, reunited with friends they saw only twice a year. The young Tellers did not play with these other children. They sat around fires on the outskirts of the camps, listening, as always; separate and studious and seemingly older, as always.

Desert's red sand—large, far, shining. Oasis pool—black water, tall green palm trees—

"Enough, girl!"

Alea blinked. Her Telling images vanished and she saw only Old Aldira's scowl.

"Dull. Flat." The Teller was pacing, waving a hand at the smoke that was rising from her fire. "I always say the same things, and you never heed me. If a Telling does not *enrapture,* it has failed."

"But we can only Tell the way things look," Aliser said as Alea swallowed and tried not to cry. He was frowning, which made the red freckles on his nose seem to widen. "How can a Telling be … enrapturing if we just—"

"Please, Aliser," Old Aldira said in a tired voice. She knelt across from the two children, her fingers kneading the white fabric of her skirt. "Your defence of Alea is, as usual, endearing but misplaced. It does not matter that you are only able to Tell appearance. If there is no passion at the beginning, there will never be any. I have taught more Tellers than anyone else, and I can swear to the truth of this. Alea, you will try again—but now Aliser will have his turn. Perhaps *he* will succeed."

Aliser smiled at Alea before he began. She smiled back, because his eyes were so bright and encouraging and because it would hurt his feelings if she did not.

Sand around the oasis red and sparkling, up and down like frozen water. Oasis pool dark with shadows of palms, tall trees—

—that rustle in the hot wind, though the water beneath is still. The wind is on your faces, blowing sand that stings your cheeks. You close your eyes. A horse whinnies, a baby cries, a woman begins to sing. And then you feel hoofbeats throbbing against the soles of your bare feet, and you draw your dagger, and it is cool and smooth in your hand.

Alea opened her eyes as the strange voice echoed into silence. She put shaking hands to her cheeks, which felt sand-raked and hot.

"Who are you?" she heard Old Aldira say, and Alea too looked at the one who had Told.

He was a boy, she saw with a shiver of surprise. Not much older than she was; tall and slender and dark, grinning down at them with his arms folded across his chest.

"I am Aldron," he said in his boy's voice, the words flat and dry.

How can he Tell like that and then be normal again so quickly? Alea thought. She wound her own arms around her waist.

"Aldron of the Tall Fires caravan. You have likely heard of me."

Aliser scrambled to his feet. "We certainly have not," he said. Alea watched his hands open and shut at his sides. "And why should we?" He was a full head shorter than Aldron, but broader. He drew his shoulders back and thrust his chin up. *As if that will make him taller,* Alea thought, and felt a sudden stab of pity and shame.

"As for you," Aldron said, "your feeble Telling is proof that the Goddesses gave you their colours but neglected to bless you with their greatest gift. What good are Alnila's red and Alneth's green if you have no voice to honour them?"

Red-haired, green-eyed Aliser took a stumbling step toward him, which Old Aldira halted. "Silence," she snapped, "both of you. And sit." They did, though Aldron hesitated as if he would not. They did not look away from one another. "Aldron, this is Aliser of the Twin Daggers caravan. Now greet each other civilly. Your pride should make you friends."

They did not speak. Old Aldira sighed, but Alea saw the lines around her narrowed eyes and knew she was smiling, though not with her mouth.

"And who," Aldron said at last, turning to look down past Aliser, "are you?"

Alea took a steadying breath. "I am Alea. Also of the Twin Daggers caravan."

"Alnila warm you," he said, "and Alneth succour you. Alea." She smiled as he did, slowly, like flame blooming in wind.

~

Aldron came often to Old Aldira's fire as the leaves in the wood began to fall and the green grass turned gold. "Doesn't your Teller have a fire?" Aliser demanded once when Aldron appeared beside the wagon. "Or your family? Or are they tired of you too?"

Aldron did not answer for a long time. Alea watched his dark eyes move from their fire to the smoke of the fires near theirs and over to the distant trees.

"My Teller is very old," he said at last. "He hardly knows that I'm not there. And I don't have a family."

Aliser's mouth fell open.

"Aliser," Old Aldira said sharply, "don't gawk. Aldron, there is no need for you to explain."

"My parents died," he said. He was looking at Alea now, and she nodded once, as if this would help him continue. "Of the marsh sickness. My grandfather took me to my caravan's Teller and then my grandfather died. I barely remember him, and I don't remember my parents at all."

Aliser was staring at the ground. He picked up a stick and tossed it into the fire, which spat fitfully but did not rise. "Oh," he said.

Old Aldira clapped once and rose from the bottom step of the wagon. "Very well. Now that Aldron is here, perhaps he can show you both how to make your colours sharper. Colours only, Aldron—nothing more complex than that. Let's begin with the palms ..."

That night Alea looked very carefully at her own family. Her mother Aldana was holding the new baby to her breast with her right arm; with her left she was reaching for herbs, sprinkling them in the soup, stirring with a wooden paddle. "You will be just as beautiful as she is," Alea's father Aldill often said to her, and she always smiled at him, though she did not believe him. She had Aldana's hair—long and heavy and black as scorched wood—but she did not have her grace at dancing, and she doubted she would ever be as tall.

Her father was sitting with her older brother Alder, trying again to teach him how to skin a hare. Their faces and hands swam in the firelight, and the hunting knife glinted as Alder turned it. "No," their father said, "no, no, listen to me ..."

Her sister was in the wagon. Alea heard her babbling words that were not yet words and heard their grandmother laughing. The wagon would be glowing inside, with firelight and woven blankets, and the ivy and flame that were painted on the walls and roof—their family's own design in paint and cloth, made to please Alnila of the Flame and Alneth of the Earth, who blessed all families.

"Alea!" her father bellowed from the other side of the fire. "Come here immediately and show your brother how to do this *neatly*." She rose and went to them as her mother sang the baby to sleep.

~

Rain began to fall and did not stop. There were grumblings that the wagons would all be washed away by the time Alnila's Night came; and some Alilan commented, only half in jest, that they would soon be forced to seek shelter in the nearby town. People huddled in their wagons, coaxing the fires in their stoves higher. The smoke that billowed from the wagons' chimneys was swallowed by lowering cloud.

Alea stayed with her family for five days and nights—longer than she had for many, many seasons. One murky morning she could not stay any longer.

"How strange to see you so eager," her father said over the baby's wails, "when only four seasons ago we had to drag you flailing and weeping to Old Aldira's wagon."

Alea shifted from foot to foot in the doorway. The door was already open; rain was blowing against her leggings and cloak. "Yes, Father, I know. But I'm older now, and I'm learning things there."

"Go on, child," her mother said, gesturing with her free hand. "And hurry, before we're all soaked."

Alea glanced at her father, who was smiling at her now, and then she ducked out into the darkness of water and mud and sky.

Aldron was in Old Aldira's wagon; Aliser was not. "Come and sit," the Teller said. "And have some cider, girl, you're shivering."

Alea sipped her cider, trying not to slurp. Across from her, Aldron tossed a small pillow into the air over and over again. He sighed several times, and yawned, and did not look at her. Old Aldira leaned forward and swung the stove door open with a poker.

"Although you are both particularly vivacious today," she said as she fed a log into the fire, "I feel I must effect a change in mood. Aldron, use your prolific Telling powers to convince us we are warm."

He straightened and set the pillow down on the bench. For a moment there was a stillness. Alea gripped her bench, steeling herself against the blast of Telling that would surely come. But when Aldron opened his mouth, only a whisper emerged. A single flame kindled between them—orange, with white at its heart. It flickered steadily. She watched it, and his solemn face beyond it, and she began to speak her own words into the murmuring quiet.

Her flame was blue and very slender. He smiled when he saw it, and Told his orange flame closer, so that the two twined and rose and there was a fire. She saw sweat on his cheeks and felt it on her own forehead, beneath her hair. This Telling was an illusion, as they all were, yet her body and Aldron's did not know this while the images formed. Their fire crackled and spat. The noise would be his, she knew, but still she Told her small part.

Warmth, she suddenly thought. *Old Aldira said warmth, not just fire.* Her blue flame vanished as she Told the desert sun, bloated and white. Aldron instantly added sand, which scalded her feet and hissed over the floorboards. She Told a cauldron of steaming soup; he Told its bubbling and a smell of onions. She Told cloaks and blankets, and he made them heavy and soft. Then she covered him in fur like a winter animal's, and he covered her, and the Telling dissolved in laughter. They laughed and laughed—children's voices, high and giddy. When Aliser came in, they were still smiling.

~

After the children had gone, Aldira sat without moving for a long time. She was always tired after Aldron's visits, drained by the restless energy of his body and by the power of his words. Drained by her own need for these words. When she finally rose and walked across the wagon, she felt something shift beneath her foot. She bent and swept her hand over the place and felt sand. She brushed it into her palm and stared at it: real sand, where there should only have been a memory of Telling. Fine, white, dry sand, never touched by sunlight or blown by desert wind. She curled her fingers around it and said, very quietly, "Twins protect him."

~

Rain turned to snow, and the trees stood stark and jagged against the sky. The air was thick with smoke from the wagons' chimneys, and from the town's, where the black roof tiles were now piled white. The Alilan gathered branches and logs from the woods and began to stack them in the centre of the camp. The main fire of Alnila's Night would be built here, with the smaller family fires radiating outward from it like sparks. Children raced around the growing pile, imagining darkness and dancing.

"Pay attention to the Telling tomorrow," Old Aldira told Alea and Aliser the day before the celebration. "Try not to allow yourselves to be swept away by the words. Likely you are still too young for such control: the power of all Tellers together is considerable. But try to listen to the words beneath the images. Try to understand how we are making our Telling strands and how we weave them together."

Alea did try, at first. She watched each Teller stand—ten of them, representing each of the caravans. She could not see their faces; they were ranged around the other side of the fire, and their features were blurred by flame and smoke and the night that hung between. The rest of the Alilan sat or knelt or stood. Alea could feel them around her, stretching back to the smaller fires and even beyond, to where the horses whinnied and pawed at the snow.

One voice began. The image was the same every time, and every time Alea's heartbeat quickened when she heard it: a single wagon, a single family, held motionless by snow that spun and drifted around the wagon's wheels. A second voice joined the first. Alea saw a streak of light high above them, plummeting from the stars that were the fires of the Alilan dead. The light grew, lengthening and brightening, until it was a woman's hair, a woman's arms reaching toward the wagon. Alea trembled a bit, as she had when she was very, very small, huddled against her mother's knees. The fire goddess towered, a coursing plume of blue and orange and red; then she extended her fingers. Flame showered the snow and caught on a bush, and the family leaned toward the fire, their faces amazed and thankful.

Alea lost the separate threads. There were other voices now, and other figures. More wagons, and lines of horses: the growing strength of the Alilan, blessed by Alnila's gift of fire as her earth sister Alneth slumbered. The Alilan danced to show Alnila their gratitude—and Alea realized that she was dancing too, whirling among bodies that were real. *Old Aldira will be angry with me for not listening right*, she thought very dimly, before her brother swung her up onto his shoulders and she shrieked with laughter and dizzy joy.

Aliser found her after the dancing was done, when all the Alilan except the children and the very old were disappearing into the woods or the further reaches of the plain. ("Where do you go?" she had demanded once, and Alder had chuckled. "Remember: Alnila is the goddess of fire *and* passion." Alea had stared blankly at him and he had laughed at her loudly, until she hit him.)

"Wasn't that beautiful?" Alea said, still breathless, and Aliser nodded.

"Beautiful," Aldron said as he stepped into the light, "but tame. Easy. I could do better all on my own."

Aliser sneered. "Really? You're a fool, Aldron. And you're too proud."

"No Alilan can be too proud," Aldron replied. He was so still that his lips hardly seemed to move with his words. "*You* are a bore. You have no idea how to be brave or different. My Tellings will be new. They'll change things."

Alea stood up between them. "Tellings don't change things. They can't. Old Aldira says that the Goddesses made it so that we could never use our Tellings to make changes in the real world. Someone did it once and she was punished by the Goddesses—"

"The Goddesses!" Aldron scoffed. "Don't bother repeating your lessons to me. That old woman's teaching you to be afraid of your own power." He looked down at her and all she saw were shadows, in his eyes and flickering over his skin. "I thought you were different from Aliser."

She made a sound like a laugh, though she hardly heard it through the anger humming in her ears. "There's nothing wrong with Aliser."

"Clever," Aldron said to Aliser, "making a girl speak for you."

Aliser shouted and lunged for him, and Aldron stepped neatly away. Aliser stumbled past him into a pile of snow.

"Stay with him, then," Aldron said to Alea, and he walked away from them into the darkness.

"He *is* a fool," she said as Aliser cursed and shook snow from his hair.

The next day, as the caravans prepared to take their separate paths, she threaded her way among blackened wood and wagons that were unfamiliar to her. "Where is the Tall Fires caravan?" she asked someone, and he pointed, and she wandered and asked again. She was no longer angry; she needed to find Aldron, to tell him something she was not sure of yet. But when she came to the right place, the wagons were already gone. She saw them in the distance, black spots against the plain. She stared at them until they disappeared. Then she stared at the grass, bent and broken beneath the snow, and she thought, *I feel like that grass,* though she did not know why.

FOURTEEN

She has forgotten him, Aliser thought as the wagons rolled across marshland into the lake country. He watched Alea frowning into spring light as she Told sight and the beginnings of sound; he watched her smile and turn to him when her Tellings were done. She never mentioned Aldron, not even once. When summer came and the wagons turned toward the red desert, Aliser felt dread in his gut. Surely now, so close to the oasis and Alneth's Night and the other caravans, she would speak of him. But she did not.

Their caravan was the first to arrive at the oasis. She and Aliser waded into the still, dark water and laughed at their wet leggings and the rippling shade of the palms. "Our Tellings don't make me feel like this," she said as she leaned over and dipped her head into the pool. She raised her face and her plait swung behind her, soaked even blacker than it usually was. Aliser wanted to touch it, not as he used to when they were smaller and he tugged at it until she screeched. He wanted to weave his fingers through it like the red and white ribbons she wore.

"Come with me," he said to her one morning when the sun was still low. "My sister says we can ride Sandar now, before it's too hot."

Alea looked at Old Aldira, who was pursing her lips. "May we?" Alea asked, and the Teller sighed.

"I know that we will accomplish nothing this morning if I say you cannot. Go now, quickly—and pick me some watersage. At least make it a partially useful ride."

"Not too far!" Aliser heard his sister call as he urged the horse away. "And no galloping!" He lifted a hand but did not look back.

"Hold on," he said to Alea, and felt her arms tighten around his waist.

Sandar cantered away from the wagons as the dawn clouds came apart in sunlight.

They followed the river that flowed from the oasis pool. It was high and wide, even though the rains had passed weeks ago. The banks were thick with colour: green fronds and stalks and leaves, pink and blue petals that were closing now, as the sun rose. Bushes dotted the sand; they too were covered in leaves and folding blooms.

"Look how beautiful it is," Alea said when they were sitting with their feet in the river and their backs against a tall rock. Sandar was beside them, snorting and shaking her head so that her red mane flew.

"Yes," Aliser said. The leaping place looked small from here, just a rock like the one they were sitting against, when really it was so tall, nearly a cliff.

"I guess that's why the Perona fight us for it," Alea said, and Aliser frowned at her.

"Well, they shouldn't, and they won't dare to again. It's Alneth's place, our place—where we've been taming our horses forever. Anyway, we beat them last time they challenged us for it."

"I know," said Alea, and was quiet.

"Imagine," Aliser said, wanting her to speak again, "we'll be taming our horses here soon. Getting our fighting daggers. And after that we'll be able to fight."

"And Tell," Alea said, frowning herself. "In front of everyone. Imagine *that.*"

"I can. It'll be glorious. We'll be so strong by then and everyone'll be so proud. Let's practise: I'll try to Tell thunder or maybe horses running, and you can—"

"No," Alea said. She drew her feet out of the water and pulled her knees up beneath her chin. "Let's just sit here a bit longer and listen. Old Aldira says we have to listen all the time now, to make sure we can Tell sounds right."

He tried to sit as she was, motionless and facing the oasis, but he could not. He shifted and splashed and looked sidelong at her, so that he could see her plait hanging against her white tunic and her brown feet resting on the sand.

"Listen," she said as they rose at last.

Aliser groaned. "I've been *trying* to, but—"

"No—listen. I hear something."

After a moment he did as well. A rumbling, drumming sound, too weak to be the wild horses, and anyway it was too early for that. Soon after, voices—some singing, some yelling. He and Alea stared northward with their hands shading their eyes.

"It's another caravan," she said quickly, her voice strangely high, almost breaking.

"Yes, so let's go back. Except—wait—we forgot Old Aldira's watersage. We'll have to find some, maybe closer to the oasis ..."

She was not listening to him. "Which caravan is it?" she said, but not really to him. She was straight and still, beginning to smile—and he knew with a suddenness like falling that she had not forgotten after all.

~

Aldron walked around their wagon as if he had been there only the day before. He sat down on the third step and looked at them, one by one. He looked at Alea last and longest, Aldira noted, and she narrowed her eyes.

"Greetings, Alea," he said in a voice that was deeper than it had been before.

"Greetings, Aldron," Alea said. Just four words between them—but Aldira heard them heavy and warm and living. Telling words. She shivered, as if the wind were not desert-hot and languid.

"How generous of you to join us again, Aldron," she said. "Aliser was about to Tell birdsong, I believe. Weren't you, Aliser?" she added, more loudly.

He shifted his eyes from Aldron to her, very slowly. "Yes," he said in his own deepening voice.

"And then," she went on, though she knew she should not, not with such keen longing, or such fear, "Aldron may treat us to a display of what *he* has learned since we last met."

"Certainly," he said, and she nodded briskly.

After a moment Aliser Told the sweet, high notes of woodland birds, rising above the red sand into the silence of the sun.

~

Two days later, Alea was on a horse again. This time she was flying, squeezing her eyes shut against air that seemed to be buffeting her face into a new shape. She had no breath, though she thought she might be crying out beneath the noise of hoofs and wind.

When the horse slowed and she opened her eyes, there was no camp behind them, no distant palms, not even the towering rock of the leaping place. The river here branched into three, shallower and more slender than the one near the oasis. Alea asked, "Where are we?" in a voice she could hardly hear.

"Does it matter?" Aldron was rubbing the horse's sweat-slick coat with a piece of red cloth. "Or," he added, glancing at her with one eyebrow raised, "are you afraid?"

"No!" she said, more loudly than she'd intended to. "No"—more quietly, though it still sounded like a lie. She rose shakily from the sand and laid her hand on the horse's twitching flank. "You haven't told me who lent him to you."

"No one." He was smiling down at her—enjoying her shock, she knew. "I borrowed him from someone who's busy. I do that sometimes. No one ever notices. And I know how to take care of horses—better than their owners, mostly. Don't worry: we'll return him in time. If you're better now, I'll show you the place I told you about."

"Better?" she repeated, flushing—then turned as he walked away, and fell silent.

There were buildings behind them, clustered in two wide semicircles. Some were large and others small; all were conical, covered with climbing plants. In the bare patches among the plants, lizards basked, motionless, nearly as golden as the stone. Each building had a black door with a downward-pointing claw set in its centre.

"I found this place at the last Alneth's Night gathering," Aldron said. "Come inside with me."

He led her to the smallest building and pulled the door open, covering the claw with his own fingers. Inside, sunlight shivered on the curved walls and on a staircase that wound into shade. Alea followed him down. The darkness felt like water on her skin.

There was a light ahead of Aldron. *A flame,* she thought, and was surprised that she had not seen him holding wood or kindling it. Its glow took them along a corridor and into a large round room, where she stood and gaped. The walls around them also stretched up to a conical point; they swam with carved lines and ridges that had no shapes but seemed to. When she looked back at the sand floor, she saw stacked barrels and scattered stools and a low table strewn with dead heartflowers.

"Whose place is this?" she asked, and the walls surrounded them with her voice.

"*Was* this. No one's used these buildings for a long time. Maybe they were the Perona's. Or someone before them. Now they're mine."

She touched a stool, brushing fingerprints into the dust. She peered at the marks in the orange light; and then the light grew white and brighter, and she saw that Aldron was not holding a torch.

"What are you doing?" she said, though it was not the question she wanted to ask.

"Providing light," he said, mock-solemn, the corners of his mouth quirking.

"But you're not Telling now, you're talking to me. And before that you were quiet. How did you Tell this light when you were being *quiet?*"

"I made it," he said. She realized she was leaning on the stool now, hardly standing on her own. "I Told it in a whisper at the top of the stairs, and it stayed. It's real. I've been teaching myself, and it works now." He gestured to the table. "I Told those flowers too, at the last gathering time. But they're still here."

He drew his palm over one of the heartflowers. It crumbled immediately. Alea shook her head over and over, as if this would keep her from seeing the flame or the dust that had been petals and leaves.

"No," she said, "that's impossible. Alilan Tellers can't create—they can only show. We can't—"

"But *I* can." He took a step toward her. "The Goddesses have given me a more powerful gift, and I'm learning to use it. I'll be the strongest Teller ever. I'll Tell great things: changes, victories ..."

"Aldron." She tipped her head and tried to see his eyes, which flickered away from hers. "You mustn't Tell these things, even if you can. The

Goddesses forbid Tellings that become real. They warned the very first Tellers that such things could destroy us, and so they made it so we couldn't do this. That's why we're warriors as well as Tellers: we have to make our victories with our bodies, not our words."

"Why," Aldron said in a low voice, "would they give me this gift if I'm not allowed to use it?"

She swallowed. *If I asked him for water, he could Tell it for me. It would be cold* ... "Does it frighten you?"

His mouth and eyes were very still now. "No," he said at last, and the flame shuddered as he turned his face away.

FIFTEEN

Alea had no voice. She heard words and felt them in her mouth and knew that they would be swift and true—but she had no voice to Tell them. She stood before the people of all the caravans, in the shadow of the leaping place, and was silent.

It's because of the pain, she thought. The pain of limbs and belly, all her muscles and all her skin, everything burning and bruised. She had walked to her wagon afterward. She had wept as she drew off her leggings, had hardly been able to step into her skirt. Her woman's skirt, stitched by herself and her mother, kept carefully folded until this day—and Alea had shuddered in its clean folds and cried as blood snaked down her legs.

She was still dizzy from the long fall and the longer ride that had followed. She did not remember holding on to the horse's mane, but she had, somehow, she had clutched so desperately that her fingers still ached. She had not lifted her head, not even when her body was balanced and steady. She had kept her eyes lowered and stared at her hands and the golden mane. When the horse turned to gallop back to the oasis, it was not because she had urged it to, with words or pressure from her legs or arms; it was simply following all the horses of its herd that were also turning that way, directed by their new riders.

And now she could not Tell. *My woman's skirt, my first dagger, my horse standing beyond the fires, Aliser and Aldron beside me* ... She felt tears again and swallowed furiously until they thinned away. Aliser had held her hand as they walked to the leaping place, and he had caught her when she slid from her horse's back after that first ride. "We are warriors now," he had said, his lips warm against her neck. She had leaned into him, wrapped her torn arms around him so that she would not fall.

Aldron had appeared only moments before all the Tellers rose on the sand ridge. He had not spoken to anyone, and he was so tall that his raised eyes did not even seem to graze the assembly in front of them. Alea had looked up at him and willed him to turn to her, to smile or make a silly face, to lighten the heaviness of her body and the night with scorn or humour. But he had stood straight and quiet, alone among them.

Four Tellers had already begun, one at a time, weaving images of Alneth, towering above the desert with sand and palm fronds and water streaming from her outstretched hands. Aliser, to Alea's left, had joined them, Telling roots and the burrows of animals beneath the earth. And now it was her turn. She opened her mouth as if the words would burst forth on their own—but of course they did not, and she closed her eyes so that she would not have to see the confusion and pity on the faces of her family.

~

The air is thin atop the leaping place, and the sun is too bright. The colours of the horses blur and change. You stand and grip the rock with your bare toes, and then the pounding is directly below you and you step out into the sky—

Aldira forced her body out of the Telling. She heard herself whimper as she angled her head, so slowly, to look at Aldron.

It should have been Alea; she was next, directly after Aliser. She had not begun at the correct time, and the others had spun out their own words to cover her silence. They could have done this for longer, waiting for her to summon courage, but her voice had never come. Aldron's had instead, and the others had faltered and died. The image of the Goddess shuddered into darkness; plants and water, her gifts, twisted in brief confusion and vanished. Aldira saw Aldron's face clearly for a moment, before his Telling gripped her again.

Your body falls slowly, though the wind is fast, reaching into your ears and nose and open mouth, and wrenching out your breath. You are falling slowly, but the ground is surging up toward you—the ground that is heaving with the backs of horses. You try to find your legs and hands because you will need them, even if only to die—

Aldira screamed his name, or hoped she had. *Stop, stop*—her own words were minuscule and colourless beneath his. Not permitted, this next Telling—the joining never, ever Told: too sacred, too full of anguish, left to silence, always. Young Tellers knew this, knew to Tell only the first fall and then the first ride—but Aldron was not slowing or changing the course of his words.

Your head snaps and you are blind and your bones separate from their sockets in fire and blood. Blood in your mouth, your teeth sunk into your tongue, grinding flesh—

Aldron's words ended in a cry. Aliser's, Aldira knew as she rocked on her knees in the sand and retched. When she could raise her head, she saw Aliser standing above Aldron, who was curled on the ground like a sleeping child. Aliser was staring down at his fist, which was cradled in his other hand. Alea was sitting with her hands over her mouth, looking at no one.

It should have been me, Aldira thought. *I should have been the one to stop the Telling—but I was helpless. I am old, Goddesses, just as they all say …*

She heard a child wail. A man shouted, and another, and the crowd rustled and began to move.

"Wait!" Aldira cried as she rose, and they did. They looked at her, as did the other Tellers. She saw their fear, felt it like rising water against her skin. "Do not come closer. We must wait and be calm. When he wakes, we will speak to him. Remember that he is young, and the young do not know well enough how to channel their power—"

"Please, old woman," said Aldron, each word steadier than the last, "do not embarrass me, or yourself." He was standing with Aliser and Alea behind him; he must have taken a pace or two forward as Aldira spoke.

"Let us sit together," she said, her own words unwavering, "and talk about this thing you have done."

He laughed. "Why not speak as plainly as you usually do, old one? This *forbidden* thing. This forbidden thing I have *unwisely* done." He walked toward her.

She drew herself up and stared back at him. "Forbidden and unwise, yes. You have sat more often by my fire than your own, and you should know what is right—what we Alilan hold dear or reject, and why. Your power has always been great—I know this, and now so do all of us. But power must be borne with wisdom—"

"Complacency," he said, directly in front of her, speaking very quietly. "Surely you mean borne with complacency and obedience. Wisdom is something you have never taught me."

He turned and walked away from her, down the gentle slope and into the crowd, which parted for him. When he had disappeared among the wagons, there was a brief stillness. A great held breath, Aldira thought as she herself tried to draw one—and then people were stirring and milling and calling to one another.

Someone grasped her arm. Before she turned, Aldira saw Alea pushing her way toward the wagons. Aliser took a few running steps after her, but when she too slipped out of sight, he stood still.

"… can we do? Does his caravan have any …" Aldira brushed at her companion's words as if they had been sandflies. She watched Aliser's face and the tiny movements of his body, and she felt a dread so keen it was almost desire.

~

Alea bent low over Ralan's neck. She urged him to a gallop and he bore her east, beside the rain-swollen river.

The moon was high by the time she reached the clay buildings. She saw them very clearly, and the horse that was standing among them. Her own horse reared when she started to slip off his back. She stroked him and murmured in his ear and waited until he was calm before she went to the door with the claw at its centre.

Her feet found the way even in the complete darkness. She had descended these steps many times since Aldron had first brought her here, sometimes running to keep up with him, sometimes walking carefully, quietly, in case he was already working in his carved chamber. She had watched him Tell a dagger, a loaf of bread, a goblet, into being; and also, each time, a heartflower, which he would bestow upon her with a grin or mock solemnity. But the first thing he always Told was light; she would see it spilling into the corridor and follow it to him.

There was no light tonight. She dragged her fingers along the wall until they found the entrance to the chamber. She stopped and listened but heard only pulsing silence. She felt her way into the chamber and along the wall to her right, her bare feet scuffing the packed earthen floor. The carven shapes were cool. She recognized them, even though she could not see them. This wave-form was halfway round the chamber—and this triangular bump was on the other side, high up, nearly back at the entrance—

Her hand touched skin. She stood motionless with her fingertips on the line of his jaw and her thumb on his chin. She felt his fingers slide along the inside of her arm and twine with hers, lightly, shiver-touches on her knuckles and palm. She stepped forward so that her forehead was against his chest. Still only the slightest touch: his hips, the tops of his thighs, his cheek whispering over her hair as he bent his head to find her in the darkness. They turned, struggling out of clothing, trying not to leave each other's skin as they did so. She was against the wall now. He put his hands under her thighs and held them apart and thrust up into her—and he cried out, once, before he began to move again. The stone ridges pressed against her flesh, and all her bruises and her bones echoed with pain, and she felt a new tearing over the others that had already opened wide that day. But she held him with her legs and her arms, with every ragged muscle, and was silent.

"Don't tell Aliser," Aldron said later, when they were lying among their clothes. "And make sure to get a bleeding draught from your Healer as soon as you can."

Alea dragged herself up until she was sitting. "Make a light. Now. I need to see your face when you say things like that."

He did nothing for a moment. "What colour do you like best?" he asked at last, not mocking, no smile in his voice.

She eased herself back against the wall, very gently, so that the carvings would not dig. She pulled her skirt with her and held it against her breasts. "Blue," she said.

She did not hear the beginning, but she saw it: a shimmer in the dark, a flutter like a falling leaf. His words grew louder and the blue grew brighter, and she turned to him as he Told her light.

"There," he said when he was finished and the chamber was rippling around them. "Can you see my face well enough now?" He crawled over to her and kissed her once on the mouth. He drew the skirt out of her hands and down and kissed her on each breast.

"Your Telling frightened everyone," she said when he had settled himself with his head in her lap. "Even Old Aldira—she talked to you so quietly afterward. She's never quiet."

He blew a slow stream of air against the skin of her belly and she wriggled and laughed, even though she did not want to. "And were *you* frightened?"

"Yes," she said, thinking, *No, that's not the word for what I felt. You Told the fall and the joining and I felt more pain than I had when those things happened to me. It was slower and brighter and more real than anything I'd experienced myself …*

"But not enough." He looked up at her without blinking, his eyes black beneath the blue glow. "You came after me anyway."

She sank her fingers into his hair and felt the bone beneath, and tears rose in her eyes.

"I'm surprised," he said after a moment, "that Aliser didn't come after me as well. He's far too earnest, but he's no coward."

"And that's why you don't think I should tell him? About … this?" She tried to straighten her legs—they were numb, leaden—but he did not move his head.

"Yes," Aldron said. "I'm sure he'd use his new dagger on me even more quickly than he did his fist. Anyway," he went on, "you and I will be travelling soon. Separately. And you're with him, aren't you?"

There was no scorn or jealousy in his words, only a lazy sort of disinterest, but she turned her head and lowered it so that her hair hung between them. "Yes, but I don't love him."

Aldron took her hair in his fist and moved it away from her face. "I recommend," he said as he pulled her down to him, slowly, his knuckles white, "that you avoid loving anyone."

They returned to the oasis separately, just before dawn. Alea's parents and sisters were sleeping—even Alnanna, who had woken at sunrise since she was a baby. Alder slept at his own fire now, with his own children.

Alea tugged her sleeping sheet aside, and went very still. There was a purple heartflower on her pallet, its petals velvet and dark with dew. She knew it would be soft if she picked it up, that it would have a weight and a scent. She did not touch it. She shivered in the sunless air and felt the tenderness of her body, inside and out, and she smiled at the flower he had made.

~

The wine was deep red, nearly black within the pewter. Aldron wrapped his fingers around the goblet's stem and lifted it. A rich, fruity scent rose, and the liquid lapped a bit against the sides. He put his lips to the edge, very slowly, giving her more time. Alea spoke faster, no space between the words, and she leaned forward as he tipped the goblet up.

"No," he said, setting it down on the table beside the bed. "Closer maybe, but no."

She lay down with a thump and glared at the ceiling beams. She could hear the rain again, now that her Telling had ended. It drummed on the shutters and dripped into a shallow pool on the floor. Her body was puckered with cold. "I knew it wouldn't work. I don't understand why you keep making me try."

He laughed. "I make you, do I? The same way I make you meet me in this town you claim to despise?" He leaned over and bit the skin in the hollow of her hip, then dodged away from her slap. "Put some clothes on, woman, and come have dinner in that hateful warm room downstairs."

She *had* been horrified the first time she had come here. She remembered this, though it was a vague memory as she sat at the massive round table beside him and watched him laugh with his town friends. He was already slightly drunk. They had had real wine before she tried to Tell it, and now there was the usual dinner mead. She drank, but not much. Already she half wanted to leave, to walk out beyond the town's wooden walls to where Alilan smoke curled above the plain. Half wanted only— for she would return to the camp alone. She could only touch him here, and so she tolerated the narrow streets, the buildings that blotted out the stars, these men and women who lived motionless as trees on their small piece of earth.

"So, sorcerer," one of the men was saying, "will you show us a trick this time?"

"Quickly," his female companion added, "before your pious friend can say it's sacred to your goddesses and stop you." They all glanced at Alea and laughed. Alea tried to laugh too, until they glanced away again.

Aldron looked around the room, his gaze slow and deliberate, and Alea's nails dug into the underside of the table. "The fire," he said after a moment, "look at it."

The fireplace was large and deep, permanently soot-layered. The flames were high within it, their crackling audible beneath the noise of the room and the rain on the shutters. Alea looked back at Aldron. She watched his lips move and heard his voice, itself a pattern of rain or sparks, though she could not hear the words.

The fire died silently and completely. Something tugged at Alea—a protest, a wrongness that she did not try to name as she, like her companions at the table, gaped at Aldron. He smiled, especially at the woman Pareya. Then someone at another table called to the innkeeper and a murmur of confusion rose.

"Can't understand it," the innkeeper muttered as he passed Alea. "Fine dry wood, and there's no smoke now ..."

Much, much later, Pareya said, "That was well done, but not very exciting."

Alea did not know where they were. Somewhere deep within the town, with houses leaning in and strangers jostling. She stumbled when she looked at anything except her feet. *I am as drunk as the others,* she thought, quite coherently. She trailed behind the group, clumsy and slow for the first time she could remember. Every few steps Aldron fell back to find her. He pressed her into doorways, against walls still damp from the rain that had passed. He drew his fingers over her skin, each time a different place: her cheeks and her neck, her belly and thighs. She grasped his hands and made him clutch her, hard, so that she moaned—and then he laughed and pulled away again.

"Ah," he said to Pareya now, as Alea drew closer to them, "you wanted excitement. Please be more precise next time you demand a trick."

Pareya raised one dark brow. "I demand another now," she said. "Sorcerer."

Someone whistled and someone else said, "Look out, Medwel, you're about to lose her to the horse man," and Alea began to feel sick.

"Very well," Aldron said. He seemed to look at Pareya for a long time—too long, the silence between them too thick. Alea took one unsteady step toward him. He turned just then and gazed at the buildings, the passersby, the small, distant sky.

"No." Alea's tongue felt swollen and dry against her teeth. No one looked at her. Perhaps she had not spoken.

Something rattled above their heads. *Pebbles,* she thought, peering up with the rest of them. Pebbles against wood—a shutter, which flew outward with a crash as a second handful of invisible stones danced against the wall.

"Who's there?" a man called.

Aldron was standing with his face upturned, eyes almost closed. His lips were hardly moving. More pebbles spattered, against flesh this time as well as wood.

"You!" the man bellowed, his fists swinging above them. "Get away or I'll—"

"Run!" one of Alea's companions cried. She wrenched herself around so slowly, as if her feet were caught in bog or tangled in the creepingvine that grew in the lake country. Pareya shrieked as she dodged away. Alea tried to order her limbs, her muscles, her wine-thick mind. She moved forward, and Aldron caught her hand and pulled her after him into an alley.

They pounded through darkness. She heard Aldron and the others ahead of her, tripping and cursing, laughing breathlessly. They pulled each other up over walls and wound through more alleys and streets, some empty and others scattered with people who shouted at them or joined them for a while before disappearing.

Everyone fell away, though Alea did not notice this until Aldron heaved her up and through a window and she saw their inn chamber, and him—only him—lurching toward the bed. She sat down heavily on the floor, which was still wet, and felt the rainwater spreading slow, dull cold into her skirt and skin.

"Well," he said, "that was entertaining." His voice sounded slurred or muffled. She thought, *Maybe still the drink in him—or me,* even though her own head felt abruptly, painfully clear.

"No," she said. "It wasn't."

He was on his back now, rolling his head on the pillow to look at her. "You pretend disapproval," he said, his voice still strange, "when actually you're thrilled to be included in these things."

"No," she said again, though his words sounded mostly, horribly true. "This—you—just make me tired."

"I thought you liked that." A whisper of mockery; he was barely smiling.

"I mean your tricks, your energy—the waste of it all."

"So you'd have me create only pretty things, or useful things? Or—"

"Not create at all." She got to her knees, resting her knuckles on the floor. "You toy with this power and use it to impress people, and you don't seem to see how dangerous it might be." His face was turned away. He was very still, one arm hanging off the bed, loose and heavy. "Aldron?" she said, starting to shiver. He had not Told a fire yet.

"I didn't just create, tonight," he said at last. "I'm disappointed that you failed to notice this."

Alea's teeth were chattering. She wrapped her arms around herself, for warmth and to keep herself from crawling to him. "The fire," she said, and knew. *He's right, I should have noticed instantly, but I was so distracted by those people* … "You Told it away."

"Mmm. Destroyed it. Wasn't sure I'd be able to, and the words were so different—but it was easy, once I'd started. It made me tired, though—I don't know how I walked for that long—and then Telling those pebbles, and the running …"

"No." Now that she wanted to go to him, she could not, so she spoke instead, quickly, and it was fear that finally warmed her. "Stop this. All of it. You'll hurt yourself or someone else—you'll change things beyond what's permitted—"

"Permitted?" He was looking at her again, his eyes steady and unblinking. "You're no different from all the others—only concerned about conformity."

"That's not true, I'm concerned about you. Look at you! You can't even move now. Imagine what will happen if you stretch your power any more. Please—turn your Telling back to what's right and good. I'll help you—"

"Go." The fingers of his right hand twitched once and remained slightly bent, gripping air. "Go back to Aliser. He's an amazing man, never asks questions, always Tells nice safe pictures and maybe a wind or a storm, but only if the Goddesses wish it. He'll make you very happy."

Alea rose, clenching her teeth against stiffness and tears, and walked to the door. She opened it and stepped out, closed it as quietly as if he had been sleeping, though she wanted, suddenly, to shake the inn with slamming.

The plain was bright with Alilan fires. She skirted them and went instead to the line of horses behind the wagons of her caravan. She whistled four notes and heard an answering snort, and she almost smiled as she found her Ralan in the darkness. She murmured into his mane, reaching around his neck to bury her fingers in it. She touched something, not horsehair, and her words trailed away. As Ralan nuzzled her, she drew the flowers out from where they had been tangled: two heartflowers, leaves and stems twined together, petals velvet and slightly creased, as if they had just opened. Alea held them to her face and breathed in their scent of sun and spices. Then she slipped them into her skirt waist and walked toward the fires, where the Alilan danced beneath their endless sky.

SIXTEEN

Aliser found Alea just before the leaping. She was standing with her mother and youngest sister, though she had not been there a moment before, had not, in fact, been anywhere near the oasis for most of the day. Alea was holding one side of her skirt up, fanning her legs with it. As he watched, she twisted her hair up as well, lifting it away from her neck.

"Where've you been?" he asked after he had slipped unnoticed to her side. That question—the words of it so old and thin and useless that he swore, one more time, never to say or even think them again. But then, as always, he heard her answer and the lie in it, and knew he would keep asking until she spoke the truth.

"I went to pick watersage," she said, taking his hand and holding it to her cheek. Her skin was dry and fever-hot. "And I practised Telling for a bit."

"On your own," he said, marvelling at the flatness of his voice, "as usual."

Alea leaned over and kissed him. "Yes," she said against his lips. "And now," she went on, drawing her face away, "I'm back, since it's almost time."

The horses were coming. The youths atop the leaping place were all looking northward, so high above the oasis that they could see the herd. The Alilan gathered on the ground and on the smaller rock outcrops could only hear and feel the approach. The sand shuddered and Alea gripped his hand, and Aliser allowed these things to dull the edge of his anger.

The horses emerged from the dazzle of distance and heat, and he sucked in his breath, remembering when he had stood far above the camp, awaiting his own leaping with Alea beside him. He watched as the horses' colours bloomed—bay and black, white with red patches—and gasped with the other Alilan when the herd swerved as if it were one animal, thundering toward the leaping place.

One of the youths above screamed. Very few people looked up; someone always cried out just before the leaping. Often there was a cluster of them left after the others had jumped. They would slither down the rock, alone or with someone else close beside, faces turned away from their families and the horses. This time, though, there was another scream, and another, and words began to form and fall.

"Goddesses, no—*no*!" Aliser heard, and he looked back at the horses that were not just horses any more.

Riders dotted the herd. As Aliser watched, more appeared, swinging up from beneath the horses. Cloth veils and robes cracked, and new voices screamed blood and exultation into the wind. "Swords!" Alea cried, and he saw them—three-pointed like arcs frozen in descent—and he shouted, "Perona!" before he turned and ran.

~

Aldira no longer watched the leaping. The beauty of white cloth against brown limbs against desert sky and rock was too small and fleeting a thing; it was the horror of crushed bones and lashing, bleeding bodies that remained each time, like a Telling that would not fade. So she stayed in her wagon now, waiting for nightfall when she would join the other Tellers on the sand ridge. It was easier to Tell glory in the dark.

She heard the first screams and closed her eyes briefly. *A bad one, this season,* she thought as the screams continued. She heard the drumming of hoofs—and then voices, so unexpected and familiar that she ran to her wagon's door.

Aldira stood for one long moment on the top step. She saw in a glance that the Perona rode this time without their usual trappings of metal and leather. The horses seemed bare and wild, but they moved beneath their robed riders with the grace and restraint of long training. She saw the Perona riders sweep the Alilan before them. She saw scattered Alilan running to the wagons for their weapons or their sleeping children, and others pressing on to where their own horses stood. They were too far away, the Perona too close. She saw Alilan falling beneath swords and hoofs, and she sprang down the steps and flew, her body young with fear.

Closer to the riders there was only chaos, images blurred and meaningless. An arm lying without a body; a toppled horse; a gout of blood that came from nowhere. Aldira stabbed with her dagger but did not feel it sink into flesh. Pain burned along the length of her left leg. She fell to one knee, her own cries louder than the battle. Suddenly Alea was above her, her arms encircling and firm. Aldira bent her head into Alea's shoulder. She listened to the hammer of hoofs and death, and wept for the Alilan's breaking.

She felt Alea stiffen. "Listen, Aldira," she said. "By the Twins—listen to him!"

At first Aldira heard only the same screams, of horse and human and metal. "To whom?" she cried to Alea, who was straining to her feet, eyes seeking and wild. As Aldira too tried to stand (her left leg numb now, though she did not look at it to see why), different shrieks began. They were distant—at the rear of the Perona army—but the noise and motion of the battle broke, as if the fighters were listening. And Aldira heard him for a moment before she heard his words: a man's voice, but still also a boy's, rising in a passion and power beyond the Alilan and their Goddesses.

The Perona horses reared and twisted, trying to evade showers of thorns and clouds of biting insects. Their riders clawed at their faces, tearing veils away to reveal blisters and open sores, as if each had been struck at once by the same disease. Their swords fell unheeded to the sand and many Perona followed, pinned by arrows and daggers that had come from no hand.

The Alilan watched, motionless and mute, as Aldron drove the Perona back into the desert. Shrieks and blood and torn cloth billowed behind them; but soon there was only a pall of dust, and silence. Still the Alilan stared.

Alea moved first. Aldira heard her make a strangled sound. She turned, somehow, and watched Alea run to the foot of the leaping place. She tucked the ends of her skirt up into its waist and climbed, swift and sure. When she reached the top, she knelt, and all Aldira could see was her bent head, her black, shining hair. Moments later Aliser joined her. He climbed down soon after, edging from handhold to toehold with Aldron slung over a shoulder. The descent was very slow, and all of the Alilan had drawn together below by the time Aliser lowered Aldron to the sand.

Aldira reached them last. There was a deep cut from her thigh to the back of her knee and down to her ankle. She clutched the top of her leg as if this would stem the bleeding, and dragged it after her like a piece of wood. She felt no pain from the wound; it was the place behind her eyes that throbbed.

Aliser was standing above Alea, who was sitting cross-legged with Aldron's head in her lap. Aldira limped toward them and people made way for her soundlessly. When at last she halted, someone began to bind her leg wound. She leaned on this person and winced as the dressings were drawn tight, but she did not look away from Aldron.

His eyes were open, fixed on sky. His arms and legs lay straight, but they twitched constantly. The ground beneath him was scored with the shapes of his fingers, his heels, his sweeping calves and forearms. His skin looked yellow. *Fever,* Aldira thought, though she did not touch him to see if this was so.

The sun sank. Aliser still stood; Alea still bent over Aldron; the Alilan who waited were still silent. Others had left to tend to the injured or to build fires for the dead. Aldira heard muffled weeping and cries, and saw the flames rising, a red-orange glow at the edge of her vision. And then it was dark and torches were distributed, and as Aldira reached for hers, Aldron turned his head and vomited onto the sand.

Alea wiped his mouth and he groaned, his heels gouging hollows. His fingers clawed at his own face. Alea grasped and held them until he calmed. She bent and murmured something Aldira could not hear. Aldron answered: two words, low and rough and unrecognizable.

"Speak." Aliser's voice was loud and steady. "Speak to all of us before we cast you out."

"Aliser!" Aldira hissed. "Wait for—"

"Cast me out." Aldron's words were ragged but very clear. "Cast me out, when I've just saved you."

Aliser lunged for Aldron, holding Alea away from both of them with one tendon-corded arm. "You," Aliser said, drawing Aldron up until he was nearly standing, "have broken our Goddesses' only law. But you knew this. You knew it, and yet you proceeded."

"Look behind you," Aldron said. "Our dead are burning. There would have been more if I hadn't broken this law. Even you might have been among them."

Aliser took a step back. Aldron crumpled to his knees and Alea slipped her arm around his waist.

"I would gladly have died," Aliser said, "fighting among the Alilan of all the caravans, with my dagger and the strength of my body. That is how Alneth and Alnila commanded us to meet our enemies—not with a cowardly, twisted Telling."

Aldron laughed. "You're just furious that it was my power that saved you. My power, which is greater than any you'll ever know."

"Great power?" Aldira had to lean forward to hear Aliser's voice. She saw Alea's fingers dig into Aldron's side. "Look at you. You can't stand. If you weren't leaning on her, you'd be face down in the sand. You may have power, but they're punishing you for it—our Goddesses, who are no longer yours."

Aldron swallowed; Aldira thought she heard it in the silence. Even the cries of the wounded and the grieving had thinned to nothing in the falling darkness.

"And do the Goddesses speak often to you, Aliser? Was it they who gave you the right to pronounce judgment on me?" Aldron shook his head. "I cannot accept this judgment from you. You know nothing of—"

"Aliser is right." Alea glanced up at Aldira. She looked ten years old again, her eyes wide and helpless, her mouth open. Aliser nodded once and crossed his arms over his chest.

Aldira kept speaking. She felt tears around the hard edges of her words and was too weary to be surprised. "You have always known what should and should not be, and you have always made light of this knowledge. Your power may indeed be considerable, but it grows uglier every time you misuse it."

Aldron drew a quick breath and Aldira held up a hand. "No—listen to me now. You may have saved us today. Tomorrow you may ruin us—even if you do not intend to. So you must never Tell change or destruction or creation again. If you are to remain among us, you must swear this."

Aliser said, "Don't give him this chance! And don't believe any oath of his: he's a liar who cannot feel remorse."

"Aliser." The crowd shifted after Alea spoke. Aldira noticed that Alea's parents and sisters were in the first ring of onlookers. Her brother pushed his way forward to stand with them as Aldira watched.

Alea rose, though she kept her left hand on Aldron's shoulder. "You're angrier at me than you are at him. Let Old Aldira decide what should be done."

Aldira felt them all looking at her, rustling and muttering as they craned to see her better. She remembered, in the moment before she spoke, that she had once relished being the one to decide. "Perhaps I am too lenient, but I say again: swear that you will never use your Telling power to effect any sort of change in the world. Swear this, and stay among us."

Aldron put his hand up to Alea's and their fingers knit and held. "I cannot," he said, gazing up at Alea. She looked steadily back at him, her face pale beneath the light of the new stars.

Aldira waited for him to say more. She was suddenly dizzy. *My wound,* she thought, and knew that this was only partly true. But he did not speak again. He rose, holding both of Alea's hands, and stood before them all.

"Then you will leave the Alilan," Aldira said loudly, slipping with relief into the space where only words existed. "You will leave and never again be welcome among us. And we will never speak your name—not even to curse it. You will be a silence to us. Beginning now."

She turned away from him and from Alea, and for a moment her eyes were filled with darkness. The person who had been supporting her—Alon, she saw when her vision cleared, only a boy, whose Tellings were sloppy and too quick—stood and took her arm. She leaned on him and he led her away, back among the crowd, which parted again then closed behind and followed. The Alilan of all the caravans walked together to the fires of their dead, and Aldira led them, holding a torch that guttered slightly, as if a wind had touched it.

~

"No."

Alea thrust a tunic into an embroidered sack and did not look at her mother.

"Alea—no. Do not go with this … person."

"Sleep here with us tonight," Alea's father said, and she shrank from the confusion and tenderness that tangled in his words. "Decisions hastily made one day can be unmade the next. Stay with your family, little foal."

A belt, a pair of hide boots, a copper armring. Her mother's hands fastened on the armring and pulled it away. "If you truly mean to go, you will not take Alilan finery with you. You will take nothing except what you must wear or use." Aldana's voice was flat and edged both, like a dagger, and Alea lowered her head over her sack.

"Very well," she said, so softly that she could hardly hear herself.

"Why?" her father demanded. She heard him pace to the wagon door and back toward her bed. He would be grinding his fingers through his red beard.

"Because," Alea said, "I love him."

Her mother grasped Alea's jaw and turned her round to face them. "For how long?"

Alea's throat was ash, and when she swallowed it was ash as well, rough and dry. "Since we were children, I think."

"But you never spoke to us of this," Aldill said. "Not even to your sisters. How could you keep this … love to yourself?"

Alea laughed. It was the only sound she could make that would be contained by the wood above her, and the air, and the distant net of stars. "And what if I had told you? 'There's a young man with no family and a dangerous power—may he eat at our fire tonight?' You would have forbidden me to love him."

"We would not." Aldill put a hand to her cheek and held it there, his palm a hollow warmth. "We would have worried, yes, and perhaps tried to guide you to a more suitable young man—"

"Like Aliser." She pulled herself away from him and walked to the door, which she opened.

"Yes," her mother said. "And why not? He is a good, strong Alilan man, and he has loved you with a patience you do not deserve."

"In that case," Alea said, looking at Aldana for the last time, "he deserves someone better than me. And now he's free to find her."

They called her name as she ran down the wagon steps. Her siblings were waiting by the fire. One of her sisters clutched her hand, and both were sobbing, but Alea did not look at them as she fled. She heard Alder's feet pounding close behind her for a time, but she ran faster, and soon no one followed her.

Aldron and his horse were waiting by Ralan in the Twin Daggers caravan's horse line. Aldron was sitting with one hand raised to his horse's face. Alea squatted before him and took his other hand.

"Can you ride?" she said. He shrugged and opened his mouth to speak, but the voice that came was not his.

"It makes no difference whether he can or can't." Alea rose and turned to Aliser. Five men stood behind him; she saw the separate glints of their daggers. "You can't have imagined you'd leave the Alilan on horseback? Or that you'd stoke your sad little fire with wood hacked by Alilan daggers?"

"You can't do this." Alea backed up until Ralan nibbled at the cloth of her blouse. She put an arm around her horse's neck, not looking away from Aliser's face. "You have no right to take these things away from us."

"Haven't I?" More men were approaching, silently, holding torches and daggers. "He's been cast out. You've chosen to go with him. Neither of you is Alilan now—so you must leave behind the things that made you so. Or I'll force you to."

Aldron laughed as he drew himself to his feet. "I see you required some support to make this threat. I'm flattered."

Aliser's eyes did not move from Alea's. "After you walk away from this place, these men and I will join the rest of our people and ride in pursuit of the Perona army. We will face them honourably and Tell our triumph to the Goddesses. We will be forgiven."

"Aliser." She walked to him slowly, willing him to keep looking at her, willing herself not to stumble. When she touched his hair—not as fiery in the darkness—he flinched and she heard the hiss of his indrawn breath. "You've loved me so well, and I've needed this love. And though you may not believe it, I've loved you in—"

"Stop," he said through gritted teeth. "Say nothing more."

"If the Goddesses can be forgiving," Alea continued, feeling the tremor in her voice as if it were in the earth, "so can you. Please, Aliser—we've shared so many seasons, and you're so dear to me, truly ..."

He blinked at her, lost for a moment, frowning so that the freckles across the bridge of his nose seemed to flatten. Then he stepped back, away from her touch and her eyes, and said, "Go now. *Now,* Alea."

Her horse and Aldron's were surrounded by men. Ralan pawed at the sand and pulled his head away from the man who held him. Alea saw this as she went to Aldron.

"Well, then, my little heartflower," he said, and pulled her in to him.

~

They placed their daggers side by side on the ground, hafts out, as if giving them directly into Aliser's hands. She glanced at her horse so quickly that Aliser almost did not see it. He knew he should rejoice in her pain, but he felt nothing. The daggers lay on the sand and his men stood solid as stakes around the horses, and his own horse waited to bear him into battle—but he felt nothing.

He watched Alea and the nameless man loop their arms around each other's waists and lean their heads together. He watched them draw apart, but only a little; their hands were still touching as they began to walk. They walked along the line of horses, away from the torchlight. Soon he saw only the white of her blouse and leggings. He imagined her hair and limbs, darknesses slipping into a greater darkness, and he turned sharply and called out to his men.

As they gathered to return to the main camp, four notes sounded—a whistled fragment, nearly a melody. Aliser's voice died mid-sentence as the notes came again, and again. He knew the almost-tune. He looked at Ralan, saw the horse toss his mane and flare his nostrils. When the last whistled notes had faded, the horse threw back his head and bellowed, his hoofs churning the air. "We'll have to kill it, and the other too," Aliser heard someone say, but he did not answer. "Aliser? Should we—"

"Leave me," he said, and they did, one by one, until he was alone. They had taken all the torches, but he had no need of more than starlight for what he had to do. He picked up her dagger and turned it over in his palm three times. It would likely be sharp enough; she took care with such things.

Ralan was standing on all four hoofs now, his breath gusting from nostrils and mouth. Aliser walked up to him and laid a hand on his neck; he felt sweat and the coursing of blood beneath thick hair and skin. He drew the edge of her dagger across the place, and it was sharp enough.

SEVENTEEN

Nellyn woke to sun and birdsong. He did not open his eyes right away. He lay and listened to the singing, and to the rustling of wind through dry-tipped leaves. Some of the leaves had already fallen; he felt them crackle beneath him as he stretched and rolled onto his side. He still did not open his eyes. He listened for Lanara, who always rose hours before he did, just as he always walked or sat for hours after she had fallen asleep.

"It's right that you're sleeping like this," she had said once, a few months after they had left Luhr. "You were so sick when you were trying to sleep at the same time I did. This is more … natural."

Nothing will be natural again, he had thought with a rush of pain and surprise that had subsided, bit by bit, as he breathed. *She is right. This is how I spend my nights and dawns and mornings. This is the river that carries me now.*

When the journey began, it had been so difficult waiting for sleep. He had not strayed far from their wagon: too raw and frail, too alone. He had heard lynanyn and paddles in water, and had known that these sounds were memories but also real now, somewhere. As they drew further and further away from Luhr, he had begun to wander more at night. He was less fearful listening to sounds that were not memories. Night creatures, wind, thunder: he listened and walked and found that his body was at home again in darkness.

Lanara was writing; he heard her writing stick scratching on one of the many pieces of parchment she had brought with them. He heard herb water bubbling as well, and smelled it, and he opened his eyes at last with a groan of thirst and contentment.

They followed the broad forest path while the sun edged westward. Its light fell through half-stripped branches, and Nellyn remembered other light, other places: a waterfall surrounded by jungle, a field of bare black rocks, a mountain wreathed in smoke and spitting fire. This forest was the most peaceful place he had yet seen. The leaves shone as they turned in the breeze, and every sound seemed muffled, even that of the horse's hoofs.

"It's lovely, isn't it?" Lanara said, lifting her face to the sky. "I wouldn't mind another few days of this." But a short time later, trees and path ended at a plain of crackling gold.

"This is lovely too," Nellyn said, wading into the grass. Lanara said nothing. He turned back and saw her sitting very still on the wagon's bench, the reins slack in her hands. He turned again, following her gaze, and saw wooden walls and a tower, and smoke rising into the dark blue sky.

"This must be Galhadrell," she said. "I wasn't expecting to reach it for another few days, but this is it—I'm sure ..." She looked down at him. "It's been so long since we slept in a bed. And it's not a very big town, not even as big as that one we stopped in when we were a week away from Luhr."

"No," he said, aching because he heard and saw her longing, and because she was trying so hard to be careful of him. "It looks like quite a nice size. So let's go—it will be dark soon."

The bed they found, in an inn so ancient it leaned, was a delight. It was high off the floor, with a straw-stuffed mattress and brown sheets worn smooth by travellers' limbs; with flat pillows and a headboard that creaked. He had slept well in the wagon and on rock and cushions of vine or moss, but this bed lulled him even further away than sleep. He stayed in it for nearly two days and two nights. Lanara often joined him, sleeping and not sleeping. Mostly he lay alone, looking at the room as he had once looked at the clay walls of his hut. These walls were plaster, white smudged grey by the soot from the fireplace across from the bed. The floorboards were cracked and dotted with holes through which, Lanara had discovered, the dining room below could be glimpsed. She left the shutters open in the morning; he woke to sunlight and cloud-streaked blue.

He left the bed only when midnight was well past and Lanara was asleep. The town's streets were nearly empty those two nights. He saw shadows of cats and dogs, and even a few people; he stepped back into doorways to watch them. He was not afraid, as he had been in Luhr. He saw the animals and people, saw that they were alone and purposeful in the darkness, and was content to watch them pass.

On the third day Lanara said, "So—are you ever going to leave this room when there are people around?"

"Maybe," he said, pulling her back down to lie beside him. She laughed as he kissed her, and dragged her fingers down his back so that he wriggled away from her.

"Because you know," she said, twining a strand of his hair around her forefinger, "I've met some very friendly people. Townspeople mostly, who come to eat here in the evening."

Nellyn moved from his side to his back. "Oh," he said. The sky above the roofs was grey today; no rain, but the clouds looked heavy and full. *Like other clouds I have seen,* he thought, and wished he could burrow into the blankets until he was blind.

"Come down with me. I know you like the food here, and I'm tired of carrying it up to you. Come and meet these people."

He followed her down the stairs later, just after the rain had started. He heard it against their shutters, and against the roof when they were in the corridor—but he could not hear it at all on the stairs above the dining room. There were so many voices, and a constant clatter of plates and mugs, and the spit and crackle of the fire in the wide stone hearth. He had heard these sounds from the bedchamber, but they had merely been ripples. Lanara squeezed his hand and they both stepped onto the next stair—and then suddenly all the noise stopped, and leaves began to fall.

Lanara let go of his hand. She raised her arm, tried to catch one of the leaves, a crimson one, which still looked smooth and bright. It reached her hand and passed through it: a leaf without substance, surrounded by a forest of others, all vivid and silent, all gone as soon as they touched the floor below. Nellyn watched them, and he heard their silence, and when the last one had vanished, he did not want to move.

"Come on!" Lanara cried above the burst of applause and shouting that had risen. "We have to find out who did that ..."

She led him down to a round table. All of the people at the table were looking at the hearth—or rather, Nellyn realized, at the man who was leaning against the wall beside it. He was tall, dark-haired and dark-eyed, smiling through a rough sheen of beard.

"Who is he?" Lanara hissed to a woman who was sitting at the table. "Is he the one who made the leaves?"

The woman nodded and rose, grasping Lanara's tunic sleeve. "Aldron!" she called, and her voice was very loud as the clapping and shouting faded. "Aldron, here's Queenswoman Lanara, who's never met you before. Why not show her something spectacular? I've seen you conjure up balls of lightning and a mass of spinning daggers. Surely you could offer her something more than a bunch of leaves?"

The man inclined his head, still smiling. "Greetings, Queenswoman Lanara," he said. "And apologies, Pareya," he went on, looking at the other woman, "for the leaves are all you'll get of me tonight."

One man at the table laughed; another glowered. Nellyn glanced from one to the other, then at a woman who had set her stool a bit apart from theirs. Her hair was as dark as Aldron's, drawn back and knotted at the base of her neck. Her eyes were on a spoon she was turning over and over on the tabletop. She stopped moving it only when Aldron kissed the top of her head. She frowned at him as he sat down on the stool next to hers. He whispered to her and produced a slender-stemmed purple flower from beneath the table. The woman took it, though she continued to frown.

"So, Queenswoman Lanara," Aldron said after he had taken a long drink from a silver goblet, "what brings you to this corner of nowhere? The thin mead? The leaning buildings?"

Lanara laughed. She sat down across from him and gave some answer Nellyn did not try to hear. He was still looking at the woman and her flower, and as he looked, she raised her head and saw him.

"Greetings," she said after a moment. "I'm Alea." She smiled and set the flower down on the table.

"And I am Nellyn," he said, smiling back at her. "Greetings, Alea."

~

My Queen, after months of fairly lonely wandering we have met two people who are already our friends. They are of the Alilan tribe, but have been travelling on their own for over a year. The man, Aldron, says this is because the strict rules of the Alilan were limiting them and they needed to be free for a time. I hear in his voice that this is not the true reason—or perhaps it is only part of the reason. And I see in the woman Alea's face that there is much more to tell. Of course, I am eager to learn their story—all of it. I read about the Alilan as a child, in the Scribeslibrary. I remember what the scrolls looked like, and how I shivered when I read this new name. How I wish I could see one of these scrolls now! But I will exercise the patience I learned with the shonyn. I will talk to Aldron and Alea, and listen. I hope that I will witness another instance of Aldron's Telling—an Alilan power, he says, that enables him to conjure up visions and make them seem real (though they are not). I will enjoy their company (Aldron in particular is warm and enthusiastic about our conversations) and our shared time in this town, which is attractive and pleasantly large. Nellyn and I will stay here as long as Aldron and Alea do. We continue to feel that our journey is benefiting us, and (as urged by you) are in no hurry to reach Fane.

I have written so many letters to you, and only a few times during our travels have I found a Queensfolk delivery post from which to send these letters back to Luhr. By the time we reach Fane, our wagon will be full of scrawled-upon parchment. We will need an entire boat to return these scribblings to you! And you will need weeks to read them.

I wish I could speak to you—you and Ladhra both. Nellyn and I have encountered wonders. At least we have Aldron and Alea now to keep us company for a time. We will share our stories with them, and perhaps they will soon share theirs with us.

~

Nellyn found a stream the night after he and Lanara met the two Alilan. He was walking along streets he had not seen on his other nights here. He passed people huddled around sullen fires, and houses joined by torchlit walkways that arced high above his head. He heard a child crying, though he could not tell from where; he heard a man shouting and another answering him, and their anger made Nellyn shiver. He turned a corner, and as the voices faded he heard water.

He followed the sound to a place where the houses dwindled away and trees began. The trees were squat and gnarled. He put a hand to one of them and felt bark still moist from yesterday's rain, and leaves, and a smoothness that was fruit. His hand froze for a moment, then traced the shape slowly. He knew already that it was nothing like lynanyn (too small, too narrow at stem and bottom), but he lingered anyway, until the water noise drew him on.

The stream was about three paces wide. When he took off his shoes and stepped into the water, he discovered that it was knee-deep and numbingly cold. He followed the stream among the trees, looking at the familiar reflections of moon and boughs and his own moving body. His foot brushed one of the small fruits (ripe, fallen), and he thought, *This is the first time in so long. We have seen rivers and lakes, but I have never touched them in this way, and here too there is fruit …*

The trees ended at the town wall. Nellyn put his hands on the dead wood; he bent so that he could see the glimmer of water, which disappeared beneath the wall. There was a low door to one side of the stream. He lifted the latch and pushed the door open and ducked out onto the plain.

The tiny stream curved away, shallower with every step, and was soon swallowed by earth and grass. He turned around, feeling the grass whisper and cling, held to his legs by the water that was drying on his skin. In four paces his feet were dry, and he slid them back into his shoes.

He wandered back toward the wall and gatehouse towers, where fire flickered. He gazed for a moment at the torchlight and the stars above it. When he looked back down, he saw a woman standing outside the main gates. Her back was to him and all he saw was dark cloth and darker hair, which fell smooth to the middle of her back. As he hesitated, she turned her head into the light.

"Alea," he said when he was beside her. She started and he held up a hand, almost touched her arm. "I am sorry. I thought you heard me," he said as he looked at her wide eyes and the shaking fingers she raised to her mouth.

"I didn't." Her voice was steadier than her hand. "You were so quiet. Or I wasn't listening."

He nodded. "When I listen only to wind and earth, I also am deaf to other voices." She turned to him and he saw her face clearly. "Why are you sad?" he asked, though "sad" was not the whole word for her eyes and her white, stretched skin.

She did not answer for a long time. He waited, very still.

"I miss the earth when I'm in there." She gestured behind her with one hand. "And tonight I … thought I might see something." He listened to a second, longer silence. The grass sounded like his river. "Wagons," she continued in a rush. "I thought the Alilan wagons might start arriving."

"But they did not."

She shook her head. "There would be fire," she said, and he looked with her into the emptiness of the plain.

"So you are waiting. That is why you are here, in this town?"

He saw the flutter of Alea's lashes as she closed her eyes then opened them again. "Yes. We've been travelling for so long, seeing no one but each other—and for so long we've avoided the paths of our caravans. But this year, when autumn came to the forest, we couldn't keep away from here. Aldron says we'll only look from a distance, but I know he wants to be among the horses and the fires. Like I do."

"But if you want to return to your people—" Nellyn began, and Alea said loudly, "No! Please—you don't understand—we can't return." Her words trembled into a quiet that he knew would endure beyond his waiting. *I might understand,* he thought, but he saw her sadness and her struggle and did not say this.

"We should go back to the inn," he said instead. "It is getting colder. And they will be waiting for us."

Alea nodded and turned. They walked together to the wooden walls and in.

~

Aldron drew the bowstring back until it was level with his left ear. He held it there, squinting and smiling at the same time. He had been smiling since Lanara had handed him the bow. He had touched—slowly, with his fingertips—the dark wood, the arrows' golden fletching, even the leather of the quiver. "May I?" he had asked, and smiled as if he were hungry.

His first arrow landed flat on the damp earth of the inn courtyard. His second lodged in the outer edge of the sackcloth that stretched over the straw and wood of the target. His third thudded into the centre. They watched it shudder into stillness.

"You told me you'd never done this before," Lanara said.

"I haven't." He looked down at the arrow in his hand and angled it so that the sunlight glanced off its metal tip. "But I've had experience with other weapons. I used to throw my dagger—probably because I was told not to."

"Where's your dagger now?"

Aldron nocked the fourth arrow and loosed it. It buried itself in the centre and the other arrow trembled with it. "I left it behind. It would have reminded me too much of people I wanted to forget."

"And did you leave your horse behind for the same reason?"

He turned to frown down at her. "How do you know of Alilan ways?"

Lanara handed him another arrow, which he took without looking away from her. "Queensfolk have travelled far and written about many people. I've been reading their tales since I was a girl."

"So you found out about Alilan horses from writings," he said, one eyebrow raised. "What else did you learn about us?"

"That's all I remember clearly: horses, another tribe—in the desert, I think—something about storytelling. These were all second-hand accounts, though." The sunlight was beginning to slant. She put up a hand and peered at him beneath it. "Why don't you give me more details?"

"I don't write," he said, and she heard him smile. She laughed as he nocked the last arrow and sent it out, shining and singing and straight.

That night, as they all sat again at the round table, Lanara turned to Aldron and said, "Don't think that your little jest distracted me. I still want to know more about the Alilan."

He took a long swallow of wine and wiped his mouth with two fingers. "About the Alilan, or about why I left them?"

She felt as if she were dwindling beneath his eyes. *He is afraid of what he hides,* she thought, *and he wants me to be afraid as well.* She said very softly, "Whichever is more interesting. Whichever you'd prefer not to talk about."

He stared at her and she held herself still, hardly blinking. Then Pareya, who was sitting near Alea and Nellyn, cried, "Aldron, listen: this one's from a place where people sleep during the day and wake at night! Isn't that the silliest thing?"

The noise of the full dining room seemed deafening in the silence that fell at the round table. Nellyn looked at the woman as the others looked at him. She shifted on her chair and frowned.

"The silliest thing, Pareya?" Aldron said. "Hardly."

"I'd like to hear more about this place," Alea said quickly to Nellyn. "If you don't mind telling us."

Lanara let out a slow breath as Nellyn began to speak. He gazed steadily at Alea, then at Lanara. When he struggled to find words, he gazed at the shutters that were latched against night and chill. Lanara thought, *He never told me all this when I first asked him,* and felt a rush of warmth at the change, and her part in it.

~

Alea and Aldron nodded or smiled at Nellyn as he spoke, but they did not interrupt him. *Maybe it is obvious,* he thought, *how difficult it is for me to say these things.* For although he did not explain time and understanding and madness, what he did describe was painful enough: lynanyn in the river, moonlight on silver leaves, the steady fanning of blue curtains. As he spoke, he saw the images, but blurrily, as if the words stood between himself and his memories. When he told them of the Queensfolk ships and the tents on the ridge, his voice faltered and he turned to Lanara. She smiled and laid her fingers lightly on the back of his hand. Then she spoke of the same tents and ships—and also of Luhr and Ladhra and her own sun-moulded house behind the palace.

Lanara's words were effortless and light; Nellyn watched Alea and Aldron lean forward and change the way they listened. Aldron began to ask questions, which Lanara answered and which led her to new stories. She glanced at Nellyn often as she spoke, sometimes serious, sometimes smiling, and he felt himself bending toward her too.

Pareya rose and left them when Lanara began to talk; the tables around them emptied as she continued. The innkeeper fed logs into the fire for a time, and shuffled over to bring them more wine and bread, but soon he disappeared as the others had, silently and unnoticed.

"I think I'm losing my voice," Lanara said at last. The other three stirred and stretched. "And you haven't said one thing about yourself," she added, and Aldron sighed dramatically.

"How regrettable that it's so late and we're all so tired," Aldron said as he pushed his chair back.

Nellyn saw Alea look up at him and thought, *She is so sad, because of him.*

"Soon," Lanara said, half smiling, and Aldron raised an eyebrow at her before he turned toward the stairs.

"Thank you," said Alea, looking from Lanara to Nellyn. It seemed to him that she wanted to say more, but after a moment of hesitation she smiled quickly and followed Aldron.

"They're fascinating, aren't they?" Lanara said when she and Nellyn were back in their room. She was sitting on a low stool in front of a basin of water she had heated over their fire, squeezing a wet cloth against her forehead, her neck, her breasts. She shone like dark wood in the firelight.

"Yes," he said. He lay on their bed with his hands behind his head and the blanket drawn up to his chin, and watched her as the wind blew hard against the shutters.

EIGHTEEN

My Queen, the Alilan began to arrive today.

Nellyn and I were walking in a market—though even writing "market" makes me think of the open sky and wide ground of Luhr's market, and here the space is vastly different. Here you enter what appears to be a private home and climb to the second floor, where the rooms are small and connected by a corridor. When you follow the corridor, it turns into a bridge over the street below—and on the other side is another house with tiny rooms, each one containing wares and a seller, and another corridor that also becomes a bridge … I realize that these enclosed spaces are necessary, since there is so much rain and snow here—but I still found myself looking up at the wooden beams and soot-stained ceilings and longing for the hot wind of home.

We saw a chamber stacked with green baskets, each one holding a wriggling knot of snakes (apparently the rodents here are numerous—though I can't imagine why the townspeople prefer snakes to mice!). Another room was strung with dried herbs and spongemoss, and the smell was delicious. My favourite chamber was full of painted wooden leaves that hung from the walls and ceiling and even lay on the floor. When we first stepped inside, we thought we were in a living forest. I bought two scarlet ones (oak) and two golden ones (elm, the woman told me). I'll give you and Ladhra one of each when we see you next.

As we were about to cross yet another bridge, we heard someone cry, "The horse people are coming!" The crowd around us began to push and jostle, and we were swept along with them to an archway that led out onto the town wall. We peered over the wall with everyone else (though Nellyn was hesitant to at first: he's discovered he has a fear of high places).

"Accursed filth," the woman beside me grumbled in the thick accent of this town.

I turned away from the distant wagons (so distant they looked like insects in the grass) and asked her why she spoke of them this way. She eyed me with obvious distaste.

"You're a stranger yourself if you need to ask," she said. "Those horse herders are troublemakers. Every fall they camp outside our forest and for weeks we get no peace. They drum and hoot all night until the snows come—and then they leave, and our fresh white grass is battered down and stained with black wood and horseshit." She spat over the wall. "We've sent elders out to ask them to go somewhere else, but they've always refused. We don't want violence, of course—we're good people—so we tolerate them and count the days until winter." Despite the rancour of her words, this woman watched as avidly as the rest (such petty people—and so insensitive to those not like them!).

The wagons drew closer and I could see the horses that pulled them, and other horses that rode apart with single riders. Before they halted, though, I told Nellyn that we should go find Alea and Aldron, who would doubtless want to know about their people's arrival. We returned to the inn but found it empty—and now, hours later and darkness falling, we still have not seen them.

~

The fire had burned down to glowing ash when Nellyn stepped into the dining room. He closed the door behind him, shutting out the billowing rain. He stamped his feet and peeled off his cloak and moved toward the stairs.

His vision (as keen in darkness as in daylight) sharpened as he walked. He saw a shadow beside the fireplace, saw it shift and bend, and he stopped and turned to it. "Aldron," he said quietly, and the Alilan man raised his head from his knees. Nellyn added a log to the fire and poked at it until it caught, then he drew a stool over to Aldron, who was still staring vacantly at him.

"Oh," Aldron said at last, thickly, "you. The one who wakes at night." He lifted a bottle from the floor at his feet and tipped it to his mouth. The liquid that trickled between his lips and down his neck looked black. Nellyn saw that Aldron's skin was already veined with wine, some of it dried, some still glistening. His eyes too were black.

"Lanara sent you to torment me with questions, did she? 'What are the wagons and why are you not with them and what crime did you commit to be alone in the world?'" He drank again. This time the bottle fell when he put it down. Nellyn watched the wine spreading against the floorboards and remembered when he had dropped a goblet on a balcony high above the desert.

"No," he said, "I have no questions like that. But I will ask—where is Alea?"

Aldron grunted. "Don't know. Probably lurking round her caravan. I told her, they won't listen to you, they'll pretend they can't even see you. And that's what happened—just like I said. Not sure why I went with her. I *knew*. She's probably crying and watching them now. Crying and spying. Twins *rot* them," he shouted, and kicked the wine bottle so that it rang and splintered against the stone of the fireplace.

Nellyn swept up the glass with the ash brush and pan. Aldron watched him with narrowed eyes. When he was finished, Nellyn sat back down on the stool.

"You're a strange one," Aldron said.

Nellyn smiled. "Lanara thinks so too. Though not as much as she used to, maybe." He studied Aldron carefully: shaking limbs, cold-puckered flesh, eyelids drooping and swollen. "Let me help you upstairs."

"Alea!" Aldron shouted as Nellyn half carried him in the door to the sleeping chamber—but the room was empty. A room like the one Nellyn shared with Lanara, except that the bed had a different headboard and was pushed against a wall. When he tried to guide Aldron to the bed, the man wrenched himself upright and stood with his arms outstretched.

"No, no—not on the bed. The bed is fine for waking pleasures—but sleep, no. We Alilan sleep on the ground." He dropped to his knees on a blanket that lay on the floor. Nellyn knelt beside him, took his weight as he slipped onto his back.

"I'll make a fire," Nellyn said. He heard Aldron mumble a response—and then his voice and words changed, and Nellyn sat back on his heels.

Fire, fire, flames on stone, flames born orange and white and blue, born of twins, Alnila fire and Alneth wood, fire and wood, burn with me, burn.

Nellyn held up an arm against the blaze. Aldron's voice rose and rose until Nellyn was deaf with the pain of it. If he cried out, he did not hear himself. He scrabbled toward the door and opened it as Aldron began to wail. The noise followed Nellyn into the corridor, where he stood and leaned against the wall. He panted and waited for the wailing to stop—which it did, very slowly.

Lanara did not stir as he slipped under the blanket beside her. *Wake up,* he thought, draping his arm over her hip. *I need you to wake up*. She lay still, breathing deeply—and although he soon matched his breath to hers, he did not sleep.

~

"Let's see if they're in their room." Lanara took two long steps toward Aldron and Alea's door.

Nellyn ran forward and caught her hand as she raised it. "Perhaps they're tired. Or not there."

She wondered why he had moved so quickly, and why his eyes were so wide. "It's nearly noon," she said, frowning and smiling at the same time. "And if they're not there, it won't matter if we knock." She knocked. She heard silence—but the kind of silence that falls suddenly between people who do not want to be heard. She knocked again and called their names. Just as she was about to knock one more time, the door swung open.

Alea was wearing a cloak, holding a full sack in one hand. She was very pale. "Are you leaving?" Lanara asked, and Alea glanced back into the room Lanara could not see.

"Yes. Soon—when Aldron is … ready."

"You were going to leave without telling us?" Lanara said. "Why, when we've enjoyed each other's company so much? Are you returning to your people?"

Alea shrank back. She was looking at Nellyn now. "No," she said, more breath than word—and then a voice that did not quite sound like Aldron's said, "Let them in, Alea—she won't leave until she's seen us both."

He was lying in bed, propped up on pillows, one blanket tucked around his waist and another wrapped around his shoulders. Lanara saw his chest, bare and heaving with shallow, inaudible breaths. She looked at his face and took a step backward.

"What's wrong?" she said, the words too loud for the room.

Aldron looked as if he were trying to smile. "Nellyn didn't tell you about my night of excess?" He glanced at Nellyn. "I seem to recall that he swept up some broken glass and carried me up the stairs. Though I might be mistaken."

His voice sounds wrong, Lanara thought. *Squeezed thinner.* "You're not suffering only from drink," she said, and Aldron rolled his eyes.

"Twins protect me—I've never met such a keen-witted woman. Of course it's not just the drink. Didn't Nellyn at least tell you about—"

"Stop!" Alea cried, as Nellyn said, "No." Lanara stared at each of them in turn.

"You didn't," Aldron said in his splintered voice, and Nellyn shook his head. "Well, then, I owe you thanks for your discretion as well as for your company last night."

"Someone," Lanara said slowly, each word bitten short, "tell me what's going on. Now."

Alea sat down on the bed. Aldron lifted a hand and traced gentle circles on her back. She was still wearing her cloak, still holding the bag.

"There's very little to explain," Alea said as Lanara pulled a stool out of a corner and sat down. "Aldron was drunk last night and Nellyn saw one of his Tellings. A very strong one."

"It was real." They all looked at Nellyn, who was standing with his back against the door. "The fire did not just *seem* real, it was. Not like the leaves, before. I felt the heat and I heard the flames."

"Yes," Alea said quickly, "it might have seemed real to you, but it was just a Telling. Just words. Aldron's power is very great. Much greater than mine."

"Oh, I don't know," Aldron said, "there was that sandstorm you Told when you were fourteen ..." She turned and glared at him. He glared back until she smiled. She leaned back a bit, against his hand.

"But look at you," Lanara said to Aldron. "Why are you so frail? You seemed fine after you Told those leaves."

"Because he hasn't Told anything complex in a long time," Alea said as Aldron opened his mouth to answer. "Not since we left our caravans. The leaves were image only; the flames were image and sound and sensation. Complicated Tellings exact a price. It was a shock to his body last night, feeling this power again."

Lanara frowned. "So why haven't you Told in so long? And please," she added, not looking at Alea, "answer me yourself this time."

Aldron shrugged. "As she said, I was drunk. And I was drunk because I had just been reminded of the people I left and why I left them."

"And why was that?" Lanara asked.

Aldron laughed, then coughed. "I'm weakened indeed, to offer you such an opening. The Alilan didn't agree with the things I Told. Or how I Told them. You'll have to be content with that."

"Ah," Lanara said. She looked at Nellyn. "So you saw him Tell this alarmingly realistic fire and you didn't tell me about it." She heard the anger in her voice, felt it like a sandfly's sting and the heat that comes after.

"No," he said. "I did not know how to explain it with my own words. I did not want to speak until I knew how to."

He was so calm, standing as he had the first time she had spoken to him, his feet as solid on these floorboards as they had been on the sand. She said, "You didn't want to … How could you not tell me? You tried to stop me from knocking. They would have *gone* and you wouldn't have—"

The fountain sings. Water darkens the stone—water falling from the mouths of carved fish and whorls of shell. A lacemoth hovers, and the sunlight draws rainbows from its four wings. Wind scatters the water; wind hot and dry and rough with sand.

Lanara closed her eyes. When she opened them, the fountain was gone—but she still felt water on her cheeks and the backs of her hands. She breathed away the scent of the desert, though she longed to hold it. *Father,* she thought, and nearly saw him.

"Well, then," Aldron whispered. He was lying flat now, with his head turned on the pillow.

Lanara cleared her throat. "You've never seen my city. How did you do that?"

"You told us about the fountains," he said. Alea moved, settled his head on her lap. "So I Told one."

"Why?" Lanara was very cold. She drew her hands up beneath the green-edged cuffs of her tunic sleeves. "Why, when you were already so weak?"

"Because you were angry."

~

Nellyn watched Alea's eyes after Aldron Told the fountain. When Lanara spoke afterward, Alea tucked her head down against her shoulder. Aldron reached up a hand to her and she held it to her cheek.

"Where were you going?" Nellyn asked. His own questions still surprised him. They all looked at him. He thought, *They forgot I was here. Again.* "Today," he added, when no one spoke, "you were leaving. Where were you planning to go?"

Alea said, "We weren't sure. Just … away."

"Well," Lanara said in her brisk, decision-making voice, "he's obviously too ill to walk anywhere. And we have a wagon." Aldron raised an eyebrow very slightly and Alea sat even more motionlessly. Lanara turned to Nellyn and tilted her head in a question that wasn't really a question. He nodded as he so often did, answering yes because she was so strong and certain—but also, this time, because Alea was beginning to smile.

Lanara turned back to the two Alilan, said, "So, have you ever seen the ocean?"

~

It's been so long since we wrote to each other. I've half expected a letter from you in every town we've stopped in, but there's never been one. At first this made me angry—though I should probably write "angrier," since I'd been angry ever since you wouldn't say goodbye to me. Since before then, actually, when Nellyn was sick and you and I had that awful conversation. But now that so much time's gone by, I'm just lonely; that's what's left of my anger. I miss you. I miss your letters. So even if you don't respond, I'm writing to you now. This letter will feel like a ribbon between us—a long ribbon made of words that stretches from my writing stick to your hands. This will make me happy, for now (but do write—please).

Maybe you've been curious; maybe you've been reading my letters to your mother. If you have, you'll know that I haven't written any in a long time. We've been travelling east through empty countryside for the past many months, and I wouldn't have been able to send a letter even if I'd written one. But now we're close to our destination: today we met a man on the coastal road who told us that three more days of travel will bring us to Fane. It's been a fascinating journey, and I must admit that I feel some regret knowing it's almost over. I'll describe it a bit, as much for myself as for you. (Your mother the Queen will receive a more formal letter from me, of course, concerning this portion of our travels.)

After we met the two Alilan on the Gelalhad Plain (your mother should have the letters from this period), we passed through several other towns and then came to the city of Dorloy. The local elders greeted us warmly. They do your mother's work well and seem eager to have visitors from Luhr. After Dorloy our path became much lonelier. We camped in marshland with no company except noisy, long-legged birds (exactly like the ones we named in the first Throne Chamber!) who apparently don't mind the cold. The marsh gave way to a long stretch of rocky outcrops, shelves and gorges where a river flowed far below. We lay on the rock as snow fell and watched the stars turning and blazing above us.

It was here, among the river canyons, that we discovered the Alilan woman was carrying a child. Nellyn noticed first; he mentioned to me that she looked different. I remember he said, "She seems pale and flushed at once." She and Aldron admitted that they were to have a baby in the early summer. Nellyn and I have enjoyed watching her belly grow beneath her skirts and cloaks. She was ill for about a month—she lay curled on her side in the wagon and ate nothing; will I ever be able to bring myself to do this?—but is much better now. She says she can feel the child moving within her, and sometimes Aldron puts his hand on her and smiles.

I've learned no more of them during our travels together than I did while we were in the town on the plain. They left their people because the Alilan did not approve of Aldron's Tellings; this is all they've said to me. I sometimes wonder whether he hurt someone, though I'm not sure why I wonder this. He's Told for us a few times—just gentle, quiet things, but I can feel something much more powerful beneath them. And he looks so haunted (which, of course, I find compelling—no, don't laugh at me!). Perhaps the reason for their exile is one that would shame them to admit, for the Alilan are, apparently, a people who value honour and strength as Queensfolk do.

We approached the Eastern Sea from the north, since I wanted to avoid the Sarhenna River. "I cannot," Nellyn said when I asked him if he would mind passing by his old town again. These were his only words, but I saw the grief in his eyes. (I must admit that this intensity of feeling surprised me. I thought that he'd been missing his village less as time went on.)

The ocean awed all of us. It was midday when we came to the wide, flat road that runs along the coastal cliffs. All we could see was icy water and sky, nearly the same silver. I thought of my desert home and of the fountains we Luhrans worship, and I almost wept because this sea was so vast.

As the road led us close to the edge of the cliff, we saw an amazing thing. Below us, drifting near the cliff's base, was what looked like a range of jewelled mountains—but mountains that moved. *They were transparent but also colourful—pink, blue, green, which we saw clearly when the sun came out and struck them—and they spun slowly, though we could feel no wind. They're made of ice, Ladhra—they're mountains of ice that dance! And they also sing, as we heard when we lingered to watch them. There were delicate high notes and rumbling low ones, and when two mountains touched one another, these notes soared. Now, close to Fane, their numbers have increased. How I wish you were beside me to see and hear these wonderful things! You must ask your mother to let you come here very soon.*

We turned south on the road and almost immediately met other travellers: fruit sellers and basket makers and families making their way to Fane, even in this deep cold, to seek a different life. And Queensfolk—how excited I was when the first rode past! She reined in her horse to talk to me (it was she who told me the name of the frozen mountains: icemounts). She is from the Pedharhan Woods and is working as a boatwright in Fane and other coastal towns.

So now we're three days away, and while I'm sorry that this long journey is coming to an end, I'm also excited to begin my life in the second most glorious of Queen Galha's cities. Nellyn is eager to see the signal tower and learn with me how to tend it (the letters that your mother gave me before we left Luhr—from the current tower keeper—have been very helpful). I think Alea and

Aldron will stay with us for a time. Maybe they'll decide to settle near us; they'll need a true home once their baby's born.

I know that I'll be able to send this soon, that I'll soon share stories with Queensfolk who've also met your mother, and perhaps you; that Nellyn and I will soon have a place that's ours. A second life is beginning for us now—and I want to share my excitement with you as I always have. "You have such trouble expressing your emotions, Nara"—I can hear you saying this, can almost imagine you rolling your eyes at me. Allow me my giddiness, will you? I'm happy. And the only thing that would make me happier would be to unfold a piece of parchment and see your writing upon it …

~

"Look!" Aldron cried. He tugged the horse to a stop and stood up at the front of the wagon. Lanara was already on her feet beside him. They had drawn back the canvas that covered the wagon's interior, since there had been no snow in days and the sky was clear and blue. Nellyn helped Alea up onto the inside bench and held her arm as they too looked down at the sloping road and where it led.

At first Alea saw only colours: lines and splashes and swaths that had no form because there were so many of them. She blinked and peered, and gradually saw shapes she knew. The blinding gold was pointed roofs sheathed in metal; the red scattered among the gold was roofs lined with tile. Scarlet, blue, green and yellow were the houses themselves, tiny and vivid as distant flowers. A river snaked among the houses, and its ice-churned surface was silver in the sunlight. The river's blur ended at the sea. Its water was enclosed here, drawn smaller on either side by arms of cliff. *A harbour,* Alea thought. Another word—like "ocean"—that she had heard and used until now without having seen its reality. Icemounts ringed the outside of the harbour, sealing it; within was a forest of naked trees. As she thought, *Ships,* her baby jabbed her, very high, nearly at her ribs. She poked the place herself, with three fingers; she felt something hard and pointed that lingered a moment, then drew away. *Well, dearest, here we are—thank the Twins. A bed will be wonderful after this wagon that has no walls except flimsy cloth ones, and no paint, and no iron stove to truly warm us …*

"Seen enough?" Nellyn asked, and Alea smiled at him. He lifted a hand to help her down—but as she reached for it, the wind shifted and she heard a sound, a low, steady booming, faint but suddenly audible.

"No," Lanara said, and they all looked at her. She was open-mouthed, pale in the sunlight that turned everything else to colour and shining. "No!" she said again, the word a wreath of steam on the air. Nellyn walked along the bench until he could touch her back. She twisted round and dug her fingers into his shoulders.

"A Queensbell," she said. "I've heard one twice: after Galha's mother died and after a group of Queensfolk was killed by rebels in the north. It rings only to tell of danger and death in the Queensrealm. Nellyn ..." She turned back to the town below them.

"Maybe it's a different bell," Aldron said. "Warning a ship away from rocks, or—"

"No. That kind's higher, more like music. I know what this one is."

Another sound swelled behind them—a sound so familiar that Alea wrenched herself around on the bench, thinking for a moment that she would see someone she knew. Even as she looked, she felt foolish and lost—for it was three Queensfolk galloping, bent low over their horses' necks. Lanara shouted after them, but her voice disappeared beneath the pounding of hoofs. The ice that filmed the road was cracked and scattered by their passing.

"Hurry," Lanara said as the riders dwindled on the road. "I must know what's happened. *Hurry.*"

Aldron flicked the reins and the wagon lurched forward. Alea burrowed a numb hand beneath her two cloaks and three blouses and pressed it against the taut skin of her belly. *Where are you, little one? Let me feel you—please*—but she felt nothing except the jolting of the wagon and the wind that rang with grief.

NINETEEN

Leish no longer looked like himself. Sometimes, in the shadows of first light or dusk, Mallesh's gaze would fall on his brother and continue on before snapping back again. *I do not recognize him any more,* Mallesh thought. *I do not know him any more.* This Leish was a gaunt, stooped man who kept his head lowered as if anticipating a blow. His skin looked worn, even though Mallesh soaked it every day in the mud and water the selkesh gathered from the jungle that had trapped them since they left the sea. Others were ailing as well, and several had died, their bodies weakened from the ocean voyage and unable to absorb the fruits and water of this strange land. Leish was not like them, Mallesh knew; he was not tormented by an ailment of the body but by the song he heard in his mind.

"I can hear nothing else," Leish had said a few days after they had hidden their boats along the coast near their landing place. "Not our land or the sea we crossed. Not even this jungle. I can hardly hear the words I speak aloud. Can you hear me? Mallesh?" His hands sought and gripped Mallesh's until he tugged them away.

Mallesh heard what all the selkesh but Leish did: the hot, dry place beyond the jungle, and the hum of the water and people there. But to Mallesh and the others the notes were one great noise. He tried to separate the strands, to see them clearly, each alone—but he could not. Only Leish saw them; so it was Leish who led the selkesh army.

"I hear the water beneath the sand. I hear how it will take us to the tall city." His eyes were wild. Mallesh tried, once, to recall what Leish had looked like beneath the water of Nasranesh, spinning in bubbles of laughter as Mallesh pursued him. He could not remember; it was as if this Leish had never smiled or swum. Mallesh said to the others, "My brother will guide us to our new place"—but now he thought, *This is not my brother.*

The selkesh scrambled after Leish, over fallen, rotten trunks and through pools of stagnant water. When he halted, they halted with him. Mallesh watched them watching Leish, and he shuddered because he thought he might hate this man who was no longer his brother. "Follow me!" Mallesh cried, so loudly that they would have to look at him. They did, though quickly, glancingly—so he called even more loudly, until it seemed he had no voice at all beneath the strangling leaves and vines.

He tended to Leish at night—washed his flaking skin, placed slivers of fruit between his lips. And Mallesh spoke to him, his voice lowered to a whisper he knew no one else would hear. "We've met no people since those fishers on the coast whom you told me not to kill. There's been no one else. Why? Why are there no people in this land?" Beasts howled and water dripped onto broad, flat leaves. "And when will this cursed jungle end? Are you silent now because you no longer have answers to give me?"

Mallesh whispered night after night—until one night Leish lifted his head and said a word. Mallesh drew back from him sharply, so that water sloshed in the skin he held. They were kneeling within a ring of plants whose stems and leaf veins glowed silver. Leish's eyes were wide and bright. He rasped the word again and this time Mallesh heard it.

"Tomorrow."

Mallesh had imagined hearing this word; he had felt a surge of excitement and joy in his imaginings. Now, on his knees in the jungle mud, he heard the word and looked at the man who had spoken it, and he felt only dread.

~

The selkesh army came to the edge of the jungle at dusk. The massive trees had been dwindling around them all day. Now they were gone, replaced by crooked cacti and jumbled boulders and sand that seemed scarlet, washed by the sky. A road curved away beside them, leading around the jungle, and stretched out broad and flat before them. The road glittered. The selkesh discovered when they set their feet upon it that it was made of crystal-flecked stone.

Mallesh noticed none of this when he stepped beyond the last straggling line of trees; he saw only the sheen of what lay at the end of the road.

Towers: now he knew what this word meant, though they were still small with distance. A smooth and gleaming wall (a word that until now had meant something crumbling beneath the sea, or short and squat and made of river stones, mud, reeds). And there beneath what his eyes showed him was the song of this place, abruptly clear after weeks of confusion. Water and green, above and beneath; gentle, delicate notes spread amongst the roar of sand.

Mallesh laughed. His men turned to him, some of them beginning to smile. He cried, "Behold, children of Nasran, our home in the west! Hear how it shines—hear how it calls to us, awaiting us as Nasran foretold. We hear its glorious song as no others can. Truly, we have been chosen for greatness!" He paused to draw breath from his heaving chest. "Let us stay here until we are all assembled. We shall linger for a time among the trees and decide how we will approach—for until now I have not seen this city and so have not been able to—"

Mallesh stopped speaking as Leish brushed past him. Leish, tall and unbowed, walking, not shambling. He strode out almost to the road and stood there alone, dark against the sky that was ablaze. The selkesh watched him. Mallesh felt the weight of their awe and expectancy, and he trembled with anger—but he too watched Leish. And when Leish did not move, even as sunset faded into blue-black and stars, Mallesh went to stand beside him.

"What do you think of our new place?" he said, just loudly enough that some of those behind them could hear. Normal words—words that would shape and strengthen.

"Our place?" Leish's voice was still rough, but it sounded familiar now, like the seasong Mallesh could hear, faintly, behind them. He cleared his throat.

"It's beautiful, isn't it? I can imagine how Nasran felt when she led our ancestors out of the ocean and beheld the earth and trees for the first time. My joy too is—"

"Mallesh," Leish said. He turned and Mallesh saw tears in his eyes and in the new, deep creases of his cheeks. "Do you remember when you were a child and you first saw the place whose song you'd only heard before? Was it the northern river branches?"

Mallesh frowned. "No. The spring that begins on the slopes of the mountains." He crossed his arms over his chest and looked back at the city, which was just a blot against the sky.

"Do you remember how you felt when you saw the spring? That place you'd only heard until then?"

"Excited," Mallesh said. "Of course. I don't remember exactly." Though he did, suddenly, vividly, and his heart began to hammer as it had when he was eight and full of wonder. "But why ask me this?" he went on quickly, digging his fingers into his upper arms. "You should be thinking only of what is happening now—especially since you're obviously stronger. And why is this? Why are you stronger—what do you hear? What—"

"Mallesh," Leish said, and Mallesh stiffened at this second gentle interruption. "I remember what you said when you saw your first song-place. You told me that it was so beautiful you could hardly look at it, and that you wanted to protect it forever. That's how I feel about this place. Now that I can see it."

"Excellent," Mallesh said before Leish's words could echo and twist in his head. "Then we desire the same thing." He looked away from his brother's eyes. "Now that you're feeling better, you'll be able to assist me in planning our attack. I'll send some scouts in to discover what they can about the central building—and I plan on a night approach, perhaps a group at a time ..." He squinted into the distance, but the city was invisible. Wind hissed across his skin. It was very cold, and he rubbed at his forearms. *We'll go back among the trees where it's warmer. Maybe make a small fire. Use the last of the mud and refill our waterskins—who knows when we'll find—*

"Help," Leish said. "Help me lie down—I can't ..." He wobbled, then sagged. Mallesh caught and clutched him.

"He is much recovered," Mallesh called as he led Leish back to the sheltering trees. "He will soon be himself again." The nearest selkesh murmured this news to the ones who stood behind them. Mallesh heard his words shiver and change and dissolve away from him.

"Can you hear a way in?" he whispered a few moments later, as he dribbled water onto Leish's bare arms and chest. "Is there somewhere closer that we can all stay until we're ready?"

Leish was silent for a long time—long enough for Mallesh to soak his skin and wrap his clothes back on. "Yes," Leish said at last, so softly that Mallesh could hardly hear him. "Tomorrow."

~

Baldhron was sure the Queenswoman guard hadn't seen him, even though he had set a statue rocking on its base as he squeezed behind it. He pressed his back against the corridor wall and his cheek against the ivy-wound likeness of the Eighteenth Queen. After a few moments he eased his face around the statue and parted the ivy with his hand. As he watched, the Queensguard stretched, twirling her bow by its tip, then scraped at a crack in the wall with her dagger. She straightened when she heard (as Baldhron did) the sound of sandals slapping on stone. The door beside her opened only an instant later.

Ladhra did not even glance at the Queensguard as she walked into the hallway. Baldhron waited until the guard had gone back to chiselling at the wall before he slipped out from behind the statue and followed Ladhra.

"My Princess," he said when he was a pace behind her. She flinched and half turned, and he smiled.

"Baldhron," she said. "Not content to ambush me in the Queenswood, now? Careful—I'll have to warn my guards about you."

"Ah yes, your guards." She began to walk again; he hurried to match her stride. "The one back there looks especially fierce. Perhaps she'd yawn in my face?"

Ladhra snapped, "What do you want this time, Baldhron?"

"What I always want," he said, trying to keep his words light and smooth. "To see you when you're not surrounded by people. Now that your friend Lanara's gone, this is an easier thing to do." Lanara's departure had in fact profoundly annoyed him. Ever since the arrival of the selkesh, he had included her in his plans of conquest. He would thrust the relevant scrolls into her hands; he would watch her read and crumble.

Salanne, daughter of Bralhon, has died at Queen Galha's command (from a wound taken in a skirmish, the official account will say). I have determined that her husband Creont suspects that his wife and consort-scribe Malhan engaged in illicit relations—but he shows no signs of suspecting the circumstances of her death. Their daughter remains a close confidante of the Princess; the Queen obviously has no desire to extend her revenge to the child. The Queen has not yet punished Malhan. I believe she will not. He is her memory and her future, and she would suffer if he were not with her. Only Salanne and her family will suffer now.

Lanara's distress could no longer be a component of Baldhron's greater victory. He chewed at his lower lip, looking away from Ladhra's face as he did so. He saw that she was holding a piece of folded parchment. "A letter," he said, steeping his voice in a glee he nearly felt, "from the very same Lanara?"

"No." She pressed the parchment against her side, frowning. "Not that you need or deserve to know this."

"Ah, I see. You and she have quarrelled? I do hope she's still able to do your mother the Queen's good work with wisdom and courage?"

Ladhra rounded on him and stepped forward at the same time, so that he was forced to fall back several paces. Again the wall was at his back. He straightened his spine against the stone and looked at the curve of her dark cheek and the moist gleam of teeth between her lips.

"I have no idea," she said, and he smelled sweetleaves and mint on her breath, "how you possibly expect me to welcome your company when you persist in being so unpleasant to me. I have told you, both in writing and in conversation, that I do not return your affections. Your insistence on forcing your company upon me is incomprehensible." She stepped back.

A deep, gasping breath escaped him before he could stifle it. *Come, now,* he told himself, *you control these meetings, not her. Show no weakness.*

"I never mean to offend," he said. "Only to impress upon you the constancy of my esteem."

She made a sound very much like a growl. "Baldhron, I *know* … I know. Please—it would be kinder to both of us if you left me alone. Truly. Just …" She rolled her eyes and turned on her heel, then looked back at him. "And I know you have better things to do than lurk about, waiting for me. For instance, shouldn't you be at your lessons now?"

"My lessons," he said, "yes, indeed I should—" but she was already walking away from him very quickly, clutching the letter so tightly in her hand that the parchment crumpled. He smiled again.

He did not go to his lessons. He was always exhilarated and desperate, both, after he saw her. He could not possibly take himself to the Scribeslibrary, where he would have to bend over carefully selected texts, words that were hollow and wrong; where Galha's consort-scribe would blather about truth, wisdom and the glorious line of queens. No—he would descend to the only place where the perfumed stench of the palace could not reach him.

Pentaran was on guard duty again. "So," Baldhron said, gesturing impatiently for the man to follow him into the library, "have there been any new entries these past few days?"

"Only a partial one," Pentaran said, hardly stammering this time. "There are rumours of a Queensfolk revolt in the west—no supplies, some sort of sickness, violent local tribes. Nothing's been confirmed yet. Calhia's waiting for word from the scribe in Blenniquant City. There's been nothing from the palace, of course."

Baldhron walked out to the middle of the bridge, his favourite vantage point since it was higher than the ledges along the walls. Pentaran sat down at his feet. After a moment Baldhron joined him, thinking, not for the first time, *I must allow a certain degree of equality. Let him think he can be at ease with me, if it makes him more loyal.* He peered down at his reflection, which seemed very close; the water was high now that the autumn rains had come. He and Pentaran were silent.

When a splash sounded from the tunnel that led south from the reservoir, it was very loud.

"A fish, maybe, or a frog," Pentaran said, but he frowned. He leaned over and said, "If it's a large fish, it might be slow—we could—" and then his reflection and Baldhron's shattered as creatures rose from the water.

Pentaran shouted as they surfaced, ranks of them, filling the pool and the southern passageway. He tried to scramble to his feet, but Baldhron held him by the wrist and hissed, "No—stay like this, don't let them think you're threatening them." Pentaran stayed, though he made another noise, this one more strangled than the last, and put one shaking hand on the dagger in his belt.

Baldhron thought, *The southern tunnel runs beneath the city wall. It is desert on the other side. Desert pierced by well shafts.* He was pleased by the clarity of these thoughts and by the calm he felt. *I have never seen these creatures—not even in the marketplace. They are strangers.* He looked down at them and felt a smile, though he did not let it touch his lips.

Their skin was green-brown and deeply lined, like a turtle's. Their eyes were round and white, and their mouths were round as well, though Baldhron could not tell if this was just from exertion. *But they are like men,* he thought, noting their long, wet hair, the cloth that wound around their necks and chests and upper arms. He waited. The upturned head of the one beneath him was nearly touching his right foot. Water dripped from the water-men's hair and chins—the only sound, and it echoed from the glass-encrusted walls.

At last there was a different sound: the strokes of a body moving with its head and arms held above the water. Baldhron watched the water-man swim to the eastern wall. He pulled himself out of the pool and Baldhron saw that the cloth strips wrapped his body down to mid-thigh, that he was strikingly tall, and that there were webs between his fingers and toes.

Other water-men, all equally tall, emerged from the water. Soon the ledges on both sides of the pool were lined with them. They all looked at the man who seemed to be their leader—all except for one. This man sat with his back against the wall beneath the thirty-second hanging sack. Baldhron noticed him because he was so motionless and because he seemed different—paler, thinner, the cloth strips loose around his body. He was looking up at the lanterns and the walls. He did not appear to be blinking.

The leader drew a short hooked dagger from the cloth over his chest, not taking his eyes from Baldhron's. He spoke two bubbling, frothing words. Baldhron watched his lips stop moving, but the words pulsed on. *I know—I understand,* he thought, and he reeled, in memory, through the marketplace and the Scribeslibrary until he remembered. *These sound like fishfolk words.* Not exactly the same, but close enough to the language he had studied to be comprehensible. As the water-men began to pull an assortment of small weapons out of somewhere (scabbard-pouches within the layers of cloth?), Baldhron swallowed and wiped his palms slowly on his tunic.

"Kill," the leader said again, more loudly, and stepped onto the bridge.

TWENTY

"Stop! Wait!"

Mallesh stopped. He heard the selkesh behind and below him murmur, but he looked only at the slight, pale man on the bridge. The man who had spoken words Mallesh knew. Mallesh waited, curiosity overcoming for a moment the need for a first kill in this new place.

I will see what they say, he thought. *This cannot hurt us. There are only two of them, both quite small.* Mallesh himself felt swollen with strength. The underground swim had been exhilarating; he had not realized how exhausted he had been since they left the ocean. This water was very deep, and so cold that his teeth ached after he drank it. He had rolled his body over and over in it, after Leish had led them to the desert well and down (such a narrow, crumbling tunnel—but they had heard the pebbles dislodged by their feet splashing far beneath them and had slithered quickly on into the earth).

"This way!" Leish had cried, and they had followed him into the rippling darkness. They had sliced through the water, drinking it, feeling it cleanse and harden their skin and everything beneath it.

Mallesh had heard the river's song clearly once he was far below its water. The song was very different from that of his own, faraway river—but this one seemed to welcome him and draw him on, and he rejoiced in its strangeness.

Mallesh had worried, when they entered the river, that Leish would never surface. He had hoped for this as well, with a sickening, humming intensity. After he had swum for a time, someone had grasped his hand and pulled him to the surface. He blinked and saw a faint glow up ahead, and Leish beside him. Mallesh tried to smile at him in the flickering light, and they waited together for the other selkesh to join them.

"Quietly," Leish had whispered when they had all gathered. "We are within the city walls now. The loudest people-singing is above us—but there could be other men down here, too few to hear. Maybe there, where the light is."

But there were only these two delicate-looking men in the chamber of the shining walls. Mallesh's pulse had quickened when he brushed the water from his eyes and saw them: only two, surrounded by all the selkesh with their throwing spears and knives. He almost heard the strangers' blood, singing like the river that had brought them here.

And then one of the men called out and Mallesh hesitated. As he did, leaning on the ball of one foot, the man spoke again.

"Who?" It was the only word Mallesh understood, though the man spoke others. *Yllosh words,* Mallesh thought, and remembered the ones they had met on the ocean, the ones who had doubted and mocked him. *Who is he to know these words?*

"Selkesh," he said in slow syllables, drawing his feet together and his shoulders up and back. The man inclined his head in a gesture that was unfamiliar to Mallesh. After a wide-eyed moment the man's companion did the same.

"Where?" the first man said, again adding other, unintelligible words. He moved carefully into a standing position with his hands held before him. Mallesh noticed the dagger hanging at his belt in a pouch of blue and green.

"Across the sea," Mallesh said, gesturing to the tunnel as if this would encompass desert, jungle, a rolling, heaving space of salt water, and the swaying trees and vines of the land beyond. The man's lips formed a sound he did not make. "Why?" he finally said. Only the one word this time.

Mallesh heard his men murmur again. He tightened his grip on his knife and took another step along the bridge. "We will take this city. Our city."

"Our," the man repeated, then, after a pause, "Your city. Your …" His face changed. Mallesh had never seen a face like this, but it was enough like his own that he recognized the clenching of shock and fear. The fear, though, was swiftly gone. The man's eyes narrowed and his lips pressed together and the muscles of his jaw relaxed a bit. Mallesh thought, *A pity—he is obviously a man of valour.* As the murmuring around him swelled, he strode forward with his knife raised.

"No!" the man cried as his companion leapt to his feet. Mallesh was three paces away—so much taller and stronger, deafened by the triumphant song of the city.

"No—wait"—one pace away, the knife reflecting lantern light and glass—"I help you. *Help you!*"

Mallesh looked down at the man. The chamber was quiet except for water that dripped from limbs and weapons. The man craned to meet his eyes. He whispered the words again, again, steady as the sound of the water. When Mallesh turned to look behind him, the words softened into silence.

Leish was standing where the bridge met the ledge, his eyes steady and bright. His mouth shaped a word that Mallesh understood, though he could not hear it.

Mallesh turned back to the small, pale man. "Yes," he said. "You help."

~

Baldhron's scribes gathered at midnight. They slipped through the rain, cool at this hour, and down well shafts throughout the city. They arrived in the library chamber in twos and threes, all of them silent. Baldhron stood on the bridge and watched them come.

They looked at the water-man—Mallesh, his name was—who was standing beside Baldhron, most of them only briefly. Others stared at him. Baldhron saw some who frowned, some who gnawed at their lips and others whose faces were still and closed. When Baldhron began to speak, they turned to him, but their expressions did not change.

"Thank you, truth-scribes, for answering my urgent summons. What we decide here tonight will change history." He tried to look at each of them; it was so important to make them feel included, important, vital. "Beside me is Mallesh, a member of a race called the selkesh." They all turned to Mallesh now. He gazed back at them impassively. "He does not understand these words. He speaks a language related to that of the fishfolk, who were selkesh kin long ago. Many of you were, as I was, instructed in this fishfolk tongue. For this I suppose we must thank our teachers." A ripple of laughter, nervous and relieved at the same time.

"Mallesh's men have spread out into various of our chambers. There are many hundreds of these men. There is, in fact, an army of them."

He had expected a gasp at this point, but none came. He stood a bit taller.

"They have come here because even in their land of Nasranesh, far across the Eastern Sea, they have heard of this great city." *Don't mention the singing—if I don't understand it, neither will my men.* "They were inflamed by tales of Luhr's majesty and beauty, and Mallesh decided that they must see it. He decided it must be theirs." *Mallesh and his brother, the sickly looking one whom the selkesh seem to esteem more highly—but he's such an unimpressive figure; mustn't mention him either.* "The selkesh journeyed across the sea and through the Mersid Jungle. They discovered the desert wells and used them to gain access to the city. They are an intelligent, worthy, courageous people." *Who planned to take Luhr with fish spears and filleting knives.*

"There are many of them, all as large and strong as Mallesh. They will make an attempt on the palace whether we offer them resistance or not. So." He paused for a moment, tried to look stern as words spun in his head. "This is our moment of choice, come sooner than I had anticipated. The selkesh are here to reshape history. We could warn the Queen—and perhaps be mentioned at the bottom of the last page of *Galha's Triumph Over the Fearsome Sea Folk.* We could flee so as not to be involved in what transpires. Or we could aid the selkesh. We could act *and* write this history—it could be ours."

Light leapt from the glass-set walls as people stirred and turned to one another. *They're frightened. Great Drenhan, let me speak wisely ...*

"And what if we aid them," called the woman named Serenhan, "and lose?"

Baldhron held up a hand to quell the muttering that had risen. "We will not lose. We know more about the palace and the city than any Queensguard. There are many of us and more of them, and look! *Look* at him! We will show them how to take the city and they will do it."

"And then what?" Serenhan again, with her strident whine of a voice.

Baldhron felt his cheeks grow hot. "And then the selkesh install us as the official scribes of the new realm. And then we tell truth, always, in the light of day and above the ground. We teach them and all of our people to read and write, and everyone will understand and revere and share our power."

"What of the rest of the Queensrealm?" Serenhan asked, not as shrilly as before. "Luhr is the centre, but it's not the only place where Queensfolk rule."

Baldhron nodded, feeling his flush subsiding. "We have allies in all towns and cities where Queensfolk hold sway. I will—would send word to these allies, informing them of the proposed date of attack, advising them to be ready to seize control of their own places. With Luhr captured and the Queen dethroned, all will be chaos. Even with modest numbers, our people will prevail."

Some were nodding now, though most still frowned. "Baldhron," one man said, "this is a great risk to our lives, but also to the lives of others. My … my brother is a Queensguard. Others here have loved ones who live or work at the palace. If we …" His voice wavered into silence. He was biting his lower lip hard enough to turn it white.

Baldhron thought, *Sentimental sap*. He nodded and pursed his lips. "Of course, all palace folk will be endangered by an attack. And as you have said, some of them will be our friends and family. The many among us who have no families, or who were sent here from distant homes, are now the lucky ones—imagine!" A murmur of assent rose from these orphans and misfits, so many of them, grown to adulthood without ties of blood or place; with only each other, drawn together by Baldhron and the truth he had discovered in this room.

"We will try," he went on, attempting to address those who did have palace or Luhran ties, "to avoid harming your loved ones. If you know that they will be on guard the night of the attack, I will make sure that you are sent to where they are, to prevent their injury. Only come to me and tell me, and I will try. But," he continued, his voice rising, "I cannot promise to eradicate the risk. Battle is quick and confusing, and some of you may make mistakes. Remember this. And remember that no glory is achieved without some measure of grief."

"You are right," another man called. "But so far we have spoken only of individual lives. What of our *way* of life? Luhr is our city, whether—"

"Galent," Baldhron snapped. "How dare you speak of the Luhran way of life as if it were something to be prized. All of us know that there is corruption here—lies invented by the Queen and perpetuated by her consort-scribe. Most of us have known someone who has been lost in her service. My mother, who drank Galha's poisoned wine. Your uncle, Galent! Your uncle, who was crushed in a mine shaft Galha ordered collapsed." Baldhron had them now; they held themselves rigid, poised, and their eyes never left him. "We all know such stories, we have recorded them—and now, so much sooner than we expected, there is a chance that they may be heard. We can rid this land of its lying Queen. With the selkesh's help, we *will* do this thing."

For a moment there was no sound. Then someone shouted his name, and others took up the cheer, and the library dome rang with the thunder of their voices.

~

The marketplace began to stir just past dawn, only an hour after Leish and his two companions had slid over the lip of the well. He watched the palace towers brighten as the sky cleared; he watched men and women and creatures that seemed neither male nor female emerge from tents, wagons, wooden shacks, other places he could not see. By the time the sun had risen, he could smell food cooking and hear the clatter of wood and the slap of cloth being folded away from stalls.

"Leish." He turned to look at the Queensman who had accompanied Dashran and himself. *Pentaran,* Leish reminded himself, dividing the name into its rough, awkward syllables.

"We walk. Baldhron say walk, show place," Pentaran said.

Mallesh had chosen who among the selkesh would first see the city. "It can't be me," he had told Leish. "I won't go up until the attack. You must go and bring me back a thorough description of what you see. Of *everything.*" He had spoken with an urgency that was almost anger, and Leish had shrunk away from him—again.

Even if Mallesh had not sent him, Leish would have had to go. They had been beneath the city for weeks. Baldhron had been explaining the layout of the palace and city with drawings (which Mallesh and Leish now understood) and his increasingly fluent selkesh words. Each day that they had remained in the underground water tunnels had increased Leish's restlessness. His weakness had begun to ebb as soon as he led the selkesh into the river; but the city's song was so close that it was a constant, muffled boom, and he knew that only seeing it would help to ease the pressure in his head. But Mallesh had chosen him—so he had climbed into the dark, open air, and he had sat down hard on the sandy ground and listened to a song that was as clear now as water.

"Yes, Pentaran," Leish said slowly, so that the man would understand. "We will walk."

There were so many songs in this place. Earth, water, stone and Queensfolk lifeblood made up the deepest, most resonant one; above it were notes that were played and chanted and called across hot wind. Leish listened to all of these notes together, and he felt nearly whole, nearly at peace for the first time since he had heard the call of this land from his own shore. Only nearly, however, for beneath his feeling of calm was the insistent stab of desire.

Mallesh was right, Leish thought, blind for a moment to the riot of colour and forms around him. *I do feel his need, for more—for* mine. It was this need that made him speak to cruel-eyed Baldhron, and learn from him. It was this need that would drive him into the palace beside Mallesh, seeking blood. *Even though this search will forever twist the song that is in me now,* he thought, and shuddered.

"Leish—look at that … and there, see how they're watching us? We should walk faster …"

Leish turned to Dashran. The man's eyes were wide, leaping from face to face before swivelling to meet Leish's. Sweat had darkened his upper lip from green to black.

"I tell you, Leish, that one's staring at us—and look, she's going away, probably to say she's seen us …"

"Dashran." Leish touched the back of his hand and felt the tremor there. "These people are nearly all strangers. We are like them—no one will notice us." Dashran did not respond, just looked around and trembled.

"He all right?" Pentaran asked haltingly.

Leish nodded. "Yes. Nervous because of the crowd, but all right."

And perhaps Dashran would have been, if the woman with the horns had not stepped down from a tumble of rocks and stood in front of them. Leish saw that she had talons instead of fingers; her long skirt hid her feet. Her black hair was like the ocean water Leish had swum through near his shore: black, but also glowing with other colours. The two horns that curved up from her hair were silver-sharp.

She fixed her black eyes on Leish and spoke. Her words were also sharp, and they needled at him until Pentaran held up his hand. He talked rapidly to her and she answered, more loudly than before. Pentaran took a step closer to her. She spat three last words, looked again at Leish and leapt up the rock pile.

"What did she say?" Leish asked Pentaran. Dashran seemed frozen. His cheeks were sweat-darkened now.

"She iben," Pentaran said. His eyes slid away from Leish's. "She say ... nothing."

"She did say something—to me," Leish began, then stopped as Dashran gripped his arms and began to moan. "Water. Quickly—he needs water."

Pentaran led them away from the iben woman (whose eyes, Leish saw when he glanced back, were still on him), through the crowd of buyers and sellers and gawkers. Just as Dashran stumbled and cried out, Pentaran said, "Here—fountain."

At first Leish saw and heard only the water, a tall, graceful plume of it, rising in a flurry of notes from a wide-mouthed bowl. He smiled in recognition—and then he saw who floated in the fountain and stood beside it, and the singing seemed to die.

One of the yllosh said, "Nasran-kin," and all of them looked at Leish and Dashran. The yllosh in the fountain drew themselves up. The water that fell from their scales was so bright that Leish had to close his eyes.

"Why are you here?" The question was not asked harshly, but Leish felt Dashran stiffen.

"I need water," he rasped, and the yllosh-woman shook her head.

"No—not why are you at our fountain, why are you *here?* We have never seen your kind on these shores."

"We are here now," said Dashran hotly. "And what business is it of yours?"

"Tell him quiet," Pentaran muttered to Leish. "Queensguards there." Leish looked to his left and saw them: three women and two men, watching the fountain from about ten paces away. He knew who they were because Baldhron had told him about the palace colours they wore, and about the weapons they carried slung over their shoulders. Leish thought they looked as fierce and graceful as he had expected when he first heard their people's blood-song.

Leish turned back to the fishperson and said, "Please," imagining how furious Mallesh would be at him for using this word. "Let my friend soak for a moment, then we will talk more."

"Talk now," the yllosh-woman said, her eyes on Dashran.

"By Nasran," he shouted, "I will not take orders from your kind—you *filth*"—and he lunged forward with his hooked knife in his hand.

Leish cried, "No!" Before he could move, one of the Queensguards was between Dashran and the fishperson. Dashran did not stop. He threw himself against the Queensguard with a howl, and his arm swept up and drove the knife deep into the skin of her neck.

Leish heard Pentaran somehow, through the roaring in his head. "I go," Pentaran said, his lips nearly brushing Leish's ear. "I tell Baldhron." When Leish turned himself around, the man was already gone. The yllosh too were gone. Only Dashran was there, kneeling in the dust beside the motionless Queensguard. Dashran, the dead one, and the four others. Two of them wrenched Dashran to his feet. The other two strode to Leish. They wrapped their hands around his arms and he heard the city's song begin its change, and he wept, in joy and fear, for all of them.

TWENTY-ONE

Pentaran was doubled over, sniffling and gasping from his flight through the tunnels. He was favouring one ankle; he had blubbered about slipping on the damp stone. *He is such a child,* Baldhron thought, *with no more self-control than he had when he was twelve. I never should have taken him in; his beggar's life would have suited him better.* Baldhron snapped, "Say nothing until you can speak clearly, then tell us what has happened."

As Pentaran attempted to calm himself, selkesh and scribes began to gather in the library. Mallesh swam to the bridge and held himself very tall in the water.

"Where is my brother?" he said in a long, low hiss. Pentaran did not look at him.

It's a good thing I was here at this hour, Baldhron thought as he laid a steadying hand on Pentaran's shoulder. *The water-man might have killed him for his lack of coherence.*

"Tell us," Baldhron said, patient because Mallesh was not—and Pentaran straightened and took a breath and told them.

He spoke quickly, in the Queenstongue. Baldhron repeated the words in Mallesh's language, letting this activity blunt the edge of his own sudden fear. When he had finished translating, he looked down at Mallesh. "What we must do," he began, but the water-man slipped silently beneath the pool, and Baldhron's voice trailed away. *Queensrot,* he thought savagely—but before he could turn to any of the others who were waiting, Mallesh launched himself bellowing onto the ledge.

"Mallesh!" Baldhron shouted as the big man ran toward them, but Mallesh's roar was the only sound in the chamber. He came to a quivering halt in front of Baldhron.

"This time," Mallesh said, "I want *him.*"

Pentaran whimpered. Baldhron wondered what Mallesh would do if he cried, "Yes, please take him! Eat him for all I care!" He said instead, "No. Mallesh, be still now. Listen. Queensguards didn't see Pentaran, they only noticed selkesh men—Dashran for killing, Leish because he was with Dashran. Pentaran was right to run away. He had to tell us."

Mallesh was panting; Baldhron could feel the hair on top of his head stirring. "He could have fought for Leish," Mallesh said.

Baldhron shook his head in a way he hoped would suggest patience and solemnity rather than incredulity. "No. A Queensman cannot fight a Queensman—or four. Four! Pentaran would die. Or the Queensfolk would take him too, scribe and selkesh together—very, very bad for all of us." Mallesh finally met Baldhron's eyes. "Of course you are angry and upset. But we must all be slow and careful now."

"Yllosh!" Mallesh spat. His people cried out the name as well, like a curse. "It is their fault! They provoked Dashran as they tried to provoke me on the ocean. They mocked me there and now they have—"

"Wait," Baldhron said. The fear was cold now, and he shivered as if he had just emerged from the water. "You met ocean fishfolk? You spoke to them?"

"Yes," Mallesh said, his answer a grudging question.

"Then the ocean fishfolk will tell their lake kin, and they will tell Luhran fishfolk, and they will tell the Queen. The Queen will look at Leish and Dashran and she will know there are many more. She will ..." He could not think of the word in their horrid, slithery language. He stood numb and open-mouthed until Mallesh said, "She will suspect."

"Yes," Baldhron said, forcing thoughts out of his numbness. Thoughts, words, certainties.

"So we must attack now," Mallesh cried. Selkesh and scribes called out together, their two languages made one by their many voices.

Baldhron held up his hand and the noise abated. "No," he said, and he smiled as he began to tell them what they would do instead.

~

The messenger found them on Queen Galha's private balcony. She and Ladhra were leaning over a game of arrowmark, talking quietly. Malhan was sitting by the door, sharpening writing sticks and dropping them into a tray at his feet. Ladhra heard this rattling, and she heard ivy hissing in the wind that still breathed last night's rain. She smiled at these steady, comforting sounds—and then frowned as she heard rapid footsteps and a shout from the Queensguard posted inside the door.

"My Queen," the messenger gasped when she had stepped onto the balcony. "A Queensguard is dead and a stranger has done it."

There are no strangers here, Ladhra thought as, only moments later, she followed her mother down the tower steps. *We know every race and creature of the realm, and some from beyond it.* She tried to keep up with Galha when they reached the corridor that led to the Throne Chamber, but she could not.

"Malhan," the Queen snapped over her shoulder, "stand in front of your throne—don't sit. Ladhra, hold my bow and quiver and be ready to hand them to me."

Ladhra said, "Yes, Mother," but Galha was listening to a Queensguard, nodding, her head and body angled away from her daughter.

The Throne Chamber was muted today, with no sunlight to strike fire from the gems or rainbows from the water. Ladhra had always hated the end of the rainy season, and Lanara had always scolded her for it. "Why can't you enjoy this grey?" she had said once. "It's cool and it's gentle and it's *different.*" Ladhra had scowled at her. "Different, yes, but Nara, it's grey! It's dull and ugly. I like my 'different' to be pretty." She remembered Lanara's laughter and her rolling eyes, and she thought, *Why have I been angry at her? I'll write to her as soon as this is over.*

"Bring them in," Galha said, and Ladhra wondered again at how the Queen's voice, even pitched low, filled this vast room. When Ladhra was a girl, she had believed that the water creatures in the channels and fountains here went still when Galha spoke, listening, waiting, admiring as Ladhra had (such a simple, childish admiration; she hardly remembered it now).

The door to the Throne Chamber opened with a crash that made Ladhra blink. She saw seven figures, but they were blurred by the fountain spray. She squinted and leaned on Galha's bow as she tried to see them better. They came around the central pool—four Queensguards and one fishperson forming a knot around the two other figures as they walked.

Then the Queen called, "Stop there! Show me the strangers!" and the knot drew apart.

They are like lizards. Dark green, tough-looking skin; narrow faces; round eyes. *Tall, strong man-lizards—but their hands and feet look like a frog's. I must see how Malhan describes them ...* Ladhra realized she had taken a step back even though the lizard-men were still at least thirty paces away.

"Ladhra—my bow, one arrow," Galha said quietly. Ladhra passed her the bow and fumbled in the quiver. The arrows clattered and chimed before she drew one out.

"Which one killed my Queensguard?" The Queensguards pointed to one of the lizard-men and backed away from him, pulling the other stranger with them. The murderer stood alone. Ladhra saw that his mouth was working (words, skin, bile?). He closed his round white eyes.

"Look at me!" Queen Galha cried, and his eyes opened as the arrow flew and found his heart.

Ladhra heard her own gasp over the sound of his body falling to the stone. *How did she do that? I didn't see her nock the arrow or draw back the bowstring—I didn't hear her ...* Ladhra turned to Galha, who was motionless even to her fingers on the bow. Ladhra noticed for the first time that her mother's skin was the very same red-brown as the wood.

"Bring the other one to me."

The remaining lizard-man looked calmer than the other had—but perhaps not; his features were just strange enough to be unreadable, or misread. The Queensguards prodded him over the last two bridges and across the crystal-woven stone until he was standing in front of Galha. She handed her bow back to Ladhra and took two steps forward. She and the lizard-man were of a height; they looked, straight and steady, into each other's eyes. Ladhra waited for him to glance down, but he did not.

"He does not understand our language?" the Queen said without looking away from him.

"No, my Queen," said one of the Queensmen. "But his own language is close to that of the fishfolk. We have brought one of these fishfolk with us so that you may question the murderer's companion. This is the same fish-person that spoke with the strangers, before the killing."

"Tell me about the killing," Galha said, and the four Queensguards did, while the fishperson stared at the ground and the lizard-man stared at the Queen. *Look away from her, you fool,* thought Ladhra, but he did not.

When the explanation had been given, Galha was silent for a long time. "My Queen?" one of the Queenswomen ventured. "Would you like—"

"Take him away from here," Galha said in a voice that did not rise this time above the sounds of water and leaping fish. "Lock him in the chamber beneath the north wall and give him nothing—no food, no water—until I come to him. Post no guards. I want no one else to know of him, and you must not call attention to yourselves by altering your own routines. His presence here will remain secret until I have decided how best to proceed."

The fishperson lifted its head and opened its mouth, though it did not speak right away. Since her mother did not seem to notice this, Ladhra said, "Yes? What would you say to the Queen?"

"It is only ..." the fishperson began in its voice that sounded like phlegm and bubbles, "that ... to leave him without water for too long will cause him hurt. Maybe even death."

"Ah," the Queen said, "I see," and the lizard-man looked away from her at last as she began to smile.

~

Mallesh was bending over him, smoothing mud into his skin, dribbling water into his mouth. Leish watched the water tremble before it fell. He opened his mouth wide but felt nothing. Mallesh bent closer. He was whispering, but Leish heard only the dripping of the water he could not taste. "Help," he tried to say, but his throat was swollen shut. As he struggled to breathe, Mallesh's fingers came down around Leish's neck and pressed. This he felt—and he writhed on the damp jungle ground, his own fingers clawing at rotten leaves that were suddenly stone, then coral—

He opened his eyes and saw Dallia. She was suspended in front of him, her dark hair drifting around her like silken seavine. Her hands and feet were moving in tiny circles that kept her above the coral floor—but not coral, Leish saw: stone. And stone walls behind her that seemed to be dry, though she floated and bubbles came from her mouth when she said his name. She smiled and reached for him as she so often had, among the bones of the Old City near the shore. He reached too, and was nearly touching her when a door in the stone behind her opened.

Dallia vanished, and the water with her. Leish curled his body up as tightly as a snail's and tried to swallow something that was not sand. Even his saliva was sand. He would crumble and scatter—

"Get up."

He squeezed smaller.

"Get up, selkesh." There were hands on him, shaking and prying and unfolding him. He opened his eyes and saw that he was standing. Two Queensmen were holding him under his arms.

"Now." He recognized this yllosh-woman. He stared at her, waited for her and the two Queensmen to disappear as Mallesh and Dallia had. But these people remained—and then, abruptly, there were more.

The Queen walked into the stone chamber. The Queen and the younger woman who had been with her in the enormous room of water and light. *The daughter,* Leish thought, struggling to remember the information cruel-mouthed Baldhron had given them. *And the man—the Queen's mate, the one who writes things.* The man stayed by the door; the women came so close to Leish that he could see the liquid sheen of their eyes. Brown, he saw, and thought he could almost taste the colour. He watched the Queen's lips move as he had in that other room, and he heard her voice again, speaking words he did not understand.

"I know you call yourself selkesh." Leish moved his head, which felt like a boulder, and looked at the yllosh-woman who had spoken. "The Queen says this. She also says: I know you come from a land called Nasranesh, across the Eastern Sea."

It hurt to think. His head ached because his body did; and his thoughts stabbed insistently against this larger ache. *So the yllosh-woman by the fountain,* he thought slowly, *this is she—and she has told the Queen who we are. Nothing is safe any more.* He remembered that long ago he had dreamed his land bleeding and dying, that he had woken in Dallia's arms.

"I know you and your companion were not alone. I know there are many of you, and that you crossed the Eastern Sea in boats. I know you have never before left your land."

He had known. He had dreamed of rivers and plants screaming; he had seen Mallesh's desire, and the boats growing skeletons and skin by the shore. He had known—but only later. Not that first bright afternoon, when he had heard a song so vivid and distant that it had to be spoken of. He had been a boy—O Nasran, just a boy, proud and afraid.

"Where is your army now?"

She was very tall—taller than Baldhron or any of his men. Her daughter was a bit shorter, her skin not quite as brown as her mother's. Leish wondered whether her long black hair would drift like seavine in water.

"Speak, selkesh."

His head dropped heavily to his chest. The Queensguards jostled him. One of them grasped his chin and tried to force it up. His head was a boulder or the stump of a fallen tree.

When the water dripped onto the back of his neck, he swung his head up and around, looking for it, knowing it would vanish. But he felt it again—on his arm this time—and saw that the yllosh-woman was holding a waterskin, tipping it over Leish's cracked, dry flesh. "Drink," she said—her own word, not the Queen's—and angled the mouth of the skin against his lips.

He managed one long swallow before the Queen spoke sharply and the water was taken away. He felt it gush out of his mouth and down his front, and he gave a hoarse cry because he knew that it was already drying.

"Tell me where your army is and you will have more." The Queen turned the skin in lazy circles so that the water within it sloshed. Several drops spattered onto the floor.

"No." He had to try several times to say the word. When it finally emerged, it was barely more than a whisper. The Queen was smiling before the yllosh-woman spoke the word.

"Thank you," Galha said.

He hung between the Queensguards and gaped his confusion, and still she smiled. "You may not have told me where your army is, but you have confirmed that there is one. For which I thank you. I will return later with a bit more water, and you will respond with a bit more information, and soon this will be over."

She murmured something to her daughter that the yllosh-woman did not translate, and the Princess too smiled. Leish thought, *Mallesh will kill you both,* and just for a moment his hatred of them was so pure that he believed this. But then they left, and the hatred turned to him in the empty room, and he clawed at his own flesh until blood dried with the water on the floor.

TWENTY-TWO

Ladhra ran her fingers slowly down the red wood of the Queensstudy drawers. Her lips moved as she read the dates on each drawer. "Do not murmur as you read," her mother had said when Ladhra was a child. "And do not let your lips tell others what you are reading. Words are for you alone, unless you choose to share them aloud."

"Or I could share them with my writing," Ladhra had said. "I could write to my people and they could read—"

"No," Galha had interrupted, "you know you could not. Not with anyone outside the palace—for most of our folk cannot read. You can, and scribes and Queensguards and their children can, as can those who do my work far away. But that is all. I have told you this before, my dear: remember it this time. Remember that words are the Queen's power—and written ones are the greatest mystery of all, to our people. You must guard this mystery well."

Ladhra pressed her lips together, her cheeks as flushed now as they had been every time Galha had scolded her as a child. *She's not even here,* Ladhra thought as she pulled open one of the drawers, *and yet I still obey her.*

She frowned down at the pages that lay stacked before her. Malhan's tiny, neat letters flowed across the parchment. She skimmed the close-set lines, bending down to see them better.

"I'm sorry, Ladhra," said Galha from behind her, "that in my brief absence you required something. May I help you find it now?"

Ladhra straightened, flushing again, a child again and always. Her mother was standing beside the table, the fingers of one hand resting lightly on the wood.

"I didn't hear you come back in," Ladhra said, even though this was not an answer and she knew that it would make her mother shake her head, just once, and look away from her as if to gather patience from the air.

"That is not an answer," the Queen said, her eyes lifted up to the arrowslit windows that were so high and so useless.

"No, I'm sorry. I was looking for the record describing the strangers' arrival. I'm going to write to Lanara and I wanted to see how Malhan ..." Her voice trailed away as Galha lifted her hand from the table and waved it in a languid, looping shape.

"You'll find no such record. Malhan has not written of this event."

Ladhra shook her head. She glanced at the double doors. They were closed, and Malhan stood with his back against them. He was looking at Galha.

"But," Ladhra said, "this happened two weeks ago, and he's such a quick writer, even though he has to record everything. He writes especially well when he describes momentous things like Queenswrit Eve—so I wanted to see how he'd describe the strangers. The selkesh. I thought I'd look for this while you were gone, so that we could discuss it later ..." She looked down at the parchment again, as if the words would be there now, beneath the date; as if her mother had been wrong.

"Come, child, sit with me here"—and Ladhra did, still staring at the open drawer. "It's true that Malhan watches and remembers everything, but he does not write everything. At night he sits with me here and we decide together what should be written. This is a precious time, and a vitally important one. You will value it as I do when it is your turn to rule."

"But the selkesh are strangers. You ... Justice was done when one of them died, and the other is now our prisoner—and yet none of this has been written?"

"You will discover," the Queen said, "that sometimes you must know how a story ends before you tell it. This discernment is one of the greatest skills a queen possesses." A tiny frown puckered the skin between her eyes. "I myself had ascertained the truth of this before I was your age, and without direct guidance from my mother. I had hoped that you would display a similarly subtle wit."

The table was so smooth. Ladhra tried to see a line or nick in its wood and could not. "So I've failed some sort of test," she said after a moment. "Because I didn't even know it *was* a test."

Galha rose and closed the drawer. Its latch caught with a slight, final sound. She remained standing, though Ladhra, still staring at the table, only saw this peripherally. "You must not be sullen," Galha said. "You must never show an excess of sensitivity, for people will—"

"This is us," Ladhra said. She lifted her head, anticipating anger and needing to see it. "Us alone. Surely I can be permitted an honest emotion in the privacy of our own chambers?"

Galha's lips were pressed thin and pale, and her voice, when it came, was higher than it usually was. "Privacy? Not here, Ladhra. Not in your life, though it may have seemed like something you had when you were a child, running around the palace like a wild thing." A tremor ran through these last words. She paused and swallowed and looked briefly at Malhan. When she continued, her voice was steady again. "When you were a child, you believed you were alone. Now that you are a woman, you must entertain no such illusions." She took four long strides around the table and stopped with her back to her daughter. "I fear for you. You have not apparently learned the many lessons I have tried to teach you, and yet you may be called upon to rule sooner than either of us expect. And what if you should prove to be the one blessed with Sarhenna the First's mindpowers, as no queen since her has? What then? I fear for this realm."

Ladhra's chair scraped as she pushed herself away from the table. She felt a fluttering in her throat. She wondered whether Galha would see it, and was furious with herself for wondering. "I am sorry that I disappoint you," she said over the fluttering. "But how am I supposed to take responsibility if you give me none? How can I truly learn these lessons you want to teach me if you never let me *try* things?" Her voice was perilously close to cracking, but she did not stop speaking. "You keep me beside you nearly every moment of every day, and you say this will help me learn—but all it does is bore me. Let me learn how to be a worthy queen, even if I'm not destined to be the one with mindpowers. Let me go into the city and meet my people, or travel on my own to another Queensfolk city to see how it's governed, or accept trade goods here at the palace in your place—anything, as long as I'm *doing* something!"

The Queen glanced at Malhan, and they smiled at each other. "My dear," she said, turning back to Ladhra, "I am pleased that you at least have some of my spirit." She took a step forward, her hand raised to touch Ladhra's cheek, but Ladhra walked past her, past Malhan. She pulled the door open.

"And I'm pleased that I amuse you," she said. She wanted to say more, but she was already in the corridor and would not look back at them. She walked quickly. She heard Galha call, "Let her—" but that was all; she was beyond the voice, following the staircase that would take her away.

Ladhra meant to go to the Queenswood; she wanted shadow and silence and the illusion of solitude. But when she stepped into the corridor that led to the western doors, someone called her name. *Run,* she thought. *Just run.* She slowed. The call came again, closer, and she stood still.

"Thank you, Princess." Ladhra frowned at the fishperson's watery voice and gesturing hands, which were covered with scales. She had seen the fish-folk in the marketplace motioning to each other. She knew that they spoke in hand signals when they were in the deep waters of their homes, but surely they could use their voices when they were together in the air? This one continued, "I am W——" *(completely unintelligible names).* "I translate for"—its white eyes darted around the empty hallway—"the prisoner."

"Yes?" Ladhra said, looking past it at the sunlight that swam on the flagstones by the door. The rains had passed, but the earth beneath the trees would smell damp. "What do you want?"

It glanced again around the corridor. "I am sorry to seek you out in this way," it said quietly, "but your mother would not listen to my words, and I fear she will suffer for this. And so I come to you."

Ladhra said, "And? What were these words that the Queen did not listen to?" She felt the silence suddenly, and the stillness of the bright stone. *I'm alone now,* she thought, and leaned closer to the fishperson.

"The prisoner is dying. At first, as you know, the Queen visited him every day, and each time she brought water to give him. But when he would not answer her questions, she began to come less often—and only she gives him water. I told her of his increasing weakness, but she refuses to allow me or anyone else to aid him. If he dies, she will find out nothing—so I thought that you … that you might …"

"Well?" Ladhra demanded, though she felt the shape of the words that were coming, and her heart raced.

"That you, who have such influence, might prevail upon her to help him. You seem wise and strong and not so … determined as she is. I wanted to come to you rather than to provide him with water secretly. I wanted you to know my honesty and tell her of it. But most of all I wanted you to impress upon her the prisoner's fragility, since I cannot."

Ladhra took two steps past the fishperson. Her palms were slick with sweat; she pressed them against her leggings. "I may do all of these things," she said slowly so that her thoughts would have time to grow solid before she spoke them. "I may. But first," she went on, turning back to look at the fishperson, "I will go myself to see him. *I* will bring water to him."

The fishperson walked over to her—though it didn't walk, really, it glided, as if it were swimming through the air. It stood in the sunlight. Ladhra had to close her eyes briefly against the dazzle of its scales.

"I will take us to him by a different path," Ladhra said, "one that is not guarded. Until I have ascertained his condition, I will attempt to avoid involving my mother the Queen."

"I see," the fishperson said. Ladhra thought, *Do you? I very nearly do not.*

"Well, then," she said. "Good. Come with me"—and she walked quickly away from the doors that would have taken her, alone, into the Queenswood.

~

Mallesh lay at the bottom of the well and looked up at the sky. The circle of brilliant blue wavered as he breathed. He watched the bubbles dissolve and the water smooth, and then the distant sunlight returned to taunt him. From time to time the hole above darkened and a bucket came clattering down, and he had to kick away from the wall into the tunnel beyond until it had been pulled up again. Each time, he glided back to his place at the foot of the shaft and watched the bucket's slow, bouncing upward progress; each time, he imagined grasping it, pulling so hard and so suddenly that the person holding its rope would hurtle down into the water.

He was here because of the sky, and because he was alone. He would have thought it inconceivable, back in his own land, that he would seek out solitude from the army under his command, but this is what he did now, at least once a day. The scribes seemed to sneer at him—at all of the selkesh, but at him in particular. Baldhron treated him with respect, though Mallesh was never sure what the man said when he turned and spoke to his own people. Sometimes he smiled in a way Mallesh distrusted, and then all the Queenspeople smiled a bit; so perhaps even Baldhron was mocking him.

The selkesh were also beginning to show signs of disrespect. They muttered to each other in small, tight groups that broke reluctantly apart when Mallesh approached. Several times he had come upon gatherings of them beneath the water; he had watched them direct each other to distant tunnels before he slipped among them and they scattered with false smiles and excuses.

"We were talking of home. That is all."

"We were going to see the other waterways—these ones are dull to us now."

They lie, Mallesh thought. *They are talking about me.* Back in the jungle, or on the earth of Nasranesh, he would have attempted to talk commandingly to them of faith and leadership. Here, snared in rock so far below the sky, he fled from them.

Mallesh watched the well circle dim for a moment. *A cloud.* He drew a thin stream of water into his mouth to remind himself that he was thankful for it, and for this place—but he thought again, *A cloud,* and remembered mist dissolving from the treetops around the gathering pool, and again he cursed himself for the yearning that made him weak.

He swam back to the main selkesh pool very slowly, turning his body around in the water. When he surfaced, he saw some of his men on ledges and rafts, sleeping with their legs in the pool, and he saw others who were awake and waiting. He knew they were waiting: they were still and silent, standing in a line against the wall nearest him.

"What is it?" he asked them as he pulled himself onto one of the sleeping rafts he had ordered them to make, before Baldhron had told them they could no longer go to the jungle for wood and plants.

One of his men lifted his hand, as Mallesh had instructed them to do if they wished to speak. "We are ... very hungry," the man said. "Hungry and weak."

Mallesh stared at the man's fingers. The fans between them looked thin and red-gold in the lanternlight. "You know," he said, standing up carefully, "that I can't allow anyone to go back to the jungle to gather food. Baldhron has told us that the Queen is sending her guards out of the city to search for us. She knows there are many of us, though Baldhron's palace contact has assured him that Leish did not give her this information." He saw their eyes flicker at one another when he spoke his brother's name. He continued more loudly, "The scribes are bringing us as much food as they can—and we still have cut seavine from home. This will have to suffice until we go above." His own innards ached with emptiness, but he did not speak of this, or even think much about it.

"As to going above," the man—*Who* is *he?*—said, "we would like to know why you keep us here when Leish is a captive. Why has no attempt been made to free him? If the Queenspeople will not help us with this, we should do it alone."

His last words came quickly, and when he had finished, he bent his head. His seven companions were already gazing down at their own feet. Mallesh looked at the row of them and swallowed a shout.

"Leish," he said, "is alive and safe. The Queen will keep him alive because she needs him—this is what Baldhron has told us, and I believe him. Baldhron has aided us and we will continue to require his aid—do not forget this." He wanted to spit to clear his mouth of these last words, but he smiled instead and waited for the men in front of him to smile back, reassured and strengthened by his own certainty.

"What if Baldhron is lying?" another of the men asked, still staring at his feet. "About Leish, about helping us? Why should we believe him? And," he added, looking up and into Mallesh's eyes, "what would we have done if we hadn't met this person whom we now need so much?"

Mallesh imagined himself lunging across the water, grasping these men in his hands—their necks or forearms, twisting and wrenching until they cried out his name. But he stayed still, perfectly still, so that the raft would not tip. He breathed until he was sure his voice would not tremble.

"Nasran has blessed us. She has steered us to people who will aid us—but not because we could not have triumphed on our own. No: because now our triumph will be greater. We will rule this new land, and our scribes will record our greatness with writing implements and words so exact that they will never confuse those who come after us. Think of our carvings at home—the oldest of these are mysteries to us now. But this writing will give our people and our deeds a kind of permanence we selkesh have never before known. This is why we will wait, as Baldhron has urged us to." They were all looking at him now. He saw their fear and awe, and he almost smiled. "If you do not wish to be part of our victory, go home. Go back to Nasranesh and sit by your hearth pools and try to hear the song of this city that is so beautiful and so great."

They shook their heads one by one, but before any of them could speak, Mallesh dove. He sliced to the bottom of the pool and out into a tunnel, and there he swam faster, so that the stone walls blurred and the water seemed as thin as air.

He had left the chamber to allow his words to echo among the men—but also because hearing his own lie had shocked him. "This is why we will wait, as Baldhron has urged us to." *Not entirely a lie,* he thought as he sped through the water. *But mostly. I tell my men to wait a bit and a bit more so that they will remember who it is that leads them, so that they will stop murmuring Leish's name instead of mine.*

This thought was believable, nearly forgivable. But as Mallesh swam, he heard other words, buried half-formed. He cried out in streams of bubbles and hammered at the walls with his fists, as if pain could dissolve these words that grew clearer with every river-breath: *He may die he may die he may die …*

TWENTY-THREE

Leish hears nothing but singing. He hears so many songs: white stone and spray, ocean swells and blooming coral; even the quiet deep of his own hearth pool, ringed round with the sweetness of selkesh lifeblood. At first the songs of Nasranesh were faint, but they soon surged above the other notes and he knew he was going home—back to the sunken city, to the river mud and the trailing vines and the leaves that smelled of mist at first light. He thinks he hears his mother and father and Mallesh, and even though he knows that he should not be able to hear their individual strands, he grasps at this singing and sends his own shining through the water toward them. Home, *he sings, and he is washed in joy.*

He hears his name. It is very clear, and he turns his head to this sound that is harsh and strange and spoken, not sung. "Leish, Leish"—the voice is not right, and it pulls him out of the water, spluttering and retching until the sea and all the songs are gone.

He opened his eyes and saw that she was with him, her dark hair falling around her face and shoulders. She held a golden horn crusted around its rim with jewels. She tipped it and he opened his mouth and tasted water. "Dallia," he tried to say after he had drunk, "thank you"—but his voice was gone, and this woman, he now knew, was not Dallia. She was that other dark-haired woman, and he was lying in his own filth on hard, dry stones, and he remembered everything . He wanted to roll away from her as he had before, but the water kept flowing into his mouth and he kept swallowing.

Wollshenyllosh the yllosh-woman was kneeling beside him. He knew her name, though he did not remember when she had told it to him. He blinked at her, realized that it was she who held the drinking horn to his lips. The dark-haired woman was standing by the door. He felt dizzy and tried to focus his eyes on both of them in turn, to keep them motionless and solid.

The dark-haired woman spoke. "The Princess Ladhra bids you eat," Wollshenyllosh said, and Leish saw his own hand reaching for the piece of fruit the yllosh-woman was extending to him. He bit and his mouth filled with sweetness, and he cursed this pleasure and his heart, which continued to drum within him. *Now she will ask me questions,* he thought, and waited again, sickness churning in his gut where the emptiness had been.

Long minutes later the chamber rang with silence. He glanced at Ladhra through heavy-lidded eyes and saw that she was still standing beside the door, looking at him. She had not moved when his eyes closed fully. *Wait,* he thought weakly, already spinning into a sleep that would be dark and dreamless.

Ladhra came to him many times after this, most often alone, though occasionally with her mother and the silent, brown-clad man who always stood by the door. The Queen seldom visited Leish now, and when she did, she did not linger long. He noticed, as he grew stronger, that Ladhra did not look at him when she was with the Queen; she studied the floor or the wall above his head. She never spoke. Only Queen Galha spoke, in short, sharp words that Wollshenyllosh hardly needed to translate for him. Leish would shake his head and press his lips together and the Queen would turn on her heel and sweep past the guards and her daughter, who still would not look at him.

But then Ladhra would come to the stone chamber on her own and stand by the door as Wollshenyllosh gave him water and food. *Perhaps she and her mother expect me to break because of the water and the silence,* he thought, but he did not believe this. There was no challenge in Ladhra's eyes and no expectancy in her limbs. She simply stood and watched him as he watched her.

He waited for her. At first this was because of the jewelled horn and the fruit or bread or cheese; soon it was because of the woman who brought them. He sat up against the wall when she entered, even though his stiff skin cracked and bled a bit each time he did so. *She looks like the sky,* he thought once, *or a living tree in a place that has been burned.* He waited for her and pulled himself taller when she came, and he forgot, while she was with him, that he should hate her.

One day she pointed at him and spoke. Wollshenyllosh said, "The Princess Ladhra wishes to know why your skin bleeds."

Leish said in his new, splintered voice, "Tell her, then."

Wollshenyllosh blinked and curled her own webbed hands against her sides before she turned to Ladhra. The yllosh-woman did not look back at Leish after she had finished speaking.

Ladhra left soon after, though she had not been with him very long. He lay down and slept and woke much later in the stone silence he had determined was the palace at night. Ladhra was kneeling beside him with a torch in her hand. He rolled his head on the ground and saw, blurrily at first, then more clearly, that he and Ladhra were alone in the chamber, and that the door was open.

"Come," she said thickly in the yllosh language. "Leish—come with me."

~

She had memorized the night palace as a child, slinking around corners, running so lightly that her bare feet made no sound on the moonlit flagstones. There were fewer guards at night, fewer torches and lanterns—and more shadows and wells of darkness that drowned familiar shapes. Lanara had always been worried that Creont would discover her empty bed; Ladhra had prowled alone.

The moon was nearly full tonight. She waited until it rose to the level of her tower window before she opened her door. She stepped carefully down the stairs, holding an unlit torch in her left hand, trailing her right along the wall for balance. She pressed her ear to the thick door at the bottom of the stairs and waited until she heard the guard's footsteps advance and retreat twice, regular and measured. The third time they retreated, she pushed the door open, pulled it smoothly closed and turned to her right. She did not glance left; the guard's back would still be to her, but only for a few more paces. She ran to the corridor's turning, her bare feet as silent on the stone as they had been when she was a child.

She had never been afraid before on these nights; nervous, yes, that she would round a corner and bump into a Queensguard—but never afraid.

Tonight the fear seemed to creep like cold, up from the floor and into her flesh, from toes to belly. She shivered with it, and with the excitement to which it was joined. *My mother does not know. No one does, except me—and him, soon ...*

She had planned to visit him once—to give him water and relish the absence of guards and Queen. And she had done this. She had watched the fishperson tipping water against his chapped lips, had enjoyed his relief because she alone had given it to him. His convulsive swallowing had sounded very loud in the chamber and the empty corridor outside. She had offered silent thanks for her mother's decision to leave the prisoner's door locked but unguarded. After he had eaten the piece of scarlet mang, he had looked at her. She had held his gaze until his eyes closed. Then she had ordered the fishperson to remove all traces of water and fruit from his skin, and she had left the chamber.

She had returned the next day, and the next. Day after day, thinking each time, *Just once more;* each day staying longer, to stretch her dizzy exhilaration further.

She tried to remember, as she ran through the darkness, when she had begun truly to see him. Perhaps the first time Galha had requested her company for "another attempt on the prisoner," when Ladhra had stood beside her mother and met his eyes. Their round whiteness had been so unexpectedly familiar that she had had to look away. *He knows me now,* she had thought. *I know him.* Even though this could not be; how could it, when he was a stranger who did not understand her language? A stranger like the one Galha had killed, rightly, in the Throne Chamber, the one for whom Ladhra had felt no pity. Yet she had seen Leish's eyes so clearly that day, and she had flinched when her mother ordered a Queensguard to beat him until he lay like a bloodied animal on the floor.

Ladhra had shuddered in her bed that night. *I will not go to him again. I swear by the First that I will not.*

But she had, of course, again and again, and she had seen his seeping skin and his filthy clothes and his strange, hollow eyes as if she had been looking on them for the first time. She realized that the straightening of his mouth when she entered was a smile. She noticed that he sat up now, and smoothed his long, lank hair behind his ears. But he only did this when she came alone. When the Queensguards thrust open his door for Galha and her daughter, he stayed on the floor, his eyes half closed and his limbs heavy.

He did not stir now, though the door swung open with a slow, climbing screech. She knelt beside him and touched his shoulder. When his eyes blinked open, she spoke some of the fishfolk words she had learned—and she spoke his name. She watched him listen to her voice. He looked at the door and back at her, and she crouched so that she would be able to support him.

He was heavy, and much taller than she was. She slipped an arm around his waist and willed him to stand on his own. He did, after their first shambling steps, and by the time they were halfway up the tunnel, she was holding on to him only lightly. The torchlight showed her new black patches on his already stained clothing. She felt the blood as well, a slow, wet warmth against her fingertips and palm and wrist.

It took them a very long time to reach the door behind the thrones. Both of Ladhra's arms were numb, one from carrying the torch and the other from half carrying him after his initial strength had ebbed. They leaned together against the door. When their gasping had subsided, she took a key from her belt.

The Throne Chamber was layered with white and silver and shadow. The moon was hanging directly above the glass tower. Ladhra noted its position, calculated how much time they had and drew him quickly on. She urged him across the winking flagstones to the edge of the vast central fountain. Only when they were standing with their feet at the edge of the pool did she notice his trembling and look up into his face.

He's listening to something, she thought. His eyes were open but unfocused; his head was bent, but he did not seem to be looking at the water. The webs joining his fingers and toes were stretched taut and thin. After a time he turned to her and she knew that he saw her, that he hoped and questioned and feared because she had brought him to this place.

"Swim," she said, relieved that she remembered the word, and "Please," because she wanted him to know that this was something wished, not commanded.

Leish was shaking so violently that she expected him to fall into the water. He stood for a moment longer, his toes now curled over the rim of the pool. Then he leapt up and in, his long body a gentle, silent arrow. She saw rings expanding and receding where he had entered the water, saw fish pebbling the surface in surprised flight. And then, for almost an hour, there was nothing. She sat with her legs in the pool and waited for his head to appear, but it did not. *Perhaps he was too weak for this,* she thought, and imagined plunging in herself to grapple his body into the air. *Perhaps he can't breathe.* But she knew that the selkesh were fishfolk kin, that he would be able to breathe as easily under water as above it; and so she waited as the moon's path shifted on the water and the gems and the backs of drifting lake creatures.

He emerged at last with a roar. Not his own voice—that of something beneath, something large and invisible whose bellow tore the water into waves. Ladhra flung up a hand to shield her eyes from the spray. When she looked back at the pool, Leish was there, bobbing close enough to touch. He drew himself over to her and she clenched her limbs still. *O First Queen, First Mother, what have I done, he is changed, he is strong and sure as a warrior …*

She lifted her chin when he slid from pool to stone. His dark skin glowed; the water hung upon it like a net of beads. When he raised his hands, she flinched just a little. He gestured to her left hand with his fingertips and she turned it up. Her palm looked soft and fleshy; she tried to close her fingers over it, but he gestured again and she left it as it was. He extended his other hand—a fist, she noticed—and eased it slowly open above hers.

At first she thought that the four hard, smooth objects that fell into her palm were stones. When she held them out into the moonlight, though, she saw that they were shells, two round and two straight. They were translucent, thin as the webs between Leish's fingers, because there were no living creatures within to darken them. She smiled at him, wondered whether he would know what this meant. He smiled at her.

He did not need her help on the way back to his prison. He walked in long strides and she followed, watching the torchlight on his skin that looked now like scales. When they reached his door, he turned to her. "Thank you," he said slowly and clearly. "Ladhra."

She waited for him to speak again or move toward her, but he did not. She stepped forward and touched her cheek to the damp cloth over his chest. She placed her hands lightly on his hips and closed her eyes. His heartbeat was rapid and very loud. After a long, motionless moment he eased himself away from her, back into the empty room.

Baldhron hardly ever slept any more. Luckily, sleep had never been something he'd had much of, or needed. For the past many years there had been lessons to attend in the mornings; Ladhra to seek out in the afternoons (when the student scribes were expected to study independently in their library); the Scribesrealm to visit at night. He had not slept a full night in his bed in the Scribestower since he was a child, though he had always been careful to begin and end the night there.

He was less careful now. He knew that his absence from his bed would be noted, perhaps commented upon, and he made sure to mention to his chamber fellows that he had several women, both in the palace and in the town, who required his presence on a consistent and wearying basis. He explained his occasional absences from lessons the same way. "Tired," he said to one of his teachers, "worn out—must tell those insatiable women that I need some rest …" Because he had always been a gifted student and would soon be finished his long training, his teacher sighed and rolled his eyes and allowed Baldhron's frequent truancy to continue.

He now spent all his afternoons and nights with the selkesh and the scribes, and some of his mornings in class. This meant that he had lost the thread of Ladhra's daily doings, which made him irritable with his men. This irritability in turn made him impatient with himself, for it proved that his shadowing of the Princess had become a necessity, a dependence, rather than the voyeuristic pleasure it had once been.

He remembered how amusing it had been to compose those first letters to her, years ago. He had laughed aloud writing them, as he knew she had laughed reading them. He had planned to needle her, to work his way into her life and observe her reaction—this poised, proud girl who would be the next lying queen. But as he continued to write and she continued to laugh, something had changed. He saw her scorn as she read his letters or spoke to him, and his amusement turned slowly to anger. And then one day, as he stood before her among the shadows of the

Queenswood, she had said, "I could never love someone like you—forgive me, but this is the truth." Her pity had been new and unexpected, as had the desire that racked him then along with the rage—shocking, stabbing desire like a sudden illness or a wound. He had turned and left her. Later he had been proud of his restraint. *I was my own master,* he thought, *despite my need. It must remain thus.* For the exercise too had changed. He courted her scorn and pity because he knew that he would master her someday. When he and his scribes revealed the truth of the Queen's corruption and the realm convulsed in chaos, then he would take Ladhra and watch her despair.

The arrival of the selkesh army had made Baldhron's nebulous plan an achievable one. He taught them and fed them and assuaged, with infinite patience, their growing restlessness. He told them that they would wait until Queenswrit Eve to attack. He explained that the palace and city were poorly guarded on this night, for Queensfolk were inevitably drunk and sleeping by midnight after the earlier festivities. He declared to his own men that, by striking on this night, they would forever alter the meaning of the date, which was so sacred, so beloved of the Queen's ignorant people. The new rulers would change its name and its memory; from then on it might be called Scribeseve, or something to do with Truth or Victory. This idea so thrilled him that he risked selkesh discontent. He knew this and regretted it, but also knew that the revolt could take place at no other time.

"Wait!" he commanded the selkesh over and over, as their bodies hollowed and their eyes darkened. "Wait one more month. We can only triumph on this night, when the moon is dark and the city is weakened. Believe me: this will be the perfect moment."

He would shake her awake. Perhaps there would already be screaming; perhaps Ladhra would be sitting up, confused, rubbing her hands over her eyes. In that case he would push her back again and pin her with his body. He would not cover her mouth; he would let her scream until she realized that no one would come for her, until the other screams made her own more like the mewling of a kitten. She would be broken even before she knew what was happening in her palace, her city, her realm.

He envisioned going to her in more and more detail, until this unspoken plan was as intricate and delicious as the other. Only his certainty of success and imminence enabled him to sacrifice the afternoon hours that he had often spent as Ladhra's shadow. Soon she would be his whenever he wished; his army needed him now.

One night the men beneath the city seemed more content, quieter than usual. Most of the selkesh were sleeping; Baldhron did not allow himself to think that this was due to the lethargy of confinement and slow starvation. His own men were mostly above, since he had ordered them to be more cautious in these last few weeks and to remain visible to any who might be questioning their recent absences. Baldhron murmured to one of his scribes that he would be back in a few hours, well before dawn. Then he swam to the marketplace's well shaft.

Why go up now? he thought as he drew on one of the dry tunics that hung at the base of the shaft. The sky was much lighter than the air beneath the ground—because of the moon, which was full. Deep night already, moon risen and bright. *She'll hardly be about at this hour.* But it had been so many weeks since he had lingered at her tower door, and perhaps tonight he'd go further, tamper with the lock every time the guard turned his back, run up the twisting stairs to stand against the door to her chamber. Baldhron climbed the well shaft as swiftly as he had once scrambled up the cliff above his cave.

When the moon waned to invisibility, the palace would be his. He attempted to imagine this as the Queensguards nodded to him and opened the doors, and as he slipped through the darkened corridors and took his customary place behind the statue of the Eighteenth Queen. He had spied and hidden for so many years that an end to such an existence was almost impossible to envision. But he did. He half closed his eyes and saw himself striding down the middle of the hallway, smiling at the guards, who would bow from the waist …

Ladhra's door opened. Baldhron stiffened and watched the Princess pull her door quickly shut behind her, unnoticed by the guard who was fifteen paces away, with his back to her. Baldhron's surprise held him motionless for a few long moments, and she was nearly at the corridor's turning before he leapt after her. He knew the guard was about to begin his march back to the door. Baldhron ran, glad for his bare feet and the swimming that also gave him speed on land.

She was difficult to follow, for she was moving even more rapidly than he was. He tried to keep an appropriate distance between them—and then she would round another corner and he would have to sprint to keep up. Once he hurtled around one such corner and nearly collided with her. She was standing with her arm extended, holding a torch—which he had not noticed until now—to another that stood, lit, in a wall bracket. He waved his arms violently in order to stop himself before he touched her. Somehow she did not hear him or see his ridiculous flailing.He followed more carefully after this, even when she opened a door he had never seen before, one hidden by flowering vines as thick and heavy as a wall hanging, as he discovered when he pushed his way through them. The door was low and unlocked, and opened onto a stairway that stank of sand rats and mildew. Baldhron eased the door open and shut so that there would be no wind to tug at the torch flame—but she was already at the foot of the stairs, disappearing into a tunnel. He thought, *Sweet Drenhan, how have I overlooked this place?* and felt a prickling that was both excitement and anger.

He was calm and lucid until the moment she stopped at another door and raised her hand to it. As she did this, he remembered the words of a fishperson he had spoken to in the marketplace. "The selkesh man is alive—ill, but alive—and being held in a chamber that is not known to any palace folk except the Queen and her family."

"And how do you know this?" Baldhron had demanded.

The fishperson had stared at him with its inscrutable underwater eyes and said, "Some questions cannot be answered and should never be asked. Would you, for example, answer me if I asked why you and your comrades throw vast quantities of food down the wells here every night? And why you slither down after it?" Baldhron had stared back at the fishperson, his voice vanished. "Well, then," it had continued, "let us not concern ourselves with such questions. Now, if you please, my payment ..."

When Ladhra entered this new door, Baldhron began to feel dizzy, so dizzy in fact that he did not think to hide himself in case she returned the way she had come. She did not; she turned the other way when she finally emerged again, her arm wound around the selkesh prisoner's waist. Baldhron watched them lurch almost out of sight, then he stumbled forward. He followed, blind to the strange tunnels through which he was passing, seeing only her skin and the other's, her shadow on the wall, rippling and bending and larger because it was not just hers. He halted when she opened a door at the top of another stairway. He watched her enter the chamber or corridor beyond, with the water-man beside her. When the door had closed, Baldhron stepped back into the tunnel and waited. He might have waited for minutes or hours; he had no idea afterward. He shivered and did not think to blame himself, as he normally would have, for this evidence of physical and mental weakness. He did not think at all.

When he heard the door above him open again, he pressed himself against a wall within a side tunnel. This time the water-man walked ahead of Ladhra. He was no longer stooped and shambling, and his breathing, which before had rasped, was now silent. They returned to the prison room and stood together. The water-man said, "Thank you, Ladhra." She reached out her hands, not to support or aid him this time, not for any other reason than to touch him: his hips, wrapped in strips of cloth that looked wet-dark, and his chest, against which she laid her cheek and her long black hair.

Baldhron's dizziness evaporated. He leaned forward so that he would see clearly what the water-man would do, where he would touch her before Baldhron launched himself into the light. But the prisoner did not touch her. He stood very still, then moved her hands off his hips and turned into the room behind him. The door closed with a deep, shuddering sound, and Ladhra stared at it. Baldhron could not see her eyes, but he could see the rigid bones of her hands.

His instincts, restored and perhaps even keener, told him to remain concealed, told him to pause and consider how he would wound her best, now that she had twisted the threads of his plans. So he stayed there as she walked slowly toward the stairs that would return her to the moonlit palace. He stayed there after that, so still that a sand rat drew very near and snuffled around his feet.

When he finally did move, he ran. He ran along corridors and over covered tower bridges until the doors he sought were before him. The four Queensguards there stepped toward him, arrows nocked to bowstrings.

"Please," Baldhron gasped, "I must see the Queen."

TWENTY-FOUR

The day after Ladhra took him to the room with the deep fountain seemed like the longest Leish had yet passed as a captive. He tried to hear the song of his brother's army, so that his thoughts would be appropriately occupied—but he could not. He had heard no selkesh blood below the city since he had left his people by the stinking pools. *Maybe I cannot hear this song because we do not belong to this place,* he thought, and imagining Mallesh's fury distracted Leish for a time. He tried then to hear the fountain and the underground river that fed it, but these notes were difficult to concentrate on. Leish reached for a different song, fainter but possibly more compelling. When even the delicate, distant music of Nasranesh could not hold his attention, he curled up and tried only to sleep.

The fountain chamber had looked different in the darkness. At first, weak and confused, he had not recognized it. But then Ladhra had led him past the thrones and he had remembered them in grey daylight, and the sound of the fountains and channels that had seemed so loud as Dashran bled silently onto the stones. Leish had almost fled after he remembered this, even when she spoke and he realized what she was giving him—perhaps especially then. For how could he accept this gift from her when she had stood beside the Queen and watched Dashran die?

The pool was quite deep. All his misery had fled as his skin and lungs breathed the water, which was somehow fresh and clean. It had taken him a long time to notice the bottom of the pool. He wove slowly down to it and looked at the layers of bones and bleached coral, and suddenly the water tasted foul. He had plucked up four shells for Ladhra, since they were the only beautiful dead things there, and he did want—Nasran help him—to give her something beautiful.

I am thankful to her, he thought as they returned to his prison. *I am strong again*—and he had hated his need and his pleasure.

Leish sat up with a groan. He touched a hand to the place where her head had rested, and summoned again images of Dashran dying, and the selkesh—his friends, his cousins, his brother—swimming beneath the city. He waited for these images to restore—or, more accurately, engender—a feeling of purpose. This did not happen—for he also waited for her.

As if she will return. I turned away from her. Even if she did return, I wouldn't be able to explain this. She should never come here again. Soon my brother and Baldhron will end their waiting and attack, and either she or I will die. She should stay away.

He was still awake at midnight when his door swung open. He rose as she entered, and because he could not explain to her in words she would understand, he crossed the floor and fell to his knees before her. She put her hands in his hair and he wrapped his arms around her hips. She rocked him, so gently that at first he thought the motion was only his own body's shaking. She raised him up until he stood against her, wound in her arms and her unbound hair and her breathing. After a time she eased herself away and tugged on his hands, and he smiled at her smile and went with her.

This time she swam too. He surfaced after a brief, deep dive and saw her in the water, still clinging to the edge of the pool. He laughed and dove again and she met him beneath. She clutched his waist and burrowed her head against his belly, and he drew her to the other side of the pool so quickly that she did not need a breath. He lifted her into the air and she spluttered, coughed, put her hands on either side of his jaw and pulled herself up to kiss him. When they drew apart, he watched her take a breath, then he took them both beneath again and found her mouth and her skin. She bit his lip when she needed air—so soon—and he let her slip from his arms. He saw her surface through the moonlit ripple of the water; saw her legs, which had kicked so frantically, go still. He saw her hands reach for the rim of the pool. He saw that she was not waiting for him or looking at him, and he took one last water-breath and kicked himself upward to find out why.

The Queen was standing there, so close that he could see the sheen of the pearls that held her shoes closed. *Not sandals,* he noted numbly. Pale, white, soft things—shoes for a bedroom, for night and privacy. He moved his eyes from them, knowing he should not, knowing he must—but she was not looking at him.

She spoke her daughter's name, soft and low. Ladhra did not stir in the water beside him. Only when Galha called out over her shoulder did Ladhra move—abruptly, clumsily. She was looking where Galha had looked. She fumbled her way out of the fountain without shifting her gaze. Leish saw something in her face that made him want to bury himself among the rib cages and the hollow pores of coral at the bottom of the pool. But he rose up after her and straightened, dripping, on the stone, and saw the man who was standing between the thrones.

~

"You," Ladhra said, the word thin and vanishing as the water she had borne with her into the air. Baldhron inclined his head in a gesture that could almost have been one of humility or graciousness. She clenched her teeth, which had begun to chatter. "Why is he here?" she said, turning, looking at last into her mother's face.

"He informed me of—"

"Yes," Ladhra interrupted. Her bones seemed to be chattering now, grinding inside her skin. "Of course he did. But why did you allow him to come here with you?" She did not recognize Galha's expression. She expected fury or indignation or at the very least disappointment, and she knew what forms these would take—but she saw none of them.

"He is here," the Queen said quietly, "because he cares more about this land than you do. You needed to see this."

Ladhra heard herself laugh. "Really. Really, Baldhron? Is this so?"

He smiled and moved his head again. Silver light shivered from his eyes to the pitted flesh of his cheek. "It is as the Queen has said," he replied evenly. Ladhra thought, *Nara and I used to laugh at him.* She thought too of the man who stood beside her, and wanted to scream, *I've been such a fool, Nara,* as if her voice would reach east, all the way to the sea.

"There are two guards outside this chamber," Galha said. "They will take you to your tower."

"And lock me in?" Ladhra said, cringing at her petulance but too cold and distant to repress it.

"You know that I must," Galha said, and these words trembled a bit. "Though it grieves me. It does grieve me, Ladhra."

Ladhra shook her head and half turned so that she would not have to see her mother's eyes. She met Leish's instead. "And Leish?" she asked, still looking at him. "What will you do to him?" The silence was so long that she glanced back at Galha.

"Go now," the Queen said, and Ladhra finally heard anger, finally saw it in her lips and the skin beside her eyes.

"I am to blame," Ladhra said. "Do not—"

"Go," said Galha.

Ladhra walked past her mother, around the fountain, over the bridge that led to the thrones. Baldhron stepped back as if he were giving her room to pass. "My lady," he murmured, and she ran the last few steps to the door, where the guards were waiting for her.

"Tomorrow?" Mallesh repeated.

"Yes." Baldhron had already said this several times.

They were all assembled—as many of them as would fit—in the largest chamber, where they had met that first day. Mallesh had no idea how long ago that had been—one month, two, three? Would the fireblossoms have fallen yet around the gathering pool? The only thing he was certain of, as he looked at his men, was that they had been down here long enough to grow thin and pale and sick. Even this chamber, where the selkesh did not usually come, stank of them. Their own place was worse. When Baldhron had grimaced and demanded to know what the odour was and how to remove it, Mallesh had said, "It is our skin rotting. We need air as much as water—fresh air, not what is in these tunnels. To be rid of this smell we must go above."

"Well, then," Baldhron had said, "I suppose we must learn to endure it."

But now, weeks later, Baldhron was saying something different. *He* was different: loud and flushed, gesticulating at the maps and weapons that hung from the stone walls. He declared that the plan had changed.

Something had happened that would distract the Queen; she was no longer thinking about the selkesh army. This army would attack tomorrow.

"But," Mallesh said, groping for words through the aching of his head, innards, flesh, "you were so certain before that we had to wait. What is this thing that has happened?"

He saw Baldhron's flush deepen. "I cannot say exactly—just that it has to do with the Queen's family. For the first time in years she is concerned with something private that will keep her from noticing other things until it is too late."

"But the guards," Mallesh said, thinking more clearly now because there was something wrong with Baldhron's words and the voice with which he spoke them. "You told us the palace on Queenswrit Eve would be quiet, hardly guarded—but that is not so now, even if the Queen is distracted, as you say. Why—"

"Listen," Baldhron interrupted, and the muttering that had risen with Mallesh's words subsided. "My scribes have spent these months feeding you, teaching you about the palace and the realm and the use of real weapons. You are ready. But if you do not wish to join us, after all our efforts to aid you, we will do this thing alone." Now it was the scribes who murmured. Baldhron swept his gaze over their ranks until they were silent again. "I have led you this far with as much wisdom as I have. My first plan was promising—but the mark of a great leader is his ability and willingness to change his strategy, if such a change will lead to a better outcome. I ask you to trust me as you have until now. If you cannot, we will bid you farewell and carry out the attack ourselves."

Leish, Mallesh thought, and wondered with a tired, bruised pang how many of the other selkesh were thinking this. Leish would have known what to do and say. He would have led, in his quiet way, even though leading had never been a thing he wanted. *May Nasran wash me with forgiveness,* Mallesh thought, *for I am glad he is not here, and I have hoped for his death, yet he is the only one who could help me now.*

"And if we do join you tomorrow," Mallesh said, "and the attack fails, what then? For as you know," he continued quickly when Baldhron glared down at him from his place on the bridge, "a great leader should consider all possible outcomes."

Baldhron cleared his throat. "Yes. Of course, yes. If … such a thing transpired, we would use these tunnels to reach the Sarhenna River. This river and its tributaries would lead us swiftly into wild places where we would not be found. From these places we could escape the realm."

Mallesh nodded, as others did. Even if Baldhron had only now formulated this plan, as his voice and manner suggested, it was a good one. *Though I will not flee,* Mallesh thought. *If I do not conquer here, I will die here.*

"If you want to speak to your people," Baldhron said, "we will await you in—"

"No," Mallesh said, straightening his cramped, weak limbs beneath the water. "We do not need to discuss this. It has been our desire since we arrived to attack this city. You convinced us to delay, now you command us to proceed. We will do so. It is what we longed for even before we left the shores of our own land."

He watched his men shift and smile. He saw their exhaustion and their hunger smooth away a bit as they rose up from the pool to grasp the swords and straight daggers and axes the scribes had taught them to use. They already carried their own hooked knives, honed and hidden against their chests. They all looked at Mallesh, their oozing, stinking skin aglow almost as the metal was.

Mallesh also rose and took up his sword. He faced Baldhron across the water. "Tomorrow," he said.

TWENTY-FIVE

"The palace is shaped like a flower. Imagine rings of towers instead of petals, each ring, each tower, guarded. The centre is the Queenstower. We will have to work our way from the outer layer in. Years ago there were wells within the palace as well as outside it, but this Queen's mother constructed a different system of pipes that would bring water to the fountains and kitchens of the palace. These pipes are too narrow for us to use. So we will send men here, to the western wall where the Queensfolk houses are, and here, to the back entrance by the palace crypts. Mallesh and I will lead a larger contingent through the marketplace to the main doors. There are always people about in the marketplace, even at night—we will have to be quiet and careful. While we do this, other groups will surface in the wells nearest the city wall, which has two gates. The guards here always face the desert. Our men will remain at the gates while the rest of us do our work inside the palace. Be silent and swift, wherever you are. Use the moon's light, but be wary of it. Distract and ambush if you come upon a large group of guards or some that appear very alert. Surprise and shock will carry us into the palace, ring by ring, until we reach the Queen. By the time we do this, there will be no one left within to come to her aid.

"You know your groups. Make ready now. We move together, two hours after midnight."

Baldhron had said more, Mallesh was sure of this, but he could not remember. He was amazed, in fact, that he had remembered as much as he had. The singing of the city's stone and sand and water was so loud that he felt feverish. *It will pass.* The thought took shape slowly. He gripped it and clung, and the singing seemed to ebb. *It is so powerful because I am finally above. Soon I will be accustomed to this new place and my strength will return.*

He dug his bare toes against the packed sand of the marketplace and lifted his face to the sky, carefully, so that the nausea he had felt when he first did this would not strike him again. He was still a bit dizzy: the stars spun as they flickered, and the darkness among them spiralled like an ocean waterspout. And there were the towers as well, which seemed to curve in toward each other as if the wind that high were so fierce that it bent the stone. Mallesh raised his arms, spread his fingers apart, blinked at them and at the sky and palace behind them. He was heavy with desire.

"Mallesh," Baldhron said, "come—it is time."

Mallesh and Baldhron led their forty scribes and selkesh among the odd structures of the marketplace. These forty would hang back at the main doors; only the leaders would step up to the guards there, who might be perplexed or curious or even suspicious, immediately before they died. Mallesh fingered his spear, concealed beneath a cloak given him by Baldhron when they reached the outside. No metal clanked or gleamed as they moved, and the few folk who were awake at this hour simply nodded at them. "A large group of friends," Baldhron had said, "walking without haste or apparent direction, disturbing no one. This is how we will appear to anyone who sees us."

"The doors are just around this turn," Baldhron murmured now. Mallesh swallowed. His throat was already dry, though the cloth beneath his cloak was still damp from his swim to the well shaft. As if he sensed Mallesh's thirst, Baldhron said, "Would you like to drink one more time before we proceed? There is a fountain just here ..."

Mallesh drank deeply, head down, eyes closed. When he straightened to allow his men to drink as well, there was a yllosh-woman standing with Baldhron.

"Wait," Baldhron said, raising his hand to silence the noise that was rising in Mallesh's throat. "Do not act in haste—remember my counsel."

Despite the sound in his own head like a whirring of starmoth wings, Mallesh heard a low growl from his men. "We have no time to waste on yllosh scum," he hissed. "We go now, before I do this one harm."

Baldhron took a step toward him. "Listen to me. This is Wollshenyllosh, the fish ... yllosh-person who witnessed your brother's capture and Dashran's murder. The same one who has acted as translator for Leish and the Queen these past few months."

Mallesh glanced at Wollshenyllosh. She was looking at him steadily. He could find no mockery or malice in her eyes, though he wanted to. The noise of his hatred receded a bit, making room for thought. *Baldhron is not surprised to see her. Why do we linger here, when he was so eager to begin?* "And what," Mallesh said, "does she herself say of these things she has seen and done?"

Wollshenyllosh was silent for a moment. Mallesh heard the song of the city again, and closer sounds, like windbells and creaking wood and distant voices laughing.

"It is true," she said at last, "that the quarrels of our people are ancient and strong—but they are between us. When drylanders intervene in our affairs, we are not happy. For although we are not friends, we are kin."

Mallesh felt splinters beneath his nails and loosened his hold on his spear.

"So when this Queen killed your man—even though he had tried to attack one of ours—we were displeased. And your brother Leish, I have discovered, is brave. And," she added after a short pause, "we know where you and your people have been this past while. We have known almost since your arrival—but we have not informed anyone. Though we could have, perhaps for great reward. This is what I say to you."

Mallesh closed his eyes as a surge of dizziness rocked him. When it had mostly subsided, he cleared his throat, tried to think as Leish would. "I see," Mallesh said in the most confident tone he could muster at such low volume and with such sickness in his gut. "And I thank you for your discretion." His tongue felt heavy against his teeth. He had been prepared to scream and draw blood with spear and knife, not to attempt diplomacy with a yllosh-woman who *knew,* who had known all along ... "If, then, you are so impressed by my brother's character and so annoyed at this Queen, why not aid us in what we are about to do? There might be reward in this as well." He thrust the words from his mouth as if he were trying not to taste them.

Wollshenyllosh's smile was kind, perhaps regretful, and he stiffened. "We will not intervene—not for the Queen and not for you. We leave our lakes and oceans only to come here, for our people are fascinated by the dryland goods we trade for, but we do not involve ourselves in the lives and disputes of others. No reward is worth the risk of never again breathing our home waters."

Mallesh felt the towers above him, and the sky whose stars were arrayed differently from the ones he knew. He trembled for a moment, and sensed the selkesh behind him trembling, and he forced anger from his confusion. "Why are you here, then?" he demanded, ignoring Baldhron's swift, "Quietly, Mallesh!" Mallesh shook Baldhron's hand away from his arm. "Why are you here?" Mallesh repeated. "To awe us with the wisdom and morals of your people—to belittle and shame us yet again?"

Wollshenyllosh gazed at him so evenly and for such a long, silent time that she did not need to speak her "No" aloud. "We will not fight with or for you," she finally said, unclasping a bag attached to her seavine belt. The scales on her hand and forearm glittered as she moved. "But, as Baldhron requested, we will aid you in another way."

The key she drew from the bag was long and slender. She held it up by its notched end. Mallesh frowned at it, then at Baldhron, who was smiling and holding out his own hand.

"Thank you," Baldhron said after he had plucked it from her fingers. "You have done well. When next we meet, I will make sure that you receive some form of compensation, even if you continue to insist that you do not desire it."

"Perhaps we will not meet again. I will soon return to my home waters—after my people and I see where your strokes lead you tonight."

She slipped away from them, and there was no flash of moonlight on scales to show where she had gone.

Mallesh turned to Baldhron and spoke so that he would not begin to tremble again. "Give me the key. And show me the way to Leish, once we are inside."

Baldhron opened his mouth to reply, then closed it as an old woman shuffled by, peering, pursing her cracked lips. When she had passed, with several backward glances, Mallesh looked again at Baldhron. He was no longer holding the key.

"Of course you wish to free your brother immediately," he said. "It would be my first desire, if I were in your place. But think, Mallesh: he will be weak and sick. He would be a hindrance to us in the first lightning strike of battle. Safer to leave him where he is. We must continue with our plan: you take your men to the eastern towers, I take mine west, and we meet in the northern corridor to begin our assault on the next layer of towers. When we have successfully taken the palace, we will free Leish together."

Mallesh knew his men would expect him to protest. He *should* protest—he, the compassionate brother and leader. But he bowed his head as if in resignation, and said, "You are right. He will be safer where he is, for now." When his men began to whisper, he rounded on them and snapped, "Think of him—think only of his well-being," and glared at them until they too bowed their heads.

"Excellent," Baldhron said. "Now—shall we go inside?"

~

All the wells of the Queenscity swarmed with shadows. Scribes and selkesh climbed out into sandy squares, broad lanes, the fragrant, rustling spaces of enclosed courtyards. Some of the selkesh faltered when they stood in the open air again after so long, but the scribes urged them firmly on. In one courtyard a dog barked—but the garden was empty when its sleepy owner looked out upon it.

Luhr slumbered as the shadows filled its streets. They flowed like countless river branchings, down to the southern wall with its great gate, across to the eastern wall with its smaller one. They were swift and silent, seen by no one except some speechless drunkards, a madwoman who clapped at their passing, lovers half blind with need.

The two Queensguards at the eastern gate were sitting with their backs against the wall. One was sleeping; the other was eating an end of bread, lifting it up to examine it after every bite. The bread made a small, muffled sound when it fell from his fingers. He made no sound, though his eyes widened above the dagger lodged in his throat, and he looked as though he would speak a question, or a curse. When a second dagger—held, not thrown—sank into the other guard's chest, his eyes opened, blinked, fixed, and he breathed a whistling sigh.

Four guards manned the main gates: one at the top of each watch-tower and one in each of the tiny rooms below. The tower doors were unlocked and well oiled. The guards within were sitting on stools, looking out barred windows at the moonlit sand. One of them did not turn; the other did, and nearly had time to cry out. The guards above were leaning out over their sections of wall, talking about the dangers of the sandstorm season. They talked for two minutes, five; then they turned away from each other to pace along the walls, stretching and rubbing at their eyes, looking at nothing. Two daggers and two short arrows flew; one guard grunted and the other screamed, but no one in the sleeping city heard them.

~

The Queensfolk homes at the palace's western wall were quiet. Pentaran motioned some of his companions up the twisting staircases that led to the highest houses. When they had disappeared, he led the rest of his men to the houses midway up the cluster. He heard their breathing—the selkesh were especially loud, whistling and gurgling—and the patter of their bare feet on the clay, and his own heartbeat pounding above these other noises. He was certain that people would hear this and stream from their houses, but all was dark and motionless, sunk in the deep sleep that comes in the hours after midnight.

He halted at a door and put his hand to its wood. He tasted bile in his throat and in his mouth, and swallowed desperately until it dissolved. *Now,* he thought. *Now, before you vomit on the stairs*—and he nodded once at his men and pushed the door open.

~

"I know these two," Baldhron whispered to Mallesh. They were standing behind a wooden stage draped in canvas and dyed linen. Mallesh glanced around the post nearest him at the two Queensguards who stood straight and silent on either side of the palace doors. "They were lovers," Baldhron went on. Mallesh heard a smile in his voice. "She has recently cast him off for another. We'll take her first. I'll walk up to them, leaving space for a clear shot. One of my men will use a bow and arrow on her. I'll order another to shoot him as he's turning to her."

He knows them, Mallesh thought as Baldhron murmured to the scribes. *These are his own people.* He sheathed the sword Baldhron had commanded him to use once they were inside the palace. He shrugged the cloak off his shoulder so that his spearhead caught the light. As if this had been a pre-arranged signal, the selkesh approached. Baldhron conferred with his men and Mallesh spoke to his quickly, tersely. He saw that Baldhron had not noticed this, and made sure that he still did not notice when Mallesh and another selkesh stepped out past the stage. They stood close together and drew back their arms. Their spears had already found their marks by the time Baldhron lunged out of the darkness.

"You fool!" he hissed. Mallesh felt spittle on his face but could not wipe at it; his shoulders were pinned by Baldhron's knees. The ground was hard and cool beneath his head, and Mallesh nearly smiled with the joy of feeling it there. "I told you what we would do—"

"What *you* would do," Mallesh said, and felt all the months of his confinement sloughing away like an ocean eel's skin, leaving everything from eyeballs to toenails translucent with newness and strength. "It was an overly complicated plan. Two of them, and us with our spears—this was the better way."

Baldhron pushed himself up so roughly that Mallesh knew there would be bruises on his chest and shoulders. "They could have seen you," Baldhron said. "They could have dodged your throwing sticks and screamed for help."

"They did not," Mallesh said, easing himself away from the ground without wincing. "They did not expect to see us—so they did not see us until our spears were in them. We selkesh have hunted creatures in water, huge, limber creatures that plunge and twist, yet we hunt them with our spears and haul their bodies onto our shore. This was not such a hunt."

"And you are not dealing with sea animals now!" Baldhron spat. Scribes and selkesh were beginning to emerge from behind the stage, two or three at a time, their eyes wide. "You hunt people now—and you have no idea—"

"Baldhron," Mallesh said, hearing his own voice as if from far away, as if he were drunk or ill—though his head was clear and his limbs were coiled with power. "You are upset that I took this action without telling you. Maybe you are angry that the first Queensblood was spilled by selkesh. But remember: you are aiding us. That is the way of it."

The men had all gathered now. Baldhron's eyes darted to them and to the unguarded doors that were so close. His chest heaved as a drylander's might if he had been diving. "Indeed," he said after a moment, not looking at Mallesh. "We are giving aid to you in this place *that only we know*. Do not act without my agreement or knowledge again. Do not, Mallesh."

He did turn then, and Mallesh met his gaze, allowed his head to lower just a bit. He could hear the palace; he was near and strong and no longer concerned with the pride that had tormented him when Baldhron had given orders beneath the city. "Very well," he said.

Baldhron nodded once. "Retrieve your spears, then," he said. His voice sounded different, thinner, the words pressed by air. "We must go in now, before anyone passes by here. We have already lingered too long."

"Very well," Mallesh said again, and heard his laughter ring like waves against the city's song.

TWENTY-SIX

"Did you hear something?"

"Hmm? No. You were probably half asleep again. I tell you, you've been dozing every few minutes since midnight."

"It's the baby. He used to be wakeful at night and sleepy during the day, but now he's older, he's awake in the day too, when I used to sleep."

"Ask for a few nights away, then—just enough to get yourself rested. And anyway, he'll change. Mine did, though I admit it seemed ... What? What's—"

They were green and brown, like creatures risen from the earth of the Queenswood after the rains—like the trees themselves, so tall. There were others among them, these ones familiar. All of their mouths were open, but they made no sound—just ran and raised their arms and loosed their wood and metal before she could get her own arrow nocked. Her bow clattered against the stone by her feet. She heard this, and a grunt from the man beside her. She saw him pitch forward, though not clearly; her eyes were full of mist that would not blink away, and now scarlet like the mourning ribbon the Queen wore in her hair when she grieved for someone lost. *Me?* the woman thought, and fell.

~

The child should have been asleep. His grandmother would flog him if she found him here—but she slept longer and longer each night; and he was twelve now, old enough to come and go a bit without her knowledge. And anyway, he was pursuing his passion: the stars, the pictures they made, the shadows on the face of the moon, the luminous trails that sprayed across the darkness like the path of a giant sand snail.

He bent to scratch a notation on his skymap. It was getting bigger and bigger all the time; soon he would have trouble hiding it in his bedchamber. His grandmother would flog him for this too. Parchment and writing sticks should only be used for scribes' tasks—this is what she thought, what she had told him since he could remember. He was to be a scribe, as his mother had been. He went to his lessons and concentrated and was praised by his teachers—but only here did he feel joy.

He had not brought a lantern with him tonight; the moon was full, and his house was the highest of all the Queensfolk houses by the palace. The brightness of the moon made it difficult for him to see the stars surrounding it, but he would wait, and the moon would set, and he would look at its neighbour stars then, if he wasn't too tired. For now he peered at other, farther stars, and sketched their positions on his map, which had small round sections for every hour of the night.

At two hours past midnight he heard noises among the houses below him. His own house was silent. He was so relieved by this that his limbs felt like water for a moment. He leaned out over his flat roof and tried to blink away the dazzle the moon had left in his eyes. He saw dark shapes running up the staircase; it was the scuffing of their feet that he had heard. He looked at them for a few breaths, then crawled all the way back to where his roof met the palace. He should not be awake. He should not be here now—but surely these men were not coming to find him?

He closed his eyes when he heard the slight squeak of his door. Perhaps they *were* here for him; perhaps they were going to talk to his grandmother before they came up. He whimpered and hugged himself and his skymap, even though he knew he should probably be running or hiding or doing some other clever thing to avoid detection.

Long minutes passed without further disturbance. He was straining so hard to hear that his ears felt the silence, like a cloud that muffled and breathed at the same time. Nothing, nothing—then the creaky door again and the scuffing footsteps. He crushed the skymap against him and waited for someone to vault up onto the roof—but no one did, and the footsteps moved away.

When he was sure that they were gone, he slid back toward the edge of the roof. The men—he saw them clearly this time, though some looked much too tall to be Queensmen—were on the landing below his, pushing open the door to that house. He saw other men on the landing below that. Men everywhere, dark as insects, scuttling in and out of houses with flashing steel. He had been moon-blind before; he had not seen these weapons.

His door gaped. He slipped inside. A short time later he slipped out again. He was crying, holding a kitchen knife that dipped and wove as if he were drawing a star pattern on the air. He stood and wiped his cheeks with the back of his free hand. He saw that the men were far below him now. He put the knife between his teeth and climbed, hand under hand, foot under foot, down the long, straight palace wall that supported the cluster of houses. He climbed carefully but quickly. When he reached the sand, most of the men were still above him. He removed the knife from his mouth and turned—and looked up into the face of someone he knew.

"P-Pentaran," he stammered. One of his teachers—here, now, holding a blade as those other men were. Pentaran staring down at him, his mouth agape; Pentaran about to say something. The child cried out and sprang forward. He ran through the shadows toward the palace doors, faster than fountain water or the arc of a dying star.

~

"You are an artist," the female Queensguard said just before she took another short, noisy sip from her soup bowl. "I can't imagine why no woman has yet forced you into marriage." Her four companions chuckled. "Is that eastern redspice I taste? Or pepperflower?"

"Neither," replied the burly guard who was the chef. "And I'll never tell. Unless, that is, *you'd* like to marry me?"

Though there were only five of them in the stone vastness of the kitchen, their laughter sounded loud and full. They were sitting cross-legged on top of the broad wooden counter that hours ago had been scrubbed and swept clean of the day's food. They had coaxed the fire back to life and, after much preparation, set the soup over it. The soup's scent was like their laughter: large and nearly living in this cold, darkened chamber.

"Must be off," one of the men sighed.

"Nonsense!" cried another. "You've only had one bowl of soup and two cups of wine! And our watch only ended an hour ago."

"One more cup," the woman insisted, pouring, spilling red droplets onto the wood.

"No—I really should go," the man insisted, pushing the cup back toward her. "There've been too many nights like this recently. I need to sleep."

"Poor wee dear needs his rest," she trilled as the man slid off the counter and walked over to the wall where all of their bows were leaning. He slung his bow over his shoulder and turned to scowl at them; they were calling mock-aggrieved entreaties, holding out their arms. When he disappeared up the short staircase that led to the corridor, they dissolved again into laughter.

There was a long moment of silence after the laughter. Then, from just outside the door, came a short, twisting scream. The Queensguards leapt down—cups and bowls tipped, fell, rocked—and ran for their bows and the stairs.

The corridor seethed with men. Lizard-men—by the First, what *were* they?—and Queensfolk, all of whom turned from the body on the floor when the door crashed open. The Queensguards fumbled for their daggers, which until now had only been drawn in pretend battles, or to subdue drunken palace intruders or adolescents who stole in from the city to prove their mettle to their friends. The guards parried, mostly, until the woman sprang forward and slit a lizard-man's chest from right to left. When he faltered, she jumped up and sank her knife into his neck. He was so tall that she had to wait for him to fall before she could retrieve her blade, through gouts of blood and the last bucking of his limbs. But then there was someone else standing in his place. She rubbed the blood from her eyes and readied her dagger, then gaped at him.

"Nalhent?" she said, and he fell back a pace, his own dagger shaking in his hand. *"Nalhent!"* she cried. He took another step back, his mouth working soundlessly. A lizard-man pushed past him, thrust a hooked knife into her and wrenched it, deeper and around, until she fell.

The one named Nalhent turned and ran. Another Queensman called after him. All the Queensmen hesitated, looking at the corridor and down at the dead on the floor and, wildly, at each other. Then they too ran. The lizard-men turned as well, just long enough for the Queensguards to lunge and stab. "Go!" the chef cried to one of his companions who had reached the edge of the fighting. He fled, weaving so that none of the attackers would be able to throw a knife with any accuracy, and the lizard-man who tried to follow was cut down by an arrow.

After they had killed the two remaining guards, the lizard-men pounded down the hallway in the direction the escaped one had taken—but though their strides were long and desperate, they did not find him.

~

The Queenswood was on fire. The child had smelled and heard it even before he crawled over the body of the dead Queensguard at the palace's western entrance. The fire had reached the top branches of a few of the smaller trees; the larger ones stood above the shower of sparks, as yet untouched. The child coughed and tried not to breathe too deeply, though this was very difficult since he was running. He dodged among the trunks, weaving, turning, not thinking about where he was going. When he stumbled into a clear space among the tallest trees, he sat down heavily and sobbed. He tasted smoke at the back of his throat and wondered whether his tears would be black. He lay down as he cried. The earth was soft with the moss and the springy, spreading plants that had grown after the rains.

He must have slept. When he sat up, the web of leaves above him was ablaze. He swore and scrambled to his feet. How could he have slept when he had to do something? when he had to tell someone about the men? He stood very still. A picture was forming, slow but clear, and he knew what it was, where he had to go. He ran again, very fast, through spiralling, flaming leaves.

He was a very good climber, even now that he was twelve and his legs and arms were longer and clumsier. He found the base of the tower that jutted into the Queenswood and pulled himself up against its stones. This was one of the older towers; the stones were rougher, the surface less sheer than those of the newer towers. He scampered up, slipped, continued more slowly. He thought briefly that he could have tried entering the tower from within the palace—but he kept climbing. He had seen the silent spread of men among the houses; they would be inside the palace too, maybe posted at its tower doors in place of the Queensguards they had killed. Better to make this attempt from the outside.

Below him, wood shrieked and cracked. The fire was spreading; he heard its roar increasing, like the sound of a great beast goaded into rage. He rested with his cheek against stone that was still cool, and closed his eyes. He knew that he could not look down, especially now, when the flames might blind or frighten him. Up, up, up, rest; repeat. At some point his knife fell from between his numb lips—but that was fine, he was nearly at the first window; and in any case, what had he really expected to do with a knife?

He had often examined this tower in daylight, thinking he might climb it one day when he had nothing else to do. The lowest window was barred; the one above it was not. When he reached it, he saw shorn metal that must once have been bars. The strangest thoughts flitted through his head. *Did someone escape from here once? Why hasn't anyone ever noticed and replaced the bars? Did someone know I would need to climb up here someday? "The boy will save us all—make sure to leave him a way in ..."*

He dropped to the landing beneath the window and lay there, shuddering and sweat-sodden. He did not allow himself much rest; he dragged himself up through the darkness, stair by stair, like a wounded dog. His dog-boy whimpering sounded odd, probably because he could not feel himself making this noise. He wanted to sleep again. The darkness tugged at his eyelids and his head—but he shook it off and began to count the steps. He was at eighty-four when he reached for the next step and found only empty space. He had to stand up now. And after he did that, he would need even more strength. He lay and imagined that he was the Summer Archer, that each of the points of his body was actually a star. He was massive and powerful, spread above the eastern horizon, each of his movements a rumble.

He reached for the rope and felt it, though he did not open his eyes to look at it; rope as thick as both his legs together—but with his new star-arms he would have no trouble holding on. He pulled it in against him, wrapped himself around it. He would fly, in this darkness that was his open sky.

The boy swung himself off the wooden platform. At first he simply hung, swaying slightly. He shouted once—the Archer's bellow, like thunder—and bent his body violently back and forth, until he and the rope were climbing up and plunging down together. Somewhere far above him, the Queensbell began to toll.

TWENTY-SEVEN

I must still be sleeping, Ladhra thought. *I'm sleeping and dreaming of him.* But as she looked at Leish, she felt her eyes blinking and dry as they always were whenever she woke too soon. And his face, above the lantern he held, was not as she would have dreamed it. His rounded lips were drawn back, but not in a smile; one of his eyes was closed. At first she thought he was winking at her—but she stirred on her bed, focused her own gaze more clearly, and saw that his eyelid was swollen shut and that there was a long, glistening line of blood on his cheek. She rolled onto her side and said his name in a hoarse, just-woken voice. He lowered his head and she spoke his name again more loudly—and Baldhron stepped out from behind him.

"My lady," Baldhron said as she scrambled to bury herself in bedclothes. Her mother's guards had taken away her dagger when they locked her in here. Locked her in—she glanced at the open door. "Ladhra." She turned back to him, attempting to scowl as if this were only another encounter in the Queenswood or in the sunlit space of a corridor.

"How did you get in?" she asked, gripping the sheet in both hands so that he would not see their trembling.

He lifted one shoulder in a shrug that would have seemed lazy if his eyes had not been so steady and bright. "I killed the guards," he said, "and took the key."

She laughed—but then she looked again at Leish, who was bleeding and whose one open eye was white-wide, and her laughter withered.

"I thought," Baldhron went on, "that you might wish to see your lover." There was a vein pulsing on the left side of his forehead; she watched it and did not speak. Perhaps if she waited, kept him here long enough, a guard would pass by and see the untended door and creep up the stairs, dagger at the ready …

"Go," Baldhron said in the yllosh language, shoving Leish forward. "Go to her." Leish came to a stumbling halt about five paces from the bed. Baldhron walked to him, wrenched the swinging lantern from his hand, forced this hand up so that it seemed to be reaching for Ladhra. "Go. Touch her."

Leish smiled at her. *I know his smile now,* she thought, and her eyes stung with half-risen tears. He smiled at her and did not move.

"Very well," Baldhron said. He continued in the Queenstongue, "Stand back, in that case." He pushed Leish over to the wall across from the bed, pressed first one then the other of his arms against the hanging tapestry there. *He looks like a tree,* Ladhra thought, and *I'll run for the door*—but Baldhron had turned to her again, and the distance to the door was so great, so open, and the stairs would be dark …

Baldhron set the lantern on the floor. "My men have taken the palace. We've cut our way in this far and have only the final ring to breach. I thought I might bring you with me to witness this. I thought your mother might want to see you before she dies." He paused, nudged the lantern forward with his foot. "I watched my mother die, you know," he went on. "Your mother killed her. I was eight, and I saw my mother die."

Ladhra had to scoff; it was what she would have done if he had cornered her beneath the trees. "I always knew you were addle-brained," she said. Normal; everything normal, the same—night that was really day, guards down the hall approaching. "But you're obviously entirely mad. I pity you more now than I did."

Baldhron took several long strides toward her. She held herself as tall as she could, watched him check and smile very slowly. "Mad?" he said. "No." She saw a dagger in his hand where there had not been one before, and his arm drawn back, his body twisting round to throw. She screamed as the dagger flew. She screamed, and screamed again, until she knew that there would be no footsteps on the stairs.

~

Leish felt no pain at first. He heard Ladhra scream and saw her eyes go to his right hand, so he too looked at his right hand (a strange, awkward look, since his right eye was sealed shut). He was surprised to see a knife lodged in the web between his first and second fingers. He had not seen Baldhron throw; he had decided he would not look away from Ladhra. He could hear an ending in the song of the palace and the city, and he would not let his eyes leave her face. Except that she screamed and he followed her terrified gaze and saw the knife—and in the heartbeat it took to do so, pain seared up along his inner arm and into his chest. He tugged his right hand down and felt a tearing, but the knife was sunk firmly into his flesh and the thick wool of the tapestry behind him.

This pain made him forget his eye and his cheek, which Baldhron had hammered with his fist when he had first come to Leish's prison chamber. "Mallesh is waiting for us," Baldhron had said. "The attack has begun and it's time for you to join us." But Leish had seen the tremors in Baldhron's lips and jaw and hands, and he had shaken his head.

"I will await my brother here," he had said, "since I am too weak to fight."

So Baldhron—tall enough to do so—had struck him in the face and thrust the point of a knife against the hollow of his throat and hissed, "You come with me. Walk ahead. Turn—*now*."

Baldhron had not lied about the attack, Leish soon saw. Every palace door they passed was flanked by dead Queensguards. Some selkesh as well; Leish looked at them and heard the song of Nasranesh, sudden and piercing as a wail. He remembered his dreams of blood, and Mallesh atop the gathering pool stone, and the boats and weapons piled along the shore. He saw these fallen selkesh and wanted to sing his grief against their skin—but Baldhron nudged him on with his knife, and Leish walked past them all.

Occasionally they heard cries from around corners or behind walls. Each time, Baldhron turned Leish and forced him in another direction. "So it's not just my brother you're avoiding," Leish said the third time this happened. Baldhron spat at him, then held Leish's wrists together behind his back so that he would not be able to wipe his neck dry.

They had passed through countless doors into countless hallways when Baldhron paused. This particular corridor was empty and lantern-lit, unlike the others, which had been dark and littered with bodies. Baldhron drew in several deep, slow breaths and prodded Leish around a turn.

One of the two Queensguards standing outside an ornately carved door had called out sharply. Baldhron had smiled and bowed his head to them, and Leish had seen them relax very slightly.

"Help me," Leish had said loudly in the yllosh language, but they did not understand. They frowned and looked again at Baldhron, who spoke to them in a tone of restrained urgency. He gestured at Leish several times and mimed some actions: a lunge, a warded blow. Leish imagined him saying, "This man is the Queen's prisoner, and he has escaped. He tried to attack me, but I fought him off." Leish felt the trickle of blood beside his swollen eye and wanted to laugh at his own helplessness. Baldhron talked on. Leish heard him say the Queen's name. They were directly in front of the Queensguards now. One of them began to speak but stopped when Baldhron held up a hand. He said a few words, and he and the Queensguard stepped away from the door. Before Leish could move, the woman's throat was cut and the dagger was hissing past him, and the other guard cried out and slumped at his feet.

And now the same dagger was in him. He forced his gaze away from it, to Ladhra, who was still sitting in bed clutching the bedclothes over her drawn-up knees. The pain in his hand and the tortured singing in his head nearly blinded him—but he held her in his vision and smiled so that she, at least, might find a place of quiet. He would touch her hair with his uninjured hand; he would draw it down to cradle her head where it curved to meet her neck. He would tell her of the songs he heard, all of them, even the ones that were now being torn thread by thread and remade in patterns that horrified him.

Baldhron's head was moving, Leish noticed, back and forth, tracing the line from Ladhra's eyes to Leish's. Seeing the quiet? Baldhron howled—an animal sound, or a wind trapped among rocks—and drew back his arm again, and a second dagger sank into Leish. Into his other hand, which was still splayed where Baldhron had set it against the tapestry. The middle web: the largest and most fleshy. This time Leish made no sound, just closed his eyes and sang a high, steady note inside his head. When he could breathe around the new pain, he opened his eyes.

Baldhron's face was so close to his that he could smell the sourness of his breath. "Where now?" he murmured, jerking the dagger out of Leish's right hand. "Hmm? Where next, fish-man? Any gills under that cloth, I wonder? Or perhaps I should ask her that." He took three steps back—enough for Leish to see past him. Ladhra rising, the bedclothes falling away from her body. Rising and slipping off her bed, smiling at him as if she would simply cross the floor and touch him. Her bare feet were silent on the flagstones. She took two paces, paused; then she ran.

Baldhron stumbled sideways as she launched herself onto his back. She scrabbled at his face; she wound her legs around his waist and forced his head back. Leish only watched for a moment. He reached over to pull the dagger from his left hand—but he suddenly felt feverishly hot and dizzy, and his fingers groped in vain for the knife that seemed to be receding into a distance of heaving waves and bending trees. He heard a dull, heavy sound and looked slowly around. Baldhron was lifting Ladhra off the floor. She flailed and writhed, but still he held her. She was falling backward onto the bed, and he was falling onto her, and their limbs were weaving and thrusting too quickly. Leish looked back at his hand and reached again, and this time his fingers closed around metal.

He tugged once, twice. The knife came free and he slid down the wall, sickness rising in his throat. He saw his blood, remembered the selkesh blood he had seen in this place, and he imagined that he heard it as another song, surging east toward the sea. He swallowed and struggled to his knees. He heard a low, rapid grunting and got one foot flat on the floor. Then he heard another sound.

It was music. One note only, but still music, swelling, shuddering against all the stones. It boomed again and again, and in the silence that came between, Leish heard shouting, distant but growing closer. He raised his head and shoulders and saw Baldhron crouching on the bed with his head up. Two more booms. Baldhron cried out and sprang to the floor. Leish watched him run. His footsteps faded as Leish dragged himself over to the bed.

Ladhra's face was turned to the wall. He saw the tangle of her hair, followed its darkness down to the twist of her spine and hips. In the lantern glow her spreading blood seemed to twist as well, as if it lived. He sat down and lifted his hand, saw his own blood coursing down the inside of his arm. He touched her with the fingers of his right hand, which was no longer bleeding much. He touched her hair and the small, still place between her lips. He lowered himself down beside her and hummed a bit against her skin.

~

"They were too young for the wild country," Galha said. She was pacing in front of her open window, in and out of the moonlight that lay upon the air and along the floor. "I should have known they would lose their nerve. When did our people in Blenniquant City confirm this uprising?"

Malhan looked briefly down at the parchment on his lap. "The letter is dated two weeks ago. There will have been rumours circulating before that." He gestured at the large cushion beside his. "It's late—at least sit for a moment. Let your body think it's resting."

"There's flyfever in that region, isn't there?" Galha's blue-and-green-stitched sleeping robe tangled between her calves as she turned. She shook the cloth free with a flick of her wrist. "Caltran will find someone in Blenniquant City who has the disease. I'll have this person taken to the camp. You'll have to research the symptoms, make sure the account of their illness is exact and vivid. Queensfolk are not overly familiar with the details of such fatal diseases."

Malhan said, "Dearest, do you not think we should bring the leader, at least, back to Luhr? We might discover why this thing happened."

"It happened," the Queen said, coming to a halt in front of Malhan so that he had to crane to see her face, "because they were not fit to do my work, or to be remembered for it. Because they were too young. By the First, too young, untried, all of them—how could I have sent them there?" She bent her chin to her chest. Her eyelashes fluttered against her cheeks. Malhan held up a hand and she took it, let him pull her gently down to the cushion.

"It's late," he said again. "There's nothing to be written tonight."

"Except," she said, lifting her head, "the letter to Caltran, about the fever ..."

"Tomorrow." He tightened his grip on her hand and felt an answering pressure from her fingers. She smiled and sighed, and her shoulders relaxed slightly.

"You worry about me too much," she said, and he said, "Of course I do," and leaned over toward the single candle that was standing beside them on its golden filigree stand.

As he pursed his lips to blow, running footsteps and raised voices filled the staircase beyond the tower door. Galha rose more quickly than he did; he had barely taken his place behind her when the door crashed open.

"What has possessed you," the Queen began, "to enter here without—"

"My Queen," one of the four guards said, his voice cracking, "please forgive us—but the palace is under attack. Shandhren here has seen them, outside the kitchen and then too as he was running to find you ..."

"Quiet," Galha snapped. For a moment the only sound in the chamber was the breathing of another of the guards. He was gasping, doubled over but looking at Galha. There was a smear of blood across his forehead. "Now," Galha continued, "tell me, Shandhren: what was it you saw?"

"Men," the gasping one managed to say. "Strangers. Lizard-men. And ours too. They killed my companions—and there were more of them. In some of the hallways leading here. I took the Guardspassage to avoid them."

"Impossible," the Queen said. "How did they get in? And from where?"

"My Queen," the guard who had spoken first said, his voice lower now but no less urgent, "you must summon all—"

"I *must?*" she repeated. She took a step toward him and he fell back, nodding, swallowing convulsively. "If you are so certain about what—"

The Queensbell's first reverberation drowned out her words. As it tolled again, she turned to Malhan. The eddying light made shadows of her eyes and her parted lips. The third time the bell sounded, she walked to the staircase that led up to her bedchamber. Her bow was leaning against the steps.

"I should not have doubted you," she said to the guards in between the clangings. She let her long sleeping robe fall to the floor and slung her bow over the thin knee-length shift beneath. Even now, as the bell called danger and death, the guards gaped at her. "They will be coming for me. You will all move back through the outer corridors, seeing if you can gather reinforcements or find pockets of guards who still live. If there are too many attackers, take the Guardspassage out of the palace and await me in the marketplace. They will have to emerge sometime. We will be waiting when they do."

"And you?" The Queensguards turned to Malhan with the surprise people always showed when he spoke in the Queen's presence. "Where will you go?"

She was walking up the stairway, adjusting her quiver across her back. "We," she replied, not looking at him, "will go to find our daughter."

He followed her up. The Queenstower was joined to Ladhra's by an arched, enclosed walkway. The door to Ladhra's tower opened only from the passage, and only Galha had the key. The Princess had protested this arrangement years ago, railing about the lack of privacy and fairness and autonomy inherent in the walkway and the door she herself could never open. The Queen had assured her that, if it was used at all, it would be for the most pressing of matters. And she had never used it—not even as a young mother, sleeping apart from her child for the first time, or, later, when she knew Ladhra was sick or miserable. It had been enough to know that the walkway was there.

She strode out onto the stones now as if she had done this many times before. Malhan stepped after her. The wind was strong this far above the ground, and it gusted through the wide embrasures on either side of them, snarling their hair and their breath. At the place where the walkway's curve was highest, the Queen paused. She peered through one of the openings, tilting her head into the wind. Malhan joined her. For a moment they looked together at the rivers of flame that were the great trees of the Queenswood. Then they continued on, running this time, to the door that had never been opened.

~

There was no stone under Mallesh's feet as he ran. Shells instead, and moss, flowers spattered with sea water from his body. He was slick with scales and light with air-breaths—breaths still new, damp earth still new. He was Nasran, and his people swarmed up the bank behind him, silently, pausing only to loose the weapons that would bring them home. Drylanders crumpled, silenced before they could flee or raise an alarm. His limbs coursed with power—his own and that of this place, whose song deafened him and turned his gaze to crimson. *O Nasran, I am your son and I am you; I am next and greatest …*

The noise of the waves hummed beneath his skin. The waves and the voices, rising tides that he commanded—but as he ran on, he knew that there was no ocean. A humming, yes; a deep metal sound that came again and again. In the breaks between, the voices hardened as the stone did, and Mallesh saw the palace corridor and the wide, darting eyes of his men.

He stood still, wiped sweat from his eyes and forehead with the back of his right hand. The tip of his spear was bloodied, as was the knife in his chest-wrap. He had thrown and stabbed: that much was no battle-dream. The hallway that curved to either side was empty except for torches and tall, ivy-mottled bodies: images in stone, of women with bows and bristling quivers.

"It's an alarm." Mallesh did not look at the man who had spoken. "Mallesh, they've discovered us—let's go back to meet them in the open …"

"No." Mallesh removed his knife, wiped it on his chest-wrap in two long, sweeping strokes. "We press on. We take this tower and the next one, and we find Baldhron and his men where we agreed to."

The selkesh glanced at each other. Such a tattered group, all of them thin and cracked—but Nasran's army had faced greater odds and triumphed. "Follow me," Mallesh said. "There will be no retreat."

They followed him. He went more slowly now, one shoulder almost brushing the statues. He led them to the left and up; west, he reminded himself, and north. When they reached an arched doorway at another bend, he gestured all his men to halt. "Carefully," he mouthed, then stepped around the corridor's turning.

The Queensguards were waiting for them. The ones guarding the other towers had not been; some had been bent over food or games, others had been talking. Mallesh remembered this in fractured images that came to him all at once as he saw the seven Queensguards who stood across the hallway's width, their bows raised and strung. There were four more facing the other way: eleven, when until now there had been only two.

"Now!" Mallesh cried, and sprang forward. The Queensguards did not shout. They loosed their arrows as Mallesh and his men loosed their spears. Two selkesh fell beside him. Mallesh cried out again, and again as his spear flew wide. One Queensguard went down, and then another. There were nine of them, two drawing swords as the selkesh strained closer. Nine. Mallesh threw his knife. He did not see where it landed. He saw only one last arrow, skimming from somewhere, too straight and swift to dodge. He heard another of his men scream—and then he too was screaming.

Not screaming—silent. He spun, his voice swallowed by fire. He scrabbled at his throat, felt wood; felt the fire roar as his fingers tugged and the metal in his skin tore deeper. He looked up at white stone and did not know what he was seeing until a body bent down to him and he realized he was lying on the ground. Someone said his name. He heard it; he heard everything so clearly, though his vision swam with wriggling black shapes. "Mallesh! Mallesh, they're down, but more are coming. What should ..." The man was panting, babbling. Mallesh thought, *And how do you expect me to answer you with this arrow in my throat, you snivelling fool?* There were more Queensguards approaching; he heard their hard, measured footsteps and even the clatter of their arrows. He tried to make his man understand: *Go on. Leave me. Fight the ones who are coming. Die with me if you must, but fight.* He could not. He was falling backward, away from them, his breath vanishing before it reached his chest.

Nasran, Nasran, forgive me. He was up, his arms stretched and held, his legs dragging—or so he assumed, since he could not see them beneath him. He hardly saw anything; with every jolting step the black shapes spread and thickened. Only his ears did not betray him. They brought him the whimpering of his men and the scraping of their feet, the voices that were blooming in distant corridors and the metal being drawn. *Let them take us, Nasran. Let us bleed our failure onto this singing stone*—but now he heard different voices, screaming words that were neither Queensfolk nor selkesh, and there was wind on his face. They were dragging him outside. The warning bell was very loud here—outside, in the market, where other cowards were trampling each other in their desperation. It was over, then, truly. Baldhron's planning, and his scores and scores of followers, had not helped. Nasran had not helped. Mallesh tried to twitch a hand or arm, or lift his head just a bit, but could not—and it was too late in any case: they were lifting him, bearing him slowly down into darkness and water.

It was the water that soothed the agony from his body. He felt it lapping up around his legs and waist, and it was so soft and sang so sweetly that he no longer wanted to see or struggle. When the arrow in his throat shifted again, sharply sideways, he screamed inside his head and thrust himself more deeply into the water. They had snapped the arrow shaft; the last conscious part of him knew this. Then the river rose to blunt all pain, all knowing, and he followed it away.

~

Ladhra's body is cool and supple. Leish holds her against him and uses his other arm to draw them both through the water, quite close to the surface, so that he will be able to give her air when she needs it. He recognizes the patterns of coral and rock beneath them, and he knows their singing. She hears it now as well; he feels her listening and her wonder, and he laughs up at the distant sun.

Her body was warm and stiff. The ocean's song was gone; in its place was the knell of Mallesh's new land, and a grinding sound that was very loud. Leish's eyes flickered open. Even though he yearned to dive until he became nothing in the darkness, he opened his eyes and looked past Ladhra's head at the opposite wall and the tapestry upon it. A scene of plants, he noticed, curling, burgeoning petals and stems. The plants quivered; he tried to blink them into focus but could not. Then the entire length of weaving rippled, and the grinding sound peaked and ceased, and two people emerged from behind the cloth.

Galha's eyes found him first. He saw her stillness as she looked at him. Even when she walked across to the bed, she seemed still, as if there was no breath within her. Hollow eyes and cheeks and veins; an emptiness beneath her skin, which he could almost see through. Only when she was directly above the bed did she shift her gaze to her daughter. For a breath Galha was torn, bent into a different shape—but then she saw the knife that lay at the edge of the bed, and she was still and straight again. Leish closed his eyes.

Send me back, he thought. He heard his hearth pool, with its starmoths and its river path. Perhaps he would return as one of the starmoths; for once one song was done, there was another, and who knew what its notes would be. He would draw circles in the pool and his parents would know him and be comforted. *Send me now,* he thought, and waited for the knife with a joy that was nearly silent.

A voice cried out very loudly, louder than the bell or the sudden, frantic clamour of Leish's heart. He opened his eyes just enough to see the Queen turn away from him toward the man whose name, Leish remembered, was Malhan. It was he who had spoken the word. Leish had never heard Malhan's voice, had never even seen him approach the Queen, as he did now. He wrapped his fingers around hers so that they both held the knife, and said another word, quieter and less steady than the first. She made a shuddering, dissolving sound that seemed to come from somewhere beneath her throat, and Malhan looked away from her, at Leish.

"Did you do this?" Malhan asked him, the yllosh words quick and flawless. Although he did not want them to, Leish's eyes opened very wide. Before he could find his own voice, the Queen spoke several low, clipped words that were nearly strong enough for anger. Malhan replied, slow and deliberate, and she lowered her gaze once more to her daughter.

"Did you?" Malhan said. This time Leish stirred. His muscles stretched and throbbed, and his injured webs ached, and he had to breathe away the pain before he replied.

"No," he said. He tasted old blood and swallowed, but the taste remained. His need for water was another ache, and he cringed from it, ashamed, alive.

"Who, then?" Malhan demanded, and Leish told him. "Where is he?" Leish said he did not know but that he knew where Baldhron had come from. He heard himself describing the wells and tunnels, the chambers and pools, as if he were eager to do so—which was strange, since he felt only spreading cold. The Queen had laid a hand on Ladhra's hair as Leish began speaking; as he continued, she drew it back again and lifted her eyes to his. All these words, which had waited in him during the months of his imprisonment; the words he had not spoken when she had laughed at him and had him beaten and railed at him so fiercely that Wollshenyllosh had not been able to translate quickly enough—he gave them to Galha now, one by one, each adding a bit to the numbness in his veins. He gave them to her over the Princess's body and thought that the knife would have been an easier way.

When the words were done, Leish waited again. So much waiting, these past few months—though now, at least, he was not afraid. Not even when the Queen bent down and hissed her own words into the space between them.

"She says," came Malhan's voice from somewhere above, "that we will go together to the place you have described. She says it does not matter what we find there, for no one will ever know of it. Your people attacked this city, and you alone"—he faltered, then spoke as smoothly as he had before—"you killed the Princess. This is the story that will be told."

As Malhan's voice was fading, two Queensguards, panting and blood-spattered, ran into the chamber. They stared at the bed in silence for a moment; silence, for the great bell was no longer sounding. Leish did not know when it had stopped. Then one of them spoke, and the Queen rose and spoke as well, in short, sharp words. She pointed at Leish and the guards strode to the bed, reaching with hands and metal. One of the men jerked Leish down to the foot of the bed and up, gripped him as the other man pressed his knife against Leish's throat. He did not flinch. When the guard held the dagger up, its tip was dark and wet. Leish smiled, and the knife thrust close once more. Galha called out and the guard wiped his knife onto the cloth that wrapped Leish's thigh.

"Take us there," Malhan said, such strange yllosh words that did not bubble in the throat. "Now." Both guards were holding Leish now with hands like skeins of seastrangler. He could feel the hatred in their skin. Before they dragged him out the door, he looked back at the bed. One more glimpse of pooling blood and hair—and the Queensguards shouted and struck him so that he had to turn away from her.

He closed his eyes against the noise and light outside the tower. More guards joined them almost immediately; he heard their voices and the pounding of their feet, and he heard the hissing of their arrows. They were all running except for him. The two guards dragged him between them, calling out sometimes to their companions. He smelled smoke and burned cloth and dying. He heard the dying as well, in sounds that were selkesh or Queensfolk or unrecognizable as either.

He kept his eyes squeezed shut until the air around him changed. He coughed and gasped, trying to breathe this new, fresher air, and he opened his eyes. They were hauling him through the marketplace, which seemed empty. Only the Queen, Malhan and the two guards were with him now; the others must have remained at the palace or near it, to wait for more to kill.

The well shaft was moonlit at its top stones and black within. One of the Queensguards went down first, holding a lantern that swung and blurred into a distant point of light that looked like a starmoth. The other guard pushed Leish to the well's mouth. The numbness seemed to be spreading to his skin; he did not feel the stones or the metal hand- and footholds within, though he descended swiftly. The other guard clambered down after him, then Galha, then Malhan. They crowded close together in the water. The first guard had hung the lantern from the nail the scribes' bag of clothes usually occupied; the light glanced off skin and water and penetrated nothing.

"And now?" Leish saw the Queen turn to Malhan as she had in Ladhra's chamber when he had first spoken the yllosh tongue to Leish. Leish told them where they would swim, and how. After a moment of silence the Queen did speak; a moment after that, they were all beneath, Leish in the lead and everyone holding on to everyone else like a line of baby water rats. Despite this line and the tug of the guard's arms on his thighs, Leish drew them quickly through the water. *I could shake myself free,* he thought. *I could be out beneath the city walls before they even surfaced again—if they surfaced.* His body did not seem to acknowledge this thought; it propelled him. And in any case, Baldhron would be here somewhere. Baldhron, who had promised glory to the selkesh; who had thrust Ladhra's body into a bloody knot on her bed.

Everyone except Leish and Galha coughed after their heads emerged into the air of the tunnel. She was up on the ledge before any of them. She cried out to them and they scrambled to join her. She walked beside Leish, her strides so long that he had to force his own limbs to match her pace. Once or twice he slowed, and each time felt the prick of a knife against the small of his back or his neck, where the life-vein pulsed. He led them through the torchlit tunnels that flashed with cut glass. They turned after him, crowded around him, until he had to look down into the water to keep his dizziness from upending him.

He saw selkesh, ten, twenty, more, all swimming far enough below the surface that no one would know they were there; no one except Leish, who recognized the silent shadows speeding south, east, away to where the river foamed free in the desert. He did not falter, and he looked up again almost immediately: no clues, no reason for them to lean out over the water. The knife nicked at his skin, and his people surged homeward below him, and he rejoiced even as he despaired, for this, at last, was punishment.

He slowed when he saw the glow of the scribes' pool ahead. "There," he mouthed over his shoulder at Malhan. Galha pulled an arrow from her quiver. They watched her, and she stood still, lifting her shoulders, placing her back so that she seemed as tall as a selkesh. Then a voice called from the chamber, and another answered it, and Queen Galha moved forward.

~

"Faster!" Baldhron shrieked. "Faster, you fool."

Pentaran's hands shook as he reached up to snatch another bag from its hook. He had been shaking since he had seen the child, one of his students, who had gazed up at him with eyes as filmed with shock and horror as Pentaran's probably had been. The child had run, and Pentaran had watched him vanish into the fire-limned darkness of the Queenswood. Only after the boy had disappeared did Pentaran follow. He had called the boy's name among the whistling, snapping trees, though he had not expected an answer. Pentaran's blade was bloody, as were his clothes. He had killed Queensfolk as they slept—the boy had known this. But still Pentaran called as he reeled like a drunkard over moss that was brittle now instead of soft.

He had stopped when a large, straight branch blazed down to land at his feet. He seemed to start awake. He looked down at his sword and his skin, looked up at the flames that seemed to beat against the moon. And he ran again—out of the Queenswood, away from the palace, down among the houses of the city, which still stood quiet and dark.

His feet had carried him toward the great southern gate. Beyond it lay sand and rock and freedom—space in which to dissolve and forget. But as he ran, he remembered that this gate would be guarded by scribes and selkesh, all of them facing into the city awaiting the great battle that would soon spill from the palace. Pentaran had come to a sudden stumbling halt. Not the desert—not yet. The wells instead, one last time. He would travel below the city wall, and perhaps he would meet up with someone else who was fleeing the terrible thing that had been done this night. He had found a well in a wide, empty square. As he had pulled himself up and in, he had heard the first echoing notes of the Queensbell. For a time he heard it beneath as well, as he worked his way through the tunnels with his body pressed against the wall. There was nothing but blackness here. After who knew how long, he had seen a light ahead: the main tunnel, a stretch he knew so well after all these years of sneaking and spying and feeling important. He had slithered over the wet ledge—past the place where he had stood guard so many times—and into the library chamber, thinking, *Almost there—almost away.*

Baldhron had turned to him immediately, even though Pentaran had tried to be very quiet. "Come here!" Baldhron had cried in a high, wavering voice. Pentaran had taken a step back—just a tiny one, but Baldhron had leapt to his feet with a dagger in his hand, which was steady. Pentaran realized that his own sword was gone and had no memory of where he had dropped it, or why. "I'd kill you, Pentaran, and be happy to do it. But I need you—I'm gathering up the most vital of our accounts, especially the oldest and the most recent. The tablets may survive a bit of water—the parchment I'm not so certain about, but we need to try. Come here *now* and help me."

Pentaran had been tearing open bags since then, sifting desperately through scrolls he could hardly read, drawing out ones he hoped would please Baldhron, who was obviously mad, and still gripping his dagger. Mad! This man whom Pentaran had loved since Baldhron had found him begging, starving, and brought him here, fed him with bread and words … He would try to be quick, speak a few calm and calming words that would convince Baldhron of the need to leave this place. But Pentaran's fingers were clumsy and slow, and he had not been able to speak a word since he had thrown open the door to that first Queensfolk house.

"Faster, you fool!" screeched Baldhron, and Pentaran sobbed again, and wondered why he could make this sound but not words. When he paused to draw a shaking breath, he heard another sound, a muffled slapping: wet feet on stone.

Baldhron stood and turned his head to the entrance. He listened only briefly before he thrust his dagger into his belt and tied two sacks beside it. He dove, so gracefully that Pentaran felt his own body fuse with the ledge. *I can't,* he thought. He was so clumsy in water, so slow as he flailed and strained even the short distance from well to tunnel. *Get up! Follow him!* But Baldhron was the river; Pentaran was only clay.

"Pentaran!" A woman's voice, very deep, pulsing with strength and fury that only seemed to increase as the vaulted walls sent the name back in echo. Pentaran's leaden limbs were air now. He twisted around, his nerveless arms trailing scrolls. He watched them fall and bob, light as leaves. One was so close to him that he could see the lines a writing stick had made, rows and rows of them, all blurring and bleeding. He looked down at the single scroll he had managed to hold on to and saw its letters, shaped by urgency and a kind of love.

"Pentaran." Her voice was not as loud or as low as it had been. "Where is he?"

He thought of the parchment made empty, and the desert that opened against the sky so far away. He rose, pressing the scroll against his chest, and looked at her.

"He's gone," he said clearly and quickly. "You won't find him, Galha. You'll never find everyone who—" The arrows sang his ringing voice to silence.

Book Three

TWENTY-EIGHT

The Queen, Galha, daughter of Pradnadhen, sends this message to her servants in Fane, both as information and as command.

On the night of the first full moon after the month of late rains, Luhr, greatest city in the Queensrealm, was attacked by Raiders from the sea. They numbered in the thousands, all fierce and well armed, and oblivious to the ways of civilized folk. The army massed within the jungle and beset Luhr in the depths of night, when all its residents were abed. The Sea Raiders overpowered the guards at the gates and swept up into the city, and before an alarm could be raised, they had forced their way into the very palace. It must be admitted that some Queensguards were unprepared, slain while sleeping at their posts or relaxing in a manner unbecoming of the Queen's chosen caretakers. However, it must also be stressed that this city and indeed this land have ever been blessed by peace, and the Queen forgives those who were taken unawares, for they were victims only of the comfort of her rule.

As the warning bell tolled, Queensguards turned the Raiders back and pressed them out again into the desert. The city dwellers were waking now, some of them walking into the streets, but most hiding themselves and their families in the darkness of their homes. The ones who did emerge were the first to hear of the terrible tragedy that had unfolded before the gates. The Princess Ladhra, beloved only daughter of the Queen, had been one of the first to join the fight against the attackers. She rode out to Luhr's gates and awaited the ones who were fleeing—and she cut them down with sword and bow. As the moon began its descent, the stream of Raiders abated. The Princess looked down and saw one who yet lived. She urged her horse to his side and bent to see him better—and in this moment the Raider sprang from the ground, hale and strong, and stabbed her again and again with the dagger he had held concealed beneath his body.

There were other Queensfolk at the gates by this time. They saw the Princess Ladhra's murder and subdued her killer, and they carried both back into the city. The common folk heard the tidings of her death and grieved for the woman who would have been their next ruler. Queen Galha, who had remained to defend the palace and had been unaware of her daughter's actions, looked on Ladhra with dignified sorrow and righteous fury. The Sea Raider begged for his life and told the Queen much: his name—Leish—and that of his land, and where it lay. She contained her fury and spared him, knowing that he would be of use to her. Scores of other Sea Raiders died at her hand, yet she knew that still others had fled early into the desert and escaped punishment. And so Queen Galha swore vengeance upon Leish and all the people of Nasranesh, across the Eastern Sea.

The fastest route to the Eastern Sea is overland to the Sarhenna River and thence by boat to Fane; this is the way the Queen will take in pursuit of the Sea Raiders. She has written to her servants in all the port towns of the realm and commanded them to send any boats and ships that may be fit for an ocean voyage. She writes to Fane as well, and with greater urgency. Your ships too will be required, and your harbour will be the gathering place for the fleet that will sail with the Queen at its head. She will make haste to Fane, and you must be ready to greet her and assist her through the weeks of preparation that will follow. Make ready for battle, in the name of Queen Galha, and in the name of Ladhra, who has died for this land that is strong and unbroken.

Lanara set the scroll down. It was so long that only its ends curled inward; the rest lay flat on the table. Malhan's words were stark and far too easy to read, even by accident, when her eyes swept over them and up to the face of the Queensguard who was standing beside her. She looked at him as the Queensbell tolled on and on, jarring as a fist against her ribs.

"Wine," the guard said to someone behind him. "Quickly. Better make it unwatered."

"Lanara," Nellyn said, and she turned to him. There they all were: Nellyn and Aldron and Alea. Lanara was surprised that they were still sitting on the cushioned bench where they had been before she unrolled the scroll with the Queen's seal upon it. Everything seemed the same: her friends, with their worn travelling clothes and wind-chapped skin; this room, with its tapestries and painted woodwork, and the thick glass window overlooking the wharf and water. Even her body felt the same: bruised and weary from the wagon that had jolted them down into the streets of Fane, where people had been running and calling news she had refused to believe—until she walked into this room and saw the faces of the Queensguards who were waiting for her.

She tried to smile at Nellyn. It was what she would have done if everything had not changed. "It's true," she said, "what we heard on our way here, about the attack, and Ladhra"—and then she laid her head against the scroll and waited for understanding, or a darkness that would enfold her like sleep.

~

Lanara seemed a bit better after the wine. Nellyn held the cup for her at first, but after a few swallows she took it from him, and her hand was steady. He glanced down at the scroll and saw that some of its words were smudged. Perhaps she had cried after all, though he saw no trace of tears on her cheeks or in her eyes. Perhaps it had only been her skin or clothing, lying on the letters and blurring them when she moved.

The short, plump Queensguard asked her if she and her friends would like to spend the night here, in this house that was the Queen's place in Fane. Lanara replied, "No, though I thank you for your kindness. Queen Galha sent me here to assume command of the signal tower, and I intend to do so immediately."

"Ah," the guard began, "yes, a commendable intention, but the cliff path, you see, is hardly—"

"Please," Lanara interrupted, and Nellyn was relieved to hear a familiar strength in her voice, "have someone lead us there now. We are seasoned travellers and will be able to climb the path." But then they all rose, and Lanara swayed and sat again, and although he thought, *Maybe just the wine,* Nellyn's relief vanished.

He held her around the waist as they went down the stairs. When they stepped outside, she lifted his arm away and smiled at him, too brightly. *But everything here is too bright,* he thought, *and I am tired, not seeing as I usually do*. He looked up at the house, which was very tall and broad.

Behind it was a courtyard and a stable, where they had left horse and wagon. This house was the only one on the wharf made of stone. There were shapes in the stone, edged and curved, and painted in green and blue. The other houses were wooden, their planks scarlet or yellow or orange. The doors were painted as well, and seemed brighter than the houses themselves. Nellyn thought he knew why the paint and roof tiles were so vivid: if they had not been, Fane's buildings would have been swallowed by the glare of the sea and sky. Lanara had turned to him when their wagon had come to the cliff road and they had first glimpsed the ocean. She had smiled at his expression, lifted his hand to her lips, kissed him on each knuckle. "The end of the river," she had said. He had remembered his small, bright river, and the silver-leafed trees on the other side, and his certainty that this river was all, here by the red clay huts. He had remembered the water of his town with a love that was like pain, on the icy road above the sea—for he had been wrong. All the shonyn were wrong. Here was water so vast and changing and terrible that any shonyn looking on it would feel the world's circle break. Nellyn had looked and trembled, and drawn Lanara in against him. "Thank you," he had whispered. The wool of her cap had scratched his lips.

He tried to look at the sea again now, as he followed her along the wharf, but the crowd around them was thick, and beyond the crowd were the boats, creaking at the docks. Lanara and the Queensguard walked together, Nellyn behind, and Aldron and Alea behind him; there was no room for more than two to walk abreast. People milled and called to one another. Some reached out to Lanara and the Queensguard, whose blue-and-green clothing marked them as Queensfolk. "The Queen—is she near?" Nellyn heard, and "Tell us of the Princess!" Someone grasped Nellyn's cloak and he wrenched it away without turning back.

The crowd thinned as they approached the southern harbour arm. Nellyn took a deep, steadying breath when he stepped onto the cliff path. There was no one here, and the noise from the wharf seemed muted, the air more open and fresh. The path was just a track, really, like the ones he and Lanara had seen on mountainsides, beaten down by goats and other climbing animals. He kept his right hand on the cliff wall and did not look at the sea; he had discovered in Luhr that he did not like being far above the ground. *And yet,* he thought as he squinted at the frozen mud at his feet, *this signal tower is on a cliff.* He swallowed. In order to distract himself from how steeply the track was climbing, he stared at Lanara. She was walking quickly and confidently, without looking back—and this worried him as her too-cheery smile had. She knew his fear and usually tried to calm him (in the mountains she had insisted on taking a longer, lower way when he had balked at the height of the quicker path). She did not turn to him now, or slow her pace so that he would be able to catch up. *She is alone in her mind,* he thought, *somewhere else—not here.*

"Nellyn," Alea said, and he felt her hand on his stooped back. "Are you all right?"

He straightened and smiled over his shoulder at her. "Yes. Afraid, but all right." He saw that she was leaning heavily against the rock, and his fear for himself ebbed. "And you? How is the baby? Are you tired?"

"The baby is poking me, probably because I've stopped walking. And I'm not too tired—though I am looking forward to sitting down whenever we reach this signal tower of yours."

"So let's reach it," Aldron said, resting his chin on Alea's shoulder, "before it's time for the baby to be *born*. Go! Go!"

The path ended abruptly. Nellyn lost sight of Lanara around yet another jutting corner of rock. He edged his way around it as smoothly as he could, and suddenly there was no path before him—a broad, flat place instead, with the signal tower rising up from it like a stone tree. Aldron gave a long, high whistle between his teeth when he stepped onto the cliff ledge. Alea squatted with both hands on her belly and looked up, and up.

The tower was square at its base and circular as it rose, and there was a dome of glass at the top. Sunlight flashed from the dome so intensely that Nellyn had to look away from it. Small windows dotted the stone, which was painted in red and gold bands splotched with the grey-green of some sort of plant. The door was wooden, as were the structures that jutted from the tower's base: a shack with no windows; higher up, a casement hung with brown cloth. Each window was concealed by shutters.

"Better not venture out there," Aldron commented to Nellyn, pointing at two wooden balconies that ran all the way around the tower near the top. "A dizzy spell might pitch you into the sea." Nellyn nodded and looked past Aldron. He saw only sky where the ledge fell away. He tried to breathe. *"The river is within you. Seek it out when you are not calm." There is no river,* he thought. *The shonyn are wrong. Though it does not matter, since I am no longer shonyn …*

"Nellyn!" He swung his head around and focused slowly on Lanara. She was standing at the door, which was now open. "Come," she said, and held out her hand. A familiar, comforting gesture—but when he reached her, her eyes leapt away from his and her fingers barely touched him before she drew them away again.

It was very dark inside the tower despite the candles that burned on shelves and countertops. There was a pungent odour in the air; Nellyn put a hand over his nose and mouth.

"That'll be the tallow you smell," said a female voice quite close to him. "Years and years of tallow, for the signal light and for these rooms down below. You'll soon hardly notice it."

His vision was sharpening. He saw the woman, who was large and round and had light hair that might have been blonde or white. An old man stood behind her, leaning on a piece of wood as tall as his waist. He took a shambling step toward them and Nellyn saw that he was shonyn-height—short for a Queensman—and slight as a wading bird. His tunic was blue and green, and his sleeves and leggings were stitched with ribbons of the same colour—though they were faded, threadbare clothes, and larger than he was.

"I am Drelha," said the woman. "And this is my father, Peltanan, tender of Fane's signal tower since he was a young man in the service of Queen Galha's blessed grandmother. Me, I was born here," she continued, leading them toward a staircase that spiralled up from the tower's centre. "Never imagined I'd be leaving, either, and certainly not at my age and to wed a townsman. But that I am, and may every spinster rejoice and take hope from it. Come, Father, get behind them and we'll take them up and show them what's to do. His body's slower now, you see, and it's mostly me that does the hard work, but his mind's as quick as ever. Isn't that right, Father?" Nellyn heard a grunt from the back of the line. "Now, then—that below was the kitchen—and this level's for sleeping …"

Drelha talked on and on. Nellyn stopped attempting to follow her words. He looked mostly at Lanara, though he did try once or twice to see what Drelha was pointing to. The two sleeping levels were as dim as the kitchen had been. He caught glimpses of low beds, tables, a gleaming pitcher and basin set on a chest beneath a shuttered window. They were bare spaces, though, other than the few pieces of furniture; the barest he had seen since leaving his own hut, with its curtain and pallet.

"Father, you'll want to wait for us here. His eyes are tender now, not suited any more to the upper floors." In two steps they were in a circular chamber flooded with sunlight. Nellyn's eyes watered and he closed them, rubbed at them with his fingertips until they cleared. "This here's a room that has to be bright. It's where we watch the harbour and the sea—where I watch, since Father's not up to staring at the water all day, and his hand shakes when he tries to write. See, here's the desk and the daily log. Fresh parchment here, writing sticks. The old logs are on these shelves, bound at the end of every year. I'd say there'd be generations of books here, going back to a time when this tower was just new—all the records of storms, wrecks, sightings of new ships, or weeks and weeks of calm sometimes. You even have to write about the calm days, though I couldn't say why."

They were all standing at the wide, curved window with its countless squares of glass. Thick, bubbled glass, but Nellyn could see unending water below, cliffs to his left, the icemounts that turned and sang in the harbour and just beyond, where it widened into sea. He touched the glass and the cold metal that held the glass together, very lightly, knowing that it would be solid and strong, but still afraid.

"So then, Lanalla—or is it …? Yes, yes—Lanara, of course—my Gelartan's always chiding me for forgetting names. The price of a lifetime of isolation, I tell him. He's lucky to have found me at all, up here … Lanara, yes—this, as my father will tell you, is the most important place in the signal tower excepting the lightroom itself. Two Queens have visited us here—even our revered Galha, may the First comfort her now—and each one has bade us take great care with the daily logs. You must record with precision and fine script—but you're of Queensfolk stock, of course, you'll know about writing …"

Lanara turned away from the window. Nellyn turned as well and watched her walk toward the staircase. Long, firm strides—but then she stopped, and Nellyn ran to her and caught her as she fell.

Alea's body hurt. Not just in the places she would have expected to pain, carrying a baby, but in all places—every muscle, every bit of skin, and her innards too. She walked very slowly up the tower's stairs, sometimes leaning on the handrail or lowering her head to its cool metal. *It's only winter,* she thought again, as she had so many times since coming to Fane. *And the baby won't come till the summer*. She paused and arched her back. This felt wonderful for the space of three heartbeats. *It's because I'm here, enclosed by walls. And even when I do go out, I'm bound by the sea and that horrid path. I remember my mother, only days away from birthing Alnanna, dancing by our fire as if she weighed nothing more than a spark. And the next day she rode ...* Alea shook the images away, knowing they would return. These memories were as comforting and relentless as the sea water that rose and fell against the cliff.

She climbed through her and Aldron's sleeping floor toward Nellyn and Lanara's. In the month since Drelha and her father had departed, these spaces in particular had changed. The shutters were always open during the day; light shone from the polished wood of floors and chairs and tables. Despite this brightness, Alea found her room drab. The screen that hid their sleeping mat from the staircase was brown, as was the carpet. "A very sensible colour," Aldron had said when they had examined their room for the first time in daylight. But she longed for other colours—scarlet, green, orange—and knew that these were Alilan colours and thus unacceptable in their new home. They were by the sea now, and there should be no attempt to call back the hues and textures of the lake country or the plain or the desert, the painted wagons and the blankets by the fires.

Aldron was aware of her yearning. He had brought gifts back with him on his last three trips into town: light blue, pink and yellow glass vases. He had set them on the table, the windowsill, the floor, trying to coax as much light from them as possible. She did love these things (and him for his eagerness to cheer her), but she did not touch them. They were beautiful, delicate, like tiny icemounts trembling indoors.

She stepped quietly into Nellyn and Lanara's chamber. Nellyn tended the signal light from midnight until after dawn; he sometimes slept until midday. She glanced at the sleeping screen—cream-coloured linen—but could see nothing behind it. This room was more cluttered than hers: there were several low tables and chairs, two carpets (both green), a bookcase that had somehow been made to match the contour of the wall. The old man had kept little wooden boats here. Now that these were gone, the shelves were mostly empty. Lanara had set some books on the section of shelf furthest away from the bed—just a few, in a short, neat row. Sitting cushions were strewn about. *As if,* Alea thought, *we may suddenly be flooded with visitors.* The cushions at least were brightly coloured, though they had been so dirty at first that they had all looked grey. The previous signal tower keepers, it seemed, had received few visitors.

The writing room was, as usual, so dazzlingly sunny that Alea had to stand still and wait for her eyes to adjust. As she waited, she heard a familiar sound from above: Lanara in the lightroom, scraping tallow drippings from the floor. "Some other signal tower keepers are starting to burn oil," Drelha had told them. "Oil! Candles are good enough for us and always have been. We've had many a fisherman thank us for our light on foggy days or nights." The level above the writing room was so low-ceilinged that adults had to stoop; it was stacked with candles, as was the shed beside the tower. And Lanara spent hours every morning, after she had extinguished the flames and trimmed the wicks, kneeling on the floor with a metal tool, jabbing at the tallow that had congealed upon the wood during the long hours of the night watch.

Alea walked to the window. She rolled her forehead back and forth over the rippled glass until the sweat was gone. She smoothed the damp hair away from her temples, tucked it behind her ears.

"Alea," Nellyn said from behind her, "you must not climb all these stairs. I keep telling you … Here, sit"—and she turned and let him guide her to the stool.

"It makes no sense," she said, propping her elbow on the desk and placing her hot cheek on her fist. "I'm only five months gone with child. I was strong before this …"

Nellyn sat down on the edge of the desk. He was silent. He so often was, when others would have filled the air with words. She looked down at the parchment that lay between them. "Will you read it to me?" she said. "What you and Lanara wrote about last night."

Nellyn held the sheet up and squinted at it. "My writing is terrible, even though I have been practising. I have asked her to help me, but she is too … tired." Another silence pooled between them. Lanara's scraping was very loud. "My entry is short," he continued. "It says: 'Dawn. Light fog, water calm.' That is all."

"And Lanara's entry?"

Nellyn smiled a bit as he followed the marks Lanara had made. "Longer than mine, of course—though she never writes as much now as she would have … before. She wrote: 'Midnight. Winds gentle from the north and east.'"

Alea glanced at the balcony outside the window. Long branches of wood were attached to the railing, and a collection of smaller wooden pieces extended from them. Two of these, shaped like flowers, were spinning very gently. The rest were still.

"'Water ruffled, but few waves. Half-moon risen. Icemounts in harbour quite bright. Some activity on two small boats just arrived from north. Queenshouse windows lit.'"

The scraping stopped just after his voice did. Nellyn and Alea looked up, then at each other. "Will she come down?" Alea asked.

"No," he replied. Both of them were nearly whispering. "She will polish the mirror and the glass pieces. And the windows too, though she may have already done that."

"I came up to tell you both that the midday meal is nearly ready," Alea said. "Do you think she'll eat with us today?"

He set the parchment down on the desk exactly where it had been before. "No," he said, and turned his head so that Alea could not see his face.

"I don't understand her, Nellyn," she said, her words faster, louder, because she had not expected to speak them. "Her pain, yes—of course I understand that. But we Al … the Alilan are loud about their grief. They drink and dance and weep together, for grieving must never be solitary. Lanara is too alone."

He looked back at her. She had learned to read his face, which had at first been so strange to her. The slight narrowing of his eyes, the single line that creased the dark blue skin of his forehead: these were signs of a difficult emotion for him. "For the shonyn," he said, each word as carefully placed as ever, "there is no grieving. Death, as you and Lanara call it, cannot change their days or nights. Dead shonyn are rowed to the lynanyn trees and covered with earth, there among the roots. So these shonyn continue to live, as always."

"And the ones who row them across? The ones left behind? They aren't sad at all?"

He lifted his hands, spread his fingers apart. "Perhaps, though in a different way from the one you know. I …" His fingers curled, dug against his palms. "I cannot describe these things now. I am outside them."

Alea nodded. She looked out at the sea and drew her hands in light circles over the places where her baby moved, beneath.

~

"Aldron's down in the town again," Alea said as they returned to the kitchen. Nellyn held out his hand once or twice when she seemed to be tiring, but she smiled at him and shook her head. "He's looking for a stonemason who'll supply us with some flat stones for the cliff path. He claims he'll lay them himself. Lanara's pay is good enough, he says, and the path really is awful … though with a better one I may never see him again—he'll be off to Fane every day."

Nellyn half turned to see if her expression was light-hearted or melancholy, but then they reached the bottom step and saw Aldron bending over the brick oven. He straightened when he heard them, and grinned as he tossed a chunk of bread from hand to hand. "Apologies, my sweet," he said to Alea, who had made a low sound in her throat. "I know how you hate me to pick at your bread before it's done, but it's utterly irresistible." He grasped her hand and pulled her in to him. She laughed when he popped a piece of the bread into her mouth. "Better every time," he mumbled around his own mouthful. "I say again: this settled living will make a fine cook of you."

Nellyn saw Alea's eyes shift. She walked over to the fireplace and leaned against its stone rim, stirring the soup that hung in a pot above the flames. Aldron rolled his eyes at Nellyn; this was something he often did, which Nellyn did not comprehend at all. "I brought you back a gift," Aldron said, coming up behind her. He slid one hand over her belly. The other, behind his back, held a glass vase, the fourth he had given her this month.

"Violet," she said after he had presented it to her. "It's beautiful."

"I thought," he said, taking it from her, "that we could put it here, on the windowsill beside the door. It's set in the wooden casement, you see, so the light will be even stronger, especially in the morning ..."

They all stared at the vase for a moment. *It's like frozen water,* Nellyn thought. Its edges swam and blurred in the sunlight on the sill.

"How do you pay for these?" Alea asked. She did not sound angry, but Aldron cleared his throat and took a step away from her. "Not with Lanara's Queenspay, I'm sure," she went on. "And what do we have to trade for such fine things? Aldron. Look at me and answer."

Even Nellyn could hear her anger now—but Aldron faced her when he said, "I didn't mean to, the first time—but there was a child crying in a doorway. Such a child, Alea: small and dirty, hardly any flesh on her. So I Told her something—a trifle—just a little rainbow in the air that coloured her clothes for a moment. But someone who was passing saw and offered me coins if I'd make a picture for his wife too. She was sad, he said—this news about the Princess—so ..."

"So." The word was heavy—lynanyn falling from a branch into the river. "How many times? And for how long will they be trifles?" She crossed from the fireplace to the window and laid her head against the wall. "How can you continue to make a mockery of this kind of Telling? You know how careful I've been not to Tell at all, ever, though this causes me great pain. Swear to me, Aldron, promise me that you'll never try to change anything with your other ... gift."

Nellyn stood very still. He understood little of this exchange, just Alea's fear and anger, and Aldron's discomfort. Aldron angled his head to the side and tucked his chin against his collarbone. Nellyn thought, *He must truly be ashamed*—but then he saw Aldron's lips part and heard something, only a whisper, like wind between stones. Alea must have heard it as well, for she lifted her head and turned it to look at the vase beside her.

Nellyn blinked. There was a flower in the vase, slender, with dark purple petals that clung tightly together—the same kind as the one Aldron had given her in the inn, so long ago. A tall flower, fresh-cut—*from where? the frozen moss, or a hollow in the snow?—or perhaps Aldron got it in town and put it in the vase quickly when I was not looking?*—but Nellyn knew this could not be true, and he let out a long, shuddering breath.

"I swear it," Aldron said quietly as Alea went to him. She wrapped her arms around his neck; her linked hands were in his hair. "Except for this one, small use," he said, and she laughed against his shoulder, though Nellyn saw that she was also crying. "Except for this, I swear it."

I must leave, Nellyn thought. He looked at the flower and found that his feet would not move. His heart was drumming strangely, too quickly but with long spaces between beats. It was so loud that at first he did not hear the bell, and when he did, he thought the ringing must be within him, as his noisy heartbeat was. But Aldron and Alea raised their heads, and a moment later Lanara came to a slipping, stumbling halt on the stairs above them.

"The bridgetower bell," she gasped. "And there are banners—blue and green—and Queensfolk on the wharf." Her eyes found Nellyn's and she smiled, though he could not. "The Queen is coming. The Queen is here."

TWENTY-NINE

On Queenswrit Eve, Luhr's marketplace was cleared of wagons and stages and sleeping mats so that there would be room for all the people. They would gather throughout the day, until every corner of the marketplace and many of the surrounding streets were filled. The crowd would sing and cook food on small braziers and wait for dusk, when the Queen would step onto the balcony of the Scribeslibrary, in which all the records of the realm were kept. Her people would call out to her then, raising their arms, straining for a clearer view. Lanara remembered the Queenswrit Eves she'd spent as a child, hemmed in by legs until Creont lifted her to his shoulders. She had looked down at the crush, and blinked at the noise, and thought that there could never, ever be more people than this gather to see the Queen.

Lanara knew she had been wrong, on the day Queen Galha's ship sailed down to the mouth of the Sarhenna River. The citizens of Fane flooded every street, even ones with no view of water. They lined the river and the wharf, every one of the six docks and each of the boats in the harbour. They climbed up to perch on roofs, so that the gleaming red tiles were nearly invisible. They stood on balconies and leaned out of windows. Some even clambered from boats onto icemounts, where they huddled together beneath blankets. So many people, the most Lanara had ever seen in one place—and all were silent as the ship came slowly down among them.

"A little higher," she whispered to Aldron, who grunted and stood taller. She teetered a bit, clamped her legs under his armpits. It had taken a long time to push their way this close to the river, but close as they were, she had not been able to see anything except people and the bridgetower that rose beside them. Aldron had muttered, "I hope our dear ones won't be able to see us from the tower. Up you get, now. That's right, woman: up!"

She could see the river now, and the bridge, which had split into two halves. Each half was being hauled up by invisible chains and wheels within the bridgetowers on either side of the river. The metal of the chains clanked and occasionally screamed into the silence, which Lanara thought she could almost see. Seabirds called from the sky above the harbour, and the icemounts sang and groaned. Water lapped against creaking timber. All this was faint and small, almost unnoticed; it was oar strokes that everyone heard most clearly, and the heavy flap of sails.

Queen Galha stood alone at the ship's prow. Lanara saw the red ribbons first, vivid as blood or blossoms against the Queen's dark hair. Some of the ribbons were long, and fluttered beside and behind her. The ship surged closer and Lanara saw Galha's face: the sharp, firm edge of her jaw, the steady shine of her eyes. The closed line of her mouth. Lanara did not look away from the Queen's face until the ship drew level with the bridgetower and its deck became visible. Malhan was there, standing below and behind Galha, gazing up at her. Lanara waited for him to turn and scrutinize the crowd, the sailors who were heaving the Queensship anchor up and over the side, the party of Queensguards who were lining up to grasp the end of the gangplank—but he did not, he looked only at the Queen. Lanara glanced from Galha to Malhan and saw that everything had changed for them as well. Of course this was so—how could it not be?—but she shivered.

"Look," a man murmured. Others were murmuring too, and pointing. "The Raider that killed the Princess—may the First rot him and all his kind ..." Lanara turned away from Malhan and the Queen and saw the other man—or perhaps he was half a man, for his flesh looked thick and strangely coloured, and his hands, lashed together to the wood of the foremast, were wrong somehow, as if they had been plucked from a beast and attached to the ends of these arms. Strips of filthy cloth hung from his body; his head lolled, and long, snarled hair hid his face. Someone in the crowd cried out, and a rock flew and landed on the deck at the prisoner's feet, which were also tied to the mast. Lanara wanted to laugh. Such a feeble, helpless attempt. Even a hundred arrows in his chest would be as worthless an expression of hatred and grief. She watched him as the anchor sank and the mooring rope pulled taut. She willed him to lift his head and see her; she felt sick with the desire for him to do this.

The thud of the gangplank meeting the stone beneath the bridgetower made Lanara flinch. She saw the Queen take Malhan's raised hand and step down onto the deck, saw them turn together to the side of the ship. "Aldron!" Lanara hissed. "Help me down—I must get to her."

He tugged at her hand when she was beside him again, already pushing her way into the crowd. "You'll never make it there," he said, but she felt him follow her anyway, through knots of bodies and growled curses.

She was nearly at the river's edge: one more row of people. She jabbed her elbow into someone's back. She heard an oath, saw an opening, thrust her face between two sets of shoulders. The Queen and Malhan were at the end of the slender bridge that joined their ship to the shore. So close: Lanara could see the whorls of stitching on Galha's cloak and boots, and the darkened tips of Malhan's fingers, stained by decades of clutched writing sticks and words smudging on parchment.

"My Queen!" Lanara cried into the silence, and voices rose around her, scolding, quelling.

Galha turned. "Step aside!" she called. Lanara heard her, though she did not see her; the men in front of her had forced her back against Aldron's chest.

"You heard the Queen," Aldron said in a rough, low voice. The men shifted, glanced at each other.

"Step aside," Galha said again, "and let her come to me."

There was a path before Lanara now. No people, nothing in her vision except for the Queen. Lanara walked faster, faster, and was nearly running when she reached her.

Galha's skin was yellow, older. Her eyes were wide and burning-dry and webbed with crimson veins. Her voice at least was almost the same. "Nara," she said, and held out her arms, and rocked them both in the sunlight by the Eastern Sea.

~

"Malhan chides me for not sleeping." The Queen turned from the window, but only a bit; she still stood with the harbour and the sea before her. The same room where Lanara had read of Ladhra's murder, the same benches and table and wall hangings. This time, though, there were no

Queensguards present; Galha had dismissed them. "I must speak with Queenswoman Lanara alone," she had told them, and Lanara had felt a flush sweep up from her neck to her cheeks. A moment of pride among all those others that brought her only helplessness.

"I do not chide you," Malhan said quietly from his customary place by the door. Again Lanara's heart sped and lightened, for she was here alone with the Queen and her consort-scribe, permitted to see and hear them as no one else was. No one, now that Ladhra was gone. "I simply urge you to rest. You are too busy—"

Galha's laugh was hollow and grating. "Too busy! How not, when there has been so much to do? Ever since the morning after the attack. Our own forces to contact, and the prisoner to interrogate. And Ladhra's tomb fountain to choose." She did turn now. She leaned against the window and gazed into the room, though not at anyone or anything. "I could not choose one in the end, from those set aside for my family. I ordered one to be made specially, according to my own design. My daughter died a heroic and remarkable death. None of the fountains already in existence could possibly have done her justice."

The Queen's voice was high, nearly strident, but her silence was worse. Lanara cleared her throat, said, "And who … who saw her fall? Do I know them?"

Galha's eyes sharpened on Lanara. "Two of my personal guard. I'm sure you have seen them near my tower chambers. They have accompanied me here, though one of them is unwell—some sort of intestinal complaint … But we are hoping he will be able to join us on the journey. As you will, Nara. You will come with me on my own ship. How proud your mother would be! And your father."

Lanara glanced away from Galha, at the fireplace. The flames were tall and did not shudder or bend. "Yes," she said, trying not to sound uncertain, "I'm sure they would be. And I will sail with you just as proudly—more than proudly, for I long to fight beside you, to cut down the beasts who have so wounded us both …" She bit her lip as if this would steady her pulse or her voice. "How," she said after a time, slowly, raising her eyes again to Galha's, "have you kept yourself from killing him?"

The Sea Raider was still bound to the mast, nearly naked, his skin cracking in the sunlight and the fierce cold. Lanara had attempted not to look back at him as she followed the Queen to the house—but she had, and each time had felt the sickness crawl again in her stomach.

"My dear," Queen Galha said, so gently that Lanara felt for a moment like a child, cherished and comforted, "of course you do not know—how could you? There are worse things than dying, more effective ways to punish than the quickest one. This Sea Raider is mine now. He will not leave me. He will starve a bit, and his flesh will cry out for the water his kind needs for life—but I will keep him well enough to witness the destruction of his land and people." She smiled. Lanara saw deep lines in her yellow-shadowed skin, branching from her lips and eyes. "And in any case," the Queen continued in a quicker, brighter voice, "the information I have forced him to provide me with has proven invaluable. So much so that I've grown tired of translation and have employed a fishperson of his acquaintance to teach him the Queenstongue. He is sullen and quiet in my presence until I urge the words out of him. The fishperson, though, tells me he is learning quickly."

Galha's breath caught on her last word and she groped for a chair back. Malhan crossed to her, lowered her down as she waved her hand at him. "It is nothing—a brief weak spell, to be expected … and now you will chide me and try to bundle me off to a darkened room. As if I would be able to rest. When I close my eyes, I see only ugly things …"

Lanara was staring once more at the fire. It filled her vision, especially when she kept her eyes unfocused. *Alnila,* she thought, remembering the name Aldron's people gave to their goddess of fire. *Aldron* … She turned quickly to Galha. Malhan was standing beside her chair, very close but not touching her. Galha's fingertips and thumbs were together: the sign of the arrow, her reign, her strength.

"I—" Lanara began, then stopped. Perhaps it would sound foolish, this idea that had come to her so swiftly. Better to think a little more, as her father would have commanded her to do. But Malhan looked at her, and Galha lifted her head from her joined hands and said, "Yes, Nara?"—and the words came out almost as quickly as she had thought them.

"I know an Alilan man—you may remember them from Queensfolk reports—and anyway, I wrote to you about him. About his Telling power.

He can speak and make you see and hear and feel what he speaks of. It's the most wonderful thing. He Told a fountain for me once, in an inn, when he could see that I needed to be cheered, and since we came here, he's been Telling for almost anyone who asks him and has need of comfort. He's generous and careful, and his words can soothe and distract, though they don't make real things—that's not part of the gift …"

"So this is what I require?" the Queen said when Lanara's words had faded. "Soothing? Distraction?"

Lanara's fingers felt numb; she wove them together under the table. She had no answer to Galha's question, which had not been a question at all, and she could not look at her, now that she had been a fool and presumed to offer counsel.

"Dearest," Malhan said. Lanara stared at the table, which was almost as glossy as the one in the Queensstudy in the palace. "She loves you. She thinks only to help you in your grief. And her idea is a good one. Even the illusion of peace may calm you, allow you to marshal strength for what is to come."

Lanara heard the icemounts in the harbour humming and snapping. She heard voices: Fane's people were shouting now that the Queen was not among them—probably at the ship and the green-brown man who stood limp beneath the windless sails. Lanara looked up when she realized how long she had been listening to the noises outside and the silence within. The Queen was sitting still and straight, her head turned slightly toward Malhan. She stayed this way for a moment more, then stirred and nodded once.

"You are right," she said to him. "If listening to this man helps me feel stronger, do more, then it can only be a good thing. And if it does not, there will have been no harm done." She stretched out her right hand. Lanara leaned forward and took it, felt her trembling fingers wrapped in Galha's firm ones. "Thank you, Nara," the Queen said. "Now, where is this friend of yours?"

~

The patch of moss was yellow and shaped like a handprint. Nellyn was so familiar with it now that it could have been the shape of his own hand splayed against the rock. He had found this part of the tower balcony nearly a month ago, and he came to sit here every day when the air inside the tower pressed too closely against him. He reached the back of the balcony through a door in the writing floor. It faced the cliff wall, so he did not have to walk out into the spinning space above the waves. The wind always blew, always tugged at cloak and hair, but it was not so wild facing the cliff as it was over the sea. He sat on a stool he had carried out with him the second time he had come, and huddled deep into his layers of clothing and studied the moss. His thoughts, so loud within the tower stones, quieted. His breaths grew long and slow, and there was silence between them. *This moss and rock are my river now,* he thought once. *My lynanyn trees. The still, calm place that holds me but does not touch me.*

Nellyn was sitting looking at the moss the first time Queen Galha came to the signal tower. He had been there for many minutes—long enough that he should have felt the beginnings of peace. It was stormy; the wind was viciously cold and grasping even here, and the boom of the waves was so loud that he was sure they would rear up behind him and sweep him away. Icy snow stung his cheeks above the scarf he had wrapped over his mouth. The snow clung to his eyelashes and to the moss, and he caught only quick, broken glimpses that confused him.

Go inside, he told himself—but he remembered how Alea and Lanara's laughter had grated in his ears, how he had left them in the kitchen baking bread because their amusement had been as stifling as the silence of the upper floors. Lanara always seemed to be laughing these days, and reaching for his hand, kissing the back of his neck when she passed him. He woke to her every morning sliding her skin over his, taking him into her when he was still half asleep. All things he had missed and yearned for since their arrival in Fane, and yet he ached with wrongness, with fear and pain that would not dissipate. *She is happy because she will leave soon, on the ship with the Queen. She will leave and I will not, and she is happy.* He clutched his sodden cloak around him and shuddered, and sank into the cold as if it would numb the other ache in him.

The voices were difficult to hear at first, above the waves and the wind and the bell that was swinging, clanging its warning to whatever ships were sailing in the storm. Nellyn glanced toward the tower door. Perhaps

Lanara and Alea were there, or Aldron, returned from laying stones on the path. One of the voices was certainly Aldron's, though it was not coming from inside.

Nellyn rose from his stool and took several unsteady steps over to the part of the balcony that overlooked the ledge. He peered through the slanting snow—thick enough to his right to obscure any view of ocean swells—and saw Aldron. He was standing where the path ended, shouting and waving his arms. The person who was with him was swathed in a cloak. Even from this height, and with blowing snow between them, Nellyn could see the cloak's colours and the dark hair that curled out from beneath the hood. The Queen was about five paces away from Aldron. She turned her head briefly to look at the door then called out to Aldron. He fell silent. Nellyn could not hear her words, but he saw Aldron's face as he walked toward her. He was smiling—but Nellyn did not recognize this smile, it was new and strange and intended only for Galha, who spoke two last words and glanced up over her shoulder and saw Nellyn. He did not move, not even when she lifted her hand to him, stepped over to the door and in; not even when Aldron followed her without an upward glance, or when Galha's consort-scribe walked after them both. Only when Nellyn heard the front balcony door bang shut did he turn.

The Queen was alone. Nellyn looked past her and saw Malhan's face in the round window that was set in the top of the door. He was inside, watching. He stayed there as Galha walked to stand beside Nellyn.

"The last time we met on a balcony," she said, leaning close to his ear so that the wind would not scatter her voice, "the sun was shining. We were warm and comfortable. And now look at us." His eyes were fixed on her hands, which were hidden by woollen gloves; green and blue, of course, speckled with gold. He remembered the wind that had torn at him above the endless sand and the heat-gauzed city. He remembered vines and water and music, and wine that had spilled.

"I do not like high places," he said.

She nodded and gazed at the sea, which he imagined would be foaming and heaving. "Well, Nellyn," she said at last, "you are the only one I have met in the last three months who has not mentioned the murder of my daughter."

He looked into her eyes then, saw how sleepless and sunken they were. She was hardly blinking, despite the driving snow. He said, "I have no words to give you, so I am quiet."

Her brows rose toward the edge of her hood. "What—no wise shonyn expressions to soothe me? No descriptions of your people's death rituals to distract and educate me?" Her voice was hard and tremulous at the same time, as Lanara's sometimes was—but this woman was not Lanara. Galha's words were more than words, or perhaps less.

He shook his head and took a steadying breath. "No," he said, and waited, not looking away from her face.

Her lips moved: a kind of smile, stiff because of the cold, or something else. "Thank you," she said, and turned away from him as the door behind them slammed shut.

"My Queen!" Lanara cried. "I'm sorry I wasn't here to greet you—I was in the larder. Do not linger outside, please come in—we have spiced herb water and fresh bread ..."

~

Alea glared down at the sitting cushion by her feet. Lanara had already sat, as had Nellyn. Alea put her hands beneath her belly and wondered how rude it would be if she stood in the Queen's presence.

"Here—let me help you." Alea looked up. Galha was beside her, offering her hand. Alea took it immediately, reflexively. Galha's grip was firm but gentle. "I remember how ungainly I felt when I was carrying Ladhra," she said as Alea sank down onto the cushion. "Lying, standing, sitting—nothing was comfortable. Will the babe come in the spring?"

"No," Alea said. Her voice sounded very faint. "Not until early summer." She saw Galha's expression of surprise and looked away. She had had no intention of speaking to the Queen; she had willed herself to silence before stepping onto Nellyn and Lanara's living floor. But now she *had* spoken, and about the baby—and Galha had mentioned her daughter who had died. Alea flushed at her weakness, her pettiness, the clumsiness of her body.

She had never met the Queen before this moment. She had seen her at the prow of the enormous ship, and from time to time standing on the wharf watching the boats come down the river—but she had been a speck until now, a small, featureless blot of blue and green cloth and red-brown skin. Aldron, though, had seen much of her, ever since that first day, a month ago, when he had Told for her.

"What did you Tell?" Alea had demanded, and he had waved his hand at her and shrugged.

"Nothing much. A summer scene and some water—easy things, but they seemed to comfort her. She's nearly as simple to please as the townsfolk." But he had not met Alea's gaze—not then and not on the many occasions after, when he went down to the town to see Galha. He usually went with Lanara, but sometimes he slipped out alone. He would be gone for hours, most of a day. At first Alea told herself that he was merely laying stones for the path he had begun, but then he would return, pale and quiet and sick as he only ever was after a difficult Telling.

She said she worried about him. She begged him to stay at the tower. She hurled the yellow vase across the room and it shattered against the stairs. She demanded to know whether Galha was beautiful—and this question alone, among all the others that were equally ridiculous, made her cringe and long to swallow back the words until they were unsaid. He had not answered her; had walked back out of the tower, back down the half-finished path, back to the bright stone harbour house.

She looks sick. And old. Alea thought this when she saw the Queen at last. A tall, slender, strong body, its lines visible once her cloak and outer tunic had been removed—but her face was sallow and drawn. *She is sick with grief, you heartless woman,* Alea told herself, though she could not quell her relief and her shame. And then Galha had smiled and held out her hand, and Alea had shrunk from her.

"As Lanara and Aldron already know," the Queen said after she had helped Alea to sit, "my war fleet is nearly assembled."

Alea looked at Aldron, who was sitting next to her. He did not meet her eyes. His attention was on Galha, of course, who was still standing while the rest of them sat like eager students at her feet—the rest of them except for the strange, silent man who had accompanied her and now stood beside the stairs. *If only we were in the writing room,* Alea thought, *she would look striking with the storm stretched out behind her. Or the lightroom, even: she would stand among the flames and the blinking glass pieces and we would prostrate ourselves before her brilliance …*

"Only a few more boats will come and then we will be ready—but for one thing."

Lanara said, "What thing is that?"

Alea could not stop her own words; they spun away from her like leaves falling in the autumn woods. "What—something Lanara doesn't know about the Queen's plans? Something perhaps even Aldron doesn't know?" She laughed. She was a girl again, railing against her father or Old Aldira or Aliser, throwing her defiance at them all. "Even I can guess what this one more thing is: how can this great fleet sail forth when there are mountains of ice in the harbour?"

She heard the wind howling and rattling the shutters. As the minutes passed, she thought that it was reaching within, sucking away her defiance along with her voice. She stared down at her mound of belly; not a girl at all, and so far from woods and wagons.

"You are right," Queen Galha finally said, as evenly as if there had been no outburst and no awkward pause. "The icemounts are the only obstacle to our departure. There is just enough room between them to allow small vessels into or out of the harbour. You will have been observing this from your tower, I'm sure. The largest ships have reached Fane from upriver. Two lie anchored in perilously rough seas by the northern cliffs. We cannot wait for the icemounts to retreat in the spring. My ships must sail now."

"Well," Lanara said, "perhaps Alea can tell us what should be done."

Aldron gave a cry and leapt to his feet, and Alea laughed, though not the way she had earlier, and Lanara began to speak again. "Quiet, all of you!" Galha said, and they were, as quickly and clumsily as chastened children. Alea felt Aldron touch her shoulder then slide his hand down to lie against her belly. Their baby stirred and dragged a hand or foot to where his palm rested. He sucked in his breath and Alea smiled.

"It's likely," the Queen continued, "that Alea *could* tell us this—for the Alilan worship a flame goddess, do they not?"

Alea felt the wind again, this time beneath her skin. She had watched the icemounts every day. She loved their glancing, changing colours, their leaping, jagged, bubbled edges. They seemed to breathe—and they certainly spoke. She listened to them when she was alone, and she watched them dance, so slowly, so close to the freedom of the open sea. They danced. She had dreamed sometimes of Telling their shapes and hues and voices to her child. She closed her eyes so that she would not see the Queen when her next words came.

"I will come to you again tonight, since this is a high place with an excellent view. I will come here after the fires have been set, and I will watch the icemounts burn."

THIRTY

Midnight. Clear sky, calm water. Queen Galha arrived at the signal tower in late afternoon. With her came the Sea Raider captive—for she desired him to witness her first conquest, that of the icemounts—and the fishperson who acts as his translator.

Lanara lifted her writing stick from the page. "The Sea Raider captive": very detached, entirely descriptive; an amazing thing, since she tasted bile in her throat when she thought of him. She had seen the man-creature behind the Queen, approaching the tower door. It was the first time she had glimpsed him close up, for he had been confined to a cellar room at the Queenshouse since his removal from the ship. "He is unwell," Galha had said, "so we must tend him carefully. We do not wish him to die before we reach his land." He had walked to the door with his arm around the fishperson, who seemed to be bearing much of his weight. When she had finally looked into his face, Lanara saw that it was lined with cracks and oozing a clear, thick liquid. She had felt the first welling of sickness then, imagining him tearing Ladhra from her horse; imagining more like him swarming through Luhr's palace and streets. Lanara had been proud that she did not want to kill him—not any more. She understood the Queen now, understood that bitter hatred could also be patient.

The Queen had not spoken his name, though Lanara remembered it from her letter. *Leish:* a thin, weak name. She might say it to him someday, with spittle and scorn. For now she had merely looked at him as he looked at the floor. When the fishperson led him upstairs, Queen Galha had lingered with Lanara in the kitchen.

"Nara," she had said, "I must speak with you alone"—and Lanara's cheeks had flushed as they did now, remembering. She could not write of this conversation; it was a secret thing, intended for silence. "There is a change in me," the Queen had murmured. "A change I have felt since I learned of Ladhra's death and the Sea Raider attack on my city. I am growing, within. Something is growing—a heat, a light that gathers in my chest and throat."

Lanara had stared at the hand the Queen had placed on her forearm. "Could it," she had said, unwilling to reveal ignorance but almost certain already that she understood, "—could it be that what you feel is an ancient power?"

She had looked up and flushed again at Queen Galha's smile. "I think that you are right. This force within me is still gathering, but already it shakes me to my bones. It can only be the mindpowers possessed by Sarhenna the First herself. She has chosen me as her true heir in my time of direst grief and need. With her gift I shall wound our enemies as they have wounded me."

Mindpowers. Lanara clutched her writing stick so tightly that it cracked. *Will they look like lightning called down from a cloudless sky? Or will they be invisible things, forces that cause confusion among the Sea Raiders? Whatever they are, I'll write of them someday, after they've been seen and known. And I'll write that she told me of them before she ever used them.*

The Queen was on the high balcony now with the prisoner beside her, watching the fires below. Lanara reached for a new writing stick and set it lightly against the page in front of her. She wrote, revelling again in concentration and clarity:

In the afternoon, before the signal candles were lit, we watched small boats row out to the icemounts in the harbour. Deep, narrow holes were hacked into the icemounts' flanks and lit torches placed in them. Many of these torches died before the flames reached the ice; many others sputtered and caught. By dusk, most were alight. It was a marvellous sight: all the ships and boats lining the Sarhenna River, up past Fane's western limit, bathed in the glow of the icemounts' fires. And every fire was a different colour: blue-tinged or green or pink. Scarlet and gold. Whatever hue the ice had been became that of the flames. The Queen was well satisfied. I stood with her until I could no longer put off my duties. Aldron is with her now.

This will be my last log entry before the sea voyage.

"It's horrible," Alea said. Her voice was muffled, her forehead lying on her arms, which were propped on her belly.

She and Nellyn were in the kitchen. The casement shutters were closed, and the door, but still the terrible music reached them—piercing, cascading melodies that swelled together until one fell silent or another became a scattered wail that had no music in it.

Nellyn said, "Would it comfort you to see the fires? Perhaps then the sound—"

"No." She raised her head, placed her knuckles on the cushioned bench beneath her. "The Alilan worship fire, but fires made of the earth, things that once lived and are now dead. Fires that bring life." She thrust a strand of hair behind her ear. "Though what are these beliefs to me? I am no one. I belong to no …"

Nellyn walked over and stood by her. She cried almost soundlessly, though her body shuddered from her head to her heels, which drummed against the bench. He waited for a time, until she gasped and gripped his wrist. "Alea," he said, "I will go and get Aldron." She shook her head in short, snapping jerks, but when he drew his hand away and went to the staircase, she did not stop him. She did not even look up—just wept and traced circles on her belly.

Malhan, the prisoner and the fishperson were in the lightroom. Malhan nodded at Nellyn; or perhaps he had not nodded—it was difficult to tell. The chamber rippled with a light Nellyn knew: thirty-six candles that stood in a massive candelabra, their flames reflecting off a copper disc and hundreds of hanging glass pieces. But in addition to this familiar glare were ribbons of blue, pink, scarlet, green, and Nellyn had to stand still for a moment before he made his way through the colours toward the people by the window.

When Nellyn reached them, the prisoner turned to him slowly. He was very tall, but stooped as well. Nellyn looked at his body and his face and thought that he almost seemed old, like a wise one who would soon be rowed over to lie beneath the lynanyn trees. The icemounts' fires stained his skin and the liquid that ran from it, pooling in its hollows like congealed tallow. Nellyn wondered what his voice would sound like, how it would say the name Leish, which Lanara had spat like a Queensfolk curse when she told it to him.

Nellyn wiped the sweat from his brow with the back of his hand. He noticed that the fishperson was holding its scale-encrusted hand over its nose and mouth; the smell of burning fat, no doubt, which Nellyn now hardly noticed, as Drelha had predicted.

"Aldron?" he said, and Malhan angled his head toward the window. Nellyn peered through the brilliant glass and saw the Queen with Aldron beside her, standing on the highest balcony. Nellyn swallowed and walked over to the door he had never before passed through, and opened it quickly before his legs could turn to water.

He pulled the door closed behind him and took a wobbling step toward Aldron, but neither he nor the Queen looked at him. Perhaps they had not heard him: the icemounts' death songs were much louder here than they had been inside. But then he took another step, his palm slick against the lichen-rough stone, and saw that Aldron's lips were moving as they had at the inn, when he had been drunk; as they had in the tower's kitchen, when he had made Alea laugh and cry at the same time. Fire in a hearth and a flower in a vase. Nellyn gripped the stone and turned to look at the sea.

The icemounts in the harbour had shrunk to small masses that glowed only fitfully. These had been the first to blaze, for they had been easy to reach by boat. The icemounts outside the harbour had been impossible to access; some of the smallest vessels had tried, but the water there had been very rough and they had turned back. Once the harbour icemounts were alight, the ones past them had been utterly inaccessible. A few people had stood in their tipping boats and flung torches, but all had fallen short and been swallowed by waves.

Now, Nellyn saw, the outer icemounts were burning. The flames were double the height of the ice, maybe even more, undulating towers of every shade that never flickered or wavered. He walked closer to Aldron, heard the humming of his words beneath the icemounts' keening.

"Aldron!" he shouted. Aldron did not look around, so Nellyn shouted again, louder. Aldron's voice stopped and he moved his head, so slowly that he might have been racked with pain or half asleep. Nellyn saw his eyes and fell back a pace, so that his back was flat against the wall. Aldron stared at him, his mouth still slightly open. It was the Queen who said, "Yes, Nellyn, what is it?"

Nellyn ran his tongue over his dry lips. "Alea," he said. "She needs him."

Galha bent her head until it was almost touching Aldron's. Nellyn could not hear what she said, but Aldron blinked and nodded and shook himself like a sodden animal. He stepped away from the railing. His legs buckled, straightened again almost immediately.

"Thank you," he said as he passed Nellyn. "I'll go to her now." His voice was as thin and misshapen as a lynanyn husk without its fruit.

Nellyn looked back at the Queen. For a moment she met his gaze and he felt as if he were receding from her, into a distance she had created with her height and her stillness and her eyes. Then she turned again to the fires and he stumbled back to the door, heedless for once of the yawning space beneath him.

~

Alea did not move when she heard Aldron on the stairs. She noticed that his footsteps were more halting than usual but could not summon the strength to wonder why. When he touched her hair, she hardly felt it. "Love," he said, and tears rose in her throat again even though she had cried so much already. "Alea." He stroked the hair away from her cheeks and put his fingers beneath her chin. She let him raise her face up. So weak, no one would recognize her now, not even Aliser. "What is it? Why are you crying?"

His voice was flat, as it always was after a powerful Telling. She welcomed the heat of her anger, which seared away her trembling and her weeping. "Trifles, you said. And then you swore to me that you would never use your other power here, with anyone except me. Now look at you—too drained from killing icemounts to even pretend innocence."

Aldron's hand fell away from her face. He wrenched himself around—she saw what an effort it took for him to do this—and walked to the table by the fireplace. His head brushed some bundles of dried herbs that hung from a beam. His hair came away flecked with green and brown, and a bruised scent rose, but he did not seem to notice. He leaned over the table and said, in his transparent voice, "Do you not feel mad? Do you not yearn to Tell? Or are you so perfect that you are immune to this loss?"

She laughed. She thought, *Listen to me, I sound like a panicky horse,* but kept laughing until she gasped for breath. "My dear," she said at last, "I feel mad nearly every moment. I yearn to Tell, even if just a trifle. To see a dune again, or the paint of my family's wagon, or grass and leaves. But I do not Tell—not even for myself alone. I think the grief of it would be worse than the yearning."

He rubbed a palm over his hair. The bits of dried herb spiralled away from him. "I don't have your restraint. Though it may also be true that you don't have my gift—at least not as intense a gift as I have—and so can't understand me."

"Can't understand you," she repeated, speaking the words as slowly as if she were holding them up to the firelight to see them better. He turned so that he was facing her, though he did not look at her. "Let me think, then, who might understand you. Who might truly appreciate your gift and what it costs you? Yes, let me see … the Queen? Might the Queen be this sympathetic and discerning person?"

She was standing despite the tugging pain at the base of her belly. She gazed at him and saw a boy, a youth, a man, the companion of her heart and steps for almost all her life—and now, suddenly, a body spinning away from her like a spark.

"Yes," the disappearing Aldron said. And though she longed to reach out her arms to draw him in against her, she laughed another short, shrill laugh.

"In that case, go with her. Don't worry about me, or our baby: get on a ship tomorrow and seek out a destiny worthy of your lofty powers." He looked at her finally, up and into her eyes. "Ah," she said quietly after a long, long time. "I see. Far too late, but I see."

He thrust himself away from the table and took two steps toward her. He said her name in his strong, beloved, familiar voice and she cried, "Stop! Stop there." She held her right arm out, hand up; her left was draped across her belly. "Stop there," she said again, even though he had.

~

Lanara was talking, quite loudly and very fast. Nellyn felt dizzy listening to her, and he wondered why she was speaking as she was, frenetically even for her—and then she paused to breathe and he heard the voices below them. He had listened to Alea and Aldron arguing before; the staircase that ran up through every floor allowed sounds to rise as well. At first Nellyn had stood frozen with fear: their voices had sounded strange and twisted. Shonyn voices never changed this way. But he had soon learned that Alea and Aldron's disagreements passed as quickly as they began. The staircase brought other sounds afterward, which made Lanara roll her eyes and blush a bit.

He had not heard the beginning of this argument. He had come to Lanara in the writing room as he did every midnight. She had been staring out at the towers of flame that seemed to reach even the black water at the horizon. Her writing stick had been resting on a piece of parchment that was covered with words. She had looked up at him and smiled and begun to talk—as she was doing still. The icemounts, the Queen, the ships. Provisions for the journey: the fish smoked in huts by the northern cliffs, fresh water stowed in barrels and bags, thousands of strands of dried seagreen. The weather. Ocean maps that extended only to a ring of islands—emptiness beyond; who knew how long it would take … Then she had drawn a breath, and Alea and Aldron's voices had echoed in the silence.

"… hemmed in—you know this," Aldron cried. After these clear words was a jagged stream of others, all unintelligible: his, then hers, then his.

"This one is worse than the others," Nellyn said. Lanara nodded and faced the sea again. "Do you know why?" Her shoulders were rigid. He went to stand behind her and put his hands on them lightly, until he felt them relax.

"He … The Queen has asked him to join in the voyage and the attack." Nellyn pressed his fingertips against her neck and shoulders and she groaned. He knew she would be closing her eyes. She shifted a moment later and glanced back at him. "Aren't you going to ask me if he's agreed?"

"No. They would not be arguing if he had refused."

She chuckled—a sound, he had discovered, that did not always indicate amusement. Someone was sobbing downstairs; Nellyn could not tell whether it was Aldron or Alea.

"Do you think it's terrible of him?" she asked after a moment. "Leaving her now? He probably won't be here when she has the baby."

"I should not mind it," he replied, reaching for the words, placing them carefully. "Shonyn children often do not know who their blood parents are: they are raised by many, spend time in different huts. And I understand that Aldron is not happy here and needs to find another place. But … Alea is not happy either, and she will only be more sad when he goes. I understand her sadness. She will lose him as I will lose—"

"Shush," Lanara said. She swung toward him on the stool and slipped her arms around him. He laid his cheek against her hair and closed his eyes. Even so, the icemounts' flames swam before him. Their colours were so intense now, but soon they would be weaker, lowering, leaving only open sea.

"We've talked about this day," she said, her breath warm against his tunic. "Unlike Aldron and Alea. I'll come back—I keep telling you this, though I know I can't make you believe it." She propped her chin on his chest and looked up at him. "I wish you could think like a shonyn again now. You could be certain that there's no change—just me going and coming and always being with you."

He drew his fingers across her forehead and down her cheeks, to the hollow of her throat. "I wish the same thing, but only sometimes. You brought change to me and it is mine now, whether this causes me joy or sadness."

Her arms tightened around him and she lifted her head and kissed him. He had felt dread and sorrow weighing upon him these past days and weeks, and yet he stirred as she kissed him, and slid his hands under cloth, along the length of her thighs. She linked her ankles behind his legs and raised herself a bit against him, and he moaned and smiled at the same time—and then someone called her name.

The Queen was standing on the stairs. Nellyn blinked at her, as distant and slow as if he had been deeply asleep; but Lanara was standing, listening, nodding. "… much to do before we sail," he heard Galha say. "It would be best if we returned to town now."

"Of course," Lanara said. She held his hand on the steps down to their sleeping floor, then let it go, bent to pick up the things she had readied for this moment, which he had hardly been able to look at: a bag of clothes, her dagger, her bow and quiver. He wanted to cry, "Take everything! Every vial and comb and length of cloth that belongs to you—leave nothing for me to see"—but he knew even as he thought this that he did not really desire it. He followed her down and down again, to the kitchen where Alea stood and Aldron slumped. They were silent now, their faces turned, pale and waiting, to the stairs.

"It is time," Galha said, stepping from staircase to floor and into the cloak Malhan was holding out to her. The fishperson was there too, Nellyn saw, and the prisoner; he had not noticed them above.

"Fine," Aldron said. "Good." He walked to the door and took his own cloak from a peg beside it. Nellyn watched him fumble with the fastenings. He looked at Alea, who watched Aldron as well, just for a moment, before she walked to the stairs. She brushed past the Queen, past Lanara and her outstretched hand, past Nellyn. Alea went quickly up the steps, not holding on to the railing or the swell of her baby. By the time Aldron had arranged his cloak and turned again to the room, she was gone. His eyes darted and widened when they did not find her. His mouth moved without sound and he raised a hand to his forehead.

"Come, then," the Queen said. Aldron's hand fell away from his face and he nodded. He looked over his shoulder at Nellyn as he went outside, and Nellyn held his gaze until Lanara's voice and arms drew him back.

"You must get help here: promise me you will. It'll be too much work for you alone. Alea won't be able to do any, she's too uncomfortable already. The candles will be delivered next week. Stack them behind the ones in the shed—that way the freshest will be—"

He kissed her so that she would stop speaking, so that she would feel him close before she stepped away. "You haven't changed your mind?" she asked. He could feel the shape of each word against his lips. "About coming down to the harbour?"

"No," he said, barely a whisper, and she held him so tightly that he knew he would stagger when she left him.

~

Dawn. Wind strong from the northwest, some waves with white tops. Icemounts gone, river and harbour water very high, perhaps because of melting. Sky clear, light cloud to the east. Queen Galha's boats sailed shortly before dawn, are now spread out across open sea, moving quickly. Sails are bright and full of wind.

THIRTY-ONE

Nellyn is breathing in time with the lift and plunge of the poles. It is a rhythm he has forgotten without his flatboat to stand on. Remember, forget: words he does not think of or even know, with the silver leaves ahead of him, the red huts behind, the dark blue lynanyn bobbing thick in the water around. There is no horizon—just the line of trees, the river bending in rock, the sand ridge behind the huts; and these views are blurred by dusk or dawn, not seen sharp in sunlight. He senses someone behind him: Maarenn, of course. She might think it strange if he turned and spoke to her, so he looks only ahead and breathes and dips his pole into the river that swells with stars.

Nellyn opened his eyes. They focused very slowly on the handprint of moss. The palm sharpened first, then the lengths of the fingers, then the surrounding rock. He breathed himself back, his hands spread on his thighs in the same way that the moss splayed across the cliffside. The moss was green now, springy and soft and dotted with tiny red flowers. The rock was warm wherever the sun touched it. Nellyn wore a light cloak when he came to sit here. Some days he did not even need the hood, since the wind was quite mild, if still occasionally strong.

He rose and stretched and yawned so widely that his jaw cracked. He was always tired—so much work to do and, despite Lanara's urging, no one to help him with it. He enjoyed the solitude of the work, and its patterns. He enjoyed sitting at the windows in the darkness, climbing up to the lightroom at the same times every night to trim wicks and dab at fallen tallow. Dawn was his favourite time. He lowered the great candelabra, snuffed the candles, replaced the ones that had burned too low. Then he scraped at the hardened tallow and scrubbed the floor and windows and looked out at the sea, just once, before he climbed down the stairs to his bed. He slept less, and spent more energy while he was awake—but his body and mind were quiet, and his weariness did not bother him.

Today he found Alea in the kitchen, where he always found her at this hour. She was sitting at the table sorting through the baskets of fruit and greens and nuts that were delivered every two weeks. Nellyn had tried to go down to the town himself, but he had only succeeded once—enough to request the delivery services of a man he met in the fruit market. Nellyn's legs had still been shaking. The man had laughed and said he would take pity on someone who was so clearly a stranger, and charge him a particularly fair price.

"A good batch," Alea said. She smiled at him as he slid onto the bench across from her. "No rotten fruits and only a few bunches of mouldy greens. And look: your lips aren't chapped after being outside for so long. It really must be spring."

He touched a finger to his lips and felt them smile. "I am certain of it. I have not written about a storm in weeks." No more howling snow or lashing sleet or driving sheets of rain; no waves that rose and boomed against their cliff, or fog that blotted the waves away. The rain was gentle now, when it came, and never lasted long. The stars were almost always bright, in the sky and in the water.

"What did you do today while I slept?" he asked.

She paused and frowned, though he could see her smile lingering around her eyes. "Well, now, let me try to remember ... ah yes, I rested. First on my back, then on my side. Then, when I couldn't rest any more, I waddled down here and inspected fruit. I think that's everything." She set down the sunfruit she was holding and leaned back a bit, so that her hair touched the wall. He watched her hands slip up over her belly and circle there for a moment. He watched her eyes close.

"A pain?" he said when she opened them again.

She nodded. She no longer tried to lie to him. "Yes. I've had a few today." She picked up the sunfruit and turned it over and over in her palm. "Some days there are none, others many—but why, when it is so early? And the baby is always squirming—all arms and legs, and big ones at that. Did I not count the months correctly?" She dropped the sunfruit into a basket at her feet and did not reach for another.

"Perhaps you should consider moving into town to be near that birthing-woman I met. She would be able to help you, tell you what—"

"Nellyn," she interrupted, "no. It was sweet of you to look for someone, and I know you worry, but I can't live down there. And I don't want a woman from there, no matter how wise, to aid me. I've learned to be without people—so I'll do this alone too."

"Not alone," he said. "With me."

She had often told him of the Alilan way: the lighting of the birthing fire; the gathering of grandmothers, aunts, sisters, mother; the slow, unfolding dance that did not end until the baby cried and breathed. She had explained all this, sometimes tearfully, sometimes angrily; he was sure that it would not help her to know that he—not her family, not Aldron—would be the one with her when her own birthing time came. But she reached across the table now and put her fingertips on the back of his hand and said, "Yes, of course—and I am so glad of it." She sat back and kneaded the left side of her belly—one of her happy motions, when the baby greeted her and she greeted the baby.

Nellyn heard a bird singing in their silence; it must have been directly outside. There were so many different birds now, which he had not seen in the winter. Some—small and yellow with crimson beaks—were building nests in the rock behind the signal tower.

"Let's go down to Fane," Alea said. She saw his confusion—she always did—and continued, "I know I just insisted I could never live there, but that doesn't mean it wouldn't be enjoyable to visit for a day. Soon I'll be so enormous that I won't have a choice. It's spring, Nellyn. You'll enjoy the walk, once I help you down the path."

He thought, *Maybe this is just another of her excited ideas, another that will wither once this mood changes.* But two days later she held his arm as they shuffled over the moist, muddy track and then, lower down, over the stones Aldron had laid. She stopped and looked at these, which were flat and pink-tinged. "So," she said at last, "this is what he did while I sat in the tower. Part of what he did." Nellyn looked for anger in her face, listened for it in her words. He still did this even though the rage with which she used to speak of Aldron seemed to have passed with the winter. He saw and heard only sadness now.

"Listen!" she said as she stepped from the path to the wharf, gripping his hand for balance. From here Fane was a muddled roar; only closer did individual sounds become clear. Clanging pots, screeching children, the ripple and crack of carpets being beaten with brooms or oars. Music—fiddles and flutes, all manner of voices—and feet pounding on wood or hissing over cobbles. The creaking of the few boats anchored in the harbour, whose water rose and fell against pilings and stone like a heartbeat.

"These people," said Alea, gesturing to the docks, "I don't remember them being here when we arrived."

"They came with the boats. And now they are here waiting for the boats to return." Women with babies, old men, youths, all clustered around fires shielded by cloth or wooden windbreaks. Nellyn could see their fires from the tower, winking in the darkness like a strand of signal lights. He thought that Lanara would have written of them—their constancy and pattern, and who might be tending them—but he did not.

"So they've been here all winter." Alea's eyes darted from face to face as she walked among them. Some nodded or spoke words of greeting. One old woman reached up and touched Alea's belly. "Hurry," Alea said, and Nellyn felt her fingers weave among his and tighten. "There are too many of them—too many fires ..."

The makeshift dwellings extended up into the wide streets beyond the wharf; only when these streets narrowed did the tents and lean-tos thin away. Alea was panting by the time they reached a quiet, empty laneway. She had not let go of Nellyn's hand, and she held it still when they walked on. Her fingertips were slightly rough and her skin was cool; he touched it very lightly with his own.

All of Fane gleamed: stones and paint, tiles, the water that ran down among the cobbles, the leaves, new-green, that fluttered from trees and clung to walls. The river was high and brilliant between its banks of rock. *My river,* Nellyn thought when he saw it—but he did not believe this even now, so long after he had ceased to be shonyn. This river surged and foamed, reflected roofs and bridges and strangers. "The Sarhenna River": he heard Lanara's voice and remembered his own confusion, and he thought, *Yes, this is the Sarhenna River.*

~

They found the jewellers' quarter by chance, as they had found everything else that afternoon. At first Alea did not know what the place was; she merely stood and gaped at the metal and stones that hung from hooks set in walls and around windows and doors. Pendants and earrings and bracelets—and, by one doorway, a shining row of armrings. She walked over to them and looked through the doorway, into an open courtyard with a fountain and flowers and people bent over small tables, linking pieces of metal, setting gems, polishing with pieces of bright cloth. Copper and silver and gold, red and blue stones—all of them caught the sun and sang to her, in voices she had forgotten.

"Do you like these?" Nellyn was behind her, looking over her shoulder at the armrings. She touched one, despite the shrilling of the voice within her that she had always heeded until now. *Don't look, don't touch. You'll remember if you do, and it will hurt you* ... She laid her fingers against the copper and felt its warmth, and the grooves of its design, and the edges that would press into her flesh just enough to leave the faintest crease.

"Yes," she said. He stepped up beside her and she turned to him, since she knew he would want to see her face. She watched him observe her tears and her smile, and she smiled all the wider because he was so serious and so gentle.

"We will buy one, then," he said.

"No." She forced her hand back to her side. "It would remind me too much of my people. And Aldron and I promised each other that we would leave behind all such trappings ..."

"Would it comfort you to be reminded?"

She looked back at the armring. There were straight lines incised in it, and whorls, like wood with flames and smoke above. "Yes," she said. Her baby pushed at her with a palm or a heel and she stroked the place with her thumb. "It was easier to deny myself such comfort when Aldron was with me. But now that he's not, and with my birthing time coming, I need it. Comfort, reminders—I don't know ..." It was so clear suddenly: the hatefulness of her drab living floor and her rough, colourless clothing. She felt weak acknowledging it—and then there was another pain, tightening her belly from bottom to top, and she had to sit on a low wall to wait for it to pass. It did, and was not followed by another, and she looked up.

Nellyn was walking toward her, holding the armring carefully in his hand. She closed her own fingers around it, clutched it as she would have clutched the reins of her Ralan, galloping.

"Now," Nellyn said, "tell me what else would give you comfort"—and the laughter rose in her like a loosening, from stomach to throat; like a smooth untangling of wool.

~

"Are you sure I can't stay here?"

Nellyn smiled over his shoulder at Alea, who was standing on the stairs. "I am sure, yes—you can come back when I am finished. Though I am glad you *want* to be here, now."

She sighed dramatically as he turned back to the wall and the row of paint jars at his feet. "Very well. I'll retreat to the kitchen and lay my pallet out in front of the fire and—no, no, don't urge me to return—then I'll"—her voice was fading as she descended the stairs—"just settle in and listen to my skin expanding ..."

He laughed. He had laughed often in the two weeks since their visit to Fane. Alea had been relentlessly, effortlessly cheerful. She seemed to be having fewer pains, and she had been busy transforming her sleeping floor. The brown rug had been rolled up and propped against the wall of the shed; in its place was a multicoloured carpet, small (since Nellyn had had to carry it back), but so vividly and intricately patterned that it swam in his vision when sun- or candlelight shone on it. Glazed bowls lined the windowsills and the low table beside her bed; there were earrings within, and bracelets, and stones not set in any metal, which she had chosen for their hues of fire and earth.

"The walls," Nellyn had said a few days ago, and she had frowned at him.

"What about them?"

"They are so bare. Could we not colour them too?" And now here he sat, on a low stool, gazing down at red, green, orange and brown paints, smooth in their deep clay pots. She had told him which colours to get in town; she had not told him what, exactly, to paint. "You know Alneth and Alnila's symbols now," she had said, and he had nodded and begun to think. Two days of thinking; he had even planned as he slept, his dreams shaded scarlet and ivy-green.

He dipped his brush into the brown paint and lifted it up, still dripping. It did not smell like the lynanyn juice he used to mix with water for dyeing cloth, or with red earth to brush over river clay. This paint smelled thick and new. He touched the brush to the white stone and moved his hand once, again, slowly.

"Nellyn!" He started and blinked and saw that the light around him had faded. "Come and eat—it'll soon be time to light the candles ..." He eased himself up off the stool, reluctant and stiff, feeling the colours leave the air and the place where he had held them, in his eyes.

"I did not expect to be so absorbed in it," he told her later, when they were sitting together at the table.

She traced a smudge of green paint from his middle finger to his forearm. "So you're an artist. Maybe this shouldn't surprise us. I can't wait to see what you're doing—couldn't I peek ...?"

He did not allow her up the stairs, no matter how sweetly or stormily she begged him to. He painted and ate, whenever she called up the stairs to remind him, and he tended the light, thinking about painting all the time. He painted when he used to sleep—and, when he tried to sleep, his head throbbed with colours and shapes and anticipation. He would go to her, lead her up when the sunlight was clear and strong, probably around three hours after dawn. She would stand and turn around, looking; but here his imagining faltered. Would she smile and speak, or would she frown, even just with her eyes? *I know nothing of this or any other future. I do not know what her expression will be, or whether the boats will ever come back across the sea.* Only when he stood before the curving stone where he painted did he feel quiet.

One afternoon, about a week after he had begun, he was drawing a swath of green up and around, dipping his brush again and again. He would soon need to go down to Fane for more paint, though he was nearly done. Another few days, and then he would—

"Nellyn." The word was low and breathless. He heard it, then wondered if he had. He waited, craning his head so that he would hear her better if she called again. "Nellyn, come here"—each word louder, rising and tight—"come here—*help me*"—and the paint fell and flowed across the floor as he ran to her.

THIRTY-TWO

It was to Ladhra I last wrote, and although it was so long ago, my hand still wants to make all its letters and lines for her. But I'll write to you now, and hope that you'll read these words someday. Perhaps we'll read them together, with our backs against the tower stone and the cliffs beside us covered in flowers. I try to imagine your spring, and what you're writing of in the log, but it's difficult; I'm so far away. Has your ocean been as calm as mine these past two months?

It's strange. The Queen's most experienced ocean captains warned her, in Fane, that we would be sure to encounter fierce storms on our journey east. They spoke of winds that could crack the thickest mast, waves so high that the biggest boat would spin about like a twig in a puddle. But such violence has never found us. We've had a few minor storms, which even the smallest vessels have ridden out without much damage. I've heard other Queensfighters (for that's what the Queen calls us now, ever since we left Fane) murmuring about the blessings of the First upon our fleet and its mission. I am certain they are right, for the Queen has spoken to me, in Fane and on this ship, and I know that she is Sarhenna's chosen heir. Our way has been smooth, and we will prevail when we reach our destination.

Leish was seasick. He had not been before, on the journey west with his people or on the river that led to Fane—but here, surging atop the ocean in this enormous boat, he was ceaselessly, violently ill. Early in the voyage, lying spent after vomiting bile or retching nothing, he had thought, *A selkesh, ill with the motion of the waves!* and felt a thin, miserable amusement. After a time he hardly noticed the sickness; it was just a layer of wretchedness among all the others. He writhed in hunger and thirst and sleeplessness, and sometimes he convulsed with vomiting too. It was all the same.

But as his body quailed, his mind grew light and steady. Nasranesh sang to him. He did not have to grasp at the sounds from far away or conjure them himself from memory; they flowed to him across the space between them, which was closing. He did not need to look at the sea when the guard took him up on deck twice a day. He did not need his eyes at all. He heard the notes of his home, and they were so beautiful that he had no fear any more about what would come. No fear—until Wollshenyllosh's voice reached him through the singing, as it had long ago, in a different prison.

"Leish! Leish, hear me: we are entering the waters of my kin."

He tried to open his eyes. She had rarely spoken on the voyage—only sometimes when she bathed him with the water the Queensfolk gave them every few days, or when Galha came to question him. Usually he barely heard Wollshenyllosh's words. She murmured them, and some were entirely strange to him. But he heard her now, and felt her as well, holding his shoulders with her scale-edged hands.

"My home waters, Leish. Look at me!"

It was darker in their tiny cabin than it had been behind his eyelids. He had seen blossoms and treetops there, and the ruffled, sunlit surface of the gathering pool. Here there was just a wan grey light; no torch or lantern, he remembered, because they could be used as clubs or to start fires. Wollshenyllosh's scales hardly shone at all when she bent over him.

"I can take us there, I think. We need to try."

He mumbled up at her, then moaned as the cabin tipped and she slid briefly out of his sight. "To try?" he whispered between his torn lips, and then she was above him again, pressing her fingers into his flesh so that he could not return to the comfort of his song.

"We will both die in your land, Leish. She will kill us there. We must get off this ship. We would be safe in my waters."

The quiet was gone from his head. The weight of his brittle body returned, and he saw very clearly the squalor of the cabin and the silver-white of Wollshenyllosh's eyes. "You are afraid," he said, and her finger-scales dug as if she would pierce him through.

"Of course I am afraid. I know how strongly your land calls to you, for I hear mine also—but listen to me: *she will kill us*."

"Us?" he repeated, his thoughts even more sluggish than his tongue. "It is me she hates."

Wollshenyllosh let go of him. He felt for a moment as if he were falling, and swallowed over another wave of sickness. "She needed me in Luhr, even in Fane—but she will have no such need once this boat finds land." She was on her knees, reaching behind her with both hands. "I was about to leave. I met your brother and his Queensman companion and I told them I would leave—but I was curious about the attack and I lingered, and when I finally tried to take the water tunnel your people used, she was there before me, she had blocked the way ..."

Leish thought, *I have heard this before—she told me this on the river journey to Fane, and again in the house by the water*. She had been so calm in Luhr—and now she repeated her own words as if she had never spoken them before, and her eyes were wild, and she scrabbled at something behind her back, desperately, her scales striking each other like music.

"And what then?" he asked. "What will happen when we reach your waters?"

She was still at last, and her gaze was unwavering on him. "I will tell my people what she has done to yours. When they know, they will help. They will fight her boats in the sea and keep them from reaching your shores."

He sat up slowly. The room spun, but he ignored it. "Very well. How will we do this thing?"

"Here," she said, her hands working again, "here, on my back, there's a scale—the longest on my body, and the sharpest. I've been loosening it for days, but I'll need you to pull it out ..."

He shuffled around her on his knees, feeling the dampness of sea water and his own sickness, and smelling these things suddenly as he had not for so many weeks. He saw the scale, eased her fingers away from it. He ran his own hands over it and felt it lift away from her body, except for its widest part, which stuck. He moved it up and around and she stiffened. "Pull," she said when he hesitated. He drew in a breath—through his mouth, not his nose—wrapped fingers and webs tightly around the scale's slippery length, and braced one foot against her hip. He breathed out and pulled.

The scale ripped free and he heard the sound it made, briefly, before she began to scream. She screamed once, twice, then in a long, unbroken line. She doubled over so that her forehead touched the floor. Leish looked down at the scale, which was sharp and smooth at its tip, and dark with clotted blood and flesh at its base. He noticed that his own hands were bleeding. He did not look at the place where the scale had been. Her screaming wavered into a lower keening. She shifted on the floor, one hand groping behind her. He set the scale in it and watched her draw herself to her feet and lurch to the door. She went quiet there. She stood and panted and raised the scale above her head.

The door latch was rattling. "What's all the noise?" The Queensguard outside, fumbling for a key, likely surprised; these two never gave trouble. "Here, now—don't try—" He was ducking into the cabin, his eyes on Leish—only Leish, kneeling, staring back at him. The guard grunted, "Where's the fish-thing, now?" and started to turn his head—and Wollshenyllosh's arm descended, found his neck before he had truly seen her. He grunted and gurgled and fell, hard.

For a moment Leish saw only the scale, half buried in the man's skin. Then Wollshenyllosh tore it out and stepped through the arcing blood. "Come, Leish," she rasped.

He followed her, though he could not believe his legs were supporting him. Their cabin was directly below the deck—not far to go, and he could tell from the light in the passageway that it was dawn, or evening. Perhaps the deck would be empty and a quick stride or two would bring them to the sea …

She led him the length of the ship, to a ladder and a hatch above it. She climbed up two rungs and turned back to him. "Follow close behind me, on the deck and also in the sea. It will be very dark just before we reach my waters."

He nodded at her. Her scales seemed to shine more here, even the ones that were spattered with blood. He reached up to touch her, very lightly, where her scales were bright and clean. He imagined what Mallesh would say if he could see this—but it was a fleeting imagining, a shadow of another time, another Leish. "I will follow," he said, and she pushed the hatch open.

Leish saw nothing clearly at first, just a great burning glow that was the open sky. Daylight. Not dawn, not dusk: daylight, muffled by fog but as shocking as it always was, after the cabin's gloom. "There are people," Wollshenyllosh whispered as he rubbed the tears from his eyes, "but no one has seen us." She was squatting to the right of the hatch, her eyes darting. He pulled himself up to crouch beside her. His teeth were chattering and his limbs were shaking, and he gagged a bit and swallowed the bile down again.

"… sick of maggots in my bread," said a voice from just beyond the row of barrels that hid Leish and Wollshenyllosh from the boat's prow. Two Queensmen passed the barrels. Leish looked only at their legs, as if this would keep them from glancing down and seeing him. "I hear the Queen has her own private store—wine and cured meats, even some fruit still," said a different voice, and then the men were gone.

Wollshenyllosh covered both of Leish's hands with her own. "Run with me now," she said. "And after we run, our strokes will lead us home."

~

Queenswoman Grelhal's giggle was so high that it sounded like the screech of a gull. *A hysterical gull,* Lanara thought, glancing at Aldron, *which has been circling around us since we left Fane's harbour*. "Are all of your people so witty?" Grelhal was gasping, her giggling over with for the moment.

"My my, no!" he exclaimed. He had been nearly as giddy as Grelhal on the journey, though Lanara had also seen him go silent and still, as if he were somewhere alone, far away from all of them. "Our Goddesses decreed, back when time began, that only one Alilan in each caravan could have the gift of wit, for they feared there would be chaos if …"

"If?" prompted Grelhal, but Aldron did not speak again. Lanara watched his eyes narrow. As she turned to follow his gaze, she heard shouting from the deck behind them.

She had never before seen a fishperson move quickly. They stood or lay in the marketplace, stepped delicately to the wells and fountains, where they often floated when the sun was high. She had seen this one at the signal tower and here on deck, stooped and shuffling beneath the Sea Raider's weight. But now it was running in long, ragged strides that did not resemble at all the fishfolk's usual graceful, gliding walk. It was already past a group of sailors, who were looking after it too slowly—halfway to the side of the ship, and no one else had tried to stop it.

Lanara cried out and began to run as well, though she would never catch it; it would plunge over the side and be lost—and if it had escaped, where was the Sea Raider? She sped over the boards, over rope and canvas and fallen barrels—and as she did, something sliced past her with a whistle of speed.

One of the fishperson's hands was touching the ship's side when the dagger found it. Its arms flew up against the sky. Even in this murky light its scales flashed, iridescent as the wings of countless lacemoths. Then it slumped to the deck and its scales dimmed, and Lanara ran with all the others to stare down at its twisted limbs and at the place where the dagger had lodged.

"There was already a wound there," someone said, as someone else prodded the fishperson with a booted foot.

"And that's what I aimed for." They all turned to Aldron, who knelt and fingered the hilt of his dagger. "How else could I have wounded the creature?" he went on, looking up at the faces of those around him. "These scales are like armour. It was a lucky thing, this other wound." He pulled the dagger free, and the fishperson moaned and jerked so that fresh blood spouted onto the deck.

"What about the other one?" Grelhal said. "Weren't they imprisoned together?"

Lanara was already moving away from the gathering at the side. She found the thin trail of blood the fishperson had left in its flight, followed it to the small hatch near the prow. The Sea Raider was there, sitting with his arms around his knees. He looked up at her. She saw his body's shaking, the blood that dripped from his clenched hands, his wide eyes, so shocking in the horrible, cracked darkness of his face.

"Coward," she spat as if her words could also be metal. "Filth."

~

"It was a fine throw," Galha said.

Lanara turned from the sunset she was watching through the thick windows of the Queen's cabin. Aldron and Galha were sitting at the table in the middle of the cabin, a replica of the table in her tower study, though not nearly as large. Aldron's dagger was lying on the dark red wood. He was holding it with two fingers so that it would not slide with the motion of the ship.

"Thank you," he said. He lowered his eyes to the dagger. "I didn't intend to kill the thing," he continued very quickly. *As if he were confessing guilt,* Lanara thought, *or apologizing for it.* She frowned, even as the Queen smiled.

"Do not reproach yourself," Galha said. "The creature was ill—we all knew that. Too ill in body and mind to have survived the voyage to the Raiders' Land, or indeed to its own home. You delivered it from suffering, Aldron. I am very glad I gave you that dagger in Fane."

He smiled—his usual confident smile—and said, "I wish you could have seen me use it."

"As do I," the Queen replied. "But there will be many opportunities for that, soon. We are nearly there, nearly at Nasranesh—aren't we?"

Lanara followed Galha's gaze to the thick wooden pillar that stood by the cabin door. The prisoner was there, lashed to it as he had been to the mast, months before. He did not open his eyes when the Queen spoke to him. There was no need for him to answer her; shorebirds had been sighted that morning flitting among the larger gulls. Tiny birds, brightly coloured, skimming over the water as lightly as insects. And the water itself was changing, deep green-grey shifting to a clearer blue. Lanara thought she had smelled growing things, too, as she stood on the deck with Aldron and Grelhal; a scent of green, like Queenswood trees—but different, and so fleeting that she had not been able to catch it again before the fishperson had run and died.

"We are very close now," Galha said, leaning in toward the Sea Raider. "Close enough that I have posted extra guards on every deck and porthole on every one of my vessels. Your people will not take my ships the way they tried to take my city." She stayed near him for a moment, looking at his closed eyes. Then she turned and said, "Aldron, come here with me—I have a finer dagger for you, one I should have given you in Fane ..."

They went together to a long case across the cabin, by the hanging that hid her bed. Lanara watched them, listened to the low hum of their words, which she could not hear. She wandered away from the windows, her hands hovering over the furniture that would brace her if the ship tilted. She would return to the deck, or to her own cabin, to continue writing to Nellyn—but she slowed as she passed the pillar, and stopped when she saw that the Sea Raider's eyes were open.

"Ladhra." He whispered it, but Lanara started so sharply that he might have shouted. "Ladhra tell me: friend Lanara," he went on. She struggled to untangle his sounds even as she thought, *Walk by. Don't listen or even look* … "Ladhra friend Lanara—Ladhra friend Leish." His lips were flecked with bloody spittle. His shoulders strained against the rope that held him.

Lanara stepped so close to him that his features blurred. He oozed decay—she smelled it and saw it and trembled with disgust. *Disgust,* she told herself, *nothing else.* "You will not speak her name," she said slowly, so that he would hear and feel every word. Then she walked away from him.

Ladhra friend Leish—she heard it standing at the ship's side, gulping air, and later, curled in her bunk, sleepless and cold. A line of unwanted music, circling with more and more intensity—and why? Why allow the words to echo when they were a lie? *I cannot see him again,* she thought. *I'll tell the Queen some half-truth about fearing him*—and this decision let her sleep at last, with nothing in her head but the sound of creaking timbers.

"Nara." She scrambled out of her covers, one hand reaching for her knife—but then she blinked against torchlight and saw Aldron. "It's just after dawn," he hissed. "There's land ahead—wait, wait," he said, grasping her wrist as she tried to stand. "Listen: the watch on the oardeck just reported activity outside. Creatures crawling up the sides of this ship and several others. Creatures from the water. They've come to us—they imagine they'll take us by surprise …"

"You're shaking," she said. She herself felt heavy and strong now that this moment had come. She would be strong for all the Queensfighters when they quailed before Queen Galha's mindpowers.

He let go of her wrist. "Of course I am," he said, and his voice trembled now as well. "This is battle. This is what I came for."

The deck was thick with Queensfighters. They stood in rows, silent except for the occasional sound, quickly muffled, of metal sliding against metal. The Queen was at the prow, her bow held loosely, pointing toward the empty railing to her right. Lanara slipped through the rows until she was a few paces from the side. She looked behind her, at faces and swords; she looked beyond the prow at the shadows of the other boats, and the still water, and the eastern sky that was clear and silver except for a dark, rolling line of land. The wind rose; canvas and cloaks snapped. After it had died down again, there was another gusting: bodies slithering up and over, falling to the deck—and the stillness shattered into shouts and singing arrows and the first hard thrusts of swords.

"Ladhra!" someone beside Lanara screamed, and she made the name herself, with her mouth and all her muscles. She ran four paces and slashed at a figure crouched on the deck. She felt its flesh and bone, and the hot spatter of its blood on her own skin, and she shrieked her joy into the lightening air of Nasranesh.

THIRTY-THREE

Mallesh climbed up the gathering pool stone at dusk, when the treetops shone gold and the lower leaves and trunks were shadow. The features of the selkesh on the benches below him were also smudged with darkness; he wondered whether his own would be any clearer.

"My people," he cried when he was standing straight. He felt as if he were shouting, though his voice was rough and thin, like a strained whisper. When he had been pulled out of the sea onto the shores of Nasranesh, the hole in his throat had been scarred shut. He had not tried to speak for weeks after that; and when he had, this voice had emerged. The selkesh listened to it, feeble as it was. They fell silent when he spoke to them, and leaned forward as they had when he had been whole and strong. He had dreaded their compassion—but it was fear he saw on their faces when they listened to him and looked at the wound he had taken across the sea. It was their fear that had made him want to live again, after the journey across, when he had yearned each day to die.

"My people," he said again, now that they were all gazing up at him, "strange boats have entered our waters. Leish's treachery has been confirmed!" He ground his fingers into his palms to keep his hands from shaking; that the gathering would be sure to see, despite the dimming of the light. "I told you, after my return from the western land, that our attack on the stone city failed because of Leish. The Queen and her fighters had been expecting us: he informed her of our plans." The lie came easily from his mouth now, but his hands still trembled—and some selkesh still shifted a bit on their benches, uncomfortable, unsure. "Some among you have doubted me," he continued, "for I swore to lead our people to victory across the sea and yet I came back to you defeated, without many of those who had followed me. Without Leish, who was the first to hear the city's song, who was the first to desire and possess it. It must have seduced him indeed, for him to have betrayed his own people. And now to pursue them with boats from the west."

He waited while his audience muttered; a pause for effect, but also to rest his voice. It tired so quickly now, and many words turned his throat's ache into anguish. While he waited, he saw some of the selkesh turn to one another and motion with their hands. He saw Dallia among them, her long black hair shining, somehow, as the treetops did. She was not moving or talking, just staring up at him, holding his mother's hand.

She had come to him by the hearth pool he had claimed for himself when he returned. He had not been able to stay with his parents, who welcomed him home and pitied him, and did not believe what he told them about Leish. "The seasong has changed," Dallia had said, facing him across the small, dark pool. He had felt his innards twist with dread, had angled his head in an almost-nod, hoping she would say more. "I have heard it, as have others. The water sings higher now, over shapes that do not belong to it. Dead wood—boats, probably. The notes grow more shrill every hour, and our people wish to know what this means and what we will do."

He had swallowed, heard it clearly in the silence that had filled his head since he had been dragged from the river to the sea. His men had pulled him beneath the icemounts' great flanks, and he had tried to ignore the sudden faintness of the songs he knew. The river behind him, the sea ahead, the islands, the shores and people of his own home, which he should have been able to hear by now—their notes were smudges. *My wound has made me deaf,* he had thought, and this had seemed another reason to die. But he had lived, and the songs had grown no clearer even as his wound began to heal. He heard nothing clearly, only a thick buzzing through which some notes thrust, a few together, most on their own, so that he could not identify them. Once back in Nasranesh, he had found this pool and lain beside it. After weeks of silence he had spoken to the awed selkesh who had come to him to ask about the failed campaign. Shame, lies, desperation—and then Dallia, looking at him without any awe at all, waiting for him to answer her.

"They have found us," he had said, as if he had heard the changing seasong himself. "Leish has led them here. Tell everyone to await me at the gathering pool." She had stayed where she was for a moment, and he had lifted his eyes away from hers, which saw him too clearly—as they still did, even with him atop the stone and her so far beneath and the air deep blue with dusk.

"We will surprise them—we will swim to their boats and attack before they know we are there. Any of them who escape will be met here by our knives and spears." The crowd was quiet, but they might as well have shouted; he heard them. *"Why should we follow you when your previous guidance brought us only death and dishonour?"* Mallesh glared down at them, attempted to find words that would convince them.

"I will go to the boats," Dallia called as she stood. "I hear them clearly, it will just be a short swim. Who will join me?"

Selkesh cried out, offering their names, leaping to their feet. Mallesh nodded as if this had been his plan, as if he weren't relieved and furious and echoing with silence within.

Dallia led her band into the sea just before dawn. Mallesh arranged most of those who remained in a line on the shore. They waited, clutching spears and knives, and when the sun rose, their breath left them together in one great sigh. Mallesh did not sigh; he hardly felt his own breathing. He looked at the dark, distant shapes ranged across the horizon. He remembered arrows and long, straight knives and selkesh screams that had sounded in his head long after all the songs had died. He rolled his spear shaft around against his palm and his webs and the lengths of his fingers; a spear for hunting shankfish among the bones of the Old City, or red-bellied eels in the river where it broadened, in the shadow of the peaks.

Two hours after dawn, other shapes appeared on the water. The selkesh on the shore strained to see; Mallesh did not need to. "The attack on the boats has failed," he said. His shadow-voice was even lower than usual, but they turned to him with wide, fearful eyes. "Let us stand together, here. They will see us as we are: strong and unafraid, lovers of our earth and water." He was not sure where these calm, measured words were coming from; they did not feel or sound like the ones he had used before to rally his troops. But the selkesh looked at him and nodded, and the ones who still bore the scars of Queensfolk blades and arrows were the first to straighten beside him.

The small boats drew closer. Sunlight glinted from metal and wood, green and blue cloth, the water that scattered from oars. So many boats—but one came ahead of the others, a larger one, in which two figures stood. A woman, Mallesh saw—the Queen; he would have known this even if Baldhron had not told him what she looked like. She was nearly as tall as the one who stood beside her.

"Leish ..." The name hissed along the line of selkesh like a wind in the trees behind them. Mallesh heard it as clearly as if each of them had whispered it to him alone, and he flinched, though he did not look away from the selkesh in the boat. *Not Leish,* he thought. *Another from the army, perhaps—not Leish; this one does not resemble him at all.* But the eyes half hidden by swollen lids were Leish's; the long, blood-encrusted fingers were his, and the cracked lips that hung apart, awaiting words or water. Mallesh felt his lies pressing on him, squeezing away his breath and blood as the arrow had. *"Leish's treachery ... Leish's doing ... Leish has led them to us ..."* Mallesh could not move, though he knew he should: the boats were close, drawing together like a shoal of hunting fish. He could see red cloth in the Queen's dark hair, and the places on Leish's face where the moisture of his own rotting flesh had gathered.

"Leish!" A shout from the line—his father, Mallesh knew. Their father. A spear streaked toward the Queen, who slid behind Leish. As the weapon clattered against wood, her left arm snaked around his throat. She raised her right arm very high and held it still for a moment then brought it sweeping down.

As soon as the first arrows left the Queensfolk bows, Mallesh moved again. "Run!" he cried. The selkesh beside him fell with an arrow in his chest, but Mallesh did not glance down. "Back to your hearth pools. We will engage them closer, so they cannot use these weapons! They do not know our homes or our land ..." He knew that he had told them to stand only a short time before; and now, so soon, to command them to run—it would seem confused, confusing, when really his mind was clear for the first time since he had come back here. "Run!" he cried again, ignoring the pain in his throat. "Send your children upriver and fight these invaders from your pools and trees ..."

Most of the selkesh did turn and race toward the trees and vines that stood between the shore and the hearth pools. Some lingered to throw their spears before they ran back. Mallesh saw a few Queensfolk pitch into the sea while the others struggled to steady the boats. But the boats were nearly aground now, and the arrows still whined, thick and glittering, and Mallesh too leapt away from the shore.

~

Too slow, Lanara thought as she rowed. Ever since the ships and the dying Sea Raiders she had felt the world dragging around her. The killing had been quick: a blink or a single pulse of heartblood. She had thrust her sword into the first Raider she had seen, and suddenly it seemed that she was pushing the last body over the ship's side. It was then, leaning over the rail watching dead Raiders float, that her surroundings had slowed. One of the Raiders had had long black hair that spread out around her like drifting velvet. Lanara had looked away from it, at the rowboats being lowered from this Queensship and the others. Aldron had been beside her, wiping his dagger on his leggings—one side, then the other, then back to the first—slow and strangely silent, as everything else seemed to be.

She pulled the oar back against her chest. The shore ahead was almost painfully clear, the colours and textures searing her eyes so that they would remain even if she closed her lids. Hummocks of shell-spattered moss at the water's edge; a tangle of enormously tall trees behind, hung with vines that rose in the wind despite their weight of blossoms. It was a warm wind, like nothing Lanara had felt in Luhr or on her travels; warm with cool beneath, like water that has lain in a fountain's bowl in sunlight. The wind also was slow.

She lifted the oar up and pushed her body forward. One stroke closer—and now she could see the faces of the ones who waited on the shore. Their skin was smoother than the prisoner's, their eyes whiter than his yellow ones. She saw their crude spears and tiny knives, felt the shape and heft of her bow pressing against her back as she rowed. *Too slow,* she thought again, and wished the Queen had not commanded her fighters to stay their hands until she gave them a signal. A signal: her arm raised, descending—Lanara saw it, felt her boat tip as the others in it stood and nocked arrows to their bows. She was standing with them, though she did not remember doing it. Aldron was in front of her, still sitting, smiling up at her as she drew her bowstring back.

She shot four Raiders down before one of them flailed his arms and sent most scattering back among the trees. A few remained behind. She shot two of them, and Aldron felled one with a dagger, and then their boat bit sand and she sprang onto the moss and ran. She heard herself panting and realized she had been hearing this sound since the dawn attack. *Faster, Nara, faster, Nara*—each footfall Ladhra's voice, pushing Lanara from open sun to dense green shade and then to dappled river-light.

She stopped running. Nearly all the Queensfighters had, though some had slowed closer to the river. There were no Sea Raiders here, just massive roots and trunks, and rounded hills rising among them, covered in creepers and moss and flowers. And the river, slow beneath the dome of trees, glinting black in some places and gold in others. Lanara heard the river as she had not heard screams, or the thud of bodies on wood, or the splashing of scores of feet by the shore. The river sang so quietly—neither surging like the Sarhenna nor splashing like the fountain in the Throne Chamber—but Lanara went still, listening to it.

"Where are they?" someone murmured, or shouted. Lanara shook her head, tried to clear it of the sounds of water and leaves. Two Queensfighters moved slowly to the river's edge. They looked down into the water—and they were *in* the water, thrashing and choking, sinking—and Queensfighters behind Lanara were also shrieking and falling. She looked back for a moment, just long enough to see knives and spears raining down from the trees; then she was running again, through a world that was no longer slow. She ran among the hills, weaving so that no flying weapon would find her. Her feet remembered hard earth baked flat, but she did not stumble on this sinking green, and she leapt over roots almost without glancing at them. She halted a few steps from the riverbank. The Queensfighters were bobbing there, face down in the shifting light. Blood curled away from them: mourning ribbons that would thin and vanish.

"Careful." Aldron's voice sounded as if it came from far away—farther than the trees behind, whose branches bent with bodies. Lanara did not turn to him, though she let him pull her down. They crouched by the bank. She saw plants beneath the water, swaying with the current; a glimmer of fish as well, and the shadows of the floating Queensfighters. And suddenly a darker, longer shadow, sliding up from black water.

"There," she said, more sigh than word. She fumbled for an arrow—no, her sword—the thing was too close already, its face veiled in water but twisting through—and Aldron plunged a spear down, wrenched it in and deeper. The water foamed wildly. Lanara saw hands flailing, grasping the spear haft. Very quickly the river was calm again. Aldron pulled the creature up so that it lay half on the bank. He braced his foot on its shoulder and jerked the spearhead free.

"There should be another," he said. "At least one." He looked back toward the trees and Lanara followed his gaze. There were fewer spears falling, more arrows now, arcing into the broad leaves; and more Sea Raider screams than Queensfighter. She turned again to the river just as Aldron waved his spear at a patch of sunlit water upriver. They both ran—but the water was empty, the plants beneath it undisturbed except for those by the bank. "Maybe it's at the very bottom," he said, poking at the place. Lanara stared at the plants that were still shuddering and shook her head. She looked from them to the hill closest to the river; she looked up above the hill and saw a thin, broken line, almost dissolved, hanging against the sky.

"Smoke," she said, her thoughts swift and clear. "The river has underground branches that lead there, and there." She pointed at another hill, and another, all the same, all breathing smoke from fires that had been recently quenched. "These are *houses,*" she said, and raised her sword.

At first Aldron helped her hack at the creepers and moss, but she motioned him away, panted, "No—they'll try to escape into the river again—wait there." He did, and she continued alone. The earth beneath the growing things was soft but very thick. She hacked at it and it sprayed around her until it lay like drifts of snow, and still she was not through. She dropped her sword and scrabbled with her hands. She hollowed out a hole and then hit a web of roots and picked up her sword once more. *Faster, Nara, faster, Nara.* She heard a ragged cheer go up from the other Queensfighters, far behind; she heard Aldron cry out, heard his spear in the water, but she did not pause. "Got one!" Aldron called, and the last root gave way in a shower of earth and she stumbled forward, into darkness.

She stood with her sword held in front of her and breathed in moist, heavy air. As she did, she saw that the darkness was not complete. There was light coming in the hole she had made, of course, but there were also specks of it hovering in front of her—coloured specks, which winked and spun and showed her a pool of still water perhaps ten paces ahead. The lights began to spin faster and more erratically. When they blurred toward her, Lanara bent her head and shielded her face with her hand. For an instant her hair and skin felt brushed with warmth—silk or soft, soft fingertips—and her ears were filled with a low whirring. She lifted her head when these sounds and touches had passed. She did not glance behind her; she squinted ahead, saw the sheen of water and, as her eyes adjusted, moss smooth around it, and a clear stone place stacked with wood. She looked up and saw broad roots jutting from the earthen walls, shapes on these roots that might have been bowls, cups, lengths of cloth.

She sheathed her sword, which was gritty with dirt, and drew her dagger from her belt. One step away from the outside light, and another—and then she was falling.

The moss was as gentle as some new wool she had touched in a cottage near the coastal road—but there were arms around her legs, and they were wrapped hard and fierce. She heaved onto her back, carrying the weight with her; and it was gone, it was a body rising up against the weak sunlight, an arm descending. She threw up her own arm and felt the quick heat of her flesh tearing open. She stabbed with the dagger she held in her good hand and heard a high, piercing scream. The body crumpled onto hers. She grunted as she rolled it off and onto its back.

A small one, like the shonyn small ones that play by the shore. She heard the voice as clearly as if Nellyn was beside her, and she shrank from it. The Sea Raider was young, but hardly a child; he was already tall, already strong enough to kill, or try to. His eyes stared up at the earth-and-roots ceiling, so far above that it was invisible in the half-darkness. His open mouth made a perfect circle, as a Queensboy's never could. Lanara looked at his knife, which had fallen onto the moss; its blade was wet, and she held up her arm. The skin of her forearm gaped and bled, though not very much—strange, since she could see the shine of bone when she fingered one side of the wound. She tried, one-handed, to rip some cloth from the hem of her tunic. When this did not work, she grasped an end of cloth below the Raider's shoulder and unwound it. His upper arm, bare, was quite slender. She held the cloth with her chin, pulled it as tightly as she could, round and round her wound. She tied it with fingers and teeth, and spat afterward into the moss. She knelt for a moment more beside him, because she had begun to shake—but then the light flickered and dimmed and Aldron shouted, "Nara—are you all right? Come outside and help us." She rose, strong and steady, and walked again into the daylight.

There were only a few Queensfighters beneath the far trees now; the rest were digging at the hills, as she had. She followed Aldron to another one, though he did not allow her to work with him once he saw her arm and its darkening bandage. She stood and watched him and the others as, one by one, the tall hill houses were opened to sky and metal. A tangle of flying creatures burst out each time—not coloured any more, in the sun, but dun-brown. They were moths, Lanara saw, with broad furred wings and fat bodies. They plummeted within seconds, to die among the torn vines and petals. She batted at them and pushed her way into another house, and another. She watched Aldron kill two Raiders by a pool and three more in the river. She managed to catch one in the back with her dagger; two others leapt into their pool before she could retrieve the dagger. She had thrown down her bow and arrows somewhere, sometime. She did not remember this, or indeed anything except running into darkness and out of it, and cheering with the other Queensfighters when another Raider died.

The shadows of trees and hills were lengthening. Lanara looked for the sun and found it, low and red, caught among the highest branches. She shook her head, tried to swallow over the taste of rot she had not noticed until now. Queensfighters moved nearby—but not Aldron; she could not see him by the river or among the gaping houses. She had no voice to call his name, so she walked, as quickly as she could, her left arm hanging heavily at her side. When she came to the grove from which the Raiders had attacked, she heard someone say, "It's over. The Queen is waiting for us." *The Queen,* Lanara thought. *Ladhra, Luhr: how could I forget all this?* She staggered after the person who had spoken—just a shadow among all the other shadows—until the trees ended and red-gold light stopped her and flooded her eyes with tears.

It was a wide space, she soon saw, ringed with trees but flat and open. A large pool lay in its centre, reflecting the edges of the forest and the colours of the sky. *Like the Throne Room fountain,* Lanara thought, grasping at details that would anchor her here; but the fountain was not like this at all. This pool could never have shone beneath a desert sky, not even through the magic of a hundred queens. It had been born here, sprung from a river that also fed green things and flowers. Lanara shivered with longing and hatred. In the middle of the pool was a tall stone, light green and grey except for a darker patch halfway up. At first Lanara could make no sense of this darker patch—but then she saw that it was Leish, bound once more, even around his forehead. Above him was Queen Galha, standing very straight atop the stone. *Malhan*—Lanara remembered this name too, and glimpsed the man on a bench by the pool; one of a series of benches, she saw, and went to join the Queensfighters who were already sitting or standing there. Some of them were laughing; most were bloody on clothes and skin. *They have no idea what will come now,* she thought, *but I do, and I am ready.*

"People of the Queen!" Galha cried, and they quieted, gazing up at her. "Our victory is nearly complete. My daughter is almost avenged. There is but one punishment remaining."

Lanara saw something move, beneath where the Queen was standing. Aldron. Lanara squinted at him, and he shimmered in her eyes before she forced them to focus. He was not looking at the Queen but around at the trees, down at the water, into the glow of the sun. Lanara did not recognize the expression on his face. Just as she thought, *I'll go to him,* he disappeared behind the tall stone. She could not have risen in any case; her wound was throbbing from arm to shoulder to ears. It was so loud that she heard only its pulse and ache—but then Queen Galha lifted her hands and face to the crimson sky and opened her mouth. Sounds blazed at last from the months and months of silence, and Lanara cried out, hearing them, and knew that she had not been ready after all.

~

"Leish!" His father's voice is faint, but Leish knows this is because Nasranesh's song is so vivid today. It has not sparkled so since he was a boy, picking out all the strands for the first time: the ocean against the land, the river through the

land, the living colours above and beneath, stretching all the way to the peaks that whispered snow. He hears these strands effortlessly now, together and separately, all of them as beloved as the voice that calls his name from the shore. Leish calls back to his father as he steps into the water, then onto the moss. He cannot recall ever having felt such welcome from the water before. Perhaps at birth, slipping from his mother's body into his hearth pool—but of course he does not remember this.

He hears splashing: probably Mallesh coming out behind him, letting him be first to shore as always. As if Leish could ever really be faster than Mallesh, whose limbs are so much longer. Leish sometimes does best him beneath the water, when his boy's body passes through smaller arches in the Old City and Mallesh is forced to take a different way—but that is all. And whenever he asks Mallesh not to let him win, his brother sputters and blusters and embarrasses them both—so Leish does not turn and speak to him about it. Not this time, when the water on his skin and the songs in his head are so sweet.

The trees welcome him too, wrapping him in green shade and gold. Vines brush his hair and the backs of his hands, and he smells moist petals, hears roots stretching beneath his feet. He follows a dazzle of notes to the gathering pool, where he stands and dozes a bit, until someone picks him up. His father, maybe (not his mother: Leish is too big for her to lift, except in water)—but he soon feels stone against his back and knows that it is Mallesh who has carried him. Leish will wait here at the bottom of the stone while Mallesh climbs it. Leish hears his feet scuffing and settling at the top. He will talk and talk—afterward as well, asking Leish what he thought of the speech, scanning his face for a lie. Leish presses his head and neck against the stone and prepares to listen, even though Mallesh's words cannot possibly be as strong and clear as the song of Nasranesh today.

Leish was choking. Water poured down his throat and he had no breath. There were fingers on his nose, pinching and gouging, and in his hair, pulling so viciously that his head snapped up and his streaming eyes opened. Even before they did and he saw the person beside him on the stone's base, he remembered. He remembered the pain of his body, he remembered every note of sea and jungle and city and river and tower and ship. He gagged and hacked, looked into the eyes of one of the Queensmen who had been with him since the day Dashran had died, on palace stones;

since the day Leish had first seen Ladhra, as his own people starved and stank beneath them.

He heard truth now, not dream or memory. The song of his land was splintering, its sounds rising and sharp with empty spaces. And above the changing song were other sounds: screams and breaking boughs, whoops and the pounding of feet. He listened as the Queensman bound rope around his forehead and tugged it taut. Leish felt the skin there crack open as the rest of his skin already had. They had carried him here—the Queensman had probably stepped on the flat rocks that lay just below the pool—so that he would have no relief from the water; and now he cracked and bled, and he did not care. Malhan was sitting on the first bench and Queensfolk were milling around the others. Leish saw the blood on these Queensfolk and knew it was mostly not their own. This he did care about—this made him struggle against the ropes and moan, though he longed to shout so loudly that his people would hear his shame and sorrow, and his love. So that his mother and father and Dallia and even Mallesh would hear him.

The Queen spoke, from the top of the stone. "Queen" and "daughter" was all he understood, though Wollshenyllosh had taught him so many words. Galha was silent for a moment afterward. Leish looked at the last of the sunlight, among the highest leaves—not at the Queensfolk who sat on the benches, with their carvings of Nasran and the land she had found. He and Mallesh and the other children had carved some of these. Leish had chipped out a fallen drylander because Mallesh had laughed at the fish he had begun first.

Blood dripped and beaded on Leish's eyelashes and he blinked it away. He heard the Queen say, *"Now,"* her voice low and harsh and very close, as if she were directing this word downward to him. He heard his breath, in and out—and then he heard the sounds of a dream he had had long ago. Dallia had woken him, held him and steadied him afterward. He whispered her name once before this waking horror took him.

~

The roots are the first to scream. They tear from the earth and strangle in air, too high for the touch of water or burrowing creatures. The trees fall one by one, until there is no forest, no dome above the river. The cries of the bark are long and deep; the leaves chatter and flutter and slow, crushed against the ground. They turn from green to brown, and brown to yellow—not autumn, which they have never known, but a separate season that withers them to dust in a moment. The vines among them rot to threads. The flowers crumble and scatter before the wind of words and dying. Moss curls into earth that cannot hold it. Hill houses split and flatten. The wind boils over the shore and into the sea, where coral bleeds to smooth white and plant stems keen and sliver away. Fish spin and struggle toward the water beyond the wind. Animals crawl and fly and slither among the toppled trees—but there is fire now. The flames hiss over the wood and through it, they roar into the sea. The Old City burns. The moss blackens on the shore and by the hearth pools, which cry out in shrinking foam. The river courses with flame, from the sea to the vanishing pools and past them all, up and on to where the peaks weep snow. The fire thunders close around the gathering pool, against a sky livid with colours that no longer live below.

All the waters of Nasranesh sing as they die. They sing beneath the flames, softer and broken, until only a whisper remains. Selkesh walk into this whisper, long lines of selkesh, their skin pale and dry, their bodies transparent, so that rock and blowing ash show through them. They crouch or lie still or stagger, they bend over black puddles and tear at the flesh of unrecognizable beasts. Some of these selkesh stand by the shore and look out across the wide salt water. They are motionless and stooped. Such pale, diseased skin and such twisted bodies—but their song is familiar. Weak, and warped with change and distance, yet still selkesh. They shimmer in the light of the lowering fire, and then they tremble into air. Their song lingers on the cooling wind but is soon lost, dissolved by louder noises. Hissing ash and drumming stone; slow, faint water; and silence, vast and empty. The end is silence.

THIRTY-FOUR

Alea was quiet by the time Nellyn reached the kitchen. She was standing, leaning on the table with her arms straight and her head bent, so that he could not see her face.

"What is it?" he asked when he was beside her. She was breathing very quickly and her eyes were half closed.

"My legs," she said, "look"—and he did, and saw that her yellow leggings were dark, darkening as he watched. "Is it blood?" she asked, her voice climbing higher again with each word. "Is it blood or is it water? And if it's just water, what colour is it? My mother told me that clear birthing water's good, but yellow's bad and brown worse—what can you—"

"Alea." He put his hand on the curve of her spine, pressed down when he felt her trembling. "It is water, not blood. And it has no colour in it."

Her arms bent as she let out her breath. "Good. But it's still too early. Nellyn, it's much too soon—the baby can't be ready. *I'm* not ready ..."

"You are. We are. Now tell me: where do you want to be? The fire here is already high, but I can stoke the one upstairs."

She pushed herself away from the table and turned to him, stepping back to make space between them for her enormous belly. "Upstairs," she said—and so Alea did see her walls after all, before Nellyn had finished painting them. It took them many minutes to climb there. She managed the first eleven steps holding on to the railing, with Nellyn close beside her—but at the twelfth she gave a cry and twisted herself against him, and did not move again until half a minute had passed. He supported her after that, and although she did not have another pain on the staircase, she moved more slowly and clung to him with white-tipped fingers.

When they stepped at last into the room, her fingers tightened even more sharply on his forearm before she lifted them to her mouth. She looked at the stone—at the earth and ivy and wood and flames that were painted upon it—and when she said his name, it was wobbly with tears.

"I'm not done," he said in a rush. "The fire isn't complete there, and I wanted to add some stars above the flames, all the way around. I wanted you to see—"

"Hush," she said, moving her fingertips from her own lips to his. "It's beautiful—it's perfect"—and then she moaned as another pain gripped her.

At first she stayed on her pallet, lying on one side, and watched Nellyn bring towels and blankets, extra wood and water in a deep basin. She draped a sheet over herself and he pulled off her sodden leggings. He ran to her when she cried out, and knelt beside her until the pain had gone. Thirty minutes went by, and three pains, and she struggled to sit up.

"I can't lie down any more," she said, "I have to sit"—and he brought her pillows from his sleeping floor to put behind her back. "Talk to me, distract me. Tell me about your home again." He did, slowly, stopping whenever her hands rose to her belly to press and stroke a pain away. She asked him questions and laughed sometimes when he wanted her to. He watched her smile at him and at her painted room, saw her muscles relax between pains, and he felt his own body loosen with relief. *I have never seen a woman—not even a shonyn woman—birth a baby, but Alea has, and she is strong and cheerful again. All will be well.*

"Look," she said, pointing to her window, "it's dark—you should go light the candles." He hesitated for a moment, but she said, "Go on—I'm fine. And bring me some food when you come back, I'm hungry ..."

They ate fruit and nuts and bread after he had lit the candles and scribbled an entry in the log (*No wind, clear sky, smooth water:* "Modest even for me," he said afterward, and she laughed again). She talked to him now about her girlhood and her people. She often spoke during the pains; some letters became very long or very short. "My si——sters would da——nce and I——'d—*hoooo*—" He checked on the lightroom twice, amazed that these hours had already passed; her breathing and movements were his measurements now, and they seemed so slow.

And then, around midnight, she could no longer speak through the pains, which came more closely together and lasted a bit longer every time. *Waves,* he thought as she whimpered and ground her heels against the floor;

waves taller and faster against the riverbank during the first of the rains, when shonyn scurried to hide indoors. She clutched his hand while she moaned. In between, he loosened her fingers and rubbed her palms and she smiled, though from further away than before.

"I need to walk," she said after he returned from trimming the wicks yet again. She pushed herself onto her hands and knees.

"Alea, you should rest, surely—"

"Get me up."

They walked around the room once, twice; she leaned against him when the pains came. He imagined that she would tire and sit, or maybe lie down—for the baby must be close to coming now, it had been half a day since the pains began. But she shuffled on, stopping in the same places with each circuit, and he came to know each brushstroke of these places, and every bump or pit in the stone—and still she walked and leaned. He breathed with her: deep and quickening as the pain began, and lengthening, softer as it ended. He held her hips as she hung from him with her arms around his neck; he felt her breathing and her cool, dry skin. The circles they walked were shonyn, for him—shonyn nights, each one the same, blurring into the last and the one to come. A rhythm he knew with his blood.

The pains began to come even more closely together, so that she hardly took three steps before another was upon her. She cried, "Lie down, lie down," and kept crying out even after she was on her pallet. She wailed without pause and seemingly without breath, and he knelt beside her, all his certainty dissolving. She no longer looked at him, and although she still clutched his hands, when he wrapped them around hers, she did not truly seem to notice them or him. *Be with her,* he told himself to quell his fear. *Follow her in every moment—that is all.* He felt his calm returning—but then her parted lips shaped words.

Fire beats against sky and skin, outside, where there are stars—but there only because of this other fire, deep deep within. A body like a brand, a body tight and hard as metal; not a body. The flames climb and burrow, and they will always be here, scalding breath black—but not always: a break, smoke billowing in wind. The body returned. A surge and a heavy thrusting weight, another,

another, and then the space of wind again, for breathing and looking at the sky of desert, lake, woods. Pressure like falling or floating underwater, too long but no other choice—and the weight moving down and through. The body filled and open, tearing with a different fire—another body, easing slow and vast, then rushing slithering weightless free.

Nellyn heard a thin, liquid sound through his own whimpering. He blinked away the imprints of sparks and stars and saw a baby. It was lying on its side, curled limply on a blanket. Its skin was as blue as a shonyn's. Nellyn stared at it and at his own trembling hands. There was bright red blood on the blanket; also on the baby's head, flattening its black hair, and streaks of it on belly and leg. And on Nellyn's hands. Alea's hands, he saw, were clean. They reached down, holding something. A ribbon, his sluggish mind told him: a scarlet ribbon, which she tied firmly around the looping cord that joined the baby to her. The cord was whitish, with something darker inside—green or deep red. Alea's fingers held a knife now. She sawed it upward through the cord and there was a spatter of blood, but the baby was quiet. Alea's hands slid beneath the baby's head and legs and lifted. Tiny arms and legs splayed wide—fingers and toes as well—and Nellyn saw the mouth open to wail again. He also saw that the baby was a girl.

Alea set the baby down against her skin, just below her breasts. She drew a clean blanket over them both, rubbing and warming. Nellyn saw tufts of hair, limbs that were pink now except for the hands and feet, which were still tinged with blue. Alea was singing, or speaking—he was not sure which. He looked at her for the first time since her Telling. Her hair was sweat-slick, clinging in whorls to her cheeks and neck. Her face was mottled, flushed and pale. Her forehead and left ear were smeared with blood. She raised her eyes to him and he saw the pink of burst veins where there should have been white. She smiled, held up one side of the blanket so that he could lower himself down beside her, so that she could cover him too and warm them all.

Her moan woke him. He started up, saw the baby's face close to his, relaxed. The baby's eyes were open, very dark and steady, as if she knew him and everything else. Alea moaned again and shifted, and said, "Nellyn—it's not done."

He scrambled to build up the fire and gather fresh blankets. When he glanced out the window, the dazzle of the sea made him squint—day already, well past dawn. Alea cried out behind him and he ran to her, because this cry was different from any she had uttered before. "Goddesses protect me, keep me close and keep my child, my children—something is wrong, wrong ..." He set his own hands beneath the baby. She was air and earth and water at once: slippery and slight, but with a weight that surprised him. He wound her in a sheet, tightly, thinking, *She will want to feel held close—it is how she has been, all this time until now.* He set the baby bundle behind him on a pillow and covered it with a small blanket, so that only nose and eyes and wrinkled forehead were visible.

Alea was weeping. He bent over her, smoothed the damp hair back from her forehead. "Hush," he said, "you will finish this soon. You are fine. You are *wonderful.*" But still she cried, in heaving, jerking sobs, and squeezed her swollen eyelids closed. There was no Telling this time, and so he watched her bend her chin to her chest and push down. He saw new blood leaving her, and he saw the crumpled gleam of a baby's head, just a bit and then more, and more, until it was round and full and out. Alea screamed once as the body slipped free with a rush of fluid; then she was silent.

There was a thick, putrid smell. Nellyn choked and turned his head away. This baby's body was greenish and crushed and far too tiny. He took a deep breath through his mouth and looked down at it again, then quickly up at Alea.

"Let me see it," she said in a low, hoarse voice. He swallowed and tried to shake his head, but could not. He rolled the thing gently onto a cloth without touching it with his hands. He held it up—still attached to its cord—so that she would see the side of its face that looked whole and sleeping. And one hand, with its five fingers and five nails.

Alea pressed her lips together but did not look away. "What—" she said, and "Is it a ..." and he said, "A girl."

For a moment Alea did not move. Then she raised her face up and laughed. Nellyn touched her shoulder. She shook his hand away, gasped, "Twin girls! Imagine: *twin girls!*" She laughed on, even as her body convulsed once more and the afterbirth slid onto the blanket beneath her.

Nellyn did not touch her again. He cut the second baby's cord (much more slender than the first one's) and wrapped the mass of afterbirth in the bloodied blanket. He found a clean blanket for the baby—red and blue wool; Alea had chosen it in Fane on the day he had bought her the copper armring. He was gentler with this baby than he had been with the other, even though the other had wriggled and mewled and this one was so still. He wound the cloth around legs and chest and arms, drew a long piece up over the face and head, and knotted it behind. He did not know what to do with it then. He laid it near Alea, who was quiet now, her eyes closed but fluttering lightly beneath their lids. He dribbled water between her lips, and she swallowed it but did not stir, not even when he said her name. Her skin was cool against the back of his hand.

The candles in the lightroom had all burned out. Most were just stumps, drowning in bubbled tallow. The floor beneath the candelabra was so layered with it that he could not see the wood. He thought, *We are lucky that there was no fire*—only there had been, of a sort, and he shivered as he remembered it.

He left the cleaning for later and went down to the writing floor. He washed his hands in the basin there. The water was cold, and the scrubbing crystals stung his skin. He left the dirty water too, and walked over to the desk, where the baby girl lay swaddled and wailing. He set her in the crook of his left arm and jiggled her a bit. She continued to cry, her eyes squeezed shut, her freed fists waving. He slid the tip of his little finger between her quivering lips and she sucked immediately, fiercely, tugging his fingers against the hollow at the back of her mouth. It would not satisfy her for long, he guessed—but after a few minutes her jaw slackened. Afternoon light turned the sea to bronze, and Alea's daughter slept against his heart, and Nellyn breathed with her, softly, into the silence of the tower.

THIRTY-FIVE

Lanara heard wind first. The wind in the desert sounded like this; she lay and listened to its moaning. There were other sounds, though, that were not as familiar: murmurings, cries, a jagged hissing. She moved her head, felt her cheek graze stone—hot, sharp stone. She sat up and opened her eyes.

For a moment her head and stomach swam with nausea and she saw nothing but darkness. She leaned forward with her fists against her eyes and swallowed a few times. She tasted dust and coughed, and then she saw the dust. It was black, soot or ash or both, swirling around her and up against a dull grey light that must be the sky. The rock she was sitting on was also black; it was pitted, and breathing bubbles and steam. As she looked at it, she felt the tight throbbing of her skin. She remembered the wound on her left arm—but as she scrambled to her feet, she saw blisters on her right arm and leg, and scarlet flesh between them. Her right cheek was blistered as well, and the tips of all the fingers on her right hand. She had lain on burning rock and not felt it; she had slept through pain and choking ash, had woken only because she had heard a wind that reminded her of home.

In two stumbling steps she moved from rock to dirt, which was cool enough to stand on. She whimpered, tried to turn away from the wind that scraped its claws across her, but could not. Although it did not stop blowing, its direction changed, leaving open spaces that she saw before the dust rose again. She saw dirt broken by more hissing rock, and smaller stones that looked white; she saw pools of thick black liquid that simmered and spat. She saw Queensfighters, standing and kneeling, as bloodied and burned as she was. Some of them were still holding swords; one was using hers on a Sea Raider who scrabbled and shrieked and then was silent. Lanara saw a few other Raiders who lived, and many more who did not.

When she looked over her shoulder, she saw clear sky far away, beyond the billowing dust, and blue-green water that rolled in gentle waves. She could not believe in this ocean, just as she could not believe in the place whose rich, dark earth still clung to the skin beneath her fingernails.

She saw a very tall stone to her left; it was so white and smooth that it might have shone in sunlight. She did not know what stone it was until she saw the people around it. It had been green-grey before and partly submerged in water (that wide, glinting pool that had also reminded her of home). But the Queen and Malhan were standing by this white stone, and the prisoner was still tied to it, though very high up now that the water was gone. Lanara dragged herself toward them through the clutching wind. It took a long time: the dust was often too thick to see through, and she had to stop and wait for another clear patch. Twice she stepped on more of the scalding rock, and once her heel touched one of the bubbling puddles. She was bent and staggering by the time the Queen's voice guided her through one last veil of ash.

Galha was craning her head up to see the prisoner; her back was to Lanara. "… stay with me," Lanara heard her say. "You will come back to my land with me and we will see how long you will be able to live without water."

I must reach her, Lanara thought dizzily. *I must bow down before her, for she is the greatest queen since Sarhenna.* She could not move. The Queen was the same as ever: tall, straight, her words to the prisoner clear and sharp. She stood surrounded by the destruction she had wrought, and she was the same. "My Queen." Lanara's words rasped against one another so softly that no one looked at her, not even Malhan, who was only a few paces in front of her. Galha spoke again.

Lanara was about to call out more loudly when she heard another voice, a low, wordless voice—so faint beneath all the other noises, wind and steam and skittering stones—but Lanara knew it, and began to walk. She walked quickly somehow, and still no one noticed her. She rounded the stone's base and fell to her knees and lowered her head so close to Aldron's that she felt the slow, weak thread of his breath against her mouth.

"Aldron." His eyelids fluttered but did not open. Blood trickled from the side of his mouth and from his right ear. There was so much blood on his chest that she thought, when she glanced down, that his tunic was black. But then she saw the darkness spreading, and she saw the spear that lay on the ground a few steps away from him.

"My Queen!" This time her voice was quite loud—but Galha and Malhan were already above her.

"Nara. Thank the First you are alive. Come, now, we will find one of my physicians to tend to your burns, and to that wound on your arm."

Lanara leaned back on her heels, though she kept one hand on Aldron's forehead and the other on his tunic where it was wet and torn. "My Queen, I don't need tending—it's Aldron who needs help. Let your physician see to him first. There may be little time ..."

Malhan bent his head, but he did not move more than that, and the Queen did not move at all.

"He is alive," Lanara cried, forgetting obeisance and awe. "How can you do nothing? He came so far for you—he took this wound for you—why do you stand apart from him, talking to the prisoner?" She leaned forward again, smelled ash and earth in Aldron's hair. Her blistered cheek stung with tears.

"Nara. My dear, look at him—he is already gone."

"He is not." His thread of breathing, his whispering heart. She looked up at Galha. "Please: find me a healer, or someone else who will find me one. I will stay with him. And you," she said to Aldron firmly, as if she expected him to contradict her, "listen to me. I know you don't take orders well, but listen to me—hold on to my voice. *Do not leave me.*"

~

The Queen's voice was so loud that Leish could not hear it when he woke on the gathering pool stone; he heard only distorted thunder that echoed but did not fade. After a time words began to thrust out of the other noise and he understood them, though he tried not to. "... will never grow again here. Little water, little food—but your people will live. They will not find a new place. Water of other places will kill ..."

He concentrated on different sounds: voices that were farther away, metal scraping stone, a wind that screamed. So many sounds, all deafening, for they sprang against emptiness above and beneath. Against space, where before there had been the song of Nasranesh.

Leish opened his eyes: better to see rather than merely to hear and wonder. He was not sure if he cried out. All his senses flattened. Moments later they bloomed, opened wide and wider still. Light and shapes battered at him as the sounds did, and smells smothered him as if he had been a stone sinking into black water. He heard, now, the notes that remained: diseased, hollow things, very faint, rock and ooze and scalding dust. He gasped for breath and wrenched his head from side to side—and he saw the ocean. As he looked, its song rose within him again, slow and sweet, unchanged. He reached for it and then reached beyond, heard islands and even that western shore that had called to him so long ago. He heard fresh water and plants and rich, dark earth, and he choked on his own thirst and knew what the Queen had done.

"Water of other places will kill." The selkesh would hear songs of water and be unable to follow them. They would hear the growing colours of other places and be forced to remain on the dirt of Nasranesh. Her prisoners, all of them, if they wished to live—though who among them would? Who would drink from the black pools just so that they would have to drink again and again?

Leish looked away from the ocean, inland. He caught glimpses of flat earth among the sheets of dust. Flat earth, and selkesh upon it, running where the river had run before, weaving its gold toward the peaks. He strained to see them—Dallia? Mother, Mallesh? that slight one, Father?—but they were so small, fleeing and wreathed in ash.

"You." Galha was below him, standing on the fissured pool-bed. He looked down at her, squinting a bit, since forms and shadings still hurt his eyes, just as her voice still rang too loudly in his ears. She was smiling. "You will stay with me. You will come back to my land with me and we will see how long you will be able to live without water."

He thought he might try to speak. "I will not live even one day for you," he might say, or, "I will die long before you take me back to your white city." But as he was forcing his stiff, cracked lips open, he saw the woman Lanara stumble to a halt behind Malhan (so brown and still that Leish had not noticed him). She passed behind the stone, and the Queen and Malhan followed. Leish heard the women's voices but not their words. Shortly after that, the space around the stone began to fill with Queensfighters. First two, carrying bowls and sacks and folded cloth, who also went around the stone to where Lanara was. Leish heard nothing for a long time—then a scream that made him moan as well.

More Queensfighters came, some walking, some crawling, some borne up by others. All of them clustered by the stone and were examined, one by one, by the two with the bowls and bags. Leish watched this from his height and was not sure why he did. None of the Queensfighters looked up at him. They huddled together, hunched around their blood and their pain, which he cared nothing for—except when he remembered that it had been selkesh who had drawn this blood. He hung from the stone as the dust-fanned sky darkened, and he listened to the ocean's song as if it could dull the cries of the people below him and the land below them.

Every time the Queensship pitched, Aldron whimpered. Lanara had looked forward to being aboard during the rough, halting walk to the edge of the sea. Aldron had been unconscious, his head rolling with each step of the five Queensmen who bore him. Lanara had walked beside him, pressing two of her fingers against his right wrist so that she could feel the tremor of his blood. The rowboats had been lying on the sloping rock that was the shore now—many scattered and overturned, but all intact despite the fire and wind that had howled into the sea. "The Queen's mindpowers," someone behind Lanara had said. "She spared the boats even as she destroyed our enemies." Lanara could not murmur in response as those around her had. She had managed to say, "Gently, please," to Aldron's bearers as they passed him into a boat. She had sat in the bottom with him and taken his head into her lap. The waves had been high; it was a long, wet, arduous trip. She knew the other Queensfighters in the boat needed her strength at the oars, but she stayed with Aldron and imagined how much more solid the Queensship would feel beneath them.

Timbers groaned and the cabin tipped and Lanara snatched at a glass vial that fell from the bag the doctors had left her with. They had washed Aldron's wound with water and wine. This had caused him to flail and shout—so one doctor had sat upon his legs and Lanara had set her knees on his shoulders while the other doctor stitched his ragged skin together.

He had been limp again by the time the fourth stitch was pulled taut, quickly and rather clumsily, since the ship was heaving and straining against its anchor. The doctors had shown her how to apply a poultice and bandage, had stitched her own wound and given her a bag of supplies. Then they had shaken their heads and recommended that she refrain from hoping for her friend, and had ducked out of the cabin.

The ship was underway now, and the sea was rougher than it had been. Aldron slid up and down in Lanara's bunk despite the pillow she had wedged behind his head and the blanket she had rolled up at his feet. His sliding was quite gentle compared with her own. She wrapped her arms around the wooden support pole at the head of the bed and clung there as the ship rose and fell. Sometimes her legs flew out from under her when the floor dipped, and her own weight nearly dragged her away from the post—but she scrabbled with her feet, and clung, and held her breath until the cabin righted itself.

She hardly heard the knock on her door over the sound of creaking wood. "Yes," she called, "come in"—and the door crashed against the wall. Malhan held it open, bracing himself with one hand on the door frame.

The Queen also steadied herself on the frame, with hands and wide-apart feet. "Nara!" she cried. The waves were much louder with the door open, and there was another noise, perhaps thunder. "Come with me to my cabin. We have food, and you must be hungry."

"Thank you," Lanara said, nearly shouting, "but I think I'll stay here. I don't want to leave Aldron so soon—and anyway, I have some bread and water here."

"Then I will have someone move him," Galha said. "He will also benefit from the comfort of my cabin."

Lanara shook her head and tightened her arms around the post. "He shouldn't be moved now. Best to leave him as he is. Maybe when he's better ..."

"Very well." The Queen remained in the doorway. "Nara—they didn't frighten you too much, did they? My mindpowers?"

"No." A lie—but the Queen had told her about the mindpowers months ago and must not think her weak now. "I wasn't frightened. I was amazed, as I knew I would be." *But then I found Aldron behind the stone, still alive. Perhaps your senses were blurred after you used your mindpowers? Perhaps you didn't hear him?* Lanara shook her head again, forcing the questions away.

The lantern swung as the cabin angled up. Galha's smile looked lopsided in the twisting of light and shadows. "Good. Come to me soon, my dear. And I will check on you later. You and Aldron both."

The door made no noise as it shut. Lanara heard Aldron's whimpering, which had been covered by waves and thunder and voices. She let her aching arms fall and climbed over the board that ran the length of the bed. Aldron had slid against the wall, so there was a bit of room—enough for her to lie on her side, facing him. Her blanket covered them both. She rested her left arm on the pillow above his head; her right hand she placed on his chest very lightly, above the blood-splotched bandage.

"I loathe doctors," she said quietly, her lips very close to his ear. "Do the Alilan have them? They never, ever say, 'This one will recover.' Perhaps they're not allowed to, for some ridiculous professional reason. So I'll say it for them: you will recover. You must. It's spring, you know—Alea will be having your baby soon. Imagine that: a baby in the signal tower! We'll put her in a basket in the kitchen window casement—there's so much sunlight there. Have you and Alea already chosen a name? I know some people's customs forbid the choosing of a name before a baby is born. Your twin goddesses will bless you, with this child and with your own life. Alea will tend you. Nellyn will too. He's so gentle, so careful and good. When we were in the mountains, I fell on a sharp stone and he stitched the wound and bathed it every day. His touch was so light I hardly felt it." Lanara bent her head against Aldron's shoulder. "It's spring," she said, and squeezed her eyes closed against the tears that would turn her blistered cheek to fire.

~

For eight days the sea raged and Aldron slept more deeply than sleep. Lanara was able to count these days only because Galha sent a Queensfighter to the cabin every morning with food. The Queen herself came three times—though Lanara wondered whether there had been more. She slept most of the day and night now, when she wasn't cleaning and binding Aldron's wound, or dripping water into his mouth, or feeding herself when she remembered to do so.

He shivered and sweated through a fever for three days. He also shouted and muttered, though she could not understand the words. The fever passed and he vomited for another day, a dry retching that produced nothing but bile and then not even that. When this sickness passed, she kept herself from dozing as much, expecting that he would soon wake, for his wound was clean and his skin cool. But he lay silent and motionless beside her, his eyes darting under closed lids.

And then, on the eighth day, she woke from a colourless dream to find his eyes open. His head was turned toward her, his face so close to hers that it was blurry—but she saw his eyes very clearly. She smiled and touched the line that ran through the skin of his forehead. "Welcome back," she said. He blinked slowly and licked his lips. She reached for the waterskin that hung from the bedframe and lifted his head, and he drank, one hand raised a bit as if he wanted to hold the skin himself. "Now," she said when he had finished, "talk to me. Just a few words. I want to hear your voice again."

The door behind them opened. There had been no knock—or maybe there had; she had been so intent on him that she might not have heard it. "My Queen," Lanara said, struggling to sit up and swing her legs over the bar, "he is awake—look, he is here again"—but the Queen frowned and Lanara saw that his face was turned to the wall. "Aldron?" she said, but he did not stir.

"Well," said Galha, "perhaps it was a momentary thing. He is still very weak, that much is certain." She was speaking at a normal volume; the sea was quieter today.

"Perhaps," said Lanara—but when the Queen and Malhan had gone, she leaned over Aldron and saw that his eyes were open, fixed on the wall. "What is it? What's wrong?"

He lay quietly on that day and the ones that followed, and she stopped speaking to him, asking, begging him to speak to her. But although she no longer talked, she still lay beside him, hoping that her warmth would do for them both, hoping that it might dissolve the fear that was rising in her, ringing in the silence.

~

Leish was not seasick. He wondered at this dimly, as the ship bucked and plunged. The wind screamed, and when his eyes were open he saw the waves breaking on the windows of the Queen's cabin—but he was calm. His body and mind both, though he did not understand this. He had yearned for death in his palace prison chamber, in the harbour house, on the last ocean crossing. And on the gathering pool stone most of all, when he had seen what the Queen had done to his land and his people. Queensfolk had cut him down from the stone (which was white and smooth as a bone, not the same stone as before) and dragged him over the steaming rock to the shore and put him in a boat. And then, as the water tossed him and choked him, he had stopped wanting to die. The strange new calm had settled over him, and nothing had yet ruffled it—not the Queen's cabin, where she tied him yet again (*How much rope have they used on me?* he had thought once), not the rotten fruit and maggot-foaming meat, not Galha's eyes and mouth when they taunted him. He felt nothing and feared nothing, and he was not sick.

One day when the ship rode more gently on the water, Leish was unbound again. The Queen ordered this done, and stood very close to him, watching. He also watched her, without defiance or dread. They took him to a hatch, half dragging him since his legs would not hold him. They pushed and pulled him up into the daylight, which seemed very bright even though he soon saw that the sky was heavy with clouds. The only glow was far away, maybe at the horizon, where lightning spat. The wind sucked away his breath when they hauled him up onto the place where the great wooden wheel stood, above the deck. He could hardly see the deck; it was an expanse of Queensfolk blue and green. Leish's eyes skimmed over their faces, stopped abruptly when they saw two he recognized. *Lanara*. He said the name carefully in his head, as if it might change something—but it did not. *Aldron*. They were beside the hatch at the prow, apart from everyone else. Aldron was sitting on a tall coil of rope, Lanara standing close beside him with a hand on his shoulder. *They look different,* Leish thought, and that was all—no curiosity, no feeling to make him wonder more.

The Queen was next to him, a few paces ahead. She was leaning on a slender length of wood and holding a drinking horn, a golden horn with jewels around its rim and water glittering inside. Leish remembered Ladhra and Wollshenyllosh holding it, or one like it. He steeled himself somewhere very deep within, but felt no pangs in his heart, or in his body that had to be so desperate for water.

"Some of you whisper about me." The crowd, which had been silent, somehow became quieter yet. Hair and clothing blew, but these were the only movements. "You mutter that my mindpowers should be able to calm the storms that have beset us. You say that my mindpowers should have saved the boats that have been lost." Some of the Queensfolk were shaking their heads, some staring at their feet. "Our beloved Sarhenna, the First Queen, was until now the only ruler in our history to have possessed mindpowers. She spoke to her last arrow, when she and all our people were lost and starving in the desert—and when she loosed it, this arrow struck the ground above a hidden spring. She called upon her mindpowers and moved the earth. She exposed the spring and made it a pool and caused many tributaries to flow from it. She summoned green things and water creatures. The great palace at Luhr was built around this vast summoning. The pool in the Throne Chamber is the very one that Sarhenna created. The city is the legacy of her mindpowers, which were true and potent."

Galha edged her walking stick forward. "The First suffered for her act of creation. She lay weak and ill for a month, while her people rejoiced in the hope she had given them. It is said that she never fully recovered—and she certainly was never able to call upon her mindpowers again. The only thing that gave her ease was the iben prophecy of another queen who would possess powers that would make the realm even greater." The Queen lifted her stick for a moment. She seemed to sway as she did so, her legs loose and unsteady. "All of you saw what I did in the Raiders' Land. I am the queen the iben foresaw. I am the first since Sarhenna to possess mindpowers, and I too have paid for their use with my strength. For over three weeks I lay in my cabin, dreaming of dark things, sunk in fever. For days after that I could not walk. Only now am I able to climb stairs, though slowly. Yet some of you would demand more of me, and some of you doubt me and claim that mindpowers have only ever been a tale told to amuse children. How could you possibly think these things after what you have all witnessed?"

Leish heard another storm approaching. His ears and webs and the roots of his hair ached with its song, as they had when he was a boy hoping for angry waves beneath which to dive. Galha raised her head as if she smelled this storm. She looked up at the lowering clouds, then back at the assembly below her. "Mindpowers are not trifles summoned in an instant. I became aware of my own only after I learned of my daughter's murder, and yet I could not use them until we reached the Raiders' Land. Only then, at the peak of my outrage, was I able to draw them forth. It may be that I will never do so again, just as the First did not. But her gift was a lasting one, as anyone who has seen Luhr can attest. Mine will also endure."

The hatch beside Leish opened. He did not turn at first, but he heard a rising murmur and saw a surge of movement on the deck, and he looked to see what had caused them. Three selkesh were standing by the Queen, held upright by Queensfolk: one woman, one man, the last a girl-child. They struggled against the arms that held them, but only briefly; then they looked at each other, too parched even for tears.

I know them, Leish thought, and now he struggled to feel—rage, dread, fear, anything that would make him shudder and live. But he still felt nothing, not even when Galha said, "My mindpowers will live in the bodies of every Sea Raider from now until the end of their line, whenever that may be. I have cursed them thus: They will have enough water and food in their land to sustain them. Should they travel to other lands in an attempt to escape their misery, they will be able to eat—but one taste of foreign water will kill them. Such will be the fate of all these people, both living and not yet born. They will always remember the fountains their ancestors defiled, and the Princess of the Fountains, who should have lived to be a queen. These," she continued, gesturing to the three selkesh, "will be the first to prove the power of the Queenscurse. I am holding in my hand water brought from Fane. Watch now, all of you, and remember."

Leish felt nothing—no twinge or stab, and no desperation for this nothingness. The Queen tipped the drinking horn and a thin stream of water fell onto the child's skin. She made a high, trembling sound and cringed, and her parents strained toward her—but the girl was still breathing, staring from her wet arm to her parents' faces.

"A touch," Galha said, "and she is not harmed. But now a drink"—and she stepped up to the man, and a Queenswoman pried his clenched teeth open. The Queen poured water in and down. He swallowed twice, opened his eyes wide and fell. The Queensman who was holding him let him go and he lay for a moment on the wood, twisted and motionless. Then the Queensman picked him up again and swung his light, limp body from side to side for all below to see.

The woman cried, "Murderers! My land and now my family ..." Leish understood her words, knew he was the only one who would. He closed his eyes so that her gaze would not fall upon him and see his heartlessness before she died. Or perhaps she might not see him at all; perhaps his body was as absent as the rest of him.

He heard her fall. The child was crying.

"This one, though"—the Queen's voice was slow and grave—"this one is just a child—an innocent, just as my own daughter was. I will not have her suffer the same fate as her parents. I will not belabour a thing that has already been made plain. No. I am a mother who has lost her child, and I will let this child go. Her kind can swim superbly well and even breathe under water. I will set her free." Leish heard a scrabble and a scream, a distant splash. *Swim and breathe, yes,* he thought, *but it is too far and she is too small ...*

He lost his thoughts beneath a wave of noise: cheering, shouting, the clamour of bow-ends and sword-flats on the deck. He opened his eyes to watch all the Queensfolk calling out their adulation, their frenzy of joy; to watch the Queen acknowledge them with bowed head. He looked back over the throng and saw that not everyone was cheering. Aldron was gaping. Lanara was bending, maybe speaking to him. He thrust himself to his feet and tried to turn. She caught him when he fell, helped him from knees to feet, and led him away down the hatch. *He is shocked, he is sick with horror*, Leish thought, and envy was the thing he almost felt.

~

"Mindpowers!" Aldron was on his side in Lanara's bunk, rocking back and forth with his arms around his knees. He lifted his head to speak the word—though it was more sung than spoken. Lanara stood by the door and watched.

During the month since he had first opened his eyes, he had not uttered a sound. He had lain straight and quiet, or stood at the side of the ship when she had convinced him that they both needed fresh air. He had looked on cabin and sea and her with hollow eyes, and said nothing. Nothing, until the Queen had clutched her stick and addressed her people, and the Raiders had died on the deck before her. "No," Aldron had said then, very quietly. Lanara had leaned over him to ask for more words, but before she could speak, he had gripped her arm and leaned his head against her leg. She had set her hand lightly on his hair. His breath was warm and quick; she had felt it as keenly as if there had been no cloth between his mouth and her skin. "No," he had murmured again, clutching her—and a moment later he had tried to rise.

"Mindpowers!" he cried again from her bed, and she strode toward him.

"Stop." She attempted to catch hold of his hands, which were now flailing. "Aldron—" She climbed into the bed and sat down, hard, on his thighs.

"You believe her," he said. His sudden calm was as unsettling as the frenzy had been. Lanara frowned as he went on, "You believe that Galha destroyed the Raiders' Land with mindpowers she inherited from an ancestor."

"Of course. How else could she have done it?"

He did not seem to have heard her. "Have you ever doubted her? Or have you ever hated yourself for believing her?"

She leaned closer to him. "Aldron, you're still not well—your wound was grave, after all, and you must also be feeling the shock of what happened in the battle. You were right there by the stone when she used her mindpowers. You were so close. Of course you're not recovered." She wondered as she spoke why he had been standing so close to the Queen; why, in fact, he had slipped behind the stone. Questions about Galha, questions about Aldron—Lanara shrank from them all, and would not ask them.

He was looking at her, truly *at* her, for the first time since the Raiders' Land. "Recovered? No. No." His voice was trembling now.

She shifted her gaze down, away from his. "Look, you've opened your wound again." She laid two fingers on the bandage. *He's so helpless,* she thought, *so lost.* She touched his cheeks with her palms. He shook his head once as she slid her hands down his neck and onto his shoulders, beneath his tunic. His arms came up and his fingers dug bruises she would not feel into her own shoulders. He held her away and she waited, and very soon his arms fell back again, drawing her with them. She saw the ragged line of blood on his bandage, and his eyes—and then his mouth opened against hers and she saw nothing more.

THIRTY-SIX

Twin girls. The window glass was cool against Alea's forehead, a slight, small relief to her body, which was as broken as if she had fallen from the leaping place ten times, twenty. As if she had leapt onto a horse that had refused, after hours and days of trying, to be tamed. She had propped herself at the window anyway. It was just pain, just skin and muscles. She had to look out at the ledge, had to give herself to this other pain that made her body into air.

"Burn her," she had told Nellyn when he had come to her and stood by her and the tightly wrapped bundle near her. Her voice had been hoarse from crying out and from the Telling she could hardly remember. "After night comes. It is my people's custom," she had added, since it seemed that there ought to be more words, ones that might ease the worry from his face.

It was the end of spring; the sunlight died very slowly and very late. But finally it was dark, and he came back from lighting the candles and took up the bundle. She had not touched it. She had not moved except to let him peel away her soiled blankets and shift. She only moved when she was sure the wood would be stacked and ready—and it was, it was already blazing. There were two fires. She saw him throw the bloody linens onto one. The other was closer to the cliff edge, burning lower but with more heat. It had been so long since she had watched a fire burn in the open air. She could not see what was within—but she knew. The woven blanket would blacken and merge with flesh, and the flesh would dissolve, and it would take no time at all, not for such a tiny thing. *Alnila take her body, Alneth her body's ashes. Welcome her, despite my failings.*

Alea slid to the floor. She sat against the wall and noticed her other baby, which was lying in front of the fireplace. Arms and legs had thrust free of the cloth. They were waving, pulling in tight, waving again. Alea listened to its crying, watched it squirm and flail—and then Nellyn was there, picking it up.

"Alea. Hold her—please, take her. She needs milk." He smelled like smoke. His voice was muffled, as if her ears were full of water or wind, but she understood. She saw him pass the baby over, saw it fit into the angle of her arm. She felt its bumpy, round weight—the same shapes that had been within her this morning. She saw it turn its head into the skin of her breast. She raised her arm and its mouth found her nipple. One suck, a slide away, another suck, too sharp. Alea waited for it to open its mouth on a wail, then brought its face quickly to her breast again. This time the lips clamped wide and the suck was long and painless, and there was another, and another. The baby swallowed. Of course, this was the right position, the right way to get an uncertain infant to suckle. Alea had learned from her mother. She remembered watching her with newborn Alnanna, remembered asking her wondering, breathless questions until Aldana laughed and told her she'd find out for herself someday.

"The Goddesses of the Alilan have punished me." Her words still hurt her throat, but she had to speak. Nellyn was kneeling in front of her, so tired and sad, and the baby was sucking, and Alea knew these things should be important, that she should say something.

"Why would they do this?" he asked, and she almost felt warm because he had not said, "Don't be silly—of course they're not."

"Because of Aldron's power." She told Nellyn, talked in a steady stream that became a torrent. Old Aldira, Aliser, the boy Aldron, the heartflowers on the dusty table, the blue light in the walls, the snuffed fire, flung pebbles, the Perona riding away screaming. Aldron weak and sick, unrepentant; both of them leaving daggers and horses, and walking from the fires of all the caravans around the oasis. Everything: every forbidden change, every argument. Everything—even a baby sleeping and another drifting in the darkness above the Eastern Sea. She cried as she spoke, and after—for the words and their meaning, and also for the speaking of them.

"I knew the fire in the inn was real," Nellyn said at last, long after she had finished speaking. "And I saw him make a flower for you in the kitchen, when he gave you the purple vase. I think I have seen him make other things as well." She sniffled and nodded, and he smiled at her. "But look! Look what you and Aldron have made together."

Alea looked down at the black hair, the closed eyes, the mouth that still tugged even in sleep. Nellyn cupped one hand around the baby's head; with the other he drew Alea's forehead gently against his own. She leaned against him and wished, as she cried again, that it could be so simple.

~

Nellyn leaned over the soup pot and drew in a deep, noisy breath. "Ah," he said as he straightened, "it is definitely your best yet."

Alea laughed. "You haven't even tasted it yet! And anyway, summer vegetables are so much more palatable than spring ones."

"Modesty," he said, and ladled soup into a deep blue bowl.

"Not too full, remember: you always spill some on the stairs."

He tried—and failed—to look indignant. Alea was sitting in the window, and baby Alnissa was at her breast, making alarmingly loud, appreciative noises, and the sun was shining on them both. He could feel the wind even from where he stood; it was hot and damp, and it stirred Alea's hair and the herb bundles that hung from the beams. Soon it would be too hot for a fire.

"Hush, little foal," Alea said to her daughter, "you'll get the other side too." He stood for a moment, watching as Alea sat the baby up, patted her back, moved her smoothly to the other breast. He had had to remind Alea to feed the baby for three weeks after the birth. He had come down from the writing room each night, three or four times, to pick the screaming child up from where she lay, beside Alea. He had urged her with words sometimes, or without them, and she had always complied, so slowly and listlessly that he had feared for mother and daughter both. He had feared for them so intensely that he hardly slept in the morning and often forgot to eat, himself.

One night there had been only silence below him. He had waited, listened, strained for any sound other than the wind—and then he had run down the stairs two at a time. Alea was on her side, the baby was suckling, and both of them were half asleep. And shortly after that night Alea had said, "I've named her Alnissa. It's a fine old name in my caravan." She had held his hand very tightly and smiled—her first smile since the birth and the sorrow after.

The bowl was burning his palm. He shifted it to his other hand and turned to the stairs. He walked carefully, and was so pleased with himself by the time he reached the writing room that he set the bowl down too quickly. Soup surged against the side and over. He yelped an oath he had learned from Lanara and sucked on his scalded hand. He examined it, saw that it was pink but no more injured than that, then looked out at the sea.

The waves were high today. It still surprised him that the water could be so angry when the sun was shining. It had not shone much these past few weeks. He had recorded storm after storm, while the bell clanged fitfully and lightning blotted out the stars. But the sun was dazzling now, as it sank behind the tower. Bronze light, and long shadows of cloud on the far water.

Not cloud. Nellyn squeezed his eyes shut, looked again: not cloud, but spots, specks that did not waver beneath the changing sky. He remembered how they had disappeared when he had last watched them. He had written about sails and wind—meaningless, desolate words then, but he remembered them now.

The boats would not reach the harbour by the time darkness fell. He ran up to the lightroom—so much running, not shonyn—and pressed his face against the window briefly before he lowered the candelabra and lit the candles. His hands were shaking, but he did not pause to steady them. His breath was ragged, but he did not pause to steady it. He ran down and down, into the kitchen.

Alea looked up at him. She was sitting at the table, and Alnissa was sleeping on her belly in a basket lined with red cloth. "Nellyn?" Alea said, a spoon halfway to her mouth. He could not speak, but this did not seem to matter. She pushed back her stool so sharply that it fell. The spoon fell too, and Alnissa twitched but did not wake. "Nellyn—*what?*"

"The ships." She stared at him as if he were speaking the shonyn language. "I have lit the candles," he went on, "but I am going to make some fires outside, too. It will be very dark by the time they near the cliffs, and there is no moon at all tonight." She was not seeing him; she was staring through him. He left her there by the table. Only start the fires—then he would go back and stay with her until. Until.

He fumbled with the wood he had stacked so neatly in the shed weeks before. He threw it on the ledge in untidy piles that grew untidier with every armload he added. He was panting, sweating, his hands stuck full of splinters and brushed with lichen-dust—and then her hands were there, taking the wood from him. She rearranged the piles quickly, smoothly, until they stood tall and steady. She went back into the tower and emerged a few moments later. She handed him one of the torches she had carried out, and kept the other. She touched her torch to the first pile, waited for a flame to catch and grow. She tossed the torch to the top of the stack—and he finally moved, finally walked to the next one and lit it with a hand that did not shake.

When each of the fires was burning, Alea led him to where the cliff fell away, down to rocks and spray. He held her hand and breathed smoke and salt. They stood above the sea and waited, as the night came down around them and the flames called out behind.

~

Aldron did not touch Lanara as they stood at the ship's rail and watched the land take shape ahead of them. It had always been he who had touched first, these past few weeks—trailing his fingers across the small of her back or her neck, coming up behind her and leaning, slowly, pressing until she twisted around against him. She was certain people had seen them, or at least heard them. *But he always starts it,* she told herself, standing beside him, glancing at his motionless hands on the rail. *Except for that first time, he always has.*

For a time many Queensfighters clustered at the side and up along the line of the prow, shouting to each other, gesturing at the shimmering line of land. It was very hard to see, with the sun setting behind it, but Lanara thought she could make out the taller shadows of cliffs flanking the open bronze space that had to be Fane's harbour.

"You see—I have steered us true." Lanara started and turned to the Queen, who was one pace behind. The ship rose on a wave and Galha reached for the rail. "Do you not think it astounding that I was able to return us to the precise spot of our departure?"

"Yes," Lanara said, "of course."

Aldron was holding the rail so tightly that the skin of his hands was white and stretched. Galha had emerged from her cabin only a few times after her speech, and Lanara and Aldron had not seen her. They had not spoken of her—had hardly spoken at all—and yet Galha had grown larger in their silence. And now she was here, and most of the Queensfighters had dispersed, leaving empty boards and the three of them, staring at the thickening line of the Queensrealm.

"What will you do, Nara? When we return to our land."

Lanara cleared her throat. "I will … I don't know. Probably stay at the signal tower. You posted me there, after all, and I did enjoy the work." Galha was not listening to her. Lanara saw her looking past her, saw her bright, seeking eyes on Aldron.

"And you," the Queen said to him, her words low and sharp at the same time, "would you also do my service somewhere? You have been a great help to me so far."

He stared at his hands and said nothing for so long that Lanara nearly spoke again, to end the unbearable waiting.

"No," he said at last. His voice was as rough and breathy as it had been when he first spoke after his wound. Lanara had expected it to change, to assume its old strength, but it had not. "I'll travel again. With Alea, if she'll have me. And our child."

Lanara wanted, for a moment, to cry out or grasp his hands, his face, so that he would have to show her his eyes. She shrank from her need, and her foolishness.

"Ah," said Galha. "And will you travel your old paths, near Queensfolk places?"

"No," he said immediately, and raised his gaze to Galha's. "I'll go as far away as I can, into new places. I want no part of my old paths, or the Queensrealm."

"Aldron!" Lanara gasped, and he finally looked at her, his eyes empty of the desire and fear that had shone in them all these months.

"No, Nara, I am not offended. Indeed, I am happy that he will seek out a different life. Perhaps we will all do so, in our own ways. Though I, of course," Galha went on, almost cheerfully, "will return to Luhr. There will be much to attend to, much to be written—Malhan and I will hardly sleep,

I'm sure of it. Perhaps I should try to sleep now, before we land. It will be a few more hours, and after that my people will need me, there will be no end of demands. I wonder whether Luhr will be safe under the regency of my Queensguards. I'm not at all sure ..." Galha was walking away, trailing words, her hands waving as if she were still speaking to someone. Lanara saw Malhan step into her path and take both of her hands before they walked back to the main hatch.

"She's ill," Lanara said. "Her mindpowers have sapped her somehow—she's not as she was. Do you think—" But Aldron was not behind her, and the hatch in the prow stood open. Lanara laughed. "Talking to myself again, just as I did in the shonyn village." She leaned her head on her hands, abruptly dizzy. When she looked up again, the sky was deep blue and glittering with stars in the west—some so bright, so low that they made her blink.

Not stars. Fires, three of them; and a fainter shimmer above them that was candlelight glancing off mirrors and metal. Lanara stood alone by the rail, and her tears turned the fires into one great blaze, burning up against the rock and the stars, calling the Queensships home again.

THIRTY-SEVEN

Queen Galha's victorious fleet reached the shores of the Queensrealm at midnight. The Queen looked upon the torches of those of her subjects already gathered on the wharf, and there were tears of joy on her cheeks when she declared that the largest Queensships would wait until first light to enter the harbour. "More of my people will be waiting by then," she said; "let us return to them in the brightness of day, rather than beneath the cloaking darkness of night." And so it was that, while the smaller vessels made their way to the docks and the river's mouth, where the waters were less dangerous to them, the larger Queensships dropped anchor outside the encircling cliffs.

When the golden light of dawn bloomed, two Queensships led the Queen's own vessel into Fane's harbour. Queen Galha stood at the prow, as she had when first she came to Fane in her pursuit of the Sea Raiders. Then her face had been solemn and fierce; now it was radiant with triumph and gratitude. Her people awaited her in reverent silence. They stood on the docks and on the wharf; they clustered at windows and on roofs and along the tops of the bridgetowers. They looked on their Queen and were amazed. Even I, who have been privileged to witness all the days of her reign since she was a young woman, was amazed.

Queensfighters lined the decks of all the ships, and yet no names were called from deck to wharf, no hands raised in joyous welcome. All the Queensfolk, on land and ship alike, waited for Queen Galha's words.

"People of the Queensrealm," she cried when her ship had anchored at last, at the end of the longest dock. "Victory is ours!" And now the silence was shattered by voices and hands, all clamouring in relief that banished the fear of many long months.

"The Sea Raiders are defeated," the Queen continued when the crowd had quieted. "For my army attacked with relentless strength and skill, and

afterward there was a further punishment—a punishment so unexpected and so great that words will never compass it." She lifted her hands above her, forming the sign of the arrowhead. "I am Sarhenna's true heir, for I have her gift in my blood. I too possess mindpowers, and it was they that cursed my daughter's murderers and their land. Yes," she said, this one word ringing above the crowd's murmuring, "yes: my mindpowers, though as I wielded them I felt the presence of my ancestor, that queen who made us great when we were just a ragged tribe lost in the desert. But I did not destroy the Sea Raiders, though I could have. No—I showed them mercy. They will live on, in their changed land. They will live on, never to cause more grief to any as they did to me. And so," she continued after another cheer had subsided, "we have returned, and shall mount a celebration worthy of conquering warriors. In two nights' time, Fane's wharf and riverside shall ring with merriment. There shall be wine and food, music and dancing. Until then, my Queensfighters will take their ease, for they have endured hardships not to be spoken of or even imagined. Rejoice, then, people of the Queen, and welcome your dear ones home."

The cheers this time rang with names, and the waiting throng surged toward the docks. Each of the Queensships extended their walkways, and Queensfighters streamed along them, rushing into the arms of parents, children, friends. It was a scene of joy that will forever cast its glow upon this Queen.

~

Nellyn smelled the ships long before he reached the wharf. Human waste and blood, rotten meat; he gasped and covered his nose and mouth with a hand, even though the motion made him dizzy on the narrow path. *Shift away,* he begged the wind, and after a moment it did, just enough for him to place his hand back on the cliff and resume his descent.

"No," Alea had said when he asked her if she would come with him. "Let him come to me. To us." She was gazing down at Alnissa, who was lying on her back, kicking—not sleeping, as she should have been.

"Then I will stay with you," Nellyn had said.

Alea had shaken her head. "No. Go to Lanara now. She will want you to be there." She did not look at him, even when he told her he would go and said farewell. *Another change I do not understand,* he had thought as he made his way carefully through the darkness. *There was sadness in Lanara's leaving, but now there is a different sadness—for Alea, but also for me, and I did not expect it.*

The wharf also stank, with cooking meat and stale sweat—and even fresh sweat, for the air was already warm and there were many bodies pressed together, waiting. Nellyn breathed through his mouth as he walked toward the docks. At first he tried not to bump or jostle, tried to wait for a space to open before he stepped forward, but he soon realized that he would have to push if he wished to move at all. He had been in the tower the last time so many people had gathered here. His head swam with the smells, the roiling, murmuring mass of bodies. He attempted to imagine his river and the silence that lay so thickly there, after dawn; or even the tower, with its round spaces and Alnissa's gurgling cries—but he could not. He was surrounded and small, and his breath came sharp with panic.

"Here, now," someone said, very close to his ear. "There's room by me, and see—the biggest boat will surely anchor just ahead. I've a grandson aboard—First grant he be unharmed ..." Nellyn took a long swallow from the woven seagreen bag the man offered him, and for a moment the stink seemed washed from his mouth. He saw nothing except heads and backs and dark grey sky before him. He knew some smaller boats had already returned to harbour. He had seen them waiting at the bridgetowers, bobbing shadows that had not been there the day before. No one had left these boats. "Why do they wait?" the old man fretted. "Where are the sailors, and why are the largest ships still out in open sea?" Nellyn did not respond. He watched the sky ease from grey to gold-streaked blue; he heard the scream of an anchor and the splash of oars. "Oh, by the Mother of us all," the man beside him said, many splashes later, and then Nellyn too saw the largest Queensship.

He had seen so many of these ships on his river, all clean and sleek. He had seen this very ship, a shining, graceful thing between the snow-piled banks of Fane. Now it seemed to limp behind the two boats that came before it. Each of them was tattered. Their sails were torn and bleached well beyond blue and green, and their wood was gouged and discoloured. The rowboats that hung above the deck looked black, as if they had been made from lynanyn bark—but that could not be; they must have been seared by some sort of heat or flame. Queensfolk clung to the rails. As the sunlight shone brighter and the boats drew closer, Nellyn saw gaunt cheeks and sunken eyes, bandages stained black. He swallowed over bile—fear, and a stronger waft of stench—and looked for Lanara. So many faces, and the light was in his eyes. He rubbed at them and looked again, and saw the Queen step up to the prow and stretch her arms above her head.

Galha's voice was shrill, and he did not listen to her words. Some of the people around him gave a feeble cheer during her speech, but it did nothing to lighten the silence that hung over them all. He was nearly blind with the strain of seeking out Lanara's face—blind, deaf, choked with dread, and still he did not see her, even when Queensfolk began to stream off the ships. The silence shattered. He heard cries of joy and some laughter, and a wail that made him flinch. The old man was gone from beside him. Nellyn stood still as everyone around him spun and shouted. Very soon there were fewer people on the wharf and he could see the Queensship clearly. The Queensfolk coming down its plank now were leaning on sticks or being carried on litters of cloth and wood. Some were missing limbs; some looked intact in body but lay staring at the sky as if they had no life in them. Nellyn took two paces toward the dock—and finally, finally saw a face he knew.

"Aldron!" The word was a hiss. Nellyn called again, and Aldron was right in front of him in any case—but the Alilan man went past without glancing at him. Nellyn watched him for the space of three breaths. When he turned back to the ship, Lanara was there on the dock, walking slowly, looking at her feet as she set them down and raised them up again.

He had no voice at all this time. He saw that her hair was thicker and curlier than it had been, that her skin and clothes were mottled with dirt. He watched her take her small, uneasy steps, watched her stop four paces away from him and lift her eyes.

"You came," she said, her voice rising as if it were a question.

He tried to smile. "Of course. Did you think I might not?"

"I wasn't sure, the path is so steep ..."

He reached her in three strides. Her hair and skin stank as the ships had—but beneath was her smell, and he remembered Luhr, a waterfall, mountains, an inn, a wagon, all these images vibrant and fierce because he had not held her in so long.

~

Alea thought at first that she would wait for Aldron in the dark. She would sit at the kitchen table (not in the window; she would *not* watch for him) in her brown linen shift, without candles or lanterns. He would walk in and hesitate until his eyes adjusted to the dimness, and she would rise up, a silent shadow that would make him quail.

When Nellyn saw the boats and she imagined that her waiting was nearly over, she paced up and down the stairs and around each of the floors. Even when she heard the crowd in the town and knew that the boats had docked, she did not glance out the windows overlooking the path. He might be looking up; he might see her and think her eager to see him. She remained far away from the glass.

When the door opened, a little over an hour past dawn on the day of the ships' return, she was on her sleeping floor. She heard the door shut and leaned against her wall for a moment to steady herself. She traced an edge of painted flame with her forefinger and took a deep, noisy breath against Alnissa's silken hair. Then she went down the stairs, letting her feet fall heavily enough that the people below would hear her coming.

Nellyn and Lanara looked up at her when she reached the steps leading into the kitchen. Alea stopped, frozen by Lanara's filth and smell, and by her dull, darting eyes. Alea forced her own eyes away, to the spaces behind or beside Nellyn and Lanara that should have been taken up by someone else.

"Where is he?" Alea asked.

Lanara bowed her head. For a moment Alea felt the steps dip beneath her feet, and she had to grip the handrail and Alnissa to keep herself from falling. But then she heard Nellyn say, "He is not here? I saw him on the wharf. I thought he would come directly"—and Alea's rage roared again within her, so high that her head throbbed with heat.

Nellyn and Lanara had disappeared after that. Alea had heard things, dimly: the splash of water in the large copper basin that stood outside now that the days and nights were warm; voices, low and distant; and then silence. As she was feeding Alnissa in the late afternoon, Nellyn came into the kitchen and prepared a tray of food. When he was done, he opened his mouth to speak, but Alea held up her hand and turned her face away from him, and he went back up the stairs.

It was when the sunlight left the room that she thought, *I will not light candles or lanterns. I will sit here in the dark and wait for him.* But as the hours passed, the burning of her fury made her think instead of light. Scores of candles, all the lanterns in this room and hers, perhaps even the fire—though in the end it was candles and lanterns only, since they would make the kitchen hot and bright enough. She made a second lightroom in the tower, so that Aldron would see her immediately, and their baby; so that there would be no shadows to shelter him from them. She sat with her back against the table, very straight, certain that she would not doze—but she was there a long time, and Alnissa was sleeping, and Alea must have dozed after all, because when the door creaked open, her head snapped up.

Aldron was leaning on the door frame, one hand over his eyes to shield them from the unexpected light. The laces of his shirt were undone; she saw a wide piece of cloth wrapped around his chest, and the skin around it, grey with dirt—all his skin smudged and cracked. His hand dropped from his face and he blinked into the room. In the time it took him to focus his gaze, she had seen the rest: his hollow cheeks, his matted beard, his eyes, which were nearly invisible, sunk into bone. She made a sound, quite soft, but he angled his head and blinked twice more and saw her. He took two steps, looked down at his feet, then up—but before his eyes found her again, they found the basket at her feet.

He fell to his knees beside it, so close to Alea that her eyes watered with his stench and she saw the tangles in his hair. He knelt for a long time with his head bent, looking. He lifted a hand and it hovered above the basket but did not lower.

"Touch her," Alea said, her voice aching in her throat. "Pick her up. She's yours, she's your daughter"—but his hand fell back to his side. Alea leaned forward and put her fingers in his knotted hair. She drew him gently forward until his head was in her lap. "Hush," she said, even though he was not crying. She kissed him on his hair and on his skin. "Hush, love."

THIRTY-EIGHT

Lanara had been warm for two days—a deep, encircling warmth that had let her sleep as she never had on the ship. Nellyn had brought her food, and washed her, and stretched out beside her after dawn. She woke against him, watched the blue cloth he had hung sway in the wind that blew through their small window. She had never left, perhaps. She had been here, sleeping and waking, suffused with this warmth that made her heavy.

Except that she *had* been away: she could not deny this as she stood on the cliff path at the place where it turned in its descent to Fane. She looked down at the fires that burned on the wharf and up along the river. She heard snatches of singing and laughter when the wind shifted. She watched and listened and felt the weariness of her body, and its unsteadiness, as if she still walked on a deck, not earth and stone. *I can't,* she thought. *I'm so tired I can hardly stand.* Exhaustion, that was all, the only reason she turned and walked back up the path, away from the Queen's celebration.

She did not see Alea when she climbed through the tower. She had seen her only once since her return, and Aldron not at all. Lanara had not sought them out; they would all be apart for a time, resting, and that was as it should be. And Aldron had the baby now. Lanara vaguely remembered seeing it in Alea's arms when she had stood on the stairs, looking into the kitchen.

Lanara heard nothing in the tower. Nellyn would be writing in the log or attending to the candles in the lightroom. She would sit and watch him. It was all she wanted to do, which surprised her a bit. She should have yearned for the revelry and companionship of the party, and yet she was here, stepping up through silence so thick it lapped like waves in her ears.

"Oh." She said the word involuntarily, and it echoed in the writing room. Nellyn and Alea turned to her. He was sitting at the desk and she was on a cushion on the floor near him. They had not been talking, just sitting.

"You said you would go to the celebration," Nellyn said, rising, crossing to her. He touched her cheek.

Lanara nodded. "Yes, and I started to walk there, but I'm just too tired still." *That's all*—again the insistence, the pushing against something else so that it would remain nameless.

"Sit," he said. "Here—we have fresh sunfruit ..."

"Where's Aldron?" she asked when she was on the stool, a bowl of sliced fruit untouched in her lap.

Alea straightened on her cushion and tucked her hair behind her ears. "Sleeping, finally. He hasn't slept since he returned."

Lanara stared down at the fruit, pushed at one red sliver with her forefinger.

"What happened there?" Alea's voice was so low that Lanara nearly felt the words rather than heard them. She could not look up—but of course she had to speak.

"Hasn't he told you?" she said, so that she would have more time to order her words.

"No. He hardly speaks. He's weak and ill, yet the wound in his chest is almost completely healed, so there doesn't seem to be a reason for his weakness. Tell me, since you have your voice: what happened in that place?"

It was easy to talk once Lanara had begun. She talked of the voyage across, the landing, the battle, where Aldron had fought bravely and well. She talked of the Queen standing atop the tall stone in the pool; of her raised arms and the sudden blazing of her mindpowers. The fire, the wind, the curse, Aldron gasping behind the stone. Lanara described it all, growing more certain as she did so. She had not told Nellyn this much, only small bits, and he had not pressed her for more. She had been afraid to tell more, as if the words, spoken, would bring the flames and bubbling skin back to her—but they did not. She was stronger, almost herself, as she had been in the winter.

"So," Alea said, long minutes after Lanara had finished, "where was Aldron when your Queen's power burst forth?"

Lanara frowned. Alea's voice was higher than it had been, with an edge that would have been mockery if it had not also sounded like desperation. "At the foot of the stone," she replied. "Behind it while she spoke."

"Ah, yes," Alea said. "Your Queen simply opened her mouth and *spoke* the destruction of the sea people."

"Yes," said Lanara. The word sounded defiant, and she bit her lip to stop others like it from coming.

"And how did your Queen explain her sudden ability to speak magical words?"

Lanara forced herself to answer slowly. "The First Queen," she said, and told that story too, so that she would be reminded and Alea would understand—but Alea started to laugh before the tale was done.

"You're a fool, Lanara," she said breathlessly. "You and all your people. Your Queen has ruined Aldron, and no one knows the truth of it."

"How dare—" Lanara began, and Nellyn said both of their names, but Alea spoke the loudest, standing now, very tall.

"Why was Aldron not tended to after he got his wound, though the Queen and her fighters were nearby?"

Lanara ran her tongue over her lips. "She thought he was already dead," she said, but Alea shook her head.

"No. You knew he wasn't. You said you heard him, yet the Queen was paying him no attention. She didn't *think* he was dead, she *wanted—*"

"Stop!" Lanara cried. "Stop, stop—you can't know how it was, there. It was all confusion, everyone was still muddled from the visions, the power—you can't possibly understand—"

"Ah, but she can." Aldron was on the stairs, looking at Alea. "She can," he said again into the stillness, "and she does, and she hates me even more than she did before."

Alea pressed her lips together, bent her head so that her hair fell across an eye and cheek. "No, I only grieve for you. For all of us—because we'll have to go, won't we? We'll have to flee this place and these people before someone finds out what you've done."

"What he's done?" Lanara repeated. "I don't understand ..." She tried to swallow over a sour taste that had risen in her throat.

"His Telling power," Nellyn began, quietly, only to her, but she rounded on him, said, "His power isn't real—they told us that in the inn, remember? It can't change things. It's pleasant enough, but only while the images last." She spun from Nellyn's silence to theirs. "Show me, then! Change this writing stick from black to red, or tear that parchment without using your hands. *Show me.*"

Aldron was looking at her now, at last—across a space, not pressed so close to her that she could not see his eyes. He shook his head once, almost imperceptibly, and she wanted to launch herself at him and claw away this "no," whatever it was for. She did not move. She watched him look back at Alea and smile (the smile, like the head shake, a slight, shadowy thing).

"Will you flee with me, then?" he said.

~

Alnissa was crying. Nellyn heard her begin, softly, as Aldron asked Alea his question and Alea answered him. The crying grew loud and indignant, and still no one moved. Nellyn walked past Lanara, past Alea and Aldron. He walked down two floors and over to Alnissa's basket. Her face was nearly as crimson as the blanket she lay upon. He never murmured or cooed, as Alea did, but the baby always quieted immediately when he picked her up. She did so now, her head heavy between his shoulder and neck.

"I'm sorry," Alea said from behind him, "I should have been the one to come to her." She lifted Alnissa away from him and sat down on her pallet to nurse her. Aldron was there as well, thrusting clothing into a brown sack. "You're still weak," she said. "Perhaps one more night ...?"

Aldron straightened. "No," he said in the hoarse, thin voice that seemed to be his now. "I can't. How could I sleep surrounded by ... this?" He did not look away from Alea or gesture, but Nellyn knew what he meant: surrounded by painted flame and earth and sky.

Nellyn went down to the kitchen. Lanara was already there, standing by the empty fireplace with her arms crossed. She did not glance at him, or at Alea when she came down. Only when Aldron descended with a bag over each shoulder did Lanara's gaze shift. She watched him as he took his travel cloak down from the peg by the door and rolled it up. *I have never seen her look like this before,* Nellyn thought. He turned quickly away from her and followed Alea, who was going back up the stairs.

She stood touching the painted walls with one hand. The other held Alnissa against her shoulder. "I can't take anything. Nothing except the clothes I arrived with, and Alnissa's."

"The basket?" he said. Alea shook her head. "The blanket, then. You'll need it, surely, and it comforts her."

"Yes, of course—here, hold her a moment." He felt the sleeping, curled weight of her one more time, the last time that was certain in this world that was a line, not a circle. Nellyn breathed her scent and tried to hold it. *Now still always,* he thought, shonyn words that he felt within him yet, even if they were not true.

Alea put her arms around his neck, and Alnissa, between them, stirred and sighed. Alea held him very tightly, her fingers in his hair, her forehead against his. When she kissed him, he tasted salt. He tried to take it away with his thumbs and his lips; tried to stop her sadness and greet his own, for it was new, familiar, already lost. He felt her warmth, and soon it was gone, and Alnissa's too, and he was alone.

~

Lanara and Aldron were standing where they had been before; Alea noticed this, though she hardly looked at either of them. She adjusted the sling she had made from the red blanket, ensured that Alnissa was secure within. She remembered suddenly how she had felt kicks and prods on the wagon ride into Fane. Perhaps Alnissa's movements, or her sister's, or both—not that it mattered now. Only this leaving mattered.

Aldron was slow behind her on the path. Alea turned back once to offer her hand or arm, but he shook his head. She walked on, quickly. When she came to the end of the path, she waited until she heard him gasping and close then stepped onto the wharf.

She reached the first of the fires in six paces. The heat of flames and air beat against her skin, and she turned toward the popping of wood and the sparks even though she did not want to. Not her fires; and the air was moist and salt-rimed, not red as desert sand. But there were people, sitting or standing, lifting flasks to their mouths and laughing, some of them dancing. She watched from between two fires. She wanted to run until she reached the other fires, the other dancers, the wagons that were still her only home. *But no,* she thought, bitterness like fingers at her throat, and she looked behind her for Aldron.

He was well back from the first fire, though its glow reached him, lit his staring eyes and twitching lips and the hands he held trembling before him. He could not be seeing these fires, or even those of the Alilan. *He sees horror,* Alea thought, and she ran to him and took his hands, tried to smooth the shaking from them. "Come," she said, "we'll get through, we'll get out." She led him around the fires. His hand was limp in hers until they reached the brightest houses. Here he stopped, and she stopped with him and saw which house they stood before.

The Queenshouse shone. Every window was open, blazing with candles set in holders of gem-studded gold and silver. Banners of green and blue silk had been hung from the upper windows and fluttered gently against the stone. Queensguards lounged in the doorway, and many stood above as well, on the central balcony. Aldron lifted his head to look at them—but not at them, Alea realized as she too looked up.

Queen Galha was sitting at the balcony's railing. Her chair was high-backed and wooden. Its sides, where her hands rested, were carved and painted, though Alea could not see their shapes or colours. The Queen glittered as her candles did, as the fires below her did, built high to honour her.

"Let's go," Alea said quietly, even though the noise around them would have masked a shout. "Quickly, Aldron." He did not move his eyes from Galha. He followed her hands, raised to sketch an accompaniment to her words; he followed her turning head and her smile. Alea sought out hatred in his face, or even fear—but instead she saw something far and cold. "Love," she said, touching his cheek despite her own fear, "what did she say to you? What did she promise you, if you did her bidding?"

He wrenched his gaze back from where it had been. He turned to Alea, recognized her. "Nothing," he whispered.

She wanted to laugh, or snap, "Why should you lie to me?"—something easy and angry that would remind them both of the way they had been. She did not. She cupped one hand beneath the curve of Alnissa's body and drew Aldron away with the other. Away from the Queen and her docks and her ships; away from the fires, though these extended upriver for a time, until the houses crowded in against the banks; up beneath the lit windows of these houses to where there was darkness at last, and the river widening free under stars and wind-bent trees. Away from the river then too—the three of them, alone.

THIRTY-NINE

Nellyn remembered waking with joy, hearing it in Lanara's humming or the strokes of her writing stick. He remembered it in voices in the kitchen and in the scent of rising bread and burned-down candles. It had been in silence as well. But now he woke in silence that was heavy, and he heard no joy, and felt none. It was late summer, and he lay bathed in sweat beneath his light sheet—yet he was chilled, had been since Alea and Aldron had left. Lanara had disappeared then. It was as if she had gone somewhere without her body, which stayed near Nellyn, breathing and sometimes eating, but empty. He did not disturb the quiet of this body; he waited, as he always did when he was unsure or unready—but this time the waiting was difficult to bear. He was hollow with loneliness. When she had left the shonyn village, he had felt this loneliness. Now, though, he could see her, and feel her stillness as she pretended to be asleep.

One day he woke to a sound. He lay and listened. When the sound did not come again, he rose and dressed and went downstairs, his bare feet light on the wood. He intended to go to the kitchen to make Lanara a meal (she would not have eaten yet, although it was well past noon), but he stopped at Aldron and Alea's sleeping floor. Lanara was there, sitting cross-legged on the pallet. Her mouth was clamped over the knuckles of one hand. Her sobs were muffled, but he saw her shake with them, and he heard one, broken and dry.

There were two knives in front of her on the pallet. He saw when he drew closer that one was plain and the other inlaid with strands of gold and green stones. He knelt before her and said her name.

"They're Aldron's," she said from behind her hand. "Galha gave him this simple one at the Queenshouse before we left for the Raiders' Land. Aldron killed a fishperson with it."

"Why?" Nellyn asked. It was not a word he often used—but he needed her to talk, to be Lanara.

"I ..." She shook her head. "I don't remember. I think it was trying to escape. Aldron seemed upset, afterward, that he had killed it."

"And the other dagger?" Nellyn felt slow and clumsy, trying to lead her speaking—but she did not seem to notice.

"She gave it to him in her cabin, after he killed the fishperson. As a reward, I think. She valued him, you see—his skill, his willingness to follow her even though he was not a Queensman." She raised her eyes to Nellyn's. He returned her gaze, though he wanted to look away—at the window, perhaps, or at one of Alea's glass vases; somewhere clear and calm. *I have never wanted to avoid her eyes before,* he thought. Slow, clumsy, and now afraid as well.

"Don't you have any other questions for me, Nellyn?" she asked, her eyes so bright, so expectant.

"No. What questions should I have?"

She laughed. It started as a tremor that could have been sobbing but was not; when it rose from her belly to her throat, he knew this. "What should ... Why not try 'Why do you weep so for this other man?' or 'What have you done?'"

He took a very long, slow breath. "Do you want me to ask these questions?"

Her laughter was changing. It was sobbing, as he had thought it was before—or perhaps it was all the same. "I didn't think so—but all these weeks have passed, and I can't bear it, I can't have this secret, it's hurting me ..."

"Tell me, then." His voice sounded very steady. It was strange, that his voice and thoughts could be so different from one another. "Tell me," he said again, and waited.

~

Lanara watched Nellyn. She had been watching him for two days as he walked, pacing around the back of the signal tower even during the hottest part of the day. He had come inside only to perform his duties in the light-room and on the writing floor; and when she had climbed up to relieve him, he was already gone. Outside again, probably, sitting on the back balcony, staring at the cliff. When he wasn't pacing, he was doing this. He was doing it now, his hands placed lightly on his knees, his head held straight and motionless. His entire body was motionless. She watched him and felt her own limbs twitching. Even her skin was restless, it seemed, prickling and itchy.

She had nearly gone out to him several times. "Please," she had imagined saying, "speak to me. Stay with me." Her fear kept her away. *What did I say?* she thought, reaching back two short days and finding nothing but blur, and more fear. *What did he say?*

She had told him that she and Aldron had been lovers. She had told him that she loved Aldron—but that could not be, it was not true. Or maybe it was. Even if it was, it did not matter: she loved Nellyn. She had told him that too—she must have. She would. As soon as he came inside, she would go to him and tell him and he would hold her, calm her as he always did.

She walked down to the kitchen, sat before a platter of cheese and bread. Her stomach and head felt thick with sickness, as if she had been drunk for two days instead of sleepless and afraid.

"Lanara."

She looked up so quickly that he swam in her eyes for a moment. Her throat was dry—no voice, now that he was here with her. But she did not need it: he was talking, talking, too many words for a shonyn.

"The shonyn say the river is within each of us and must be sought out when body or mind are not calm. I have not been able to find it—not really since the day I left my people. I thought this was a loss, like the others, that I could bear and even understand. But now I feel it is not. I cannot find the river in me—only confusion and noise."

"This is just change." She did not know how these words had come so swiftly out of her silence. "Remember when you first understood time? You felt mad. You told me, when you found me in Luhr: you felt overwhelmed with change. This is the same. It's overwhelming, but it will pass."

"No." He swallowed, opened and closed his hands. "Or yes. Perhaps I fear either way. I do not know my mind—that is why I must return to my people. Perhaps I will find my river there, and know again how to be."

"No." Her turn to say it, and she repeated it, repeated it even when he went back up the stairs. She forced herself to stand when he came back down again. "If you discover, once you've been there for a time, that you can't live with your people after all, will you come back?"

He was gathering fruit, nuts, bread, placing them all carefully in the centre of a cloth he had brought with him. He tied the four corners together and held the makeshift bag at his side. The bag trembled, even with so much within; she felt a surge of hope, seeing this.

"I do not know," he said—and she was crying again, though she had thought herself too far away for tears. "Lanara," he said, and took a step toward her, "do not—please ... I understand time now, as you say. I understand 'future.' So how could I give you any other answer that would be true?"

He was in front of her; she could have touched him. He lingered for a moment—but no hope now, she had been a fool to think there was—and then he was past her, and she heard the door open and close.

She ran up to the writing floor. It was dusk. Sea and sky were dark, and so was the path, but she saw him anyway, a small, slow shape moving away. When she could no longer see him, she looked down at the parchment on the desk. His writing was slanted and uneven, as it had been ever since she had met him. *Sundown,* she read. *Very hot and still. Wind gentle from*—And that was all, a sentence unfinished and the writing stick lying across the page, where he had dropped it. She stared at the words, and where they ended. She closed her eyes and imagined him coming up behind her, winding his arms around her waist, murmuring, "I'll finish that later ..."—imagined it in every detail, for she deserved this pain.

~

Leaves skittered over the cobbles. Crimson leaves, golden ones, others brown and brittle; the courtyard was full of them. A red one blew up against the sackcloth target and Lanara nocked an arrow, loosed it so quickly that the leaf was pierced and pinned before the wind could find it again. There were low whistles from the Queensfighters who stood behind her, and some scattered clapping. She smiled and shrugged, and stepped aside so that the next person could take his turn.

The Queensfighters had been friendly to her since her arrival at the Queenshouse two months ago. Friendly at the meals they took together in the long, thin dining hall, and here in the courtyard, practising archery and swordplay—but she saw that they always held themselves a little back from her. They had all seen her with the Queen, in this building, on the great ship that had led the fleet—perhaps even in the Raiders' Land. There were two Luhrans among them who had seen her with Ladhra. One of them had told her this, haltingly, her eyes cast down, on the day Lanara had come to live with them. Part of her felt strengthened by this distance and the reason for it; another part longed to be truly, effortlessly one of them. She was, however, entirely relieved to be in this house, among her own people, surrounded by their voices and their blue-and-green-clad bodies. Only at night was she alone, in her tiny room overlooking the courtyard. They had given her this room as a sign of respect, assuming she would not want to share one as all the other Queensfighters did. She had accepted it, flattered, muddled by her sleepless nights in the signal tower. But soon she feared nights here as well—for despite the distraction of her days, the waking dreams still found her when she was alone. In the silence she still heard hissing rock and smelled blood and burning and fresh earth beneath her fingernails. When she closed her eyes, she saw snatches of colour that were not so fleeting that she did not recognize them: a Raider boy lying on flower-speckled moss, trails of dirt on her skin and Aldron's. She would sit up in her bed, reeling as if she were in a cabin that tipped and tossed upon waves. In the signal tower she had been too afraid to walk the empty floors and stairs; here, at least she could go out into corridors and rooms and find people who were awake, whom she would watch and listen to even if she did not join them.

"Doesn't surprise me," Drelha had declared when Lanara sought her out at her house in Fane. "Tower life's hard and lonely, not for everyone." Lanara had nodded, too tired to explain anything. Three days later Drelha had returned to the tower with a train of donkeys bearing chests, and her burly, silent husband. "Father died in the winter," she said as she stomped up the stairs, peering at each floor. "Right after the icemounts burned—what a sight, he wished he'd still been up here, the foolish old thing. Now what," she'd continued, picking something up from Alea's low table, "am I to do with the likes of this?"

Lanara had looked from the copper armring in Drelha's hand to the rows of glazed pots with their jewels to the glass vases that stood where Aldron had placed them. "I don't know," she replied.

"Well," Drelha had sighed, "I suppose I'll sell some things back to the markets—these stones maybe, and this rug—it's far too bright. As for the walls ..."

When she had set her feet upon the path, Lanara had intended to journey back to Luhr. But by the time she had reached the Queenshouse, she knew that she could not go further—not yet, not as tired as she was. And after she had been in the house for one week, then two and three, she had decided that the rest was doing her good. She reminded herself of this during the day. At night she had different reasons for not wanting to continue on to Luhr: the Queen's strangeness on the ship, the palace corridors that would still echo with Ladhra's voice and footsteps, the river journey that would take Lanara past the shonyn village. But *I'm resting,* she insisted to herself as the days grew shorter and the leaves began to fall.

"Queenswoman Lanara."

She turned to the Queensguard who had come up beside her. It was almost her turn to shoot again; she paused with her bow slid halfway down her arm. "Yes?" she said. Her fellow archers had fallen back from her. She stood alone with the guard as silence rang in her ears.

"There is a letter for you," he said, looking steadily at a spot on her forehead. "From our Queen."

But it was not from Galha—Lanara saw this as soon as she read the first line, in the same room in which she had read another letter from Luhr, so many months ago.

My dear Lanara, our Queen is unwell. She has been weak since her victory in the Raiders' Land, and her weakness is increasing, though I had hoped that being home would soothe and strengthen her. She spends much of the day in bed, though she still insists on receiving the families of those lost in the battle, or the Queensfighters themselves, who desire to meet with her. She does this every two days, by Sarhenna's pool—but this saps her energy, and I am trying to convince her to cease the practice until she is well again.

She is asking for you. Although she has not contacted you since her return to Luhr, she has been speaking of you every day, with growing urgency. I am certain your presence would comfort her as nothing else has yet been able to. I fear for her, and for this realm. We miss you, Lanara, and we need you. Come back to Luhr.

Book Four

FORTY

Leish's chain stretched almost to the water. He had walked until it was taut, but only once, and only because the Queen had prodded him with the end of her bow. She had laughed as he stood two paces away from the pool. "There," she had said in the sharp voice that had been hers back then, "your comfort and death lie there, close enough to taste—but only with your eyes, hmm?"

And with my ears, he had thought, *but this is one thing you do not know.* He heard the water, above and beneath, as he had heard it the first time he had come to this shining chamber. And the second time, when he had swum; he remembered the water against his skin and beneath it, and Ladhra's mouth on his. These memories—and the water that was so near him every moment of the day and night—did not hurt him. Nothing had hurt him in a very long time. Even the chain around his left ankle did not pain him, though it was too tight and he could see that the flesh beneath it was bloody. He was apart, away from this place and its Queen. At first this had enraged her, and she had beaten him and dribbled water down his chest and back. When these punishments provoked no response, she had stopped paying attention to him at all. She came every few days to sit on the throne to which he was shackled, but she rarely looked at him. And although he hardly noticed his own numbness any more, he did notice hers.

"Let them in, one by one." Malhan's voice. Leish had become accustomed to it these past few months, though last time he had been in the palace it had shocked him to hear Malhan speak. He spoke now because Galha did not. He stood beside her throne and murmured to the people who came to see their Queen, as the Queen herself nodded vaguely at them, and smiled, and maybe raised her hands to make the arrow sign. At night, palace servants came with nets and bags to sweep dead things out of the pool and its channels, and Leish sometimes heard their words. They said Galha's mind was still burdened by its own strength; they said she was growing frail and stooped. *I am also thin and bent,* Leish had thought, staring down at his body in the starlit dimness. *But still, they will need a very big net to remove* me *from this place.* He had no desire to laugh or cry at the thought, and was very nearly curious about this.

"All of you, now: form a semicircle here, and approach the Queen one at a time, from this end ..."

Leish occasionally watched and listened to the Queensfolk who came. "My Queen, I journeyed with you to the Raiders' Land and fought bravely, but now I cannot sleep and my head aches so that I can hardly see ..." "My Queen, I have only two children, and my elder, a boy, was a guard of yours—he died in the battle in our city, and now there is just my daughter and me, both of us untrained in any trade ..." "I am blind, my Queen. If you would touch me on the eyes, perhaps your mindpowers would restore ..." Young, old, mad, clear-eyed—the Queen nodded and Malhan murmured and they shuffled past and out again. Some of them spat at Leish; one struck him in the stomach and he doubled over, his body reacting to a pain he did not feel. Once, a child picked up his chain and tugged on it—but she was just a child, and she smiled at him after, as her father carried her away.

"Very well. You, step forward." This one was carrying a basket of fruit that glistened, red and blue, yellow, all beaded with water, and Leish's mouth filled with saliva. His body again, saying, *So thirsty,* and, *Imagine licking the water off before biting*—but his mind did not hear or understand. The night servants brought him fruit, though not much—mostly bread and dried fish and meats, which he ate and did not taste. One of the servants liked to throw the food so that it scattered around Leish, mostly out of his reach. One of the others always gathered it up and placed it closer, neatly, even though his companions jeered at him.

Just as the basket of fruit was being set down at the Queen's feet, there was a shout from the door beyond the central fountain. Leish looked away from the fruit toward the woman who was approaching, running over the bridges and across the sparkling stones.

Galha rose from her throne. Leish had not seen her stand up so quickly in weeks. She swayed a bit, and the neat semicircle of Queensfolk broke apart with some gasps and mutterings. He had not heard her speak loudly or clearly recently, either, but she did so now, though she was crying as well.

"Nara! Nara, dearest child, I knew you'd come—" And Lanara was before her, reaching and gathering, talking low and breathlessly.

"Guards!" Malhan cried, and three appeared, to lead the Queensfolk out of the chamber. By the time they had gone, Galha was seated again, with Lanara on her knees in front of her, holding her hands.

"You see?" Galha said, and Leish saw that Lanara too was weeping. "This is your only home. You had to return—it called to you." She bowed her head over their clasped hands.

"Yes," Lanara said, and looked up, past the Queen, past Leish, at Malhan. "Of course I did"—her eyes wide with fear or questions.

They left soon after that, the Queen walking between Malhan and Lanara. The door behind the thrones closed with sound Leish also recalled from the time before the ship and the river and the sea. He lay down and gazed at the basket of fruit until all the colours blurred, as if they had turned to water. He stirred only when the servants came, with their laughter and their quick words, which were harder to understand than those of other Queensfolk. They took away the basket, though the kind servant set two mang on the stone beside Leish. His chain clanked a bit as he reached for the fruit. After he had eaten, he lay down again, looking up at the tower whose glass was invisible at night. The sky seemed open and close. He tried to imagine wind on his face or the scent of night blossoms, but could not.

He heard footsteps. Quiet footsteps, not like the servants' careless ones. Leish's chain clanked again as he rolled onto his side to peer into the gloom beyond the fountain. The kind servant, perhaps, with another piece of fruit; or the one who laughed at Leish, returning to paddle in the pool and drink in long, noisy gulps—but no, Leish saw, it was neither of these.

~

Ladhra's bed was wide and firm, its blue-and-green coverlet smooth except for where Lanara was sitting. She had run up to this tower chamber countless times since she was a girl, and lain in this bed, whispering and giggling until dawn, and sleep. She had never been alone here. She looked at the tapestry, the window, the sunlight on the familiar flagstones—and she felt absence there with her, so large that there was hardly space for anything else.

"You must stay in Ladhra's room," Galha had said as they left the Throne Chamber. "It is clean and ready for you. Go there now, and rest, and we will have food brought up to you. When my own rest is over, I shall send for you." But when the food came—trays of it, piled precariously high—one of the Queensmen who had helped to bring it told Lanara that the Queen would be receiving no more visitors that day. Tomorrow, most certainly—for both the Queen and her consort-scribe were eager to see Lanara after such a long time apart.

She stared at the trays spread out on the floor and the desk and even on the broad windowsill. She could not remember eating much on the journey here. She had ridden—no ships going upriver from Fane, or none soon enough—and had hardly paused, it seemed, except sometimes for water. She had felt no hunger. Emptiness, yes, spreading into her body from somewhere else—her mind or her heart, she was not sure. She had tried to ride hard and long so that she would not sleep, but sleep had found her anyway, sent her tumbling from her horse or spinning into darkness when she had just intended to lie down for a moment.

"Aldron's Telling power ..." She heard Nellyn's voice so clearly in her sleep, though she could not bring it back to her when she was awake. And Alea's: *"You're a fool, Lanara, you and all your people."* Their words tangled with images, bright and scattered, except for one that always came clearly whether she slept or woke: Aldron dying behind the tall white stone with a bloodied spear beside him.

"Your friend." Galha had clutched Lanara's wrist as she said this at the door to Ladhra's tower. "The Alilan man."

"Aldron," Lanara had said, motionless, her ears humming.

"Yes—Aldron. Have you seen him? Do you know where he is?"

"No." She had wanted to twist away from the Queen's grip—and this frightened her as much as everything else did. "No—he's gone, just as he said he would be." She watched Malhan place his fingers over Galha's and pry them gently open. He had looked at Lanara as if something were clear and acknowledged between them. She had shaken her head slightly: *No, I don't understand. I have more questions now than I had before I came ...*

When she had seen the first glint of Luhr against the sky, Lanara had thought that her questions had vanished. She had reined in her horse and gazed at the towers and arches, the banners, the long, gleaming road across the sand. And then the Queensguards at the front gate had called out to her, saluting as if she were a returning hero, and she had known the ones in the marketplace too, who had hugged her and welcomed her home. She had sunk into the scents and colours and noises. *Yes, I am home*—except that Ladhra was dead and the Queen changed almost beyond recognition. All Lanara's questions had returned and multiplied as she knelt covering Galha's hands to stop their shaking. And now it was worse, for she was alone in Ladhra's tower, with silence and absence and piles of food she could not eat.

"If there were lies about the Raiders' Land battle," she said, so that the words would seem reasonable and real, no longer wraiths she could slip away from, "then there may have been other lies." She remembered the prisoner in Galha's cabin on the ship, hissing, *"Ladhra friend Lanara—Ladhra friend Leish."* His bound arms and chest had oozed as he strained toward her. *He was mad then,* she thought. *He will be worse now. And why would I ever trust his word above my Queen's? I will wait. Surely things will be better tomorrow, with food and sleep ...* She lowered her head into her hands.

The chamber was firelit when she opened her eyes. She was on her side in Ladhra's bed. She did not remember lying down or sleeping, but her mind and all her limbs felt light and rested. Someone had lit a fire in the hearth and all the trays but one had been removed. She ate a globe of bread and some berries and drank a flagon of water. Then she lit the lantern that stood by the bed and left the tower.

She could not ask Malhan for the truth—she was certain of this as she walked through the quiet corridors. He was never apart from Galha. She nodded at the Queensguards she passed, and attempted to look confident, unhurried: just a palace-dweller who could not sleep, on her way to the kitchens or a terrace garden. Only when she reached the last corridor did she stop and draw a trembling breath.

Gellior was on guard tonight. She felt dizzy with relief, then shame, as he cried out her name and reached for her hands. "I heard you'd come back. Thought I'd have to wait for my next day duty to see you—but here you are, and at such an hour ..."

"Yes," she said, squeezing his hands and slipping hers free. "I know it's strange—but I can't sleep. You know, I haven't been back here since ... well, since before the attack and Ladhra's death. Now that I'm here, I find I can't stop thinking about her." True enough so far—but she looked at his chest, not his face, as she continued more slowly, "I think my mind would be easier if I could see him. The ... thing that killed her. I saw him on the voyage to the Raiders' Land, of course, but I was so occupied with other things. Now that I'm not, I must speak to him."

"I understand," Gellior said, and she heard his frown. "But now, child? Could you not wait for morning? I'll let you in when—"

"No," she said, and now she looked up into his eyes. "Please, Gellior. I feel like I'll never rest again if I don't do this tonight."

He smiled, though he was still frowning too. "Very well. The night servants have already been in to do their work—you won't be disturbed. You won't ..." He bit the inside of his cheek, glanced over her shoulder. "You'll be sure not to harm him? For if I do this for you and—"

She kissed him on his grizzled cheek. "No, I won't harm him." He nodded and turned the key. She held her lantern high as she walked into the darkness, where there would be sleeping birds, and fish bound by glass, and Leish, chained beside Sarhenna's pool.

~

Leish sat up so slowly that the links of his chain made no noise, either against each other or against the stone. The light in Lanara's hand trembled, and she set it down. Her face was mostly in shadow when she straightened again. She was many paces away from him, and she did not move at all for a long time after she had put the lantern down—but Leish felt his muscles clench in a way that reminded him of fear or expectation.

"Speak," she said at last, and the word rang, though it was only a whisper. "Tell me everything," she went on more loudly, just as he prepared to say, "Why should I speak, when all you want is to hurt me?"

"Tell you ..." he said instead. He saw her flinch at his voice, but she took two steps toward him and the shadows fled her skin.

"I've read the account of what took place here when your people attacked. A battle before the gates—I read about this. About how you pulled Ladhra from her horse and killed her as your people were fleeing the city." She ran her tongue over her lips. "But you said her name to me on the ship. You said you'd been her ... friend."

He was sure now that he felt fear. It was warm where for so long there had been only numbness. It was not fear of her; he knew this after he had named the feeling and felt it grow. He feared no man or woman, no pain, not even thirst or death. But when she fell to her knees before him and said, "Tell me what happened in the city on the night of the attack," he felt himself grow small and crumpled, and he wanted to moan with the ache of it.

"No one asks about this before," he said when he could speak. The Queensfolk words were sharp in his mouth, but they emerged quite smoothly after all his listening, all the learning he had not realized he was doing. "No Queensperson will believe my truth, if I tell it."

"Tell me," she said, and he did.

~

The well shaft was slippery and stank of mildew. There had been no rain in a long time; it was possible to paddle from the bottom of the shaft into the tunnel beyond with head and lantern held above the water. The tunnel stank too, but not as much. There was more air here, more space.

"There were lanterns shining all along the tunnels leading to the biggest pool ..." They were not lit now, of course, but they still hung from old torch brackets. Careless, that they had been left here—but who would ever come to see them and wonder who had brought them? She walked slowly so that she would not fall on the moist ledge, and so that she would see where the lanterns led. She did not even glance at the glittering stones in the walls. Her eyes were steady on the lanterns, which she followed, without a false turning, to the chamber with the pool and the bridge.

"Bags hung from the walls. The scribes tended them, always opening them to add parchment or take out stone and brush it, maybe to clean ..." No bags

now, either, though she had not expected to find any. She held her lantern as close to the pool as she could without losing her balance, as if its feeble light would cut through the murk and show her tablets and scraps of cloth, writing sticks and letters that had not bled away. *"There were many scribes—maybe a hundred, maybe more. Men and women, who listened to Baldhron. He said there were people like them in other places. He said there were people like them many years ago, who wrote the truth while queens did not."* She rose and walked along the right-hand wall, which was broken only by the gem patterns. *A hundred or more here,* she thought as she went carefully across the bridge. *I would have known some of them. Ladhra would have. This cannot be true.* The wall on the other side of the bridge was rough, studded with metal hooks. She ran her fingers over them one by one, sometimes bending, sometimes reaching high. Thirty-seven hooks, and a bridge, and a pool whose southern tunnel burrowed under the city wall into the open desert and its string of wells.

So the Sea Raider was right about the chamber beneath the city, she thought as she wove back through the tunnels, *but perhaps he lied about who used it, or what they did. Perhaps only his own people used it, and he now wishes to implicate others who will never be found ...* The Sea Raider's eyes had not wavered from hers as he spoke to her by the pool. His limbs had been shaking, then rigid—yet his eyes had been still. *What he told me about Ladhra—this, at least, I must confirm to be falsehood,* she thought as she climbed back up the shaft to which the unlit lanterns had brought her. She felt limp with dread and weariness.

"There was much blood. On the tapestry was mine, on the floor beside the bed was hers." Lanara laughed a high, giddy laugh when she looked at the tapestry. She put her lantern up next to it, but this hardly mattered, for it was dawn and the chamber was full of silver light. She saw each thread, each whorl of colour. Everything was clean, even the lightest spaces—and it was impossible to leach blood from weaving completely, there would always be smudges, imperfections that a seeking eye would find. There were no dagger tears in the cloth either, or places where it had been mended. *Ladhra didn't die here. There* was *a battle before the city gates. I should never have trusted any part of the Sea Raider's account; he is a ruined man. And the Queen would not deceive me so.* Lanara backed up and her legs

buckled her to the bed. The prisoner's face was as vivid to her as if he stood before her; Aldron's face as well, pale and blood-spattered, and his body motionless on the hot stone of the Raiders' Land.

Lanara was still sitting on the bed when she heard footsteps on the stairs—slow, scuffing ones that paused often and were accompanied by a soft blur of words. When Galha and Malhan appeared in the open doorway, Lanara rose and went to them, took Galha's hand to lead her to the bed. "Please, sit," she said thickly, as if her tongue were swollen with thirst. "You should have sent a guard so that I could have come to you and spared you this effort."

"No, my dear," the Queen said, and smiled. A stronger smile than yesterday, perhaps, and her skin looked less sallow in the light, which was golden now instead of silver. "I had to see you here. I could not sleep, so intense was my desire to come to her room—to you."

Lanara felt herself smile as well. "I remember this room with such fondness. I've been looking at every detail. They're all so fresh, as if I'd just been here with her yesterday. Why, this tapestry"—she turned, gestured—"looks just as it always did. I used to stare at it in the dark, after Ladhra had fallen asleep—it always frightened me a bit, but in the morning I forgot my fear. Just a tapestry—and here it is, still."

"No." Galha was frowning, shaking her head. Malhan lifted a hand and took a step forward, but the Queen was already speaking again. "This is not the same tapestry—this is a new one. We put it up after Ladhra—after ..."

Lanara sank to her knees, dizzy, still holding Galha's hand—but searching as well, brushing the coverlet away from the flagstones. The stains were dark and long, as if a brush, in trying to remove them, had smeared them outward and ground them even more deeply into the floor.

"Nara, I have something to tell you. Look at me, child—I must see your face when I speak these words."

Lanara did look up, though her fingertips lingered on the stains. She waited for the truth—all of it. For the truth, and then perhaps for understanding.

"Lanara," Queen Galha said, smiling still, "who was the daughter of Salanne: you are my daughter now and always, and you will be the next queen of this realm."

FORTY-ONE

Nothing changed. Leish waited, after Lanara's night visit, for the Queen to come to him and beat him again; for Lanara to ask him more questions, or at least confirm that she believed him or didn't. But none of these things happened.

He had trembled as he told her of the attack. And when he had said, "Ladhra brought me here to swim," and gestured at the fountain pool so close to him, he had had to close his eyes to keep himself from seeing Ladhra turning to him, smiling, giving him this gift. Lanara had said nothing to him after her last "Tell me," and he had not heard her go, or seen her (his eyes still closed against memory). And she had not spoken to him all these weeks since. She sat on a stool by the Queen's throne and listened to the people who came to weep or stare. Sometimes she spoke to them after the Queen did. But she never glanced at Leish, never once acknowledged him with eyes or words. At first he had been tempted to cry out to her, "Tell the Queen what I told you the other night. Tell everyone gathered here, and see what they think of the truth." But he had kept silent. He would be overcome otherwise. He would need to think again and feel again; everything would change. *And why not?* he had demanded of himself the day after Lanara came to him. *Why not force change, welcome it, even—for you have no life to lose and nothing to fear*. He had been afraid again when the answer came to him. *Because I am such a coward that I need this life*. He had shied away from the words, retreated from the emotions that had made him tremble. It was easy enough to do; he had been in an empty place for so long before, and he remembered how to return to it.

"Let them in." The Queensguards moved to obey Lanara, who spoke to them more often than Galha did now, and the supplicants entered. All these entrances sounded the same to Leish: there were always shuffling footsteps, brisk ones, measured ones. The mixture of faces was the same as well: old and young, scarred and smooth, some awed, a very few angry. Always the same—and yet they were different people. Every few days Queensfolk arrived who had not been here before. Leish wondered, without much curiosity, how many more there could be.

Today there were thirty-two, too many for a semicircle, so they stood in a long, neat line. Leish watched them, blinking to clear a haze from his eyes (*thirst,* his body told him, *hunger*—but he ignored it, as ever). The grieving mother, the lame child whose parents' faces shone with hope—Leish looked past them, to the end of the line. The last person was hunched and swathed in a cloak, despite the heat in the chamber. The cloak's hood was drawn well forward and Leish could not see the face beneath it. A disfigurement, perhaps, or an illness of the eyes. He would find out soon enough, for the line was moving quickly forward. Those who had spoken to the Queen stood at the edge of the pool. They would all leave at once, as they had come in. The lame child was crying, looking down into the water.

The cloaked person stepped up to the place before the throne. The Queen murmured something and Lanara bent to listen. "The Queen bids you stand taller and remove your hood," Lanara said, but the person was doing so already, throwing back cloth and a black tangle of hair.

"No!" the Queen cried, and Lanara stood up—but Leish noticed these things only dimly, as his numbness fell away before the change that had come at last.

~

Alnissa had been crying since they arrived. Her new teeth coming through, perhaps, or all the noise around her; but it was this very noise that covered her wails, and Alea was thankful for it. "Hush," she whispered, or crooned, or snapped. Once she snatched Alnissa up from the ground, where she was rocking on all fours, and held her very close to her face. "*Why* are you so easily distressed?" she hissed. "Alilan babies are strong and brave—*quiet,* Nissa"—but then she held her daughter very close, her anger spreading inward, to where it belonged.

People were very kind to her—to both of them. Alea had not expected or wanted this; not here, where she had longed only to hate. But the people who gave them water and food and a place for their blankets were not all Queensfolk. Some were lighter-skinned, some darker. Others were not like people at all, with their horns or scales, double-lidded eyes, toeless feet.

It was someone with horns, in fact, who told her about the Queen's audiences. Alea was walking from stall to mat to well. It was her fifth day in Luhr's marketplace, and she was fascinated despite herself, and too weary from all her travelling to allow herself to rest. The man with horns was crouching atop a pile of stones. She looked up at him, swaying so that Alnissa would stop crying.

"Let me speak to you." Alea turned, looking for the other person who must be standing beside her—but she was alone here, at the foot of the rock pile. When she looked back at him, the man was slipping down toward her. She saw his talons, his cloven animal feet. The sunlight glancing from his horns made her flinch and blink.

"I will not ask for payment to tell you these words of future." He was so close to her that she could see his eyes. Alnissa had gone quiet, though she was not asleep; she was holding her head up, looking at him.

"Your return will have no ending." His voice was strange. She knew that he was not speaking his own language, but the strangeness went deeper than that, to a sound beneath his words. She stood mute and still, and he said, "Why are you here, woman of the fires?"

She found her own voice, though it was small and cracking. "To see the Queen."

He smiled. Suddenly he was just a man. "She receives Queensfolk visitors every two days, in the palace. There is surely no reason she would not receive you as well."

"Indeed," Alea said, raising an eyebrow as if he were an Alilan boy trying to court her, as if his other words were not echoing, waiting for her.

Two days later she stood before a great wooden door in a long hallway broken by sunlight. "What is your business with the Queen?" the guard before the door asked.

Alea stared at her feet in unfeigned discomfort. The palace was intimidating from the outside—but at least outside there was still sky. Within, it was a world of seamless stone and countless corridors, everything tall and long yet dizzyingly contained. She cleared her throat and glanced back up at the guard, who was smiling at Alnissa.

"I have heard tell of the Queen's wondrous powers. There is much in me that needs mending, and I thought that I might ask her ..." She let her voice trail away when the guard began to nod.

"All right, then," he said with a chuckle. Alnissa was pulling at one of the blue ribbons that hung from his sleeve. "In you go—all of you now, one by one, through here."

Alea had not expected her own fear any more than she had expected Queensfolk kindness—but as soon as she stepped through this door, she was terrified. The birds, the reeds, the fountain and pool, the painted sky that looked so real: this was a kind of magic, surely. And the second chamber, with its water creatures and its darkness—she bit her lip to keep from crying out. *This is why,* she thought as she waited to pass through the last door. *It is places like this that make the Queen's people believe her*. Alea felt a different fear then, and for a moment she thought of running back through the tunnel, back through the bird room and the corridors, until she reached open air again. But she had come so far alone—and there was rage beneath her fear. When her turn came, Alea stepped into the dazzle of the Throne Chamber without hesitation.

She saw only snatches of this place, since she had drawn her hood over her head and face. The stones beneath her feet glittered. She smelled blossoms, felt fountain spray on her feet. She peered up just long enough to see when the person before her halted. She stopped too, and stood with her own breath ringing in her ears.

She was sure that Alnissa would fuss; she had been fussing for a week, after all. But although she was entirely covered by Alea's cloak, the baby slept. She had been awake in the first two chambers, silent and wide-eyed. *As awed as a Queensbaby,* Alea thought irritably, trying to shift Alnissa's weight a bit from shoulder to hip. Irritability, not fear: she clung to it, hoped that it would sustain her until the waiting was over.

Aldron had been wrong. He had warned her, had said that this city would swallow and silence her. She had grasped his tunic and twisted, as if anger might return him to himself. Her tears had not; nor had pleading, nor tenderness.

"You are *Alilan!*" she had cried, pummelling, pulling. "We are people of honour, and we fight. Come with me. Take your revenge on this woman who has ruined all of us. Be an Alilan man again."

"Alilan," he had said steadily. He was covering her hands with his own, firmly, without anger. "Man, revenge: these are words now. Just words."

They had been in the caves then, high above the ocean he could not seem to leave. Alnissa had just learned to roll herself from back to belly. He had not touched his daughter in all their weeks of wandering.

"Go back to the Alilan," he had said as she let go of his tunic. "They'd take you back, if I was gone and you could assure them that you'd never see me again. Alea, they'd let you come home."

"And what if I did go back?" she had demanded. "What would you do then?" She had been afraid, as soon as the words were said, and had yearned to pull them back.

"There is a thing I must do," he had replied, staring out beyond their small fire at the water. "Alone. So we must decide whether I'll leave you or you'll leave me. That's our only decision."

She had left him a month later. She knew that he had been gone from her long before this—but she cried anyway, as she walked. She would not cry this time. She was no longer afraid, just uncertain, and this would change. She was the strong one now.

The person in front of her in the line was gone. Alea took two paces forward and steeled herself for more inaction—but the guard who had accompanied them from the last door whispered, "You, now." She heard a woman's voice as she prepared to look up. Not Galha's; another, which Alea knew much better. She heard it, and her uncertainty vanished in fury, and she threw back her head and cloak and began to speak.

~

"I am here to tell truth!" the woman from the signal tower cried, and Leish looked at her as all the others in the chamber did. He could not have looked away—not if someone had dragged him backward by his chain or doused him in water.

"Alea!" Lanara would have sounded composed if it had not been for the loud cheeriness of her voice. "It is a joy to see you again. Come, why don't we retire alone, to talk of—"

"No. The things I have come to say must be said before people who will remember them."

"Guards!" Galha called, and then Leish heard Malhan and Lanara murmuring, soothing. When the Queen spoke again a moment later, the terror was gone from her voice. "Very well. I shall entertain the wish of this woman, who is evidently disturbed in her mind. Tell us this truth of yours." Vaguely amused, indulgent, much as she had been with Leish a year ago. Two Queensguards had come up behind Alea, and they held their bows before them, each with an arrow almost nocked.

"You mock me—and I expected this. I knew that you would pronounce me a madwoman, and now you have, even though I've said nothing at all. So let me say it. Let me tell everyone here that you have never possessed 'mindpowers'—that the force that won your battle for you was wielded by an Alilan man, Aldron of the Tall Fires caravan."

The Queen did not speak until all the gasps and hissed comments had subsided. Alea watched her, one hand clenched at her side, the other holding her sleeping baby against her. "Where is this Alilan man, then?" Galha said. "Why has he not come to me himself?"

Alea was very still, hardly blinking or even breathing. "Because he is gone. He was sick and weak and nearly mad after he used his Telling power as you bade him to. He left me and his daughter, for he could no longer bear love or companionship."

"Where has he gone?" The Queen was leaning forward. Leish saw this and felt her cloak tug at the chain as she moved.

"Why should you care," Alea asked with a smile, "if you do not believe me?"

More murmurs. Galha rose, quite steadily, and held up a hand. "I remember him, of course. I met him in Fane. He came to me there, for he was young and hotheaded and eager for a battle. He fought well, I remember, and took a grievous wound."

"From you," Alea said. "You wounded him. You wanted him dead, so that he would never reveal what he had done for you. But he lived, and

goes on living, though he can hardly stand it—while you amaze your people with lies."

"He must have envied my mindpowers—he must have been desperate for them. He considered himself quite a warrior, yet he could never possess what I did."

Alea took a step forward. The guards behind her raised their bows, which creaked as the strings pulled taut. "Show us, then! Use these mindpowers of yours here, now, and prove that I am as addled as you say I am!"

Galha shook her head as if disappointed, or sympathetic—but she swallowed too, convulsively. "My dear, I wish that I could. Sadly, like my ancestor Sarhenna, I have only been able to use my powers once. We must be content to recall their manifestation in the Raiders' Land—"

"Their *manifestation*."

"Yes," Galha said, gesturing another guard forward. "Come, now—show our young friend to the kitchens. We will give her food and wine ..."

The guards reached for Alea. One of them looped his fingers around her wrist. The other Queensfolk were shifting, looking at each other, not at the Alilan woman. Leish drew a shaking breath and turned away from her himself, to look again at the group by the thrones. Lanara was motionless, frowning—but Malhan and the Queen were smiling, as if at something finished, or averted, or merely comical.

"Tell me, Galha," Alea cried over her shoulder as the guards urged her around and on, "tell me, anyone who was there: did these mindpowers look something like this?"

~

Lanara was on her knees, which ached; she must have fallen hard, though she did not remember doing so. Her body was just a smudge in this place where time writhed and cracked. *Where?* she screamed, without her voice. *When?* Trees and water burned around her, atop the jewelled palace stones. The wind beat at her skin and the sun shone down through the glass tower; moss blackened on the bridges around the pool. She saw the open mouths and eyes of the Queensfolk, and Galha crumpled in front of her throne; saw this through billowing smoke and ash. Lanara dragged a hand up to her face, expecting to feel a trail of blisters. There might be earth beneath her fingernails. She tried to close her eyes, to escape or return—but she did not need to, for the flames and wind hissed away and there was only the Throne Chamber again, vast and shining.

The first thing Lanara heard clearly, after the ringing had gone from her ears, was Leish. His chain was clanking in sharp, steady beats as he rocked; and he was keening, singing, almost, in words and notes that made her shiver. She heard other noises then—whimpering, sniffling, the stirring of feet and cloth on stone. Alea's baby began to babble into this almost-quiet. She cooed and chuckled and clapped her hands as Alea smiled up at her from where she was lying.

"Kill her." Lanara heard the Queen's rasped words because she was beside her. Malhan heard them as well, and Leish might have, if he had not been making his own sounds. No one else heard them. The Queensguards were standing up, looking around in confusion and fear; they too had been in the Raiders' Land. The Queensfolk were drawing close together, turning to the thrones. Lanara saw their terror. She glanced at Alea, who was sitting up, holding her head in her hands; then back at the Queensfolk and at their Queen, lying pale and racked before them.

"We are sorry, Alea of the Alilan." Lanara took a step forward and began again, trying to speak with a strength she did not feel. "We are sorry for the hardship you have suffered because of Aldron's part in the battle. We are sorry for your grief." Her teeth chattered when she paused. "We are awed too, by the greatness of this Alilan power that you possess, as Aldron did—this power that is able to mimic the Queen's so exactly while lacking its substance." It was easier already, smoother, the sentences enfolding her so that she did not have to think about their meaning. "I have long known about the magic of Alilan Tellings, about how they are utterly convincing and all the more enchanted because they are fleeting. Now I have seen one. It was indeed akin to the destruction that was wrought in the Raiders' Land—yet look! The flames did not burn, and the wind tore no flowers from their stems. This is a subtle, delicate power, one of words, not change. I thank you for showing it to us."

Alea was crying, shaking silently. One of her arms was draped around Alnissa, who was still bouncing and chattering. Lanara looked quickly from them to the Queensfolk. They were nodding, and a few were smiling—comforted, convinced.

"As you can all see," Lanara continued swiftly—she had waited too long to speak again—"the Queen has been deeply affected by this vivid re-creation. We shall attend to her needs now, and to Alea's—the guards will conduct the rest of you back ..."

They raised their hands in the sign of the arrow. Galha did not see them, nor did Malhan, who was holding her against him with his head bent to hers. It was Lanara who acknowledged them. She longed, suddenly, to rush out behind them, into the knot of the marketplace or another way, to the houses piled against each other and the palace's flank, like a honeycomb. But she smiled at them as they lifted their hands to her, and she stood very tall as they left her, one by one.

Alea was crying after all, and so weakened by her Telling that she could not rise from the palace stones, could not even pick Alnissa up to quiet her. She heard Lanara murmuring with the man in the brown tunic. She remembered how he had stood apart from the rest of them in the tower, but she could not remember his name. She did remember the prisoner's name. *Leish.* She had thought it sounded like waves when Nellyn told it to her. Leish had fallen onto his side. His eyes were open, fixed on the pool behind Alea. His limbs were limp, but she could see them shuddering. *Twins, I have hurt him so much,* she thought, *and for what?*

"... outside if you need them." Alea looked back at the brown man, who was straightening, drawing the Queen gently up with him. Galha's eyes were closed and her head lolled against his shoulder. He turned to Alea just before he led the Queen out through a door behind the thrones. Alea gazed back at him; she would show this small measure of defiance.

"I'm so sorry." The same words Lanara had spoken before all her lies, but this time they were whispered and she was sitting on the ground, as Alea was.

"Really," Alea said somehow, with her torn throat. "Ah. Well, then."

Lanara was silent for a long time. She traced a vein of crystal with her forefinger, up and down, up and down. Alea hoped she would remain silent. Alea would stand whenever she was able to, and lift Alnissa and take her far away, and she would never have to listen to another Queensfolk word. She moved one of her legs, then the other, but she was still too exhausted to do more—and Lanara was looking at her again, and speaking.

"I've always seen how much you love and miss your people." Alnissa squirmed and Alea realized she was gripping her daughter's chubby thighs. "You can never forget your home, and if you return to it, you want to protect it, keep it the same as it was when you loved it before."

"Not with lies." Alea's voice, at least, was stronger.

"How can you say that? How can you be sure you wouldn't conceal or change what you knew, if it meant that your people would be spared confusion and misery?"

Alea shook her head but said nothing. Wrung, defeated; a change more shameful than Aldron's, for he had done something to provoke it.

"Where did he go?" Lanara's face was much thinner than it had been; Alea only noticed this now. Her eyes looked fevered.

"I don't know." Alea had not wanted to say anything more in this place, to this woman who had laughed with her once. They had baked bread, rolling their eyes at Aldron's loudness and Nellyn's silence. "He told me he had something to do. I asked him if it involved your Queen—I hoped it would—but he said no. He wouldn't say anything else, just that he'd have to be alone to do it. And that he wouldn't come back to me or anyone, after." She sucked in her breath. It was strange to hear the truth of this after so many months of simply knowing it. "And Nellyn?" she went on, needing to wound, needing to know. "Where is he?"

Lanara made a sound that was like a laugh except for its raggedness. "He said he had to be alone—though he did tell me where. His village. He said he didn't know if he'd come back to me after."

Alnissa snatched two handfuls of Alea's hair and pulled herself up until she was standing. Alea gasped, and Alnissa chortled, and Lanara smiled at them. The quiet that fell then was broken only by the sound of waves—the water stirred by a great back or a fin. Alea felt the quiet as if there had been some change in her and it was her own self rippling outward, in circles.

"Stay here," Lanara said. "If you won't stay in Luhr, at least let me find you and your daughter a home somewhere in the realm."

There was no anger or scorn in Alea's almost-laugh. "Oh, Lanara, how could I stay in the land where I have known only grief? I lost Aldron here"—*and a baby girl,* she thought, but this was hers to know, and Nellyn's—"and I could never live among your Queensfolk without hating the lie of this loss."

She was rising. Everything felt light: her own body, Alnissa's. She wondered whether the shock of her Telling was affecting her belatedly, cloaking her in this calm. Maybe it would dissipate—but it would not matter, for soon she would be far away. She could see the path she would take as clearly as if it were before her now, lined with beacon fires.

"And you?" she asked. "Will you stay in a place that drives you to lie, though you do it out of love?"

Lanara did not stand, did not look up at Alea. Alea turned to Leish, who was lying exactly as he had been. *I'm sorry*—weak words even if they were true, so she did not say them. "Come, little foal," she did say, to Alnissa. Then she walked—over bridges and stones, past the guards who were waiting for her at the door. "Lanara!" one of them called. "What should we ...?" Lanara answered, clear and steady, "Let her pass, Padhrel. Let her go."

The sun was low in the sky. The air was cool and fresh, and would be cold before too long. It would be easy travelling on such an evening. Alea readied their belongings and put Alnissa to her breast. The baby was already asleep when Alea laid her in the red cloth and tied it over shoulder and waist.

She passed the rocks where she had met the horned man, days ago. She had looked for him yesterday as well, and had not seen him. Now, as then, there was a woman atop the pile. *"Your return will have no ending."* Alea had wanted to ask him why he had told her this, and what it meant. Now she thought she knew. She was sure of it, with a joy that carried her through the city and through the gates, and on into the desert.

FORTY-TWO

Lanara was speaking before the guard had closed the door behind her. She was breathless from running, and from the revulsion that had been in her gut and throat for weeks—but she spoke anyway. "I know the truth," she said, and stood gasping, looking down at the Queen.

Galha was lying on her back beneath a blue-and-green sheet. It was drawn up to her chin; her shoulders, hips, knees, toes jutted beneath the silk. Her eyes were mostly closed, and Lanara thought for a moment that she was asleep or unconscious. All for nothing, then, the sudden entrance—and she did not think she would be able to speak the same words again.

"Lanara," Malhan said quietly.

The Queen turned her head on the pillow, very slightly, and smiled at her. Lanara took a step back from the bed.

"Alea told the truth about the battle. The truth, when for months you whispered lies about mindpowers and made me imagine I knew your most precious secret." She paused and breathed, though she was not afraid now that she had begun. "And Leish told me, weeks ago, about the other battle that was really a surprise attack, mounted by Queensfolk as well as Raiders. So *you* tell me now. Tell me about all your lies—beginning with Ladhra's death."

Galha's lips were dry and cracked, and she moistened them with her tongue. Malhan lifted a goblet from the table beside the bed, but she did not look at him. "I failed her."

Lanara clenched her hands as she strained to hear the words. When the Queen had first spoken to Alea in the Throne Chamber, Lanara had thought, *Her weakness has passed—her voice is the same as it was before*. But it was not. It was an old woman's voice, trembling with air.

"I failed my daughter. I could not fail my people."

"And how would the truth have failed them?" Lanara said, her own voice softer. "It was an attack led by traitors who knew the palace and the city. It was one of these traitors who killed Ladhra—and yet his name will never be known, and you have made an innocent man responsible for her death. Surely your people deserve to know that it was Baldhron who committed this crime."

"No. No one will know about his life. When I am recovered and find him, no one will know about his death. No one will know he led a band of Queensfolk traitors. Queensfolk traitors! Imagine what confusion it would have caused if other Queensfolk had known of it. And rebellion"—she drew a shallow, whistling breath—"always breeds rebellion, in time. No: the Sea Raiders had to be our only enemy. And my daughter had to die before the gates of her city."

Malhan was lighting candles. Eight, ten, fifteen: the round chamber was like a lightroom, though the flames shone only on stone walls and wooden shutters, not glass and sky.

"Many have had to die," Lanara said. "Aldron, say. He had to, but did not: you were too sloppy, and I was too determined. Did you plunge the spear into him yourself or did you watch someone else do it?"

The Queen's hair clung to her cheeks when she shook her head. "Dear girl. I've killed many people less beloved to me." Malhan straightened. Lanara felt him looking at her, but she did not turn to him. Galha was smiling again. One of her hands moved; the silk rippled and fluttered smooth. "No one who has not been given the gift of power should ever presume to know how to wield it. Such presumption is naive and dangerous—I warned Ladhra of this several times. And now you … though your words to the Alilan woman made me remember why you must be queen someday."

"Because I lied so well?" Lanara said, petulant, heartsick, imagining what she and Ladhra could have borne together if they had known the truth.

"Because you spoke wisely. You spoke to save all of us from disaster."

"Yes," Lanara said quickly, "and I spoke only because you were so overcome by Alea's Telling that you could not. Your body's sickness tells me what you do not, my Queen. It is guilt that weakens you so. The weight of it must be unbearable. Cast it off—I will help you. Your people love you. They will still love you if you—"

"Lanara," Galha snapped, "why do you mar the memory of your other words with these ones?"

Lanara answered the question as swiftly as the Queen had asked it. "Because there must be honesty between us, at least, if I am really to be your daughter."

Galha's right arm emerged from beneath the sheet. She extended it so that her fingers wavered in the space between them. "Nara. My sweet girl." Words and warmth that Lanara had heard before, and could not endure or permit now—so she wrenched the door open and ran from them, over the slippery stone.

~

Lanara left the palace. She walked through the marketplace and the city streets beyond it, which were quieter and slanting with shade. She sat on fountain rims and listened to the lazy, droning talk of adults and to children's high-pitched chatter. She remembered when she had come to these streets and fountains with Nellyn. He had beamed at everything, and held her hand, and kissed her ears until she giggled. She looked out of the guard-towers' windows at the sand and the distant blot of jungle. People smiled at her, and one old woman bowed a bit. Perhaps she had been present for Lanara's speech to the "Alilan madwoman," as Alea was doubtless being called. Lanara bowed back.

She walked all day, three days in a row. At night she returned to the palace, each time expecting the Queen to be waiting for her in Ladhra's tower chamber—or a Queensguard, anyway, who would summon her to Galha's side. But the chamber was always empty, its fire lit and welcoming, wine and fresh water in jugs placed on the desk. No one sought her out, and Lanara did not know whether to feel relief or dread.

On the third night she stood at the window listening to the wind. Her shutters were rattling and sand was hissing against them like rain. Even during the day the air had been full of sand; the desert had been lost behind curtains of it. Lanara almost threw open her shutters, to feel her breath snatched away and her skin stung, to feel a pain that would wake her. She laid her forehead and fingers against the wood, which was humming. Then she lay down on the bed.

The fire was low when she started awake, the wind a muted whine. She thought at first that it was the quiet that had woken her, but there was another sound. She lay and tried to hear it above the pounding of her heart. A scraping sound, quite close. She sat up, scrabbled through a pile of clothing and parchment. She whimpered when she felt the cool leather of her dagger's sheath against her palm. The scraping was louder. Her door was closed; she could see the key still in it. She had been locking the door at night since she returned to Luhr. Its handle was not moving now; nor was the key.

"There was another door." She turned to the tapestry across from the bed. Of course—Leish had said this, but she had known about the door since she was a child, listening to Ladhra's indignant protests. The scraping had stopped now, and been replaced by a grating of metal and stone. The tapestry shuddered and angled outward. Lanara leaned forward, thought, *Baldhron,* even though it could not possibly be Baldhron.

"Do not be afraid," Queen Galha said.

Lanara nodded slowly. The wind's whine was between her ears and behind her eyes. Galha's eyes shone; Lanara saw them clearly in the light of the lantern the Queen held. Her cheeks were shining as well. She glowed with tears.

"I'm so very sorry. My dearest daughter—my girl …" She took two small steps toward the bed.

"I'm Lanara," Lanara whispered. She slid back until she felt the wall behind her. She could not draw her dagger from its sheath, though she held it beneath her left hand.

"So sorry, so sorry," Galha said, moving forward, raising her arm.

"No!" Malhan cried as he ran and reached for her. "Love," he said more softly, drawing her arm down again, drawing her in against him. "You should not be here. Come away." He was breathing hard, Lanara saw through the blurring of her own relief. He must have run all along the walkway from the Queenstower to the door, which had still been open.

"No," Galha murmured, "too much to do—must be sure …"—but she was letting him lead her back to the tapestry, and her eyes were closed.

He looked at Lanara before he ducked out of sight. He was holding the lantern on the other side of the tapestry; she could hardly see his face. But he paused and his eyes were on her—and then he was gone and the key was scraping the door locked.

Lanara sprang toward the other door, which would take her into the palace. She grasped the key with numb fingers and counted as she tried to turn it: "One, two, three, four, five, six"—the last number wobbly with frustration and panic. When at last it did turn, it made no sound, though the door thudded against the wall. She took the stairs three at a time, her thick leather sandals slipping, her hand clutching the rough stone wall. She had brought no light. Only the familiarity of the twisting staircase allowed her to descend it so quickly and in darkness. She did fall once, near the bottom—but by then she could see the other door, rimmed with the torchlight that flickered in the hallway beyond it.

She did not answer the Queensguard who called out after her, or the one who cried her name at the palace's western doors. She did not pause until the ground changed from stone to earth—broken earth, rough with fallen branches and sharp, dry moss. She stopped and stood panting in the ruin of the Queenswood.

She had not come here since her return. The Queen had told her of the fire: set by the Sea Raiders, of course, who had wanted nothing more than to destroy this living symbol of the Queens' power. Lanara looked up at the trees that still stood, their branches bare against the sky. She looked at the ones that lay toppled on the ground. Baldhron had come to Ladhra here when there were leaves and moist earth. She had spurned him here, as she had within the palace; she and Lanara had laughed about it time after time. Lanara could almost see him standing where she was, gloating as the leaves above him vanished into flame. Baldhron, not a Sea Raider—but she would never know it for sure. This one thing uncertain when too much else was clear.

For a time she wandered, trying to find a trunk or stump she might recognize. When she did not, she went out through the gate. The Queensguard outside it raised her eyebrows but said nothing except, "It's a lovely night, now that the gale's died down."

Lanara nodded. "Yes," she said, mostly to see if she could make her voice bland and careless. "The wind kept me awake for hours, but now that it's gone, I can't sleep."

The guard laughed. "I'd be asleep in a moment, wind or no wind!" As Lanara walked away, the woman said, "Wait, please, Queenswoman Lanara, if you would. I hear … they say the Queen's keeping to her room all the time now. That she's too ill to walk. The cooks say her food comes back nearly untouched, and it's only broth to begin with. Is …" She hesitated. Her thumbnail was digging into the wood of her bow. "Is she well?" she went on quickly. "We won't lose her too, will we?"

Lanara heard love and fear, solid, whole. She tried to smile. "I don't know." She touched the Queensguard's hand, and its white-knuckled grip on the bow loosened just a bit.

Lanara walked past the Queensfolk houses that rose against the palace wall. If she looked at them, her feet might carry her up the well-worn steps to a door she knew, and she might open it and stand waiting for a man who would not come. "You were right," she might whisper, though it would be no use speaking to him as if he were in front of her. He was not here, just as he had not been in his tomb chamber with its jewels and its delicate crystal fountain. These places did not hold him.

Luhr's streets were filled with drifts of blown sand. People would sweep them away in the morning, but for now they stood tall and silent, a desert within the city. In some of the larger squares the sand still swirled. Lanara watched it eddy over her feet and thought of ash. She tried to look at every courtyard and cobblestone and house, at every lazily swinging lantern and fountain basin. *My city,* she thought, as if thinking this now would help her to remember later.

She searched for Alea in the marketplace, after the sun had risen. When she did not find her, she asked about her. Most people claimed they had never seen her. Some said that they had seen her leave but had not spoken to her at all, ever. "She was mad," one man said, then glanced away and cleared his throat. "I heard it from someone who saw her. Her baby's the one to pity, I'd say."

Lanara went to the base of the iben stones, but there was no one at the top. She had refused one, long before, when it had offered her a glimpse of future. She might refuse again, but she wanted the choice at least. "Don't waste your coins, my lady," a fruit seller called from his cart. "They're a ragged bunch that tells only lies—better leave while there's no one there." He might remember her if she turned to face him. He might have lynanyn on his cart. She walked away, not seeking any more, just moving.

She would have to go back to Ladhra's chamber. All her belongings were there, and she would need her knife, and her heavier cloak, and some food. She should have thought before she fled. *"Too hasty,"* chided Creont in her head. While the sun climbed, she walked aimlessly, mostly in the city, for she would be easier to find in the marketplace. When the sun fell behind the great outer wall, she returned to the palace. She had wasted the day and would not be able to bear another night. She smiled at the Queensguards at the front doors, and went inside.

The sunlight had left the corridors. Lanara walked swiftly beneath the torches, slowing only when she drew close to other people. There were very few of them about now; most would be eating supper. Her own belly grumbled, but she ignored it; when she was well away, she would eat, but not until then. The guard at Ladhra's tower door straightened when he saw her, and opened his mouth to speak. "I've been in the city all day," she said gaily as he opened the door. "Imagine: all day and part of the night too, and all I want now is some food and a clean tunic."

She was already running when the door closed behind her. Up the stairs three by three, once trying for four and falling forward onto her hands. She seized the door handle, pushed with all her weight. The chamber was dark: no fire in the hearth, no window open on the last of the daylight.

"Lanara," Malhan said, "thank the First you have come."

She bent her head. Her chest was heaving and there was sweat at her hairline. It would drip into her eyes in a moment.

"I came through the walkway so I wouldn't be seen. No one must see me now, either. You'll have to go by yourself …"

Lanara looked up. He was alone, standing by the desk, tapping his fingernails against the wood, shifting his feet on the floor. "Malhan," she said hoarsely, "what has happened?"

He laughed—a high, giddy sound that soon broke and became something else. He took three steps and spoke. She heard his words even though they were muffled and she was far away from him and this room and everything else she knew.

"The Queen is gone."

FORTY-THREE

The Queensstudy was empty. Lanara knew that it would be; the guard outside had asked her how the Queen was and expressed concern that she had not been seen in so many days. But Lanara went in anyway and stood alone among the closed drawers. The candles in the candelabra on the table were lit, as were the lanterns that hung from spaces between the drawer rows. A box of writing sticks lay open on the table beside a stack of parchment.

The wood of the drawers felt warm. Lanara drew her finger along a row, over the dates—down, down, until Malhan's writing became someone else's. So many dates and queens and consort-scribes; so many words, within. *All shadows,* she thought, *though the script is doubtless fine and legible.* She almost opened one of the drawers, but the expectant light and silence drove her back to the door.

"She is so weak," Malhan said when Lanara returned to Ladhra's chamber. "I thought perhaps her study, since it's not far from her tower, but ..." He dragged the fingers of one hand through his hair. "How could I have slept so deeply?" he cried. "I knew she was unwell, and yet I slept—and in the afternoon!"

"I know," Lanara said, and laid a hand lightly on his shoulder. "You've told me—no need to say it again. And of course you're tired, you've been tending her for so long ..." She squeezed his shoulder and frowned; his tunic was damp. She lifted her fingers away and rubbed them together until they were dry. He looked up at her and she smiled as reassuringly as she could. "Come, let's go together to the Throne Chamber. You can leave through the Queenstower. Just tell the guard she's sleeping and you absolutely must get her a document of some kind, something only you'd be allowed to get. We'll use the door behind the thrones so no one will see us."

"Yes," he said, "the Throne Chamber"—vague and weak, until he rose to the tapestry and said, "Thank you, Lanara. I wouldn't know what to do if you weren't here."

She shook her head but said only, "Go now. I'll see you in a few minutes."

She sat down on the bed after he had gone. She looked at her dagger, her heavy cloak, her travelling blanket, the leather bag Ladhra had given her, which had gleamed once. *I could be at the edge of the jungle by moonrise,* Lanara thought. *Or at the mouth of the Sarhenna River in a week.* She imagined Nellyn's eyes glimpsing her, recognizing her. She would stride past the old shonyn on their flat stones and run the rest of the way, to wherever he was standing.

Ladhra's bed was firm. Lanara shifted on it, reached over to straighten the pillows. One for her head, one for Ladhra's—though of course these weren't the same ones as before. These were new, clean, never blood-spattered or flattened by thrashing bodies. Lanara rose, sucking in her breath, crossing her arms over her chest.

The Throne Chamber was very dark. It was too early for the moon, and Lanara saw, when she looked up at the glass tower, that the sky was still murky, as if the wind had pinned it with layers of sand. She pulled the door slowly toward her as Malhan waited behind. The glass tower, the fountain spray, the shadows of the thrones. She took a step forward, into the doorway, and saw Leish lying on the ground facing the pool. Another step; her eyes were adjusting, and the lantern she was holding was shedding light, as was Malhan's. She saw the water at the far side of the pool. There was some sort of creature floating there, just beyond the spray. She walked past the thrones, past Leish, whose eyes were half-lidded and motionless.

"No." She turned to Malhan as he whispered the word again, turned once more to follow the direction of his pointing, wavering arm.

Not a water creature; not a fin or a scaled belly. A woman, her tunic rounded with water, her arms limp above her head, as if she had been frozen in a dive. There were beads of water in her hair, full and glittering as the gems around the pool.

Lanara did not flinch when Malhan jumped into the pool, even though the jump and his flailing, after, soaked her. She stood and watched him grasp an arm and pull. She watched him scrabble in shallower water, wrenching at the arm and the hips. She did not move until the body turned and Galha's open eyes stared up at the tower of glass.

"Here," Lanara said as she knelt at the side, "let me help you"—and she dug her fingers into the Queen's skin and pulled as Malhan pushed. She leaned over and set her mouth against Galha's as she had seen a Queensguard do with a child who had fallen into a marketplace fountain. Lanara forced her own breath into Galha's mouth, down her throat; paused, breathed again. The child had coughed and spewed out a stream of water and begun to cry. The Queen lay still.

Malhan covered her eyes with his hand and stroked downward. When he raised his hand, her eyelids were closed. Lanara wished she could imagine that Galha was calm or asleep—but her skin was mottled and swollen, and her clenched fingers would not straighten.

"There is no glory in this." Malhan's voice was as rough as if he had been shouting. His fingers were in her hair, smoothing the moisture away.

"No. But you'll be able to remedy that, won't you? Let me see," Lanara went on, standing up so that her sudden anger would not feel so stifling, "perhaps I can practise ... Yes: She was unable, finally, to bear the loss of her daughter and the toll of her mindpowers. She died today, at dusk, in this very room, where she had ordered us to bring her so that she would be near the pool her foremother crafted for all our sakes ..." She turned away from Malhan and the Queen. "How, Malhan?" she said when she could. "Tell me how you've been able to write such lies for so long."

She expected him to hesitate or deny, but he did not. "I love this realm, and I loved her. There was a time, years ago, when I forgot to serve both—when I transgressed, and jeopardized my post and indeed my life. Since then everything that I have done has been both penance and promise. The Queensrealm will be safe while I am here to serve it. It will be safe. This is the reason for all my words."

She looked down at him. His tunic had been damp in Ladhra's tower. His words might be true, but there was a silence beneath, between and after them that was truer still. *Tell me the rest,* she thought, and her lips parted to speak. He gazed at her, his hand unmoving on Galha's hair, and Lanara bit down instead, let out the breath that might have asked for more.

"She'll need different clothing," he said quietly, almost gently. "Something beautiful. Will you help me choose it?"

~

Queen Galha opened her eyes as the last of the day's sun faded from her bedchamber. "My death is upon me," she said, and there was neither terror nor bitterness in her voice. "Take me from this room, to the place where the joy of all the queens has been."

And so it was that her consort-scribe and Lanara, who was Ladhra's dearest friend, bore the Queen to the Throne Chamber. This was accomplished in secrecy, at the Queen's request—for she did not wish to worry her faithful guards or any other of her people. She lay on a pallet before her throne and looked once more on the water Queen Sarhenna had called forth from the sand so long ago. "Let me be remembered as she has been," Queen Galha said. "Let my people say of me that my body could not compass the great powers of my mind and heart." She drew her last breath as the first stars shone above, turning the pool to silver and the Queen's smooth skin to gold.

When her servants came to tend to the pool and plants, they discovered the Queen and her companions. The servants wept and bowed themselves down before her, and they carried the news of her passing with them when they went out again. By daybreak the word had spread throughout the palace and into the city. Queensfolk came to the Throne Chamber in a line that stretched into the streets, for they all yearned to look upon her and share their grief together. Many of them were weak with fear for their realm that was so suddenly bereft of the wisdom of its leader. They were reassured by Lanara, daughter of Salanne, who told them that Queen Galha had written several documents before her death, documents that would be studied and acted upon by consort-scribe Malhan. "The Queensrealm," Lanara declared, "is built upon a foundation so firm that nothing—not even this—shall rock it." And so the people of the Queen sorrowed, but were not afraid.

~

Leish could not wake up. He was not truly asleep; he realized this after he had tried and failed several times to open his eyes completely. He was lying on his side, and he could see snatches of shape and colour: brown feet in brown sandals, and bare brown feet dusted with sand, and the hems of tunics and leggings (mostly brown, but some scarlet and others green and blue). Sunlight dancing on the fountain pool. He saw the water and heard it, and remembered that it had been dark when he had last looked on it, when he had fallen into this sluggish, nauseated place that was not quite sleep.

Maybe the blue fruit he had eaten had been rotten. He had not even wanted to eat it. He had not eaten anything in days, since the Telling that had made him, at last, want to die. Those days had passed in a sickening blur of memory and thirst. Every image he had seen but not felt, every note he had listened to but not heard—they all struck him and tore him, and he had screamed himself hoarse in the vast, empty room. He had ignored the fruit the kind servant brought him; it lay beside him and turned rank and wrinkled in the heat. For days he did not count he ignored it—and then one day he had woken from his dreams of hearth pool and violet coral, and he was angry. It was a blinding, scalding anger, and it forced him to his knees and to his feet. He had barely been able to stand. His dry skin scattered, and blood and pus welled from the sores that covered him. He looked down at himself as he had so many times since his first imprisonment. Before, he had felt shame and rage at his own weakness, and at his desire to live. Now his rage was all for others.

I will kill her. It was a thought without form or sense that first morning—but very soon it grew clearer. *Mallesh would find a way to kill her. He would be clever and convincing … I'll beg the kind servant to find a key for my chains. I'll tell him the pain in my ankle is too much to bear.* No untruth in this: the skin beneath his shackle had worn away to something pink and white, like the inside of a fish. He could see bone beneath, when he poked at the mess. *I'll have to strike him. I'll have to remember what Baldhron told us about the palace and the guards …* His head ached more than his body did. He would need strength to make these plans, and more to carry them out. So when he woke and found the blue fruit beside him, he had eaten it. *I will ask for seavine too,* he had thought. *And maybe some salted eel.*

But he had not been able to ask for anything. He had felt sick by mid-afternoon and had lain down, determined to rest for just a short time. The sickness in his stomach had crept outward until all his limbs felt sodden and useless. His eyelids had been the last part of him to grow heavy. He tried to hold them open, but he was slipping away into a place where he was still but everything else moved. The sun, which faded; the door behind him, which he heard opening and closing; feet, which passed by him in a streak of colour and speed he could not follow. The water moved then. He saw it, though not clearly; his lids and lashes hid everything but its sudden roughness. He heard a churning that subsided into lapping. He thought he heard more footsteps, though this time they were much quieter and did not pass in front of him. He strained to turn his head but could not—and the effort sent him further down, into shadow.

And now it was day again, and there were many feet by his head. He felt a shuddering in the ground beneath him and thought for a moment that the feet must belong to giants—but he heard a sound above the murmuring of songs and people. Baldhron had looked up at this same sound and fled; Ladhra had not heard it. Leish had lain in her blood and sung against her skin. The bell clanged more slowly now than it had then. It did not call out danger; something else, deep and terrible.

People were weeping. One woman fell to her knees beside Leish and rocked herself back and forth, wailing with her face raised up to the tower of glass. So many people, so many voices, yet he could understand nothing. He whimpered, himself, as he forced his waking muscles to stretch. He arched his back and rolled and stared up at standing bodies and sky. He moved his eyes and saw Lanara, with Malhan slightly behind her. Just them, bowing their heads to each of the Queensfolk who approached. Just the two of them by the thrones, and all these people mourning, and the bell shaking the palace stones. He was too late. *She is dead. She died without me.*

As the sky above the glass grew dark, the last of the Queensfolk left and Leish sat up. He coughed, dizzy with motion and the scent of blossoms that he had not noticed, lying down. It was a thick, cloying smell, and he thought it might make him sick again—but he breathed through his mouth a few times and the nausea passed. The stones were buried beneath cut flowers and lengths of ivy, and shells, rocks, bits of bark and even coral. Galha lay among these gifts—for so Leish assumed they were, gifts of dead things that had once lived. He imagined Nasranesh there as well, its moss and trees piled atop her body, starmoths clustered above her sightless eyes.

Malhan was speaking to a group of green-robed figures, five of them, their faces hidden by veils and hoods. They were all tall but stooped, as if they carried some sort of weight. They nodded, but Leish heard no voices; perhaps they had no mouths beneath the green cloth. They lifted Galha up when Malhan finished speaking. The cloth she lay on was also green. They folded it over so that her face was hidden, carried her behind the thrones and out, and Malhan followed without looking back. *And why should he?* Leish thought. *It's just me, the Queen's plaything, which even she has ignored these past few months. The pathetic, weak, silent lizard-man who survived her because no one remembered he was there.* "You mewling boy," he heard his brother say, his scorn and frustration very clear even though his voice was merely an imagining. "You've always tried to be invisible, and now you are. Will you moan about this too?"

Leish waited. A star flickered above him, and another, and there was even a moon, after so many nights of cloud and wind-sprayed sand. The servants would come soon. He would entreat the kind one to kill him, and if he would not, Leish would goad the cruel one until he lashed out. *I will be brave enough to die,* Leish thought as he waited. *It is what Mallesh would do.*

When he heard the voice, he raised his head and looked for its source, though he did not expect to find one. A waking dream, an echo of Dallia or Ladhra or someone else who was gone. But he saw a dark shape on a bridge beyond the fountain, a sitting, swaying shape with a woman's voice. It rose as he watched, and came toward him. There were no lanterns or torches, but the moon- and starlight were enough to show him whose shape it was.

"Leish," Lanara said as she sat down in front of him. "Please talk to me, quickly, before I can keep talking to myself."

Leish's throat was so swollen with thirst that he could not swallow, and he did not know whether he would be able to speak either. "What," he said, forcing air up and out, "do you want me to say?"

She shrugged. Her cheeks looked dusty in the thin white light. *Old tears,* he thought. Dried salt water.

"I don't know. You should say nothing but horrible things to me, though. Angry, horrible things that I deserve to hear."

He tried to find the rage that had made him strong only a few days ago; tried to find it and speak with it—but he had none for this woman who had been Ladhra's friend. When he said, "You pity yourself," his words were merely tired.

"Yes. Though not as much as I pity you or Malhan or Alea or indeed all the people of the Queensrealm." She gazed at him for a long time. *She sees me,* he thought, and the shock of this made him dizzy. When she rose and walked away, he watched her, willed her to leave forever, was amazed that he wanted her to return. *She does not know who I am, and she is an enemy to the selkesh—but she sees me when she looks at me, and why does this matter still?*

She returned. She did not sit, but bent and held out her hand to him. "I'm sure Malhan has plans for you, and he will probably be angry at me for this. But there should be choice. Even if it must be made between impossible things, there must be choice."

Leish took the waterskin from her hand. It was an old skin, worn smooth and dark where other fingers had grasped it. He felt the weight of water within, and heard it with his ears and his flesh and his swollen throat. He remembered the selkesh who had died on the Queensship, so quickly and silently, after only a few swallows. He remembered the Queen proclaiming the curse as hers when really it had been the Alilan man's. Such remembering was faded, though, and powerless; he held the only thing that was real.

Lanara bent still further as he tipped the skin to feel the water's shape. He hardly noticed her until pain flared in his ankle and up his left leg. He gasped and turned to her, and he saw the broken ring of his shackle in her hand. She let it fall to the floor and placed the key beside it.

"The servants will not come tonight," he heard her say through the pounding in his head. She stood by him a moment longer. He shifted his eyes from the pile of chain to his putrid ankle to the waterskin he was clutching in both hands now. He could not look at her—not even when she moved away from him. He heard the door behind the thrones open and close. He heard the fountain singing, and the river, and the sea, so far away. And beneath it all, as he sank and sank again, he heard his heart.

FORTY-FOUR

Aldira remembered that children had scattered from her when they came upon her picking berries on the lakeshore. She had only to straighten and glare and they would be gone, back to wagons or hillsides or other, more distant lakes. They did not notice her at all now. They splashed and screeched and pulled each other under and never once glanced at her—and why should they? She no longer cried out that they were fools for trying to dive so deep. She did not even scold them for taking too many eggs from the nests along the shore. She moved slowly among the creepingvine strands, plucking berries sometimes but mostly sitting, a kerchief pulled up over her head because even the weak spring sun made her dizzy. Occasionally she fell asleep sitting and woke to fishfolk shadows in the water, gathering as the Alilan fires climbed into darkness. She was always surprised to find herself there, in her body that was bent but would not bend.

"Aldira."

She opened her eyes, her hand already reaching for a berry, as if she had paused only for a moment. "Aliser," she said briskly. "What is it?"

She heard the creepingvine rustle as he sat down beside her. He'd crushed ten berries, perhaps, and a couple of new blossoms—and she had no strength with which to chide him. "Nothing," he said. "I saw you here earlier in the day. I wanted to check—"

"Don't be ridiculous," Aldira snapped, "I'm perfectly well. There are many berries this season, it's simply taken me longer than I expected to pick them." She finally looked at him. He was staring at her gathering basket, which was nearly empty, and she could think of no excuse for this, or none that would make sense.

"In fact," he said, before the silence could become unbearable, "there is something I've been intending to ask you. My niece is beginning to show signs of Telling ability—she's five now—and my sister and I were wondering whether you'd speak to her, see if she's ready for lessons."

Aldira snorted. "I thank you for your attempt to make me feel useful, but you're the Teller of the Twin Daggers caravan now. Surely you can perform this small task yourself. Or is it that it's too small for you to perform at all?"

"Aldira," he said, too quietly. She had preferred the boy Aliser, who had been incapable of speaking much below a shout, even when he hadn't been Telling. "You're considerably wiser than I am. And infinitely more patient."

"Ah, yes, of course—you say 'wise' but mean 'old.' And patient too! Patient!" *Not that,* she thought, *no—but it's true that he's worse. He may make a fine Teller, but he'll never be a teacher*.

"So you'll speak to her," he said, and she snorted again and came very close to returning his smile.

She was glad of silence this time. It was a relief to slip away from words into other sounds: birdsong, water, bees. When she looked at the trees on the hillsides, she imagined she could hear the leaves unfurling, so bright and yellow-green, though such a thought was foolishness, of course.

"Why do we not celebrate Alneth's Night here?" a child had asked her once. She had replied, "This kind of spring is easy for Alneth—a time of comfort and fast, effortless growing. While we rejoice in this, it is when we reach the desert that we see her true power—there at the oasis, surrounded by desolation. This is what all the caravans come together to celebrate." A pretty speech, and she remembered it very clearly—but she could not recall whether the child had been Aliser or Alea. They had sat together near here and gazed upon spring in the lake country, and yet she could not remember the child.

"What ...?" Aliser said, and Aldira forced her eyes open. Even before she turned, she heard a difference in the camp: no singing or laughter, no daggers scraping against flint. All the people who were usually clustered around their own fires were rising, moving together to the southern edge of the camp. "What ...?" Aliser said again, as Aldira realized which family's wagon always stood at that southern edge. Her breath seemed to disappear.

Her chest swelled even as it tightened. She thought, *Oh, Twins,* desperately—and then she was breathing again, and even rising.

"Come, Aliser," she said, and walked ahead of him over the rustling vines.

~

Every time she had dreamed of returning to her caravan, Alea had envisioned darkness. It would be night, and she would see the fires in the distance, ranged in a pattern that would grow familiar as she drew closer. She would watch them dancing: her sisters, her parents, her brother at his fire next to theirs. In the silence after the drumming, Alnissa would clap and squeal with laughter—and they would all turn and gape, and then cry out their joy and amazement. Alea's mother would touch Alnissa's black hair, which was fine and wispy against her neck, and Alnissa would hold out her arms. They would all be weeping. Alea had wept herself, imagining the scene. With Aldron she had cried soundlessly, into a cloak, aching with impossibility. Now, entering the lake country, she ached with certainty. The wagon tracks and hoofprints in the mud were fresh. She placed her feet in their furrows and said, "Nearly there, little foal," and Alnissa wriggled against her back but did not wake.

The sky was sunlit and blue when Alea saw smoke above the hills. She looked at it and at the long, thin lake she was standing beside. She knew the place; it was close to the camp, perhaps another two hours away on the path. It was mid-afternoon. If she went at a leisurely pace, she would reach her caravan around dusk. At first she did walk slowly, trying not to glance up at the blur of smoke ahead. She stared at the ground—the mud, the grass on the lower hillsides, the blossoming creepingvine around the lakes. She thought, *I should gather some berries to mash up for Nissa*—except that she did not need to do this any more. Soon Nissa would taste her first pinkroot soup, and maybe some fish if Aldana had already caught some—and it was this knowledge that drove Alea to walk faster and faster yet. When the track bent sharply to the left, around a hill, Alea did not follow it. She strode up the hill instead, a more strenuous way, but it would bring her home much more quickly. Her leggings snagged on brambles and twigs, but she wrenched herself free without pausing. Down one hill and up another. Alnissa slept soundly, even though her head jolted against Alea's left shoulder blade with every step. It would not be dark after all, but this did not matter. All Alea's imaginings streamed away from her as she came to the crest of the second hill and stood, panting, looking down at the wagons and fires of the Twin Daggers caravan.

Alnissa raised her head and made a querulous noise. "I know," Alea said, trying to laugh, fumbling with the knots in the red blanket, "you want to keep moving. We will, Nissa, I promise—but just look with me for a moment. Look there." She held Alnissa up, pressed her mouth and nose against the back of her daughter's head. She smelled like sun. "Look," Alea murmured again, and she thought that Alnissa was unusually still, that she must be seeing the scampering children, the glossy horses, the colours—*Ah, Twins, the bright scarlets and coppers and greens.* Then Alnissa kicked out her legs and made the sound that meant, "I want to try to walk holding your finger, or at least crawl," and Alea did laugh. "Not now, dearest," she said, and set Alnissa on her hip.

Her parents' wagon always rested at the foot of this hill, and she saw it from the top, though her tears made it tremble. She did not look at it as she descended; she watched only her feet. Left foot, right foot, switch Alnissa to the other hip; down past bushes and trees laced with blooms; down until the slope began to flatten. When she was steps away from the bottom, she finally lifted her eyes.

The wood of her wagon shone. Aldill would have washed it as soon as they stopped here, while Aldana was off catching fish. Alea lifted her hand and touched the wood, which was warm. She kept her fingers on it as she walked its length, from front to back. She walked slowly now that she was here. Four paces would carry her to the back steps and the fire. Just four paces, three, two—and there was no darkness to hide her.

She peered around the wagon's edge when she reached it at last. Alnissa squirmed and said "Gaa!" very loudly, and Alea shushed her, though she did not need to: there was no one by the fire or on the steps. Two children were lying beside the fire next to this one, but they were sleeping. Alea could see their closed eyes and the deep rise and fall of their chests. Alnissa burrowed against her, tugging at Alea's tunic ties. Alea undid them and nursed her, leaning back against the wagon's side, out of sight. Her head throbbed. She heard faraway voices and splashing, and a bird singing on the hillside above. Alnissa bit down hard on Alea's breast with her four tiny teeth, and Alea was about to cry out when she heard other, closer voices.

"Nanna! Your mother caught these fish for you. It would be a gesture of thanks and recognition if you'd help her prepare—Alnanna! Where do you—"

"Let her go." Alea pressed herself against the wagon. Her mother's words were very clear; she must be standing by the fire or at the foot of the steps. "You know she only runs farther, the closer you try to keep her."

"Of course I know," Aldill replied. "And I know it better every time I make this mistake. A little help is all I ask of her. A few minutes and we'd have the fish gutted and in the stew—but no, she'd rather run off to the fire of that shifty lad with the hair like a woman's ..."

Alea was holding Alnissa on her shoulder. She did not remember moving her there. She waited for them to talk again, so that she would be able to listen and stay hidden, but they did not. She heard the wet, heavy slap of fish against wood—probably the smooth plank her mother used for chopping. She heard a knife being drawn across a whetstone and the first muffled tearing of flesh. Her parents were silent. *Now,* Alea thought, and could not move, her legs mired and wobbling at the same time. But then Alnissa squealed—and Alea turned and walked around the side of the wagon.

"I'll help you," she said.

They were both kneeling. Aldill's knife froze a finger's breadth away from the fish and a potato fell from Aldana's hand. Even after a moment had passed, there was no joy or amazement, just a taut stillness and a silence that grew longer.

"Ald—he is not here," Alea said very quickly, so that she would not be able to cry. "I left him, and he'll never come back. But this," she went on, even though it was all wrong—there should not need to be so many words—"is my daughter. Your granddaughter," she added, as if this would help them understand. She bent her head against Alnissa's and closed her eyes.

The touch on her hair was very light. Alea knew this touch, these fingers. She did not angle her head into the hollow they made in case they went away. "Alea," Aldana said. Her fingers slipped beneath Alea's chin and pressed, and Alea opened her eyes as she lifted her head. Aldana was very close to her; Alea remembered only now how tall her mother was. Aldana put her palm to the baby's cheek. "What is her name?"

"Alnissa," Alea said, and then her father was with them too, reaching and laughing, and all of them stood wrapped tight until Alnissa started to wail.

"Hush, little foal!" Aldill cried, holding his granddaughter above his head. She kicked and cried louder, and Aldana said, "That's enough, now—the poor little thing doesn't know you." Alea did not look at them as Alnissa settled again into her arms. *Too many words,* she thought, *and the wrong ones*—though of course they were true.

She glanced past her father and sucked in her breath. They were no longer alone by their wagon. Other Alilan were gathered nearby, watching, and many more were approaching. She saw confusion, curiosity, anger; only when her sisters thrust their way forward did she see joy. After she had embraced them, they stepped behind her. They stood, her family and herself, and faced the growing crowd. "Alea," her father muttered, and she looked up at him—but before he could say more, the crowd stirred and parted.

"Aliser," Alea said when he stopped a few paces away from her. "May the Twins protect and succour you."

He was broader across the shoulders and chest, and his hair was a darker red than it had been—though she remembered suddenly that it always darkened a bit during the winter, away from the desert sun. His freckles were the same, as was the stiffness of his spine and head.

"You greet me in the names of the Alilan Goddesses. Why do you presume to do this?"

"I will give an answer, but I will give it to Aldira. Where is she?"

Aliser shook his head. "You will give it to me, for I asked the question—and I am the Teller of this caravan."

Alea's eyes slid away from his. She glanced over the crowd until she saw Old Aldira. She was leaning on a staff, her back and shoulders rounded and twisted both. One of her legs looked shrivelled. She met Alea's gaze and nodded, very slightly.

"Very well, then," Alea said, looking back at Aliser. "I invoke Alnila and Alneth because I have never left them. Because it is the dearest wish of my heart to be Alilan again, now that I can return unburdened and alone."

"Hardly unburdened, or alone." Aliser did not look at Alnissa as he said this, or after. His green eyes were steady on Alea's face, though there was a flush spreading up into his cheeks.

"Yes, I bring my daughter, it's true—but she's no burden to me. It's mostly for her sake that I've come back. I can't bear the thought that she'll never know her own people."

"You returned to us once before. There are many here who remember this. Do *you* not remember what happened then?"

The plain at night. Aldron had come with her, though just to the outer fires. She had walked among them alone. "I didn't want to return forever—not then. I only wanted to see my family—to see you."

"Aliser." Old Aldira's voice was also smaller now, bent out of the shape Alea had known—but still people turned to her and listened. "This is not a matter that should be discussed here."

He said, "No, it isn't. I shall retire alone and think on it."

"No," Old Aldira said more loudly, for the crowd was murmuring, "you know that's not what I meant. You and Alea and I should—"

"Alone," he said, and walked among them, away. Many others left after him, though some lingered, staring, or trying to appear not to. Alea watched Old Aldira, who brandished her staff as she commanded the idlers to be off. *Speak to me,* Alea begged her silently—but Aldira did not even look at her as she too moved away.

"Come." Aldana was standing on the top step, in the open doorway. "It will be warmer in here when night falls." Alea nodded and climbed up behind her into the darkness of the wagon. "Here's some bread for you, and a basket for Alnissa to lie in. It's long enough, I'm sure."

Alnissa fell asleep almost immediately, on her belly, as always; clutching the filthy red blanket in her left fist, as always. Alea cupped the bread in her palm and laid her head against the wall so that she could see the painted ivy and flame. She remembered Nellyn's paint in the round tower room, though already the details were blurring. This, though—this was her family's pattern, every leaf and spark beloved. Her pattern, again and always.

~

Aliser left the camp. For two days he walked the hills, hardly stopping to eat or sleep. On the first day he wandered blindly, without a destination; on the second his feet led him to a path he had taken many times before. At dusk on that day he came out of a scattering of trees into a clearing. It was flat, covered with grass and even some creepingvine, for there was a spring here, bubbling up from beneath a slab of rock. This rock was dry on its other side, and there was space enough beneath its overhang for a person to lie. There was a stack of wood there now. Aliser bent and drew some out. It was slippery with rot, and the earth beneath seethed with insects, which soon vanished. He had put this wood here many seasons ago—the last time he had come, when Alea had been with him. His place, as a boy; then their place. *You should not be here,* he told himself—but he stayed, as the sun set, and kindled his damp, smoky fire with a gracelessness that was almost savage.

It was full night when Alea walked out of the trees. He watched her come, almost expecting her to go to the spring, as she always had before, to soak her hands and face and hair. But she did not stop there; she came to him directly, swiftly. He rose to meet her and they stood on either side of the pitiful fire, staring and silent.

"Old Aldira told me you'd left the camp," she said at last, after her breathing had slowed. The hair at her temples was sweat-curled.

"And you knew I'd be here," he said, trying to sound disinterested, and pleased with the result.

"Of course I did," she said, not disinterested at all.

He shifted his weight and frowned. "So she's spoken to you"—*the pitiful old woman, still trying to cling to her authority.*

Alea smiled a bit. "Hardly. A few words, and only when I went to her. She's waiting for your decision, Aliser—she and everyone else. No one's really speaking to me except my family."

"This can't surprise you. You're a disgraced woman—a disgraced Alilan woman who's come begging for her people to forget her dishonour. Do you feel no shame for this?"

She was quiet for a long time, her eyes on the sputtering flames. "To feel shame, I would first have to feel pride. I do not—have not for such a long time. But it's because of this lack that I can come to you now and ask what I'm about to ask." She bit her lower lip; no pride, perhaps, but some fear. Aliser nodded at her to continue. "What must I do? Give me terms and I'll meet them, whatever they are. Only tell them to me, quickly, so that I can come back to you."

His mouth was dry and his lips felt cracked. He wanted to go to the spring and take a swallow of the rock-cold water, but of course he could not leave the fire. "The terms," he began, wondering at his discomfort, "yes. I'll tell you what I've decided ..." Discomfort because she had asked him for his judgment before he could pronounce it? Because she was so close to him and she was shivering as her sweat dried in the chill wind? "You must never speak that man's name, not even to yourself. You must never speak of what he was or did, not even if you think to educate or enlighten someone. You must never speak of your time away from this caravan. He never existed, and you were never away: these will be the terms. Also," he added, his discomfort swept away by the strength of his words, "if you leave the Alilan again, for any reason, it will be forever."

He readied himself to wait, for she would surely have to listen to what he had said once more, in her mind—but she spoke almost immediately. "I've come back. Forever." She wrapped her arms around herself. Her cloak was too thin for a spring night; he could see goosebumps on her skin. "Aliser," she said, forcing his name through the chattering of her teeth, "are you even a little bit happy to see me?"

He felt the rush of heat within him spread to his cheeks, to all his flesh, so that he truly was Alnila's child. He walked around the fire, and even though Alea had not agreed to his terms—not really—he folded her in his warmth and held her there.

FORTY-FIVE

The oasis pool was very high, and the green around it stretched back further than Aldira had ever seen it. People spoke of Alneth's particular blessing this season, and greeted the Alilan of other caravans with particular joy. Comradeship, an excess of green and verdant plants, cool, deep water: Aldira should have been well content. And she very nearly was, until Alea came to her.

"May I speak to you?" she asked, a tall, slender shadow in Aldira's doorway.

Aldira said, "Of course, child," and set aside the stitching she had been trying to do before she dozed off. "You haven't sought to speak to me alone for a very long time." Not since Alea's return, which could not be mentioned because it had never happened, just as her departure had not. "I worried at first that you were angry with me for being distant, for not coming to you immediately"—*Such a bother, all this dancing around the matter, but so it must be*—"though I now believe you understood this was due to no lack of affection on my part. And you've seemed happy, these past few months, which has heartened me."

"Happy, oh yes, very happy." The words themselves were bright and cheerful; it was the pause after them that set a warning flame flickering within Aldira.

"But?" she prompted, stiffening against dread and the eagerness that always seemed to accompany it.

Alea was sitting on the edge of the bench, clutching at it with both hands. She was looking at the squat iron stove, not at Aldira. "I shouldn't say. I shouldn't, for I am happy, truly. And yet there is one thing I need to tell someone—one thing, out of so many. I can't tell my parents, who'd be too grieved by it, and I can't tell Aliser, who'd be horrified ..."

"So you're asking to tell me." Alea nodded. "Think for a moment: why do you need to say this thing to me? I cannot promise absolution or sympathy or even pity, if those are what you need."

"I know. I've been silent this long because I've known so well. But it's not pity I need. It's … I need to speak so that this thing can be real. No matter what you think of it, once it's said, it will be real."

"Ah, I see"—though she did not, yet. It might be about Aldron—a forbidden and unfortunate subject, but what else could this desperately urgent thing be? *Aldron—yes,* Aldira thought and was instantly furious with herself. But it was not Aldron.

"I had another baby," Alea said. Aldira waited for her to say more, but she did not. Her head was lowered, her face hidden.

"Ah," Aldira said again. "A sibling to Alnissa—that is, fathered by the same …"

"Yes," Alea said, apparently unaffected by the awkwardness of Aldira's words, "a sibling. Even more than that, really—a twin."

Aldira listened to the silence in the wagon and the noise outside it. Laughter and horses' hoofs, the thud and crack of palm nuts being opened, cloth dipped into water and wrung out above it. She took a drink from a wooden cup that sat on the bench beside her; a long, noisy drink, to give her time and a feeble sort of concealment.

"A boy?" she finally asked, when the cup was empty. Alea shook her head. "A girl," Aldira said. "Twin girls, and only one … what happened to the other?" Perhaps she should not have asked, should have said instead, "You've told me now, off you go." But Alea lifted her head and Aldira asked anyway, looking at her face.

"I don't know. The second one was dead already—had been for a while, I think. Her skin wasn't the right colour and she was much smaller. The Goddesses' punishment, of course—and my punishment is not being permitted to tell of this horror. I know I deserve this, but it's been too terrible, being alone with it."

"Of course it has," Aldira said very quickly, "but now you've told me and that will have to suffice. Do not think of sharing this information with anyone else—not ever. And do not speak to me of it again, for I have heard it—as you wished—and now it is done. Finished."

"Yes, I know—but I thought that Alnissa might ... that someday she'd deserve to—"

Aldira rose. She did not have her staff to hand, and she was achingly slow about it, but she stood. "Alnissa above all cannot know—not about her sister, not about her father, not that she was born away from her caravan. Such knowledge would bring her only shame and confusion, which she in turn would yearn to share. Tell no one, Alea—especially not your daughter."

Alea stood to face her, as straight with defiance as she had been at ten (except that she had glared up at Aldira then, not down). *Let that be all,* Aldira thought—yet she felt no relief when Alea turned and left the wagon.

~

Alnissa's laughter was loud and high, but Alea hardly heard it above the wind in her ears. She felt her daughter, though, wrapped securely against her back. Alea made extra knots in the sling for riding, and rarely allowed a gallop. Today the horse was galloping. Aliser's horse.

"What happened to Ralan?" she had asked Aliser a few weeks after her return. He had rolled away from her. She had traced the bumps of his spine upward from buttocks to neck.

"You know we can't speak of this," he had said, and she flattened her hand against the skin between his shoulder blades.

"It's us, Aliser," she had said. "Only us. Surely I can make a reference like this to you and be answered, with no promises broken."

He had rolled back to face her. "I said never—not to anyone."

So she knew that her Ralan was gone, likely killed as all Alilan horses were whose riders died before them. *I was dead to them all,* she had thought, and this thought had thrilled her a bit, because she had returned and was lying against a solid, comforting body; she was reborn. Now, though, reining Aliser's horse in among the conical buildings far from the oasis, the same thought made her shudder. Dead to them all, and reborn—but not fully. Never, ever fully.

For a moment she watched Alnissa walk and fall, walk and fall, and smack her hand on the clay where a lizard had been, seconds before. She tugged at vines and pulled petals off the closed flowers, and Alea swept her up, wriggling and whining. "I know, Nissa, now that you can walk you have no patience for this, but there are steps where we're going." Her daughter did quiet as soon as Alea carried her into the shade, and she even clung, going down into the darkness.

Alea nearly turned back at the bottom of the staircase. One quick, half-blind look showed her no light, no doorway—but a few blinks later it was there, blue wavering onto the hallway sand. Alea stood in front of the door long enough that Alnissa grew restless again. "All right, then, let's go in. Both of us. Now."

The blue light was as vivid as it had been when she was last here. With Aldron, of course, the two of them clutching, burning with need and secrecy. That had been a few hours before the Perona attack and Aldron's forbidden Telling, a few hours before Aliser had sent them out alone, on foot, away from their people.

Aliser had given her a dagger one night when they were still in the lake country. He had not given it to her directly; it had been lying beneath her blanket one night. They had never spoken of it. She wore it in her belt, though she had not used it yet. She supposed her first dagger had disappeared along with Ralan.

Alnissa shrieked with excitement as she grasped the carved shapes in the walls. She reached for wisps of blue light and chortled when her hands passed through them. Alea knelt near her, not touching the walls herself. She knew what they would feel like. Her fingers remembered even if her voice could not.

"Nissa," she called, low and steadily. Alnissa did not pause or glance at her. "Your father made this light," Alea said, as her daughter fell backward and giggled, then leaned against the wall to raise herself up again. *No—do not,* Alea thought, but she spoke over her own warning. "Your father Aldron, of the Tall Fires caravan."

Alnissa fell forward. Alea started up, to hug her or brush the sand from her chin, but Alnissa was already sitting, grabbing handfuls of sand and tossing them into the air. The sand looked blue for the few seconds it hung there.

I said it. She didn't hear, and even if she had, she wouldn't understand. Twins forgive me—I had to come back here, but there will not be a second time … Not for the name, and not for this chamber. She would ride back now, and she would have to lie about where she had been, but it would only be once.

As it turned out, she did not need to lie. Aliser asked her nothing, just said, "I'll do that," when she started to rub his horse down. "Nissa can help me," he went on, lifting her up and giving her the brush. Alea watched his red head bending to Alnissa's dark one, and listened to him saying her babble-words back to her, very solemnly. Alea sat in the open doorway of his wagon, which was also hers, and felt heavy with sleep and slow relief.

~

"The leaping will happen in the next three days or so," Aliser said, tipping Alnissa closer to the horse's flank. She thwacked the brush against it and he laughed. "Gently, sweetling—you're lucky he's so patient." He looked over his shoulder at Alea, whose eyes were closed. She was not asleep, though; he often watched her when she slept, and knew the difference. "Alea, did you hear me? The leaping, soon, and then Alneth's Night."

"Mmm, I heard you. And I know."

He took the brush from Alnissa and gave her the damp cloth instead, which she slapped against the horse and him and herself. He laughed again. She made him laugh, this very small person whose presence had so unsettled him, but not for as long as he had expected it to. Everything about her was Alea: her dark hair, wide brown eyes and almost sharp chin. She was silly and fearless, and very, very irritable when deprived of the tiniest amount of sleep or food. And she had begun to rub her stomach when she was hungry, just as Aliser did, large circular motions accompanied by an expression of sweetness and pleading. *She learned that from me,* he had thought the first time she did this. A little girl who learned from him and lived with him could be his little girl—he was certain of this now, as he had not been during those first few giddy, fearful weeks.

"So," he said, glancing again at Alea, "I've been looking forward to Alneth's Night. To having you take your place among all the other Tellers." He saw her eyes open, though she did not move any more than that. "It'll be wonderful to have you there," he continued, "Telling as you always used to—as you always have ..." He cursed himself for the slip. *Used to*—the wrong words, an impression of time past, and change.

"No." The word, on its own, was hard, but she softened it with others. "I don't think that would be a good idea. I haven't Told in a long time, and you know how nervous I always was, in front of so many people. And anyway," she added, swinging her legs down onto the step, "I wasn't ever very good at it. Never as good as you were."

"You were! You were just as good as I was"—*though neither of us was ever as good as he was.* A sharp, clear thought, as all the forbidden ones were. *And hers? What must her thoughts be like?*

He walked over to her and up the first two steps, so that he could reach down and touch her cheek. She put her hand over his and held it, clutched it, in fact; and though he felt the desperation in her fingers, he called it love instead.

~

"Leaf!" Alnissa cried. She was lying in a pile, a scarlet, bronze, russet pile.

"Leaves," Alea said, bending over to tickle her. "Leaves, Nissa!"

"Leaves," Alnissa repeated, writhing away from her mother's hands. "Tree, cloud—no, mama, no!" She was gurgling, choking with laughter.

So many words already, Alea thought as she sat back against a tree trunk. She could see the wagons of several caravans from here, and the tall, golden grass—but she could not see the town. *She's so young still, not even two until next spring, and yet she speaks so clearly.* Alea's pride was fretful and tentative—for what if her daughter made a leaf with her words someday, or felled a tree? *No, love—for you I wish a life of listening, not speaking.*

Although Alea could not see the town, she could see its smoke, darker and thinner than the smoke of the wagons on the plain. She wondered how much longer she would be able to remain seated. She had kept the town in sight since their arrival a week ago—not that she ever looked at it directly. She glanced at it, slid her eyes over it while she was pretending to be searching for something above or beside it. Every glimpse of wall and rooftop made her breathless. She paced among the wagons and the trees—especially the trees, since she hoped they would make her own body feel rooted. But she was more restless every day, and every night too, when she would slip to the edge of the camp and watch the torches flickering in the gatehouse towers. *Twins,* she thought, *make me calm, make me content.*

She knew that Aliser was worried about her. She was away from him more and more. When she returned to his wagon, he was always waiting and trying to seem as if he wasn't, burnishing his dagger, carving wood. He would look up at her and feign surprise, as if he had not noticed that she was gone. She groaned out loud, thinking about it, and Alnissa ran to her, pressed her crackly, earthy body against hers.

"Alea," Aliser whispered that night, "are you asleep?"

She pulled the blanket away from her face. "No, are you?"

He did not smile. "When Alnila's Night comes, why don't you stand with us? I was just thinking ... you could stand fifth or sixth: the middle Tellers are always less noticeable than the first or last."

She sat up, dragging all the layers of blankets with her. "I told you no in the desert," she said slowly, "and I'll tell you no here."

He sat up beside her. "You claim insecurity, which I still say is foolishness—"

"I claim insecurity because it's an easier thing than the truth." *Keep talking,* she thought. *It's what you've been wanting, isn't it?* "You've forbidden me to speak of my time away from the Alilan, but if you're to understand why I won't Tell, you must know something of that time. During my entire absence I only Told twice, and both of these Tellings were excruciating. I'm afraid now. What if my Tellings here, among my own people, were tainted by these others? What if, caught up in Telling passion, I Told something of my time away—some image or event? A boat, say, or a palace—"

"Stop." He leaned forward and gripped her upper arms. The blankets had fallen away from her. "Stop before you say something that will make me lose you again."

She twisted her arms and his fingers loosened. Her skin felt bruised. "Are you so afraid of what I might say? It was a few years, Aliser, a few, compared with all the years we've seen together since childhood. Tell me why you refuse to hear about them."

"Tell me why you insist on sharing them with me." When she opened her mouth, he clamped his hand over it, his palm and fingertips digging until her eyes watered. "No—don't tell me. I have no desire to know what kind of woman you were during those few years. You're back—I've allowed you this much grace. Be thankful for it." His hand lingered a moment more and then it was gone, and she was doubled over, holding her own hands to her aching jaw and cheekbones.

He was not there when she finally looked up. She stood, lifted herself onto the balls of her feet—not to seek out his shadow, vanishing among the wagons; to find other shadows, of wooden wall and rooftops, sharp against the sky.

~

I am too weary for this. Aldira's staff was thick and tall, but even it was not enough tonight. She might have to sit down even before her turn came. She could not remember ever having seen a Teller sit during a Telling. *This will certainly be my last Alnila's Night,* she thought, and tried to straighten, tried to stand in her place as if she were a younger woman.

The Telling began. Aldira blinked away the snowflakes that were clinging to her eyelashes. The snow was already thick on the ground, and more was falling; it shone in Alnila's colours of heat and flame. Aldira attempted to concentrate on the Telling—the second Teller was speaking now, and the Goddess-shape was beginning to appear far above them—but she could not. She saw Alea in the glow. She was sitting with her parents in the first row of onlookers. Alnissa was in Aldill's lap, only her wide eyes visible among the blanket folds. Alea was not concentrating on the Telling either. She was staring at the ground, so motionless that her shoulders and hair were heavy with snow. When her mother brushed some off, Alea smiled at her and gestured to the lights of the Telling. "Watch that," she seemed to be saying, "not me."

She was very thin: her face, her hands, all edged with bone. Aldira had observed this the last time Alea had come with Aliser to her fire, over a month ago. Aldira had not asked if she was feeling unwell. She had asked nothing because Aliser was there—and even if he had not been, she would have kept silent. She had hardly spoken to Alea at all since their conversation at the oasis. She had watched her, though, as happiness turned to worry turned to this new thing that stretched her skin taut. *Not proper to meddle,* Aldira thought, watching Alea still through the spinning snow.

Aliser's Telling thread began to weave among the others. It would be Aldira's turn after his. She invoked the Goddesses, silently, and begged them for clarity and strength. His images were polished and smooth, but just as bombastic as they had always been. Aldron's, though—the sound and touch of wind, the pressure of heat on skin … Aldira stamped her feet and threw back her head to clear it of snow and all thoughts that should not be.

She nearly felt quiet as Aliser's voice swelled beside her. Her gaze steadied and blurred as it always did before she Told. The people before her grew indistinct as everything within her sharpened. Correct stance, correct vision, inner and outer—but then something changed in the smudged crowd and Aldira's eyes focused.

Alea was rising. Her movements looked awkward and slow, but this might have been an effect of the swimming colours. For a time she was frozen, lit, apart from everyone else. She was looking at Aliser, and Aliser knew this. His words wavered in the air as if he had needed a breath. Then Alea walked away. She clambered over sitting bodies, ignored the faces turning to her. When she reached the edge of the gathering, she did not hesitate; she moved swiftly into the darkness beyond the Telling and the outer fires.

Aliser's images were disintegrating. Aldira forced her own voice out to cover his failing one. She Told a light so brilliant and sudden that people cried out in awe. Her last Alnila's Night, and she was very nearly Alnila herself, come to bless and dazzle. As her words flowed, Aldira forgot her weariness—but not her fear or her regret, or the sight of Alea running from them all.

~

Alea's feet remembered cobblestones—rounded ones, chipped ones, others worn hollow by wheels, boots, horses' hoofs. Fane's cobbles had always seemed to slope up, slippery with spray; these were soft with snow and lay flat. She walked slowly, hardly glancing up, stepping into the impressions of other feet so that her leggings would not get too wet. She did not need to: her feet remembered.

She heard a pulse of noise when she was still paces away from the inn. She stood before the door and listened to voices, the clanking of metal and the pounding of fists on wood. She was about to retrace her steps when the door opened. She fell back, watched three people stumble out into the snow. They did not close the door behind them. She looked into the dining room, one hand on the edge of the door. Snow gusted around her feet and faces turned to her. Someone called, "Well, woman, are you in or out?"

She squeezed onto a bench against the wall beside the door. The stools around the circular table were full, but that was fine; she had never intended to sit there.

"Something to eat or drink?"

She nodded at the serving boy and cleared her throat. "Wine. And bread with butter."

By the time she had finished her second cup of wine, the dining room was not as crowded as it had been. She could see the fireplace and the staircase that would take her up to rooms she knew. She stared at these things with such intensity that she did not notice more people leaving, and others looking at her.

"Well, well," a woman's voice said quite loudly. Alea heard it, ignored it—but then the voice said, "It's the horse-woman! Aldea, Aleena …"

"Alea," she said, and Pareya shrugged.

"Close enough. Tell me—where's the dark-haired sorcerer you usually follow?" One of the other women at the table giggled, and one of the men scowled. "Oh, and the small blue-skinned person who often sat with you—the one who sleeps during the day and wakes at night. What of him?"

Alea set her cup down on the empty bench beside her. She stood up carefully; wine and heat always made her dizzy. "The small blue-skinned person was Nellyn. I believe he's in his village now, though he was in Fane when I left there. The dark-haired sorcerer was Aldron." She felt herself smile despite the aching that had begun. "Aldron fought in a battle for the Queen and took a grievous wound and never recovered his spirits. I don't know where he is, though our daughter, who'll be two in the spring, is with me on the plain."

"Ah," Pareya said, raising an eyebrow, "a daughter. You and the handsome one."

"Yes. Aldron and I." She took her damp cloak from its peg and put it around her shoulders.

"Not leaving so soon?" Pareya said. "I wanted to ask you about the noise and lights you people were making earlier tonight. Fascinating. We watch every year from up on the wall, don't we, Medwel? But tonight's display was so much brighter. So—what are these lights? Could you make one for us now?"

Alea pulled the door open. "No," she said over her shoulder. "I won't perform for you."

She stood outside the town gate for a long time, watching the thinning snow and the colours that still hung like mist above the trees. *A return without an ending,* she thought. Her feet were numb, as were her fingers beneath her cloak. She was cold and stiff and smiling. She felt all this for one moment more, and then she walked back toward the fires. Toward her daughter, and Aldron's.

FORTY-SIX

Nellyn almost turned back. Once, three weeks away from Fane, he retraced all the steps he had taken that day. When he reached the place where he had lain the night before, he sat down and stabbed at the grass with a stick, over and over. *I was wrong to leave,* he thought, sinking the stick into the earth. *I was wrong to come back even this far*—pulling it out, watching the dirt fall away from it onto the grass that was still flattened from the weight of his body.

He slept and ate very little in those early weeks. He remembered that he had felt like this during his first days in Luhr—his head and belly light with a need he had no desire to fill. But then there had been a clear, whole joy, a different kind of need satisfied; now there was only confusion that twisted his mind and even his steps.

Go back. Life is change, and there has been a change—but she still loves you, and is that not enough?

Keep walking. Remember Gwinent, who taught you the meaning of change? This is stronger. This would make you understand things you should fear.

He left the riverbank only when he saw houses ahead. Because he hardly ate, the food he had brought with him from Fane lasted a long time. When it was finally gone, he ate berries from bushes and raw strands of rivergreen, scarcely tasting any of it. He walked beneath canopies of trees that rustled with night creatures, and among hills so thick with flowers that he stepped on them with every footfall, even though he tried not to.

He walked from afternoon until dawn in the first month, then only at night. There was a new quiet within him—or perhaps it was an old one. He lay beneath trees or among flowers and closed his eyes against the sunlight, breathing, listening, bending away from thoughts. He began to sleep, two hours, then four. One day he woke among long shadows. He saw them on his skin, saw that the sky was golden with the last of the sun. He had slept from dawn until dusk: a shonyn sleep, old and new. *Now still always*—he knew this without thinking it.

The grass turned to sand. He felt the change against the soles of his feet and smelled it, especially when the wind blew from the west. He had imagined, months ago, that he would have to run when he drew this close, but he did not. He was not impatient or fearful. He felt nothing but tranquility until he came to the place where the riverbanks rose high above him, red rock laced with crystal.

He stood on the narrow path and gazed up. He had last been here in brilliant sunshine, so brilliant that her skin had turned from brown to scarlet. She had steered the flatboat. They had slept, close together but not touching. And then she had gone away. Change after change after change; a choice made. He had had no memories in weeks; now he was weak, dizzy with rage and sorrow that were as knotted as roots, and just as solid. He ran, as if haste would return him to a space of quiet—but of course it did not. He ran until the rock walls lowered once more to sand, and the moon was gone, and the rings of stars as well.

It was dawn that stopped him at last. First light on water, on silver leaves, on blue fruit. He looked at the river and the village—but not at the ridge behind it, or the tents there. He sensed them tugging at the edge of his vision, but would not turn to see them. He stood and felt his breathing slow to match the circles of lynanyn and sun and red huts, and of the steps that had led him away, so far, and back again.

~

Nellyn is hungry. He gathers rivergreen at dusk, and fat seed pods from shore plants, and even grain from the garden plot by his hut. None of it is enough. Not when he stands knee-deep in the river and hears the splash of flatboat poles and the thud of lynanyn on wood. Not when he sees shonyn on the shore, peeling, eating, drinking blue. He looks and listens only; he does not walk past the plants to the huts or the sitting stones. He is apart because he must be, because he must relearn, in solitude, what he has forgotten.

He is ready, one day at dusk. He feels the sand beneath his feet; it is warm from the daylight. He steps slowly, carefully, as measured as the river water within and outside him. He does not look at the ridge or the tents because he does not need to. He does not need to rush toward the wise ones on their stones or the small ones at their feet. He does not need to call to them. It is one dusk among so many others. The words he hears as he draws closer are the same as ever.

No one looks at him when he comes to stand behind the small ones. He listens to the words with a joy that warms and steadies him. He moves with the others like him to the flatboats on the shore. He sees Maarenn, and raises his hand to her as always. She sees him. She stares, one hand on the black wood, the other drawn up to her mouth. He smiles at her and steps toward her, and there are wise ones between them, a long, motionless line, all of them with their backs to him. He stops, looks over a shoulder at Maarenn. Her eyes meet his for a moment more and then she is bending, wading out into the river.

"Wise one," he says to the one directly in front of him. She does not turn. "Wise one," he says again, the shonyn words another joy despite his sudden fear, "you are not content with my presence? You wish me to explain? I tell you: I try to live without shonyn ways, yes, but I cannot." Still no movement from the line. The flatboats are nearly in the deep river; the silver leaves are blinding with last light. "You counsel me when small: do not seek amazement, for it brings change. I have amazement and change, yes, but I cannot bear these things. I cannot. I return. I am here, as always. Now still always: so you say, and so I know."

They shift. One by one they turn and walk past him, back up to the sitting stones. They arrange themselves there and begin to speak again, to each other and to the small ones. When he follows, they do not look at him. Maarenn has seen him, so he knows he is here, but they do not see him. Other words rise in his throat—other reasons, and pleas. He does not speak them. He walks back along the shore, to the hut that stands alone by the plants. He slips behind the faded blue curtain and sits on his pallet. He gazes at the veins in his wrists in the almost-darkness. The branchings of his river, which carry life and calm. He gazes at them until full night hides them, but he feels them still, pulsing against his fear.

He sleeps at dawn, wakes at dusk with relief and certainty. It is a test and an illustration: they are showing him the consequences of change. He opens his curtain and ducks outside, then pauses. There is a blue bowl beside his door, filled with slices of lynanyn. A whole lynanyn sits beside the bowl. He squats, picks up the round fruit and rolls it between his hands. Its skin is firm, but the fruit within is softening: perfect ripeness. The skin peels away in one long, winding piece. He bites, and juice trails down his hand and arm. He eats and drinks, picks up the lynanyn slices and eats them too. He is restored. The lynanyn is a promise, an acknowledgment. He walks back to the village to acknowledge it in his turn.

They do not look at him. Again they sit and talk to each other; again they rise to stand between him and the river when he goes toward it. The only difference is that Maarenn does not meet his gaze. She pushes her flatboat out, beside a man Nellyn knows, a new gathering companion; a man like Nellyn, in Nellyn's place.

He does not speak to them this time. He sits by the water near his hut and watches the flatboats until they are nearly invisible, black wood on black air. He is struggling to breathe with the care and clarity he has possessed for so long. He struggles against anger, which is easy and would return him to a place of change. He falls asleep on his pallet just after dawn—but he wakes when the hut is still striped with sunlight.

There is a soft noise, almost inaudible beneath the drone of insects and the lazy lap of water, but he hears it. He kneels beside his curtain and opens it just a sliver.

"Maarenn." He speaks her name very quietly, but she startles, drops the bowl from her hands. Lynanyn slices scatter on the sand in a spray of juice and seeds. She begins to angle her body away from him.

"Stop. Sit with me. Speak to me." Her head is still turned. "Look at me."

She does. She bends to pick up the bowl and her eyes do not shift.

"Speak to me," he says again. "Please, gathering companion."

"No." A dull, flat word, this first, and he feels its weight. "Not that. You are not here."

He crawls out of his hut and sits among the splotches of juice. "I *am* here—now still always."

"Not always," she says, and he sees her discomfort, though he does not know what kind it is or what it means. He has no chance to ask her, for she walks away, quite quickly, over the sun-bright sand. "Thank you," he calls, but she is already small, and the light is too intense. He picks the lynanyn slices up and holds them, gritty and slick, in his hands.

~

Nellyn does not go into the village again. He does not see Maarenn again, though he finds lynanyn at his door every day. He listens and sometimes he hears her, but he does not go out. He wades in the river at nightfall, and walks from the water to the brown plants to his hut and back to the river: loops of steps, circles that never close. He waits and tells himself that he is not waiting.

Once, at dawn, there are clouds that do not dissipate. They are far away to the west, only a thin edge of darkness in the clear, but he glimpses them as he ducks into his hut. He stands unmoving and stiff. The thunder begins a few sleeps after. He hears it and sees that the cloud-line is larger now, and advancing. His eyes slide from cloud to Queensfolk tents, which he should not, does not look at—but he looks, as the thunder rumbles. *Like hoofs,* he thinks, and the images are too swift for him to halt: a wagon on a road above the sea; riders on horses, churning ice and frozen mud. He groans and swings around to see the river—not faces, or winter colours that are not present, nothing but the river that is his centre, always, even when the rains come to hide it.

When the rains do come, he lies on his side with his upper arm over his ear. This shuts out the noise when it is just a light pattering on the clay—but soon it is its own thunder, which he feels with his skin. *Last time ...* He writhes and claws at the ground. *No—no last time.* He has always been here; it has always been the same.

He is not alone. He sees this, in the murky light, sees a figure crouched just inside his curtain. He blinks, expecting to recognize one of his sleeping companions—and why not, if everything is the same?—but it is Maarenn. She comes to where he is lying and kneels beside him. He feels rain falling from her hair and clothing as she bends over him. She draws her wet hands across his cheeks and through his hair, and leans closer, closer, until she is touching him with her lips. He is here, pulling her down to lie against him, fumbling with cloth so that she is closer still. He is here, drinking her, breathing her—and then he is not. There is no "here"; layers, instead, other skin and other rain, another voice crying out his name. He cries out too, and closes his eyes to keep the other places from spilling into the hut. He is smothering and blind, hears only his own cries, which turn into whimpers and then to gasping breaths. He is alone. He knows this even in his blindness. There is no one with him—no one who is not smoke. Smoke blowing out over the ocean; a blanket beneath the smoke, and a baby in the blanket, and a woman with her forehead against the window glass.

He sleeps, but the images do not. He is surrounded by brightness, shapes so stark they cast no shadows. He wrenches himself awake, and then he is outside, turning his face up to catch the rain. The sky is mottled, cut with lightning that is moving eastward, trailing thunder. The rain is hard and steady; his face and arms sting as he walks through it. He slithers on the wet sand but does not fall. His feet take him up, away from the empty sitting stones and the sodden curtains, up to a ridge where sand and water are flowing together, seeking the river.

The teaching tent is empty. He stares at the stacked writing trays and the carpet where the small ones sit. *Where I sit,* he thinks; then, suddenly, in Queensfolk words, *Where I sat.* He shudders, moves to leave the words behind. The next tent is glowing. A lantern within, probably. A lantern, a candle, a tree of candles hanging, weeping tallow. Wicks to trim and drippings to scrape and bread baking in the kitchen, the smell of it rising.

A Queensman looks up from the parchment in his lap. Nellyn sees his lips move: "Greetings." A shonyn word. Nellyn feels his own mouth making Queensfolk sounds: "I have been lost. I will not return." The man stands. The lantern is on a high table, like the one on the Queen's balcony above the sand. The colours of the carpet are turning in small, smudged circles.

"Sit down with me," says the man, and raises his hand. Nellyn laughs, though he has no strength to wonder why. He goes out again into the rain and wanders down the slope. Queensfolk words pursue him: *She walked with me. My blood was on her cloth.* The huts are all the same, but there is the one, set amongst the others. His sleeping companions are inside, cowering. *They called after me from the doorway. I left them and fell and water carried me down.* The shape of the bank is changing under the rain, but he recognizes it. *I lay here with the red fish. I swept it back into the river.* He sits and sits, as the dark clouds darken further into night. He is soaked and shivering, but he does not rise until the clouds are grey once more. Even then he only stands up because there are sounds coming from the west. Creaking wood sounds, flapping wet canvas sounds. He feels another laugh rising, a wild, high one that he swallows.

He stands and watches the Queensship sail through the rain. It is moving quickly: many oars, as well as a wind blowing from behind. Quickly, even though it must stop, he knows it must. There are three people on the deck: one at the great wheel, two others at the prow. All of them are cloaked and hooded, faceless with cloth and the rain that is running into Nellyn's eyes. *A boat brought her to me. A boat brought me to her. A boat took her away, with him; and he came back, and so did she, and they were together, not together, and I left …*

Just this one boat now. One, and three people he cannot see. He watches it pass him then the sitting stones. It is not slowing at all; the oars rise and fall. When it reaches the water by his hut, he starts to run, starts to shout and wave his arms. He falls twice and scrambles up, still calling. "No no no, Lanara, wait! Lanara!" She cannot be there—this is just a madness, driving him faster, past his hut but still too far behind. "Lanara!"—her name screamed in rage and longing that are change again, this time swift and known.

He stopped running. Before the river and rain could take the ship away from him, he turned away from it. He sat on the riverbank and looked at his hut, and at those beyond it. *I've come back,* he thought, the Queensfolk words clear and heavy, accepted. *I've come back, but I will never return.* He sat, a shonyn alone in time, as the rain softened and scattered into mist above the Sarhenna River.

~

Leish kept his head lowered. The rain and wind were at his back, but he would not risk a glance up, a stray drop blown against his lips. Perhaps the Queen's curse did not extend to water from the sky; he did not know, and he would not find out. So he stood on the deck of the boat, his skin drinking what his lips could not, and felt the lightness of his limbs, and remembered that he had wanted to die.

"Why?" Lanara had asked, weeks ago, when she had returned to the Throne Chamber at dawn and found him still breathing, the waterskin still beside him. He had not answered her that day, or on the ones that followed. He had slept and woken in the burned forest outside the palace. This was where he had felt rain for the first time since Nasranesh. He was free, lying on the earth, gazing up into branches stripped by fire. Free and alive, and even he did not understand why until those blackened branches told him.

"My home is still there," he had told Lanara when she came to him on the seventh day after she had freed him. "Ruined, but still there. I can hear the blood of my people—those who survived. My parents, my brother—maybe they are among those." The rain had begun two days earlier. The ground was dark and moist. Lanara had brought him a fresh cloth to cover his small living area. He noticed that several of the twigs outside this cloth were bristling with green shoots. "I still hope for them," he had said. "And for my land. I did not believe this until you gave me the choice to die. I hope—and I will not die until I am in my own place again."

And so he was here, on yet another ship, sailing the same river he had sailed before, when he had been lashed to a mast and mostly unconscious. "Must it be the river?" he had said to Lanara when she had told him of the plan.

She had smiled at him. Her sympathy continued to unsettle him. "I'm sorry—yes. It's the quickest way." *And you're so weak and ill,* he had imagined her saying. He had nodded his agreement and understanding and tried to thrust his fear away.

It was not so bad this time. It was a different boat—a smaller one—and he was not seasick. He had lain on the deck at night, before the rains came, and listened to the diseased song of Nasranesh, and had been utterly still and certain. This certainty was the change. His body might look and feel better than it did when he was first brought this way, but it was his mind that was truly different now. He was steady, on this path that he had chosen.

"How are you?" Water dripped across his nose and cheek as he turned his head. He nodded, and Lanara said, "Good. There's food ready below, if you want some. Fresh fish cakes and sourfruit." He shook his head. Not yet, but soon. He would never be as strong as he would have been with water to drink; he felt the lack of it like a constant tremor in his flesh and muscles. But food—especially fruit—gave him some strength, even if it was a thin, temporary one. The rain gave him this as well.

Lanara stayed with him for a time. She looked out at the riverbank, frowning and twisting her cloak in her hands. He looked too, swiftly and sidelong, one hand over his mouth. He saw only empty sand, most of it blurry with rain. But she looked and frowned, and her knuckles were white—and then, several minutes later, she pulled her hood down over her face and bent her head beside Leish's.

He grunted a noise that he hoped would sound like a question, but she did not glance at him. He was about to make the noise again—perhaps she hadn't understood him?—when he heard the voice. It was high and faint, and he could not identify many of the words it called—but one he could. Her name, over and over, its syllables stretched and fading as the boat sailed on and the rain closed in behind.

She straightened. For a moment she stood facing back the way they had come. He could no longer see her face, but the rest of her was rigid, even her toes, bent against the soles of her sandals. Then she was gone, her wet cloak dragging on the deck. He followed her down a few minutes later, but he did not ask her about the voice. He ate fish cakes and drank sourfruit juice, and thought that nothing should concern him now except the sea.

~

The rain stopped a few days later. Leish lay on the deck at night as he had before, thankful to be away from the tiny cabin below deck. During the day he found what shade he could and sat there, watching cacti turn to bushes turn to trees. He heard the green as they approached it: grass and leaves, corn planted up against the banks. Sometimes these banks were lined with people who waved and called, and all the Queensfolk on the boat waved back at them. Leish always went below until the people had dwindled behind them. It was difficult, now that he could see lush, growing things, not to feel rage again. So difficult—and he had not expected this; he had been thinking only of the sea and his home. He kept himself apart even more than usual, to ensure that his anger did not escape. *No use,* he told himself as the Queensfolk cheered beneath their canopies of trees. *Don't show them this, now that you're so close.*

And they were close, suddenly. The seasong was a roar, and the river's notes rushed and ascended as it widened to meet the widest water. Leish was so consumed by these sounds that he did not notice the other until Lanara came up beside him and put her hand on his arm. He started and turned to her, and she pointed. He saw the river, and forested banks far away to the left and right. He also saw houses—just a few where the ship was, but more ahead, their paint harsh and bright. He heard the other noise as he looked at the houses. It was distant still, like a wave that will not break for a long time, but he swung himself away from it.

"No," Lanara said.

"I—I must go. Below," he stammered. "You know I can't see these crowds ..."

"This crowd you must see. I know how difficult it will be for you, but you must." She tightened her fingers on his arm, and he flinched with the need to escape from her or strike her. "Leish, it will be the biggest, but also the last."

He did not move. He stood, somehow, tall and silent beside Lanara as the Queensship carried them down again among the houses of Fane.

FORTY-SEVEN

There was rain on Queenswrit Eve. Only a light, gentle rain, but it came very early in the season, and the people of Luhr declared that this must be the blessing of Queen Galha upon them all. How fitting, then, that that Queen's last wishes were read to her people on Queenswrit Eve. They stood, those from Luhr and others from places far away, and listened to the gifts she had made all of them, writing them even as she died. As our Founding Queen, Sarhenna, implemented the first laws of the realm, so Queen Galha, in her wisdom, expanded them.

Her gifts to her people and realm were these:

That all dwellers in the cities and towns of the Queensrealm be taught to read and write.

That the scribes previously assigned solely to the study and documentation of the realm's history go out into the cities and towns and undertake the education of the populace.

That the people, having been instructed in the art of reading, have access to the Queensstudy and all its documents.

That the Sarhenna River, named for the illustrious First Queen so often venerated, be renamed in honour of the Princess Ladhra.

That the Sea Raider captive be set free in a manner of his choosing, as proof of Queen Galha's mercy and forgiveness.

Lanara let out a noisy breath and tossed the writing stick onto the parchment. She looked out the window and saw seabirds in the sky above the green-patched cliffs.

"Would you like my help?"

She turned to Malhan, who was sitting at the long table. "No," she said, picking the writing stick up and drawing it once, twice over the parchment. Broad marks, not letters; stains at the edge of the page that would always remind her of this room, with its view of spring in Fane. "I have to learn how and when to write all this down. I'm doing terribly so far. I'm only now writing about Queenswrit Eve, and that was nearly two months ago."

She listened to Malhan's silence and knew that he would say more. She had already learned much about his way of speaking and listening, but very little about anything else—and that was as it should be. "Have you mentioned yourself yet?" he asked, and she groaned.

"No. I don't know how to—" A knock on the door interrupted her. "Yes?" she called, pushing the parchment away with relief. A Queensguard entered and made the sign of the arrowhead, which she returned.

"My Queen," he said, "this wine has just been delivered by a woman from Brallent. She wished me to bring it to you rather than presenting it herself—she seemed quite overcome by the Queenshouse ..."

"Thank you, Crelhal," Lanara said, rising to take the bottle from him. "Would you drink a glass with us?"

He flushed. "I am on duty now," he began, and she said, "I know—so come back in the evening. Or perhaps I'll bring it down to the kitchen. Brallent is famous for its wine, and it should be shared."

He frowned and fidgeted with the sword in his belt. "If it is so fine, you should drink it yourself, my Queen."

Lanara tried to keep herself from frowning, though it did not matter—he was not looking at her. "You were kind to me," she said quietly, "all of you, last autumn when I was lonely, when I came to the kitchen at night because I couldn't bear to be in my chamber. You shared your wine with me then. Let me do the same now."

He did look at her finally, and nodded, a bit uncertainly.

"Was there something else?" she asked when he did not turn to go.

"Yes," he said, and cleared his throat. "The kitchen boys who found it told me not to bring it to you, but I thought it was important, and—"

"Crelhal," she said. He cleared his throat again, though he did not speak. He took a piece of parchment from the pouch at his belt, a very large sheet folded into a tiny, ragged square. Lanara smoothed it flat with her forearm and leaned over the desk to read.

New queen, new lies. We will watch you as we watched the last one. She tried to silence us, but we are stronger now than ever. We will hear your lies and show them to your people!

The letters were sprawling and uneven. The writing stick had been pressed so firmly in places that the parchment was speckled with holes.

"Where was this found?" Lanara asked.

"In a basket. It was at the bottom of a basket of eggs that was left outside the kitchen before dawn. No one saw who left it."

Lanara touched one of the holes, traced the wobbly line that led away from it. "Thank you, Crelhal," she said, lifting her head to smile at him. "You were right to bring this to me."

He flushed again and swung quickly round to the door as soon as she dismissed him.

"He doesn't know how to treat me," she said to Malhan after the door had closed. She spoke lightly, looking again at the parchment. "None of them do."

Malhan stood and walked to the window. He undid the latch and swung a pane outward, and Lanara smelled salt and fish and wet, warming earth. "You may find that it is you who does not know how to treat them."

"Ah," she said, gritting her teeth against a sharper, longer reply. He was beside her now. He would be reading the words, which were big enough that he would not need to crane or wait for her to move aside.

"There were many traitor scribes," he said, "in many places. We should not be surprised by this message."

"I know," said Lanara, thinking of an underground pool and hooks where bags had hung, full of words. "What if it's Baldhron?" she went on, touching one of the holes in the parchment.

"No." Malhan pushed the parchment out from under her fingers, to the opposite side of the desk. "I'd recognize his letters. Even if he tried to make them rough and sloppy like these, I'd know them. He didn't write this."

"Maybe not, but he could have ordered someone else to—he could be nearby, and—"

"Then we'll capture him," Malhan said, his voice rising. "We'll set extra guards around the Queenshouse. We'll certainly have no difficulty catching the person who wrote this message. Once captured, he'll tell you where the others are—including Baldhron, if he is nearby."

Lanara shook her head. "No. No one will be captured." She pulled the parchment back toward her and folded it swiftly. She held it in her palm, where it was just a tiny square again. "No one will believe them if they do speak out. I'll give them no reason to be believed."

"The one who wrote this may be unschooled and unthreatening," Malhan said, stepping closer to her, "but there will be others who are articulate and clever, like Baldhron—others who may have some sort of evidence—"

"And what," Lanara interrupted, "would you have me do when these traitors are caught? Kill them all?" Her hand was a fist, its skin stinging where the parchment's unfolded edges had cut. She loosened her fingers one by one, and nearly heard these motions in the quiet.

"So," Malhan said at last, "you wouldn't have Baldhron killed? Not even him?"

"Perhaps." She slid her eyes away from his face. "Perhaps not. It might not be enough." She sat down at the desk and arranged her own parchment before her. She began to write, with quick, slashing strokes that would keep both of them silent.

The greatest of Queen Galha's wishes she wrote last, on a fresh sheaf of parchment:

"After my death, the long bloodline of the Sarhennan queens will be ended. Let my people not fear this end. The ancient prophecy of the iben foretold the coming of one more queen who would protect and strengthen her land. I was this one queen; there need be no other after me. My final task, therefore, is to choose how the Queensline will continue. I choose a successor who has been a second daughter to me ever since her birth, and who has served me in her adulthood with sensitivity and strength. I hereby decree that Lanara, daughter of Salanne, daughter of Bralhon, be queen of the realm when I am gone. My own daughter would be well content to know of her dear friend's good fortune. Queen Lanara will be able to implement the changes I have laid out for our people and our land. With her will be born an illustrious new line of queens."

And so, on Queenswrit Eve, former consort-scribe Malhan bestowed upon me Queen Galha's bow and quiver, before all those gathered below. As every queen before me had done, I loosed one arrow upward, over the Queenstower, where the moon was rising, unobscured by the rain clouds that hung to the south. The cheer that rose was thunderous, and I was awed and moved to hear it. I held my hands up in the sign of the arrowhead, and all my people did the same, and I gazed upon their upraised hands and vowed to myself and them that I would be a queen of steadfastness, honour and truth.

~

Leish waited for four days. He forced this time upon himself, knowing it was necessary for his strength—but each hour and minute was anguish. He did not remember feeling like this before, even tied to a mast or vomiting, bleeding onto a stone floor. Now, unfettered and almost constantly alone, he looked out at the sea and could not bear the spring sheen of its water or the spring sweetness of its song.

On the fourth day he was ready. He had been sitting and sleeping in a room on the second floor of the Queenshouse, above the water and the crowd that had been gathered since the Queensship's arrival. "They want to watch you go," Lanara had said on the second day.

"They can't," he had replied. "I showed myself to them on the ship, but I won't let them watch me leave." *It would sicken me,* he had thought in his own language, *to hear them cheer for me, even if they were really cheering for you. They threw rocks at me. They killed my people. It would sicken me …*

By the evening of the fourth day, most of the crowd had disappeared. Leish looked out of his window and saw wood where before there had been Queensfolk. He saw boats and harbour water and open water, smooth beneath a violet sky. He listened to shoals of fish and anemone-blooming rocks and knew he could wait no longer.

"Are you sure?" Lanara asked when the Queensguard brought him to her. She was alone in her writing chamber. It still surprised him to find her this way, without Malhan lurking by the door.

"Yes," Leish said.

She bent to throw another log onto the fire. The nights were cool; the water would be cold. "At least reconsider my offer," she said, straightening to face him. "Let me send you in a boat."

He felt the webs bunch between his fingers. "Why? So that your people will be able to see the final mercy of the great Queen Galha? One more exciting display for the crowd?"

"No," she said, high and angrily, "so that you won't die of exhaustion before you reach your land." She sat down and ran her hands back and forth over her short hair. "Leish," she said, looking at him with her hands still on her head, "you've been a prisoner for years. You haven't had water in nearly one of those years. You haven't swum anywhere, except in a fountain, since your army arrived here. This journey may be too much for you."

"Yes," he said when he had thought of the words he needed. "But I would rather die swimming beneath the sea than travelling upon it in a Queensship."

"Ah. Well, then … When, exactly, will you leave?"

"Later tonight, or maybe tomorrow morning. I will try to sleep a bit before."

"Good. Have me woken when you're ready."

He licked his lips. They were always cracked, even when he soaked them in fruit juice or rubbed them with cooking oil. He felt a tiny crack open now, and spoke before he could taste the blood. "I will leave alone. Please." He cringed at the catch in his voice. *And so I beg her?* he thought; then, *I am free because of her.* He yearned for one simple feeling.

~

Lanara walked to the window, sat down on the bench beneath it. She could not look at Leish. *He's leaving, Ladhra,* she thought. *He loved you, and he's leaving.* "Very well," she said, angling her head so that she could almost see his face. "Go alone."

"Thank you." He lingered. His fingers were clenched, the webs folded motionless between them. He did not move, but she saw his longing. He would run from this room. "For this," he said at last, "and for the other things." His left foot shifted, as if he was feeling the purple band of scar around its ankle.

She nodded and bit her lip. "Go. Go now, Leish." He did, with a slow turn and slower steps that nonetheless seemed to blur with haste.

Lanara sat alone until the harbour lanterns were lit. As she watched the little fires bloom, the door opened.

"Lanara." She did not move except to shift her gaze to the right, toward the smudge of cliff and the wavering glow of the signal tower there.

"Lanara. Crelhal tells me that the selkesh man was with you."

She smiled, blinking against the glare of hearth and candle flames. "Yes. He'll leave tonight or tomorrow morning."

Malhan frowned and she felt her muscles tighten. "Why did you not inform me right away? We'll have to keep him here until at least midday tomorrow. By then the escort ships will be in place—three of them, I think—and the word will have had time to spread. You should wear a bright robe and walk to the end of the dock with him—"

"As drums beat and horns blare?" Lanara rose. "No. He's asked to do this alone and I've agreed. He's been made a spectacle too many times before."

"In chains, yes—a prisoner, an object of hatred and ridicule. Now he'll be a symbol of Galha's forgiveness, bestowed through the people's new queen. You know this is why we came to Fane so soon after you assumed the throne! We are here to provide your people with proof of the wisdom of their queens—"

Lanara laughed. She bent over, braced herself against the desk until she had finished laughing. "He said that," she gasped when her breath had returned. "Almost exactly that. He knew what kind of spectacle we'd try to make of him this time. I'm sorry, Malhan, it's too late. My word is given, and I won't take it back. So please," she continued as he began to speak, "let's talk of something else. Our own departure, say. I'd like to leave as soon as possible—maybe in a week, after I've met more of my subjects. And I'd like to make one additional stop upriver."

"Oh?" A small, jagged word.

She nearly smiled. "There's something I have to do in the shonyn village."

"Oh, Lanara"—a kind tone now, thickened with regret—"you're not still pining for the shonyn man?"

"Nellyn. And yes, I am. I intend to ask him to come back to Luhr with me."

Malhan strode over to the desk. "Impossible. Now is the time for choosing a consort-scribe, not dallying with men who are not even of Queensfolk stock. Surely you can't imagine that the shonyn man could be your consort-scribe? Lanara!"

"I'll change the law of Queensmarriage. I'll say Galha recommended it—we've changed so many things already."

Malhan laid his fingers on her bare forearm. "I've told you, we must be prudent. If we alter too many of the traditions that have bound our people for so long, they will become unsettled. The law of Queensmarriage will remain. We will return to Luhr and seek out an appropriate consort-scribe for you."

"We!" she cried. "We, we, we! You manipulated Galha's life and death. You won't do the same to mine."

He called her name once as she ran to the end of the corridor. Two Queensguards scrambled after her and she cried, "Do not accompany me! Fall back!" She swept through the courtyard and out into the street beyond. Too bright, too crowded. She veered into a darker laneway, glad now of the plain linen tunic she had worn today despite Malhan's protestations.

She heard footsteps when she paused in the shadows of another deserted alley. Hard leather soles on cobblestones; not even the river's muted roar or the rasp of her own breath hid the sound. She slipped around a building and watched the street behind her until two men jogged into view. She saw the ribbons that fluttered from their sleeve-ends, knew that these ribbons would be blue and green. *Malhan's men,* she thought, *sent to spy*—and she ran faster, into twisting streets and through empty tunnels. If she was lost, then so were they—and it would serve them right. She turned onto a path that sloped downward and waited for a glimpse of the harbour.

The wharf was slippery beneath her sandals; she had to lean against a house to regain her balance. It was the house at the end of the wharf, beyond the lanterns and the docks. She looked back the way she had come and saw no one, heard no pursuing footsteps. Even so, she ran again, along the last few feet of wharf and up onto the smooth, round stones of the cliff path.

She slowed after she rounded the first bend. Fane and its lights were invisible, but the moon was rising and the path before her glittered. She followed it, more slowly now that she was sure of her solitude. By the time the path became earth, her steps were dragging. She climbed up, up, her head as weightless as her feet were heavy.

The signal tower was dark below, ablaze at its top. Lanara stared at the blur of candle fire and metal until her eyes ached. She imagined knocking at the door, striding into the kitchen. "I am your Queen. I am here to scrape tallow from the lightroom floor." She imagined the log entry that would follow, and the wobbling of Drelha's second chin as she wrote it: *Visit from the new queen. Poor woman not quite right in her mind. Previous queen much more queenly*. Lanara ground her palms into her closed eyes as she laughed.

When she returned to the path, the wind was higher than it had been. She pressed herself against the rock and thought of Nellyn's fear, which had always made her forget her own. She would walk behind him again, with her hands on his shoulders. She would kiss the back of his neck when he faltered …

The wind tore at her tunic. She felt the flesh on her arms and legs pucker and rise, and wondered at how quickly the night had turned cold. She clung to a rock spur as she eased herself around a bend. She took one sideways step, and another. Pebbles slithered down the slope above and ahead of her. She watched some fall down into empty air and others land on the path, and reached out her foot to step over them. She heard a harsh scrabbling, very close. A shadow detached itself from the cliff above her. She saw it for one long moment, hanging against the darker sky—and then it was arms and a face and the flash of teeth, and a knife.

"My Queen," said Baldhron.

FORTY-EIGHT

Leish could not sleep. He lay on his back, his side, his belly; he squeezed his eyelids shut and opened them, hoping they would drift closed on their own. By the time he finally acknowledged that he was tired but not the least bit sleepy, the moon was beginning to rise. He sat up. He listened to the singing of the water that would greet him, and he breathed with it, let his muscles loosen and lengthen as they would in that water. When he opened his eyes again, the moon was high and bright.

None of the Queensguards he passed spoke to him. One of them glared at him; another smiled; most stared past him. He looked at their faces because they were the last of their kind that he would see. He swung his arms as if this would help him move more smoothly through the air that pressed against his skin.

He stopped when he came to the main doors. Malhan was standing alone before them, his arms rigidly crossed. Leish waited for a moment, flexing his fingers and webs. The salt water would sting for the first few days beneath; his flesh was nearly as tender as a drylander's.

"I must pass," he said when his gaze did not prompt Malhan to stir. Still Malhan stood and did not speak. "Malhan, let me pass."

Galha's consort-scribe smiled. "I could have made you a dead symbol, you know, instead of a living one. I very nearly did. It took me many days to decide how best to use you."

Leish ran his tongue over his lips. They would pain him the most on the journey home. "So," he said, each Queenstongue sound forced, "you wish me to thank you for my life? Your Galha knew: there are worse things than death. I have no thanks for you."

Malhan's smile thinned. He stepped away from the doors, keeping one hand on the wood. "Go, then, Sea Raider. Go back to what's left of your land."

Leish reached his hand past Malhan's and tugged at one of the door rings. He looked only ahead. Perhaps Malhan stood in the open doorway and watched him, or perhaps the door closed behind him—it did not matter. *Worse things than death,* Leish thought, *and yet the wind is gentle and the water is close, and I am almost happy.* He decided to walk directly to the end of the longest dock and dive from there, since this would likely annoy Malhan if he was watching. But after Leish had taken one pace onto the damp wood, he reconsidered and turned toward the southern cliffs. He and Mallesh and all the other selkesh had arrived in this land without being seen; Leish would leave it the same way. And in any case, a long, deep dive into open ocean would be preferable to a shallow drop into a harbour full of Queensships.

He climbed the cliff path quickly, even when the wind began to buffet him. It moaned this high up, grasping at edges of rock and sky. He listened to it, and to the singing beneath it. Soon he would reach a place where the cliffside fell sharply away; he had noticed this when Galha had brought him this way. It had been snowing then, and he had been half numb from cold and weakness, but he remembered the spot. *Soon,* he thought, as the seasong swelled in his ears.

He was nearly running when he heard the voices. They were Queensfolk voices, louder than wind or water. He slowed and heard whose they were. *Dive,* he thought, flattening his back against the cliff. *You're done with their kind. Dive* now.

~

"What do you want?" Her voice trembled, and Baldhron dug the knife's edge a little deeper into the skin of her throat.

"I want you to beg," he said. She tried to turn away from his spittle, but he forced her head up and straight. "I want you to weep and bleed. But not until after you've learned of the treachery of all your queens."

She smiled, a glinting line above the knife. "Then I'll have to disappoint you, for I won't beg or weep, and I already know about this treachery—Galha's, anyway. Perhaps you'd explain that of her predecessors?"

Not right. He shook his head, which ached from the pressure of height and wind and the nearness of a queen after his long solitude. *Drenhan, give me strength and wisdom. Help me remember the words that I've waited an age to speak …*

"I will tell you," he said. "And there may be some details, even about Galha's reign, that will surprise you." He shoved her back against the rock so that she would be within reach of his knife, but not so close that he would feel her breathing or her skin. These things would distract him, kindle a desire for flesh and death before it was time.

He began with his mother and their cave, and the kind Queensman who had praised the boy Borwold and given him watered wine. He had almost gone back there after his escape from Luhr. He had fled north through the desert, thinking only that he would go home, find his contact there, begin again with the few scrolls he had taken and the many more he would write. But after some days had passed, he realized the peril of this plan. He would be a hunted man, and the Queen would surely send her first search parties to his old home. *Not yet, then,* he had thought. *I'll seek out my people in other places*—but very soon this idea too seemed foolish. The Queen would offer a rich reward for his capture. His renegade-scribes were principled men and women, many of whom were also poor. Who knew how easily avarice would triumph over principle? So he had pressed northward alone, expecting to hear hoofbeats at his back. He crept into town at night, stole whatever food he could. His hair and beard grew thick, but still he did not show himself, certain that someone, somehow, would recognize Baldhron, the traitor who had killed the Princess.

Lanara frowned as he told her of his mother's fever and the dive that had twisted her body to its death. A frown of concern—he looked away from it, at the sheen of his blade. Her pity would enrage him as Ladhra's had. *Speak quickly,* he thought. *Be clear: she must understand the filth of her station before I take her body and then her life.*

His words *were* clear, now that he had been talking for a while. He had practised them over and over, both aloud and in his head. He had ordered and reordered them, like coloured stones that he would fashion into a vast, blazing pattern. It was all he had had to do after he crossed the northern border of the Queensrealm into the sweep of tundra beyond. He had learned to hunt, learned to sew ragged hides and pile stones against the wind. He had watched distant lines of people and pack animals wending across the waste, and seen their smoke against the stars. The words had accompanied every one of these activities. He was nearly as wild as the tree-horned deer he pursued—except for the words, which returned him to his library, and to the cheers of his followers.

"Leish!" he had cried one morning. His breath hung white in the air, and frost cracked beneath his fur-wrapped feet. "Should have killed him too! He's the one who told the Queen it was me. He's the one who led her to my library, my realm …" He had fallen to his knees, scrabbled at the lichen-crusted rock beneath him until his fingers bled. Only the words about lying queens, caves, folded notes, underground tunnels kept him from madness.

There had been a purpose to it all. He had not recognized this in those first months, as he struggled to survive, but with the swift, scurrying departure of winter came understanding: *It is not done. I must return to Galha, and she must hear me and die, even if I die with her. I must return to my people, who will write the victory of my end and hers.*

And so, just under a year after he had crossed the Queensrealm's northern border, he crossed it again. He had discarded his hide clothing before he entered the border town, and shivered in his ragged Queensman clothes, washed and mended for this occasion. He had tied back his hair and combed his beard as best he could, though it was still matted and rank. "I've been alone," he told an old woman sitting in front of a tiny stone hut. "I've been suffering from love scorned."

She had nodded at him and smiled a toothless smile. He glanced around at the other dwellings, some stone, some deerskin stretched over wooden frames. He saw two children jumping on a frozen puddle, and a dog chewing at an end of bone.

"Where," he had asked carefully, "are the Queensfolk who oversee this place?"

The old woman had squinted at him. "Gone, save one. They all answered the Queen's call to battle, months ago now. None've come back. Killed, I expect, in that accursed land past the Eastern Sea."

"What ..." He had had to clench his hands to keep them from shaking, had cleared his throat to make sure that his words were curious rather than desperately eager. "What battle was this? I've been away from the world, you see—utterly alone, deprived of news from this great realm. Please tell me, grandmother." And she had.

"Queen Galha's sick now, they say," she had finished. "Sick in her bed in the palace, and who knows if she'll recover."

By the time Baldhron was a week away from Luhr, Galha was dead. He had seen mourning banners draped over a well and heard the details from a traders' caravan the next day. He had been bold about his inquiries since the border town. He had yet another new name—but no one would know "Baldhron," in any case; there had been no public hunt. Leish was the murderer, and now Galha was dead and it was Queen Lanara whom Baldhron would kill, after he had tormented her with truth.

It had all been so easy once he had discovered she was travelling to Fane. The city was overflowing with discarded market food; he was never hungry as he waited for the right moment. After some consideration he had decided to seek out his Fanean contacts. He found only one: an orange-haired girl of fifteen whose renegade-scribe father had died ("of old age, not Queensfolk interference, I'm sure of this") the previous summer, and whose mother had died birthing her. "The rest fled," the girl, Predhanten, told him after he had convinced her of his identity. Her green eyes were wide and terrified as she looked from the Luhran scrolls to his face. "We all thought you dead in the attack on Luhr," she had whispered, and he had laughed.

"No, child, though it was a near thing. Those weakling water-men cost us the palace and many lives, but not mine."

"At least," she had ventured, "the Queen was made to suffer. We can thank one of the water-men for this, anyway." Baldhron had touched her then, suddenly empty of words. She trembled. He had been gentle with her, despite his need. She would be of no use to him if her fear grew too great for awe.

She told him Lanara had arrived only two days before he had. She told him she had written a letter and left it at the Queenshouse in a basket of eggs. "My father would have done this if he had been alive to see this new queen. And it was good to do something after so many months of uncertainty." Baldhron had praised her effusively, and her flush had made him almost unbearably restless. He needed more than this one insignificant, mostly unschooled follower—but they would come, later, after he had slain Lanara and begun to rebuild his own realm.

He had watched the Queenshouse for days from a nearby rooftop, hardly sleeping. In the end he had been asleep, had woken to Predhanten's hand on his back and the tremor of her voice. "She has left the house and evaded her guards. I heard it from a serving girl I know." He had waited, sitting cross-legged on the shortest dock, had seen Lanara slip out from beside the furthest house. A slender, dark figure, but he knew her immediately.

"Stay here," he had said to Predhanten. "When it's done, I'll return to you. We'll have to leave quickly, with only what we carry now ..." Scrolls, in his case, stuffed into his belt. Not the scrolls he would have chosen for this confrontation—the ones about Lanara's mother, which he had so longed to have ever since he had heard that Lanara was queen. Those scrolls had surely been destroyed with all the others, after he fled. He still could not think of this without a shudder. Beside the pages he had carried with him from Luhr was his knife. He had used it to hack off his beard, and Predhanten had found an old, blunt razor for the stubble. He had bled copiously.

Lanara had recognized him as quickly as he had her, even though she had met him only a few times. Her eyes had widened, and he remembered Ladhra's eyes when they opened from sleep and saw Leish, with Baldhron behind; when she realized that no guards would come to save her.

"You were wronged," Lanara said when Baldhron had finished with all the words he had prepared. She passed him the scrolls he had forced her to read despite their near-illegibility. The writing-stick markings had smudged in the water beneath Luhr, and the paper had torn—but still he had thrust them at her, and she had seemed to read. "You were wronged, and so were countless others, by countless queens."

He lifted his knife, which had wavered downward a bit as he spoke. *Tell her,* he thought. *Tell her of her own mother's death*—but he held these words back. They would be all the more powerful the longer he waited to speak them. "You seek to appease me," he said instead. She was looking at him very steadily, without the fear that might have made her words a plea.

"Appease you?" she repeated, and smiled again. "No—I merely state a truth. A truth like these others: you killed Ladhra on her bed, and then you fled, even as your followers, selkesh and scribe, died. Only a very few people in the Queensrealm are aware of these particular truths. I hope you've written them down somewhere, Baldhron, so that future generations will know of your prowess."

He lunged. He felt her draw in a breath and hold it as blood welled from the hollow of her throat. "And why don't *you* tell your people about these things, Queen Lanara?" His ears were ringing, his own blood thundering like sea.

"The deceptions that occurred before my reign will not be revealed." Her voice hummed against his chest. "Events already written will not be changed. But I swear to you that no new fictions will be written while I live and rule."

He laughed as he had sometimes laughed to himself in the northern wasteland. "I see: you will be the first truth-telling queen in the history of this realm. You will inform your subjects of the murders you commit and the poverty you nurture."

"I will not need to, for there will be none."

He laughed again, giddy with scorn and the sight of her blood on his knife. "You fool. You poor little girl. How do you intend to create this perfect place?"

She did not blink as she looked at him. Her face was so close to his that her lashes might have brushed his cheeks. "With you," she said.

The knife moved in his hand, though he did not feel himself doing this. Another dark trickle of blood appeared on her skin. "Me," he said, attempting to keep his voice flat and his muscles still.

"Yes," Lanara said. "You, as my consort-scribe."

~

Baldhron took a step back. The knife dipped, stayed down. Leish thought, *She's taken him by surprise and now she can strike*—but she did not stir. Long moments passed and she only gazed at Baldhron, her arms and back flat against the cliffside.

"A feeble attempt, Lanara." The wind warped Baldhron's words, but Leish saw them on his lips and understood. "Though I now appreciate the extent of your desperation. To even pretend to propose such a thing must be intolerable to you."

"Worse than intolerable, since I pretend nothing. You will be my consort-scribe. You will be party to every decision I make and every action I take." She pressed her lips together. Leish licked his own; he tasted salt. *Dive,* he thought again.

"You will inform your network of scribes of your new role. You will tell them that I will make appropriate reparations for whatever losses they can prove to have suffered because of a queen. You will tell them I will meet with them and employ them, should this be of benefit to my realm. You will tell them to give me all the illicit documents they may have regarding the Queensrealm."

She struggled for breath after she had spoken; Leish saw the heaving of her chest before he looked back at Baldhron. "An impressive speech," he said. "Truly. I must force myself to remember that you despise me, and that you are *Queen* Lanara. If I was fool enough to accept your terms, how long would it be before you had me killed? Would you wait until we reached the foot of the path?"

"I've told you," Lanara said clearly, despite the wind and her own ragged breathing, "that I intend to act with honour, unlike those who went before me. You mistake this desire for deception because deception is all you've ever known, or practised. It may be that nothing will sway you. But I swear on the soul of my dearest friend that I am not deceiving you now. My offer is a true one."

Leish took a step toward them. He waited for them to turn, but they did not. Another step: Baldhron's words sounded much more distinct than they had before.

"Well. Well, well. Consort-scribe Baldhron and Queen Lanara, hmm?" He smiled and slid his knife back into his belt. "Not as delectable as Queen Ladhra would have been, but you'll do."

Leish ran.

Baldhron's eyes went dark. He gasped and his lungs burned; he tore at cloth and flesh he could not see. "Lying bitch!" he tried to scream, and he heaved his body up against the one who pinned him. A Queensguard, maybe several—he would pull them all down with him when he died. Them and Lanara, who was crying out words he could not understand. His assailant raked his cheek with nails, tugged his hair back until the darkness in his eyes was washed with tears. His voice returned and he bellowed. He blinked and saw the man above him just as Lanara's words hardened in his ears.

"Leish! Leish, no! Let him go!"

The water-man's face remained above Baldhron's and his webbed fingers dug deeper bruises into his neck. Lanara appeared over Leish's shoulder. "Step back," she said. "Now." The fingers lifted, and the face, and Baldhron twisted so that his head no longer hung into the space above the sea.

"Let me kill him." The water-man's voice shook, as it had so many times in the tunnels beneath Luhr. "Or let me watch you do it. Lanara!"—a shout that sounded more like a sound his brother Mallesh would have made. Baldhron rubbed at his bruises steadily, as if he thought he would live to see them shade purple, then yellow-brown.

"No." Her eyes were very bright—with tears, perhaps, though Baldhron could not be sure since her face was bent toward Leish. "He will serve me. He must. Only his presence will force me to be the queen Ladhra would have wanted to be."

Baldhron's relief was so great that he could not move, not even when Lanara crouched beside him. "But there are two further conditions," she said, looking at Baldhron but speaking to Leish. "He will never say Ladhra's name again, and he will never touch me, either in lust or in anger. If he violates either of these conditions, he will die."

Baldhron heaved himself up so that he was sitting facing her. "How, then," he said, each word stronger, louder, "will we get you an heir?"

He was sure now that he saw tears. "Leish," she said in a voice that belied them, "go now, quickly, before I allow you to kill him after all."

The water-man stood and stepped off the path, to the crumbling edge of rock beyond it. "I do not understand," he said, craning back to look at her. "You spoke of honour. There would be honour in this man's death. The kind you speak of has no meaning to me."

"I know. And I'm sure I'll agree with you often, as time passes. But believe me, Leish: Ladhra would approve. If she knew everything I know, she would."

Leish turned his eyes from Lanara to Baldhron. *He can't believe her,* Baldhron thought. *He still sees Ladhra's chamber, and her blood.* He shuddered. He himself remembered only snatches of this—fragments of her voice and flesh tearing, and then the tolling of the Queensbell that had sent him flying away from her. He held the water-man's gaze, allowed himself a small smile of the sort he would cultivate in the palace. Leish licked his lower lip and bit down, so hard that Baldhron nearly flinched. Then he was gone.

Baldhron had leaned out over the cliff before he realized he wanted to. He watched the water-man's descent. He thought, with a quickening of envy and fear that made him forget for an instant all that had just transpired, *How does he dive in such a gentle arc, and headfirst? Surely he'll break his neck.* He watched the water close over Leish and froth just briefly. He watched the line his surfacing head made, white and straight in the moonlight. He watched the head vanish beneath and the line fold among waves. Nothing moved after that on the surface of the sea.

Lanara did not speak when Baldhron pushed himself away from the edge and rose to stand before her. She did not speak as she went back down the path. He walked very close behind her, each pace carrying him away from the squalid cave of his childhood and from the tunnels where he had hidden as a man. He would soon write a message to be distributed to all of his followers, of power to be wielded from the innermost tower of the palace. The words waited for him. For now he listened only to the ocean and his footsteps sounding with Lanara's on the stone.

He was still slightly behind her when they came to the Queenshouse doors. Predhanten would be watching, he knew. He straightened his back, smiled as he studied Lanara's hair and shoulders.

"My Queen?" Malhan's voice, though it trembled as Baldhron had never heard it do before. He raised his eyes and saw him, standing before the open doors with four Queensguards flanking him.

"I was lost in the city," Lanara said. "Queensman Baldhron found me." Malhan gaped, made a low, trailing gesture with his right hand. "I think we will drink that wine now," she continued. "You and Baldhron and I. Have it uncorked and poured in my study."

Malhan slid his gaze away from Lanara's. Baldhron's smile was gentle, beneficent. He inclined his head a bit, heard the gathering crowd murmur. Then he stepped past them all, into the Queenshouse.

FORTY-NINE

I, Baldhron, son of Yednanya, take up this writing stick with a feeling of great humility and greater honour. Even though I have not yet been formally installed as consort-scribe, I am also no longer a student; this is therefore the first entry I have made in the service of the Queensrealm in my new role. I eagerly anticipate the day when former consort-scribe Malhan (who has already set out for Luhr) will present me with the writing implements he himself used, and with the fresh parchment that I shall write upon. This day seems distant yet, for Queen Lanara will linger for another week in Fane, and after that several more weeks will pass before we reach Luhr again. In the meantime, I will record, informally, the events of her days, and ponder the import of the post she has bestowed upon me.

~

She heard him writing. She thought she could almost tell which letters he was making from the sounds that came through the wall. She tried to push her bed away from this wall. When she could not manage this alone, she called for Predhanten. The girl helped her, as silent and shrinking as she had been all the days since Baldhron had brought her to the Queenshouse. "Thank you," Lanara said to this child who had always admired Baldhron and always hated the Queen. Predhanten's darting eyes stilled for a moment on Lanara's face, and Lanara smiled at her just a bit. "You may return to your bed now." Predhanten's eyes slid away again. She did not make the sign of the arrowhead before she left, and Lanara did not command her to. She wanted to cry instead, "Wait! Let me tell you about how I too was hurt. Let me show you that we are the same"—but of course she did not. It would be too hasty; it would diminish, not strengthen, her in Predhanten's eyes. So Lanara was silent as she watched the door close.

She lay on her side in bed. She could no longer hear Baldhron writing, but she was dizzy with words.

My Queen, the uprising near Blenniquant City is worsening. Queen Galha had assured us of some sort of intercession, though she was not able to specify, before her untimely death, what this was to be. I entreat you, who have inherited her knowledge and wisdom, to guide us …

Queen Lanara, there is a crisis approaching here, and we, your servants in the far Queensrealm, request your aid …

… trade with these people is no longer tenable. I realize that this would affect the wealth of the realm, but I, and my Queensfolk companions here, can see no other way …

She rolled onto her back. The light from the guttering fire in the hearth made shadows on the ceiling. She watched them, and they seemed to twine with the words, the endless rolls of parchment, the sounds that she could still hear, after all, from beyond the wall. Her dry eyes stung with lack of sleep and tears. "Fool," she whispered, this sound louder than all the others. *Fool, to think that you'll be able to mend everything with good faith and kindness …*

Malhan would advise her when she returned to Luhr. He would surely be calmer by then. "You're a headstrong, naive girl, exactly as your mother was!" he had cried. Lanara had drawn back from him so sharply that the Brallentan wine had trembled in the three goblets that sat behind her on the desk. "She suffered for these qualities, and so will you, and there will be great peril in this for all Queensfolk. You may well undo all that your predecessors have done. I love this realm—I have told you this before. I love this realm, and this is the only thing that will keep me here—love and fear. I never expected you to cause me such fear, Lanara. Perhaps I've made an irredeemable mistake with you." He had not mentioned Ladhra or Baldhron. He had not needed to: they had been there in his quavering voice and pinched mouth, and in his eyes, which seemed to have retreated into black-smudged flesh. She had not met his gaze then; she had been shaking with shame and shock, and hatred of the man behind her, who should have died at her hand, with no one to see or know it. But she would meet Malhan's eyes when she next saw him, when she would be more accustomed to her decision. She would ask him, calmly, to tell her about her mother, and she would ask him for his help, in the wood-lined study that was now hers.

She sat up so quickly that her already aching head began to throb. She would not allow herself to sleep. She knew what would find her if she did: Ladhra's smile; Leish's eyes before he dived; Baldhron stepping out from behind a tree in the Queenswood; water like jewels in Galha's hair ... These images had woken her before. She could thrust them away in the sunlight, but they were too vivid behind closed eyelids. Even now, awake in the night, she saw them flicker beneath everything else.

I'll leave. I'll go to Nellyn. The relief she felt thinking this was so exquisite that she imagined more (darkness was kind to all imaginings that would wither in the day). She would evade her own guards, disguise herself, take a boat upriver, walk if she had to. She would find him on the bank by the red clay huts. They would not be able to stay: Malhan would look for her there. So they would go north, past Bektha and Gammuz, and she would bear children with blue-tinged skin ...

~

Today the Queen went into the city, accompanied by her serving girl Predhanten, four Queensguards and myself. Her people cheered her as she passed, and she spoke to many. Her desire is to be a queen who knows her subjects and is known by them; a queen who spends her time among them on their streets rather than above them in her towers. She is already much beloved for this, which gives her great pleasure.

Near the end of our walk, as the crowd was thinning, we came upon two girls standing at the mouth of a covered walkway. They were silent as the Queen approached, but when she spoke to them, they answered her with wide-eyed eagerness. This meeting seemed to be of particular significance to the Queen.

~

They were twelve, Lanara thought, or maybe thirteen; tall girls whose limbs were still unaccustomed to their length. She noticed the two immediately, even though they were standing in shadow. Their eyes widened as she stepped toward them, and the black-haired one reached out to clutch the other's arm.

"Greetings," Lanara said. She smiled, and they smiled back at her.

"We saw you," blurted the one with brown hair, "before you were queen."

Her friend frowned and hissed a word—her name, perhaps—and Lanara said, "Really? When was that?"

"Last autumn," the brown-haired one said, more confidently. "During the archery contest at the Queenshouse. We were in the public balcony. We noticed you because you kept winning." The other girl groaned and rolled her eyes. "Not just because of that, I mean—also because you were so quiet and … different from everyone else." She chewed at her lip. "We thought you looked like a queen," she continued at last. "And now you are, and even though this only happened because your friend the Princess died, we're glad."

"Madhralla!" the other girl cried.

Lanara put one hand on her shoulder and one on her friend's. "And I am glad that you are now my subjects, Madhralla and …?"

"Breodhran," she murmured, shy again.

"Here—take these," Lanara said, and unwound one blue and one green ribbon from her tunic sleeves. The girls gaped at them, and at her. Lanara stepped back and they made the sign of the arrowhead, hastily, the ribbons tangling in their fingers. Then they turned and ran into the darkness behind them. Lanara did not move until their footsteps and laughter had faded into silence.

"A charming scene," Baldhron said when they were back in the study. "You and the two awestruck friends."

"Yes," Lanara said evenly. She sat down at the desk and pulled a pile of letters toward her. *He won't be able to distress me now,* she thought. *Not after that walk, all those people shouting my name and waving. Not after Madhralla and Breodhran. It is they who truly remind me of my purpose.* She smiled at Predhanten when she set a cup of steaming herb water near the papers, and Predhanten nodded quickly before she looked away. This too was a reminder.

"My Queen," the guard outside the door called, "someone else has come to see you."

"Very well," Lanara said. She rose and smoothed her tunic as Baldhron took his place behind her and Predhanten sank onto a stool by the door.

"The Queen greets you!" cried the guard as the door opened.

A man walked slowly into the room. He had a beard—a thick, curly beard as black as his hair, though both were shot through with strands of white. It was the beard that confused her. The eyes above it she knew—only she didn't, she couldn't; she must be addled with the shock and sleeplessness of the past week. "Welcome," she began, as if speaking would steady her and the world—but it did not.

~

It was immediately plain to me that the man knew the Queen, and she him. They gazed at each other for long moments before the man spun on his heel and stepped back toward the door that had been closed behind him. "Aldron!" cried Queen Lanara, and he checked. I regarded him with great interest as he turned back to the room. He was as unkempt as some of the wild men I glimpsed last spring, when I was doing secret work beyond the northern border of the realm. His appearance did not surprise me, however, for I now knew him to be the Alilan man who had been driven to madness by the battle in the Raiders' Land. (Queen Lanara has, of course, told me of Aldron's lover Alea's confrontation with Queen Galha. I look forward to reading former consort-scribe Malhan's account of this incident when I formally assume my new post in Luhr.)

The Queen ordered Predhanten to leave us. When she had done so, Queen Lanara turned to Aldron. To our surprise, he spoke first.

"I looked for you at the tower. I saw that woman, Drelha, but she didn't see me. I left. I knew you weren't there any more."

"But you didn't know I was Queen." I could see from her clenched hands and rigid back that great emotion roiled beneath the steady surface of her voice.

Aldron lifted a hand to his beard. "I ... I've been away from people. As you can probably see." Perhaps he smiled; it was impossible to tell, as his beard hid the full length of his lips. "I came back here and saw the banners on the Queenshouse—and I remembered what that meant."

"Ah," said the Queen. "And what was it you wanted with Galha?"

The man blinked as if confused, and I moved closer to Queen Lanara. "I ... I was going to ask her something."

"And that was all? Just a question?"

His head twitched to one side and I shifted closer still to the Queen. "So you think I should want to kill her too. You and Alea both." He shook his head then, as a sane man might. "That was never my intention, or even a desire. I have no such desires any more."

Silence rang in the room. The waves against the cliffs sounded louder, closer than they should have, as if the very sea rose to stand in defence of the Queen.

"I made the stones on the path, you know," he said at last. "That's how Galha found out about the true extent of my power: she came up the path one day as I was Telling the stones. It was snowing. I didn't hear her, or the man." His eyes leapt to me as he spoke these words. He was obviously referring to former consort-scribe Malhan. "I promised Alea at the tower that I'd never use this power for anyone, and I didn't. Not until ..." He swallowed. "What has happened? Where is she?"

Queen Lanara said, "She died. In Luhr she never recovered her strength after the battle."

"And now you are Queen."

"Yes. And as I am Queen and you have found me, why not ask me what you intended to ask her?"

He took two paces toward her, though his eyes were on the window. I laid my fingers on my knife hilt as he replied, "I need passage on a ship. I have no way to pay for such a thing—and so when I saw the banners and realized the Queen was here, I thought I'd ask her. I thought she'd hardly be able to refuse me, except maybe to kill me."

"Passage," the Queen said slowly. "Where?"

He lifted his arm and pointed toward the water that lay white-gold beneath the sun, which had only just ceased its upward climb. "Back there. Where else?"

Queen Lanara turned to me then. "Leave us," she said in a low voice. I responded, just as quietly, that I would not leave her alone with a madman; both her reputation and her life might be at stake, as well as my own credibility as her companion and protector. She nodded her understanding. "Come," she said to Aldron.

~

"Stand with me by the window." Her anger at Baldhron gave her voice a strength it had not had since Aldron had walked into the room. He walked over to her now, stiffly. She wondered when he had last been inside a building.

"No," she murmured when they were both facing the wharf. Baldhron had retreated a bit, to the door, as if he wished to allow her a small amount of privacy. She tried to forget him, to imagine that he could not hear them if he could not see their faces. "You can't go there. Not again."

"I must." Her arm was almost touching his, which was brown and ridged with muscle.

"No," she said again. "Let me help you find a place here in the realm." Her words were echoes of others she had spoken, and she wanted to tell him, to cry, "Alea confronted Galha! Alea was strong and passionate and she Told the battle—and your daughter was so beautiful. Alea told the truth."

"Lanara." She watched his lips, then his eyes. "I did it. I ruined that place, not Galha. She promised me a chance to test the limits of my power—and I did, and I brought doom on a people that had nothing to do with me. Not Perona, not Alilan—no one I had ever known, in a land I saw for only a few hours before I undid its life and changed its course. I've tried to forget, to cure myself in a place far from there—but I can't get away from the sea. It draws me back every time I leave it. I won't have any rest or peace until I go back."

It was almost emotion in his voice that had been so flat and distant, just as it might have been emotion that had sent him back toward the door when he had first glimpsed her. She lifted her hand and touched his arm, just above the crease of his elbow. He was still, neither rejecting nor welcoming. She thought she could feel the pulse of the blood in her own fingertips. "Since you insist on it," she said, half turning so that Baldhron would hear and see each word, "I will send you there, though I fear the journey will bring you only harm. I will speak to the captains whose ships are docked. You may meet me on the longest dock in two nights' time."

"Thank you," he said. He stood with her a moment more. She stared at the window latch, which was undone though the window was closed. She did not look away even when he walked across the room and through the door Baldhron had opened

"Do you think it was wise to let him go?" Baldhron asked. "He's mad—he may do something you'll have to lie about." He was smiling, drawing a forefinger around and around the pommel of the knife in his belt. Lanara went past him, slowly, so that he would see nothing but indifference. By the time she reached the front doors, Aldron was gone.

~

The captain would not meet her gaze. "My Queen," she said in her salt-rough voice, "I have promised to do your bidding. It is just … it is the matter of safety that continues to concern me."

Lanara frowned. "Safety? You will have one passenger, and he is no threat to anyone. Your way will be quick and clear. I have already given you silver to compensate you for lost trading goods and time. I will have more given to you when you return. I have no idea why you are so reluctant."

The captain stared at the side of the ship next to them, which hid them from the wharf and the houses there. Her short hair was blowing against her cheek; the right wind, hard and warm from the west. "My Queen, it is … I am afraid. There is a curse."

"Yes. But it will not harm you or your crew or ship. I have arranged for one of my personal guards to accompany you"—she gestured to Crelhal, who was standing behind her with Baldhron—"to reassure you and act as my representative." *And to ensure that the mission is carried out correctly and completely*—though of course she did not say this.

"Ah," the captain said, and finally looked at her. "That will be a comfort. Thank you. It must be difficult to spare such a person."

"Indeed," said Lanara. She wondered what Malhan would have made of all this, or if she would even have told him. He would likely read of it, when Baldhron and his parchment returned to Luhr.

The captain glanced over Lanara's shoulder. Her eyes widened just as footsteps sounded on the dock.

"Go, then," Lanara said without turning around. "Go with the blessings and protection of the First upon you."

The captain climbed into the rowboat that bobbed on the water below them, and Crelhal followed her. They sat with their heads averted as they waited.

Lanara turned. Aldron was standing a few paces away, gazing past her at the ship that rocked gently at the mouth of the harbour. "That one?" he said. She did not reply. He looked from the ship to her and did not look away as he walked.

When he was beside her, she twisted around again so that Baldhron would see only her back. His motionless silence was almost as difficult to bear as his stare—but none of this mattered. She stepped closer to Aldron, hoping that he would flinch or move away. He did not. He stood nearly touching her, and she found his eyes, despite her fear. "Come back," she said in a low voice that shook a bit with the unexpectedness and impossibility of these words. "When you've seen it, you'll change—you'll feel differently about yourself and me and everything else. Come back then."

He raised his hands and tilted them so that their backs lay against her cheeks. She felt the roughness of his knuckles as they stroked once, twice. She almost smiled, almost showed him all her hope—but then she saw his own smile, and the pity in it.

As she drew away from him, against the flank of the nearest ship, he slid into the rowboat beside the captain. Lanara had intended to uncoil the mooring rope, but she could not move, and after a moment Crelhal did it, rocking the rowboat as he stood and reached. He and the captain made the sign of the arrowhead and took up their oars; Aldron faced the open sea. Lanara watched them, her back straightening with each oar stroke.

"So," Baldhron said as the rowboat disappeared into the shadow of the larger vessel, "you're a woman of complicated and numerous loves. A small blue fruit-gatherer, a mad poet-horseman—I'll win you yet, my Queen."

Lanara's hand lifted and landed so swiftly that she hardly felt it. Baldhron sucked in his breath, raised his own hand to cover his cheek. "We are so alike, you and I," he said. "You'll understand this someday, and then you won't be able to hate me as you do now."

"Alike?" She attempted to scoff, succeeded only because she was numb from this mad succession of days.

"Indeed. Two young children who lost their mothers. What did they tell you about *your* mother's death, my Queen?"

She felt a pressure, like fingers squeezing her throat. She laid her own fingers there and tried to knead the sensation away. *He wants to frighten you,* she told herself, clinging to the numbness that was threatening to dissipate. *He wants to hurt you—don't listen. Never listen.*

She walked past him before he could speak again. She did not see him as she strode back to the Queenshouse, but she heard him behind her all the way there, his footsteps loud and measured. She nodded to her guards and climbed the stairs to her room. A few moments after she had slammed her door, she heard the scratching of Baldhron's writing stick. She rose and opened her shutters, and then she heard only the sea, quickening before the hard, warm wind from the west.

FIFTY

Mallesh brought the hammer gently down on the chisel's end. A cloud of dust rose and hung for a moment, as all dust did in this wind-thick air. He tapped again, and again, and the stone began to breathe. He felt it beneath his hands, and he paused to draw out his welcome. There was always an instant like this, now that his skill was increasing: a flutter that rose from the cave wall and became a pulse. He remembered feeling it first when he had been carving the leaf of a fireblossom tree, there by the entrance where the sallow light was strongest; and when he had shaped the shell beside it—and now, chiselling a long, rippling strand of rivergreen. He sat back on his heels and looked at the lines he had made and those that still lay within the stone. It was so slow, the looking and the carving, and he would never have imagined, in his other life, that he would have the patience for it. When they were children, Leish had always been the one who could sit before a new row of gathering pool benches and gouge out shapes. Mallesh had always fidgeted and thrown down his tools after his own clumsy attempts yielded nothing but scars in the wood. He did not fidget here, in his cave, and he did not even touch his tools until he knew what he would do with them.

He had found the chisel and hammer—and several fish knives—at the foot of the eastern peaks. The mountain selkesh had lived here, miners and forgers whose clear pools and rivers had lain just below the line of snow. Mallesh had been certain, as he fled the fires of his own home, that they would be there still. He swam upriver as the flames rose above his gathering pool. Others swam beside him. They had not swum for long. The fire had pursued them, reaching through the water and boiling it away, so that the selkesh had scrambled onto the banks. They ran then, beside the riverbed that was deep and fissured and mute. They ran as trees toppled and burned to ash. Some of them stopped running and fell among the trees and did not rise again. Mallesh did not fall, even when his coughing bent him double and made him retch bile that burned his scarred throat. He spoke when he could, and motioned to the others to stay with him. He knew they would find the mountain selkesh, who would take them in and wash the ash from them in ice-limned pools. They would make a new home as they mourned their old.

But the silent riverbank had led them to nothing. The mountains, yes: Mallesh had recognized their shadows against the yellow sky. He had looked at them as he crouched, tearing at a tree mouse with his teeth and hands. He had nodded his head at the shadows and the others had looked at them as well. *I will lead you true at last,* he had thought, so certain, even though he could no longer hear the singing of the peaks or the ones who lived there. He had led them nowhere. The mountains were naked rock, black, brown, grey, layered with shifting dust. There was no green and no snow. The uppermost peaks were like knuckles, the slopes between like withered webs. And at the bottom were the bones of the town: scattered metal and wood, overturned anvil stones. Some of the metal had melted; tools and jewellery had fused together into multicoloured lumps. Many of the tools were intact. Mallesh had taken some, as his companions searched for the mountain selkesh who had lived there. He had not been certain, even then, why he did this. There had been some bodies, mostly old people. The rest was emptiness.

"They may have gone over the mountains," someone had said to Mallesh.

Mallesh had heard her hope, had seen it in the faces of those around him—hope and grief together. He had looked for blame when they turned their eyes on him, but had found none. What he saw and did not see enraged him.

"What do you hear?" he had rasped, as if he could hear, himself. "What singing is there, over the mountains?"

They had bowed their heads and he had had his answer; and so their hope had infuriated him all the more. "Fools!" he had shouted over the pain that rose with his voice. "The land across the mountains will look and sound like this land does. All our lands are ruined. Why search for any of our kind if we'll find only this?"

But they had searched nonetheless. They had begun to climb the bald mountainside, where once there had been paths of grass and fallen leaves. They had ignored his thin, torn cries. He had watched them until they were hidden by ash, and then he had retraced his steps, all of them, back to the edge of the sea.

He knew now that his rage had been fear. *I only ever led them wrong,* he thought once, sitting in the mouth of the cave he had found near what had once been the river. *I did not go with them because I could not have borne to be wrong again.* And so he was alone, surrounded by the silence where all his songs had been. As the months passed, he grew quieter and quieter within, until his own silence matched that of his world. Only his hammer and chisel were loud; it sometimes surprised him that he could make this kind of noise.

The rivergreen strand was not ready to be finished. Mallesh set his tools down and rose, easing his limbs straight. He left the cave, looked from sky to sea. It would be dark soon—though "dark" too had changed. Some days were so heavy with dust and cloud that they seemed to be nights; and the nights were true black, with no stars or moon to lighten them. Today the sky was yellow-brown and the dust only rose a bit from the ground. Mallesh could see from his cave to the shore, which was unusual.

He walked slowly toward the shore, already peering at the twisted lengths of wood that lay where the tide had brought them. The tide deposited wood every day, and every day Mallesh gathered it, piece by piece, and stacked it outside his cave. He did not know where the wood was from, though he had guessed once that it was whatever was left of trees that had burned somewhere else, where the fire had not been so intense. He also was not sure why he collected it. His own fires were tiny, made to cook only the meagre fare he found for himself: rodents that still lived here, in holes in the black rock, or fish that washed up half dead with the driftwood. But his woodpile was nearly as high as the cave's outer wall, and it grew a bit more every time Mallesh returned from the ocean.

He swam before he began to carry the driftwood home. He swam several times a day: at dawn, mid-morning, mid-afternoon and dusk (his body knew these hours even if the sky sometimes could not show them). When he had first come back from the mountains, he had thrust himself through the brown, empty space where the Old City had been, trying to reach water that still lived. He had had to swim a very long way—and by the time he had reached a place where the sea was clear and scattered with fish, he was too exhausted to use his spear. He had hung in the water and felt his weakness—and he had almost pushed himself further, knowing it would mean his death. But he had turned his aching body back, had dragged himself to the fire-scarred shore of Nasranesh and lain there, choking on ash and breath.

He never attempted to reach these other waters now. He circled in the murk because he had to, to keep his skin from cracking and peeling away; and although he sometimes longed for the soothing, sparkling touch of the old sea, he was mostly content. His pattern kept him quiet, and alive. Carve, walk, carry, swim, over and over, and no room or desire for more.

He took a piece of driftwood back to his cave, then returned for another. Even if they were slender and light, he only carried one at a time; he liked to take as many steps as possible. The water always felt so comforting after an afternoon of long, steady walking. He had been to the cave and back to the shore four times when he looked along the tide line and saw something that was not wood, something much larger and thicker, and pale, not blackened by fire. He stood and squinted at it, and thought that it must be a dead sea creature—perhaps a longhorned diver. Curiosity and a sudden stab of hunger drove him closer. He would smoke whatever of the meat he could not eat in the first day. He would hang it in the dimmest, coolest part of his cave …

He stopped ten paces away from the thing. Not wood, not a longhorned diver—a crumpled, sodden, dust-brushed thing that Mallesh finally saw clearly, and knew. He ran, and did not realize that he was running.

~

Leish felt the sea rising in him. It surged from his gut into his throat and he could not contain it: his skin would split and wash away. He felt his arms and legs flail against this tide, and then it was cracking him open, pouring out of his mouth and nose. This had to mean that he was dying—for selkesh did not hold water in them unless they were unconscious beneath river or sea, unless they were not breathing. But after the salt had scraped him raw, he felt his air-breathing begin and heard himself cough. His eyelids were too heavy to open, so he lay still, on wet rock that his skin was beginning to feel.

Memory was slow but insistent. He had dived, blind with rage and shame, and deaf with wind. The sea had been gentle afterward. He had swum carefully, conserving strength—but also listening. He had not heard these songs from beneath for such a long time, and they had wrapped him round and welcomed him. He must have been too careful: he remembered weariness and hunger that he could not satisfy with the sponges and oceangreen he had torn from stone. The middle ocean had hummed with darkness and food that was too deep for his frail body to reach—so he had stroked on, eastward. He had clung to Nasranesh's notes as if they were beautiful, not warped and cut with silence.

Wollshenyllosh. He had remembered her, one day or night, as he bobbed with his head above the waves. She had nearly led him to her home waters—a yllosh place, far beneath but flooded with light and growing things. He had sliced back below the surface, listening for the song of such a place. He heard it a short time later, faint and shimmering, and he spun and fumbled, seeking it—but in the end it eluded him and he was limp with exhaustion.

The rest he only remembered in bits. Fish slipping around him, his own body suspended, motionless. Dark water lightening to clear, then thickening again as Nasranesh's song grew louder. A current tugging at him, his muscles unresisting and relieved. A feeling of rising, rising, so quick that he swallowed too much water and could not choke, took it into his body and could not expel it again. He had slept then, until the sea had thrust its way out of him and left him on stone that sang of death.

He did not think he would ever be able to open his eyes. *Never,* he thought, hearing the notes that had been taken away, listening to those that were left. They had been difficult enough to listen to from across the sea, but now they were unbearable. Perhaps he would die if he just lay here. The hot, rough wind would scour away his skin and then his bones, and all would be silence.

"Leish."

The voice was so much louder than the singing. Leish groaned and tasted salt and was too weak to spit it out. He pulled his arms up over his head and pressed himself against the stone. Moss had sung here once, and living shells, and tiny flowers whose petals would close over a fingertip.

"Leish, please ..." A strange voice, so hoarse it was transparent. Leish was shaking; someone was shaking him. He swung one of his arms and felt a rush of air and then skin—firm skin, and fingers drawing his fist away. He could not. Now that he was here, he could not possibly look on this place as well as hear it. He had returned; this had been so important in a desert, in a city of bright wooden houses with red roofs. And now he could not open his eyes.

"Leish, will you not look at me?"

He rolled onto his back, one arm still draped over his face. He let the arm fall, felt dust blowing over his eyelids and nostrils. The fingers were laced with his now, warm and tight. Leish drew a deep breath and coughed once more. Then he opened his eyes and rubbed them clear. He saw his brother's face, with a yellow sky behind it.

~

Leish's eyes were closed again by the time Mallesh set him down on the floor of the cave. Leish's skin was pale and wrinkled from its immersion in sea water. Mallesh soaked it, bit by bit, in the black liquid that bubbled from a place just outside the cave mouth. He scooped mud from the bottom of this puddle and smoothed it on the ragged webs between Leish's fingers and toes. Mallesh drew his fingers slowly through Leish's hair, teasing out the knots, plucking pieces of plants and sponge that had come from the ocean far beyond Nasranesh. When he was finished, he covered Leish with a blanket he had made months ago, from animal skins; just a small blanket, which did not cover feet and lower legs, but it would warm him a little.

Leish slept for two days. Mallesh crouched or lay close to him, watching and waiting. *This is why I came back here,* he thought once. The strength and volume of this thought surprised him, for he had been so quiet, even in his own mind, for so long. Other things spun with the words: pictures, colourful and sharp. Leish sick, lying on jungle leaves, hardly blinking as Mallesh talked and talked; all that talking, and his desire for the white city, making him hard and petty—Mallesh remembered this and was thankful for the new man he had become. A man who could care for his brother without envy or anger, a man who lived where he was, deaf to all other places.

This time, when Leish woke, Mallesh waited for him to speak first. Mallesh had been bathing him again. Leish shifted, propped himself on an elbow and looked down at his own skin. He looked out the cave opening then, and a moment later he crawled to it, lifting his limbs as if he did not want to touch them again to the dirt floor. Mallesh walked behind him.

"This is what you've been washing me with." Leish was standing, one hand on the rock wall behind him, the other pointing to the black puddle. Two bubbles grew and burst before Mallesh answered.

"Yes," he said, watching Leish's eyes, seeing them widen as he heard Mallesh's new voice. Leish's voice had changed too. Mallesh wished that they did not have to speak at all. Perhaps they would not, after this stage had passed.

"And you drink it. I've drunk it."

"Yes," said Mallesh. "It's the only fresh water there is, and I'm accustomed to it now."

"You're accustomed to it. I see." Leish took several steps past the puddle and looked at the sky and the rock. He turned his head until he was facing north. Mallesh saw him stiffen before he took another step. Mallesh himself hardly noticed the gathering pool stone any more; he often could not see it through the dust in any case. But today it was visible, and Leish did not look away from it.

"They tied me there. Maybe you saw it—maybe our parents saw …"

"They're dead," Mallesh said. "Father on the shore, when the boats came, and Mother as she was running to the river behind me. We didn't see you." *And if we had? She would have stayed and I would still have run—that other person I was would have run.*

"Come inside again," he said. "There's something I want to show you before night falls." Leish came with him, like a child who moves only because he is told to. He stared at the carvings Mallesh gestured to, at the shapes and then down at the tools that Mallesh always placed so neatly on the ground.

"You did this."

"Yes," Mallesh said.

"You."

Mallesh touched the shell he had carved. It almost felt like a real shell, the ridges and serrations were that delicate. "Yes. It's calming work. And there's beauty in it—I never would have known this before, but—"

"What are you talking about?" Leish's voice was very soft, but Mallesh stopped speaking. "You chip away at this rock, and you drink black water, and you say you've found calm? And beauty? You, Mallesh my brother, who used to stand atop that stone out there and shout about the next great age of the selkesh?" Leish was shouting as well now, but Mallesh stood tall before him. He needed to hear these words; it was like tempering metal, making it pure and strong with flame. "You ranted about boats and daggers and a triumph like Nasran's—and now you live in a cave, and this, around you, is what you brought on all of us. And listen! Listen to the lands beyond ours, which still have clean water and grass and trees. If you strain very hard, maybe you'll even hear the singing of the stone city—I still do. Listen: fountains and ivy! Sand with a river beneath it! Listen and you'll hear—"

"Nothing," Mallesh said, quite steadily, with his voice of holes. "I'll hear nothing. Not the stone city, not the lands closer, or our own land. I haven't heard any singing since I left the Queensrealm."

Leish leaned back against the wall of carvings. His mouth was open. After a moment he straightened and pressed his lips together, so tightly that they went pale. He stepped to the cave's opening and looked back over his shoulder. "I don't know why you live," he said, and then he walked away, into the rising dust.

FIFTY-ONE

Even from the bottom of the dried-up riverbed, Leish could hear Mallesh's chisel. The sound followed him everywhere over the flatness that was Nasranesh. He had listened to it at the foot of the gathering pool stone, and at the edge of the ocean, and inland, where he could not even see the cave. He had imagined that the depth of the riverbed would dilute the sound a bit, but it did not. The *tap-tap* reached him still, even though he lay with earth walls rising above him.

Mallesh had finished the rivergreen strand and begun an anemone. Leish tried not to look at the carvings, and sometimes he succeeded, though only for a few days. He had tried not to go back to the cave at all, those many weeks ago, but he had failed at that too. The only one of his resolutions that he had kept was to remain silent. He had not spoken to Mallesh since their first day together, when he had shouted and Mallesh had not. Leish had vowed that his brother would be the next one to speak; and so Leish ate what Mallesh cooked, and drank what Mallesh drank, and did not say any of the words that dizzied him.

But Mallesh did not speak either. Perhaps this was good: Leish did not know if he would be able to listen for long to the voice that came from his brother's scarred throat. Mallesh whittled at his wall and trudged to the shore for pieces of wood and looked at Leish with his changed eyes and seemed content. Leish almost shouted again, several times—questions, accusations, hollow, wordless sounds—but he suspected that Mallesh would simply gaze at him as he had before, with pity and calm, and so make everything worse.

I'll follow the riverbed, Leish thought as he had so often already. If it wasn't this thought, it was *I'll go up the coast,* or *I'll see if the land over the mountains is as grey as it sounds*—but now, as ever, he rose and turned back to the cave. He ached to be away, but could not leave. Anger and uncertainty choked him as the ash did. *I dreamed of Nasranesh's destruction long before it happened. Perhaps I'll dream of something else, some other future for myself or this land, that will show me how to be.* But when he slept, he did not dream at all.

He passed in front of the cave's entrance, imagining Mallesh pausing, waiting for the daylight to return. Leish went down to the shore. He might swim, though he hated the brown water and the smooth sand beneath it that was broken only by pitted rocks. He might attempt to swim to where the fish were, though he had tried this once already and failed (still, always, too weak). But when he reached the shore, he stood with his feet in the water and did not move. There was a boat rolling with the waves to the north and west of him, a rowboat with a single person inside, leaning on oars that were motionless in the water. The person's dark-haired head was lowered. As Leish watched, the head lifted and he saw a face, also dark with hair, and eyes that found his own. Arms reached, and the oars raised and dipped, and Leish slid his knife from his chest-wrap. *Go get Mallesh,* he told himself. *Call for him, at least*—but Leish waited on the shore, alone and silent.

The man was familiar. *Baldhron*—but the thought, and the hope, was swiftly gone. Leish squinted, tried to remember, even though a specific memory would not make a difference. Not selkesh, familiar: an enemy. Leish considered throwing his knife when the boat was close enough, but he did not. He would kill the man slowly, looking into his eyes. He would not be distracted or dissuaded this time. His palm was slippery with sweat and his blood rushed within him.

The boat scraped along the stone of the shore. The man sat for a moment. He was breathing hard and his arms were shaking—but when a wave came and lifted the boat to drag it back again, he pushed himself up and out. Leish took a step toward him.

"Leish," the man said, wrenching his body around so that he was sitting. Leish leaned forward on his left foot but did not take another step. He had seen this man with the Queen, from somewhere high up: the tower, or the gathering pool stone, or both. The man had looked different then. Leish shook his head and walked, tightening his grip on his knife.

"Leish—stop, wait." The Queenstongue, though the man did not look like a Queensman. But it did not matter who he was, only that he was someone, finally, who would die.

"Do you remember me?" the man asked. "I am Aldron"—and suddenly it did matter after all.

~

Mallesh heard a splash in the quiet between chisel taps. He adjusted the tool's angle and tapped again, quite hard: he wanted this entire segment of stone to fall away, and it did, leaving a smooth, slanted expanse. Now he could draw out the edge of a coral reef—something that his anemone could cling to, and something he could add to, perhaps with the shapes of fish or crabs. Before he could bring the hammer down again, though, he heard voices; low, distant ones, but he recognized Leish's. When he rose, some words came to him more clearly, and he paused for a moment before he went out the opening. Queenstongue words, not selkesh ones; words that brought tunnels and stink and rage hissing into his quiet.

Leish was at the shore, leaning on one knee above a man who was lying on his back. Leish's right hand was at the man's throat. The man's hands were at his sides, palms up, fingers loose and curving. Mallesh saw the dull gleam of Leish's knife. He heard Leish say, "No"—a word Mallesh remembered—and then others he did not understand, a long, jagged stream of them. Leish raised his knife, and Mallesh shouted the selkesh "No!" and began to run.

When he had reached them, Mallesh said, "What's this?" in the cracked, stranger's voice he had never wanted to use again. He and Leish had been living so peacefully, with only the sounds of cooking and drinking and sleeping between them. And now this man was here, and the silence was broken, and Mallesh would have to use all of his new strength to keep some calm about them yet.

"He's Aldron," Leish said. A slender line of spittle trembled between his lips, and more was gathering at the corners of his mouth. "He did this to us. He used his voice powers to ruin our land."

The man Aldron was looking at Mallesh, his eyes rolled sideways so that the whites of them were very large. Even on his back with Leish's knee against his chest, Aldron did not look frightened or angry.

"No," Mallesh said, "that was the Queen. I heard that she spoke on top of the gathering pool stone. Other selkesh told me that the fire sprang up with her words."

"No," Leish said, "it wasn't the Queen. She told him to use his powers, but they weren't hers. I know this, Mallesh. I found out many things when I was a prisoner in the white city."

Mallesh crouched to bring himself closer to the two men. "So if he did do this," he said slowly, "why has he returned?"

Leish spat more Queenstongue words at Aldron, who answered without blinking. Leish laughed and dug his knife into Aldron's flesh, just enough to raise a thin edge of blood. "Apparently he enlisted the new queen's help and took a ship here from the harbour city. The ship dropped him just inside our waters, since the captain refused to bring him closer. He rowed down the coast until he saw the gathering pool stone, which he remembered."

"Yes," said Mallesh when Leish did not continue, "but that is only how. *Why* did he return?"

"He wants—" Leish began, and shook his head as if he would laugh again. "He insists that he has come to try and reverse what he did."

Mallesh knew Leish's expression, though he had never seen it on his brother's face before. He knew what was within, shaping the expression. "And you don't want to believe him," Mallesh said, and was not surprised when Leish twisted around to look at him.

"Such insight, Brother! I never expected you'd have gained so much from our destruction. Now, if only you could speak this murderer's language, I'd so enjoy listening to the thoughts you'd share."

"Leish," Mallesh said after a time, "let him try."

The wind was suddenly damp: rain, not just sea spray. Rain fell every few weeks, smudging the dust and stone with a darkness that did not stay. Aldron's fingers twitched as the moisture touched them, and Leish raised his face, his mouth open a bit on the water that was so fresh and so fleeting. The wind had already blown it away when he stood up. He slid his knife back into his chest-wrap and walked away from the shore. Mallesh watched him, through the night that was falling. After Leish had ducked into the cave, Mallesh turned back to Aldron.

"Come," he said in a language that would not be understood—and then he held out a hand that would.

~

Leish sat alone deep within Mallesh's cave and imagined water. It was water that had carved it out, a branch of the river that had fed the selkesh's hearth pools, perhaps, though Leish had never seen this river when it had lived. In the weak light of his brand he saw the place now: rounded walls banded with flecks of gold and crystal, rough where the water had thrust at them and smooth where it had simply flowed. He tried to hear its song as it would have been, braided with all the other rocks and waters of Nasranesh—but he heard nothing except the hum of emptiness and, beyond that, the clamour of the sea.

The footsteps sounded very loud even when they were still far away. Leish listened to them as they descended the sloping river-tunnel. When they had nearly reached him, he drew his spear toward him. The spear had been lying near Mallesh's tools, in the upper cave, and he had not said anything when Leish had picked it up. Maybe he had not noticed. It was a fine spear with a sharp, shining head and a haft Mallesh must have worked himself, since the original had to have burned. Leish set his hand upon the wood but did not pick it up.

Aldron sat down several paces away from Leish and sank his own torch into the loose sand. He waved his hand to disperse the smoke that drifted in front of his face. Leish did not; he stared at Aldron with stinging, tearing eyes and would not blink.

"I left my people," Aldron said after they had sat awhile in silence, "because they wouldn't permit me to use my powers."

No, Leish thought, *don't speak. Hold on to your voice, as you do with Mallesh*—but this was not Mallesh, and Leish had waited so long for words like these. "Don't talk to me of your people or yourself," he said, and was amazed at the strength of his voice, which he had hardly used for two years. Strength had grown, it seemed, from all of his prisons.

Aldron nodded but spoke again, as if he had not heard Leish. "Queen Galha offered me a chance to use my powers in ways I'd never have been able to on my own. I agreed to come here with her because of that."

Leish rolled his spear against his thigh and pressed it there. The wood was so smooth that he did not think it would splinter even if he dug his nails into it. "And that was all," he said. "That was why you destroyed my land: to take glory from your own power." As his words glanced from the stone walls, Leish remembered other words: Mallesh's, shouted from high above the gathering pool, from a boat on the sea, among jungle trees; Mallesh's and Baldhron's, far beneath the sand, in tunnels that gleamed and stank. Leish had cowered as they shouted—he remembered this. He pushed all of it away, himself and his brother and where they had gone. Why they had gone. The only real things now were Aldron and this place that he had killed.

"And what of your glory?" Leish said when Aldron did not speak. "Was it as satisfying as you'd hoped?"

Aldron said, "Of course not," and his voice was tremulous, higher than it had been. *Good,* thought Leish, and knew how he would hurt Aldron next.

"So you had no triumph after all, but at least you have your life. You almost didn't, I heard. The Queen tried to kill you, I heard—hardly a just reward for your service."

Aldron picked up a stone from the ground next to him. It was flat on one side. Aldron touched his finger to it, and Leish knew what it was he touched: bones and fins, a tail twisted in underwater flight. There were many such stones here, littering the ground where all the fish had died in fire and air.

"She told me, before, that I'd have to be silent about my part in the battle. The glory would have to be a private one. I knew this, and I agreed to it. But yes, she tried … she sank a spear into my chest as I was lying by that tall stone afterward. I was so weak I could hardly see her." He paused, set the stone down again. "How did you hear of this?" he said slowly, and Leish smiled.

"Your Alea told us, when she came to confront the Queen." He did not want to wait for Aldron to speak this time, so he continued, faster. "Yes: she came to the Queen's white city and told the truth of the curse before everyone who was gathered in the chamber. I was there, of course, chained to the Queen's chair, so I heard it all, even the words Alea said that brought the battle back. For a moment it was there: the fire, the dying things. She was magnificent. And the people did believe her, for a short time after—before Lanara told another story and changed everything again. But what a woman, your Alea, so beautiful—and your daughter too, just like her mother already."

Aldron rose. He walked over to Leish and stood above him, and Leish looked up, still smiling. "What happened to them?" Aldron asked, so softly that his lips hardly seemed to move. His hands were clenched; Leish felt the air between them and his own skin. He knew that there would be a ripple of wind before Aldron's fists found him.

"I will not tell you this," Leish said. *Not even if you could tell me what happened to my own Dallia would I tell you this.* He waited. Aldron was so close, and the light was so dim, that Leish could not see his expression, just the line of his cheek and the dark blur of his beard. His eyes shone flat and blank, and Leish was sorry for this; he wanted, needed, more. He sat, not steeling himself, not afraid or eager. Aldron had been wounded; Leish did not matter.

"Tell me," Aldron whispered at last, and Leish said, "No." He thought that the pleasure that pierced him was the first clear, true thing he had felt since he left Nasranesh.

"You're lucky," Aldron said more loudly, "that I'm not as petty a man as you are. I could refuse to try and heal your land."

"And I could kill you," Leish replied, though this reply made no sense, was simply his desire blurted without thought.

"Yes," Aldron said, his body and even his voice gone very still. "You could." He turned away a moment later.

Leish stirred as Aldron tugged his torch free and walked back toward the upper cave. "Do get some rest," Leish called. "You'll need to be strong tomorrow." All his pleasure dissipated as he spoke. By the time Aldron and his feeble light had vanished up the tunnel, Leish felt only fear again, old and barren as the stone.

FIFTY-TWO

The gathering pool stone was loose. Leish had not touched it until now; he had just looked and imagined that, although its colour and shape had changed, its position in the earth had not. But the earth too had changed: it was sand and dirt now, where water and clay had been. And the wind was so strong against the stone, every day, when before the days had been calm, except when storms had blown in from the sea. Whatever the reason, the gathering pool stone shifted a bit as Leish leaned against it, his feet scrambling for purchase on Mallesh's shoulders.

"I must go up there," Aldron had said to Leish when Leish had found him outside the cave after dawn. Aldron did not look at him once—not then, not a few hours later, when the light was stronger and Aldron had said, "I'm ready." He had nodded at Mallesh, who had nodded back. *A Queensfolk gesture,* Leish had thought bitterly. *Mallesh has no idea what it is he does now*. Leish tried to catch Aldron's eye when they were all standing at the foot of the stone, but he still would not glance at him. Leish was ashamed of his need to see Aldron's eyes on him—and he was not sure how he himself would look, or what he would say, if Aldron did turn to him. But he did not. He waited for Leish to heave himself onto Mallesh's shoulders, and then he climbed, his arms and legs placed carefully, almost lightly.

Leish did not think that Aldron would reach the top: the stone was too high and too smooth. Leish grunted beneath his weight, once Aldron was standing fully on his shoulders—and very soon there was no weight, and Leish looked slowly up. Aldron was above him, inching along the stone, finding foot- and handholds where there did not seem to be any. "Down," Leish gasped, and Mallesh released his ankles and let him slip free.

They walked away from the stone, back toward the cave. "We shouldn't be too close," Mallesh said. "Just in case the power is very strong where he is." Leish swallowed and shifted his feet in the dust. *The power,* he thought, and shuddered. "But we shouldn't worry if he doesn't succeed," Mallesh went on, squinting at the stone and the man who was crouching atop it. "This land will heal itself in time. I think the water is already a bit cleaner than it was."

Leish swallowed again, his throat too tight and dry for any water, no matter how clear, to soothe. "No, Mallesh, this land will never heal. That's part of what Aldron did: he brought fire and death, and he brought it for all time. Our water will never be clean again, and the water of other lands will kill us if we seek it out. This is the curse, and I've seen it work. I've seen selkesh die ..."

Mallesh's mouth was open. Leish had longed to force emotion and words from him; now that he had, he felt no triumph. "No," Mallesh said, and Leish prepared for him to become his brother again. Perhaps he would run to the stone, or get a dagger; Leish would have to restrain him. But Mallesh did not look at the man on the stone as he spoke again, loudly, the words grating in his throat. "How could you not tell me this? Our people are searching even now for healthy places, for life elsewhere—and all this time you've known about the curse? You knew and you said nothing to me."

"You've hardly been eager to rejoin our people," Leish said. "Or to talk to me." Everything was wrong—still, after so long. After a life here and away; now here again, and still wrong. His mother had always comforted him when Mallesh hurt him. Leish remembered her hands on his face, touching him because he could never look at her when she was being so kind to him.

"If this man doesn't succeed," Mallesh said, his voice rough and low again as always, "we must find our people somehow, and tell them of their danger."

Leish could not answer—but he did not have to, for Aldron stood just then, and raised his arms into the sky.

~

He was so high above the world. The open sky, the sand, the stone: he was standing on the rock of the leaping place again, watching the Perona scatter his people in distant blood and screaming. But that had been destruction—that and the other, here. Now was reversal. One more change—the last, truly. He felt the finality of it even as he felt the words beginning.

They would know: the Goddesses, and Alea, and Alnissa. All the sea folk and all the Alilan would know his heart when this eastern land was reborn. He would draw roots from nothingness, and earth from rock. He would fill the water by the shore with fish. He would sing this Telling, and at its end would be a heartflower. He had saved all his words for this song; he had not Told once since he had stood here before, at the foot of the stone. But now his voice was welling in him as it had when he was a boy on the plain, a boy in the desert, everything too large for him and him too foolish to know it. Only now did he know, and he welcomed the knowledge as he would welcome the silence that waited for him when this final Telling was done.

He raised his arms. He had to, to keep his body steady in the wind—but he also wanted to. Alnila and Alneth would see him, and although he would look tiny to them, they would understand his supplication. He spread his fingers apart. His mouth opened, and his voice *is silence. All the words of power and beauty hover in his throat and on his tongue, and then they curl away like bark in fire. The dust rises from the rock and he feels it in his mouth, smothering, clotting.*

He was nothing. The wind should lift him; he would draw apart, empty flesh from empty bone, with no flames to mark his passing. They had all known he would end this way: Aliser, Old Aldira, even Alea, though she, at least, had loved him. No Alilan rites, and no one to watch except the two sea folk and their heavy, colourless sky.

But the sky is not colourless. There may be no fire within him, but there is fire outside, drawing closer over the sea. No sounds in him to Tell, but sounds around him, still distant: a spitting of flame and a great, rolling rumble. The fire is orange and red at its edges, and white at its heart, which is a form so vast he can hardly focus on it—but it is moving very quickly, and soon he does see. Hair and arms, eyes like deep-buried coals, a body that is flame without a source, for it <u>*is*</u> *the source.*

He would not fall—not to his knees and not to the ground. He held himself tall: an Alilan man again, at the last.

As his lips make the name of the burning sister-goddess, the other appears beneath her. The rumbling ends in a sound that is both splinter and rush, and the sea convulses. Rock rises, and coral, and clay studded with scurrying crabs and anemones that reach and stroke. Hair of seagreen and eels, and a deep black mouth breathing smoke and lava that hardens as it touches the air. This sister gathers up fish and plants, snails, flowering moss, worms. They trail and cling as she spins toward Aldron, beneath Alnila's fire.

They stop above the rock of the sea folk's cave. The Goddesses are still apart from Aldron, but they are entireties, all sky and all land, and he feels their breath sting his skin with scattered sparks and earth. He cannot shape their names now; there are no more words for him. Only his body remains, small and straight and ready. His eyes are filled with flame and writhing colours—but he sees something dark beneath it all. Something dark, as small as he is, that stands, then slips away and back again. A man with a spear, a man whose eyes course with the fire and green of the Goddesses above him. Aldron looks into his eyes, across all the space that separates them. He does not look away, not even when fire and earth and spear come singing together into his silence.

~

Aldron fell with a heavy sound that reverberated long after his body had settled into the dust behind the gathering pool stone. Mallesh looked down at Leish when the air was quiet again. He waited for Leish to look back at him, but he did not; he squatted beside the black pool and stared at nothing. After a moment Mallesh began to walk alone to the place where Aldron had fallen—for there were things to do now, and they were as clear to him as the shapes that waited for him beneath layers of rock.

Aldron was lying on his side. This surprised Mallesh; he had expected to find Aldron's arms and legs splayed, or perhaps crushed beneath him. But his knees were drawn up and his arms were bent: he was curled like a baby around the spear in his chest. Mallesh knelt and rolled him over, thinking, *He lives, and he will try again to heal my land, when I have healed him*—but Aldron's eyes were black and staring, and his mouth breathed only bloody spittle. When Mallesh wrenched the spear free, the spittle thickened and gushed. Aldron's beard soaked flat, and the dirt beneath his head was stained. Mallesh did not wipe the liquid away from Aldron's skin. He cleaned the spearhead on the earth and rose and saw that Leish had not moved.

Mallesh had not seen Leish leave his side during Aldron's attempt at Telling. Mallesh had been staring at Aldron: at the working of his mouth and the wildness of his eyes, which leapt from the sea to the sky. Mallesh had not looked around him; he had not needed to. Nothing was changing. The dust still blew, and the wind still smelled of old fires. Aldron's lips had stopped forming words after a time. He had stood very tall, reaching with his fingers and arms and his raised-up head—and even though he had looked so strong, Mallesh had seen his defeat. Perhaps he should have turned to Leish then and said, "Let's decide what we should do now—all three of us, together." But he could not move his eyes from Aldron's—not until Aldron's shifted to Leish, and stayed there. Only then did Mallesh turn—and the spear was already flying, arcing gently up despite the wind. *So straight,* Mallesh had thought. *Leish could never throw like that before*—but what was "before," for any of them, now that they were here?

Mallesh leaned on the spear. Something would have to be done with the body—something different than what he had done with all the selkesh bodies he had found here after he returned alone from the peaks. Those he had dragged to the place where he thought the burying trees would have been, before; a place upriver, at a bend where the earth had been soft and deep. These could not be true selkesh burials, for there were no hearth and gathering pool waters to bathe the dead ones in; nor were there kin trees whose roots would encircle and sing. But Mallesh had hacked at the hard, cracked ground beneath the ash until he had hollowed out an enormous hole. He thought it must have taken him days to dig and days more to cover again, but he had not noticed this time passing. He had laid them all within, as gently as possible. He had placed his parents side by side on the top; their faces had been the last he had seen. When he finished, he had hauled large stones to the mound and arranged them above, so that the bodies would not be disturbed by wind or the burrowing of beasts.

He would not bury Aldron. Too much effort, now that Mallesh was a weaker man; and in any case, Aldron had not been selkesh. There would have to be another, different way. Mallesh held the spear in front of him and spun the shaft slowly between his fingers. When his hands stilled and felt the warming wood, he knew what he would do.

~

Leish felt light. He had thought that he would follow the spear up, his body just a wind, but he had remained on the earth. He was there still, though he was dizzier every moment. Dizzy, giddy, made of air, even though his land's song was the same as it had been before Aldron had climbed the gathering pool stone.

It's wrong, he thought, grinding his fingernails into the skin of his palms as if discomfort would return him to himself. *Wrong to feel such joy when nothing has changed*—but something had. He had, as Aldron had met his gaze at last, and held it. As the spear had left his hand. Aldron had not looked at the spear; his eyes had remained on Leish, so wide and vivid that Leish could see them even now. *Wrong,* Leish thought again, and drew a deep, new breath.

When Mallesh walked back toward him, Leish rose. He swayed a bit, and grasped at words he might be required to say—but Mallesh went past him, to the side of the cave. He pulled a length of driftwood from the top of the tall stack that stood there and carried it back to the gathering pool stone. He came back for more, and more. Only when he lifted Aldron's body and laid it on the pile did Leish understand, and move.

The driftwood was so smooth that it did not splinter when it was grasped and tugged, but it was also difficult to hold, and Leish dropped several pieces before he could carry any. He found, once he began, that his dizziness had no effect on his strength; he seemed stronger, if anything, balancing the wood and throwing it. It was because of him that they finished as quickly as they did. The sky was darkening already—so early, as it had in the Queensrealm winter. Mallesh bent, gasping, over the bottom of the pile. It was Leish who struck the flint, hard, until sparks wheeled and lit.

The flames spread swiftly. Leish and Mallesh retreated to the cave when the heat grew too intense. By then it was dark, and Leish was ravenous. He ate two treerats that Mallesh had cooked the day before, and drank four handfuls of black water. Mallesh went into the cave after the fire had been burning for a few hours, but Leish stayed outside. *I'll never be tired again,* he thought. He watched the fire light this place that had been Nasranesh, and he heard fire- and landsongs twining, and it was almost beautiful. He saw and heard the blaze lower, sometime after dawn. When Mallesh emerged from the cave, Leish was watching fresh ash swirl over his feet.

"I'm not tired," he said to Mallesh, to see if the hardness of his voice would weigh him down a little—but it did not.

"Maybe, but you should still sleep." Mallesh's words rippled like water against Leish's ears: loud and soft, soft and loud.

Leish did not sleep for many days. He sifted through the remnants of the fire and passed the largest chunks of ash through his fingers. He ate and drank every few hours, and ran for hours more, up the old riverbed and back again. The world bent around him. He was the fixed centre, and everything else pulsed and flowed, toward him and away.

"Swim," he heard Mallesh say one day. "Your skin is unwell."

Leish looked down and could not see his body. "No," he said, his tongue sluggish as the rest of him flew. He knew he would be light and strong as long as he did not enter the sea. The water would drag at him until he sank; here, among rocks and dirt, he would not. He did not know how to explain this to Mallesh, and even if he did, Mallesh would not understand. It was wrong; it was truth.

He waited for dawn every day, and every day the light and land were more blurred. One dawn was speckled with darkness, and Leish blinked, not expecting to see anything clearer—but soon the specks were larger, and soon after that they were clear. He felt Mallesh step up beside him, heard him draw a sharp breath. "They've come." Mallesh's water-words clung to Leish's skin, skin he could feel just a bit, though he tried not to. "They saw the fire."

Leish sat down, his dizziness turned suddenly to nausea. Mallesh took several steps away from him, but Leish could not move. Mallesh turned to look at him. "Come with me, to meet them." Leish dragged his eyes from his brother to the selkesh who were coming from north and east. He could already see their jutting bones and pale, seamed skin, and the cloth that hung from them because it was too ragged to tie. As he saw these things, the world stopped its pulsing.

"Come," Mallesh said again, and his voice was so loud in the stillness that Leish whimpered. He did not rise. Mallesh walked out alone, and then he ran, and so did all the others. Leish heard their words. They rose and spilled, and their edges gouged his skin.

The selkesh gathered that day, and the next, and the next. Days and days of returning. The sea frothed with them and the ground was covered. Mallesh went among them and spoke. Leish could hear this even from deep within the cave, and he was too weak to blot it out with the singing of a different place. He slept and sweated as far away from the crowd as he could drag himself. When he was not sleeping, he collected fossil stones and laid them out end to end until there were three circles of them, and him in the middle. Mallesh brought him food and water. Several times he tried to pour the water onto Leish's body, but Leish cried out and slapped his brother's hands away.

One day Leish heard footsteps that were not Mallesh's. He remembered hearing Aldron walking down the tunnel, and for a moment he thought it might be him. Leish would not look. He lay wrapped in his own rot yet again, and closed his eyes.

"Leish." He would not look. A prison—always a prison, and it was only his sickened mind that filled it thus. Soon a Queensguard would force him to his feet and this voice, so clear and close, would dissolve. Or perhaps it would be Baldhron, come to lead him out—and Leish would still be too weak to kill him. But the voice came again, yet, so that he felt breath on his cheek—and he felt hands as well, stroking his closed eyes and the line of his neck. Arms came around him from behind, and knees bent in against his knees. He was in Ladhra's tower again, holding her, singing against her skin—only it was he who was being held now, and a woman's voice that murmured. He rolled from his side to his back. A hand traced the length of his face. He opened his eyes, though he knew he would not believe what they showed him.

Her face was above his. No long black hair trailed down over him; it was cropped short. He looked at it, and at the livid purple scar that twisted out from beneath it, down her neck. He touched the scar, which was puckered and smooth. She drew in her breath and pressed her lips together, and he touched them too. He sat up very slowly, so that his cracked skin would not crack wider, and she sat with him. They looked at each other for a time without touching.

"Well," Dallia said at last, "we certainly make a striking pair"—and after a steady, aching moment he laughed and reached for her.

FIFTY-THREE

Nellyn woke in daylight. This was not unusual: he had not been sleeping soundly since the rains. Today, though, it was noise, not just restlessness, that woke him. He lay and listened to it as it grew louder. He thought that he might stay in his hut until the air was quiet again, but soon there were sounds from the village too, and they drew him out, shivering, onto the hot earth.

Since Galha had summoned Lanara back to Luhr, so long ago, two Queensfolk had taught the shonyn small ones. These two were coming down the ridge, laughing when they slithered sideways. They were both young men, both loud and cheerful and apparently unconcerned about disturbing the shonyn sleeping time. Nellyn had heard them before, shouting as they went down to the river, and once he had seen them shooting arrows at lynanyn and slapping each other on the back when they brought one down. Today they seemed particularly exuberant. They ran among the shonyn houses to the riverbank. One of them stood on a sitting stone and peered downriver with a hand shading his eyes. Nellyn watched him point and heard the other Queensman cry out something unintelligible. The two arranged themselves side by side in front of the sitting stones. They stood very straight and did not speak again; these things alone told Nellyn that the vessel being rowed upriver was not just another boat that would leave messages and food, or pass the village by.

Only when the sounds of oars and timbers were directly beside him did Nellyn turn. This was the same ship that had sailed past him through the rain—but now at least twenty Queensfolk stood on its deck, not merely the three who had huddled there before. The wood shone, as did the blue and green of the sails, which flapped but did not fill. Water and wind were so calm that the ship slowed as soon as the oars were drawn up. It eased to a halt before the anchor chain was even taut.

A rowboat came down, and a rope ladder. Nellyn stepped back until he felt the hot clay of his hut against his skin and tunic. He ran his palms over it, pressed down where the clay was roughest—something solid that might bear him up as shonyn time tugged. *I am older*, he thought. *This is not the boat that brought her before, and she is not here now.* A Queenswoman slipped down the ladder and into the rowboat. *Another Queensship,* a true shonyn would have thought, *and another Queenswoman rowing to our shore; these things are always the same.*

The two Queensmen waded into the river and pulled themselves into the rowboat, and one of them took up the oars. Nellyn watched them reach the ship and climb. They vanished among the Queensfolk at the rail and did not reappear until the shadows were much longer on the sand. The same Queenswoman rowed them back. Nellyn waited for the men to go back to their ridge, and one did turn that way—but the other did not. The anchor surged out of the water and long oars dipped, but Nellyn looked only at the Queensman who was walking toward him.

"Nellyn?" the man said when he stood before the hut.

"Yes." The Queenstongue word emerged effortlessly, as if he had spoken this language often since his return. As if he had spoken at all.

"I am Rilhen. I bear a message for you, from the Queen."

Nellyn took the folded parchment Rilhen held out to him. "Thank you," he said as he thought, *A message from Galha—I do not understand ...* The Queensman lingered. Nellyn saw that he wished to say more, but also that he wished not to. At last he nodded at Nellyn, smiled a bit uncertainly and left him.

The parchment was warm, as if it had been left in the sunlight or clasped tightly in other hands. Nellyn felt its warmth before he looked at it. He saw writing, upside down. He turned the parchment so that he could read it. He understood two things as he blinked down at the letters: they spelled his name, and Lanara had written them. He glanced away and back again. He lifted the parchment so close to his face that the marks blurred—but they were still hers.

He walked slowly to the plants, which the rain had made fiercely green. He placed the folded parchment on the ground. He dipped his head into the shade of the plants so that he could not see the river or the huts or the tents, only his upturned wrists, the blue-brown of their skin darker still where the blood flowed beneath. He breathed and looked and could find no stillness.

There was another breathing. It was quite soft, but he heard it in the spaces between his own breaths. He twisted his body around and saw Maarenn standing behind him.

"Gathering companion," he said, "it is not dusk. Why do you wake?"

He had sometimes thought, in the weeks following the rains, that he had dreamed her in his hut, against his skin—but now he met her steady, bright gaze and knew that he had not. "The ship is noisy," she said. "And you are also awake." She paused. "I see the Queensman come to you. I see him give you this." Her eyes shifted, no longer bright.

"Yes."

"Is it …" She frowned at the parchment, then at the plants. "It is from her. The Queenswoman who makes you leave and return."

He picked up the message, held it in his palm. "Yes. I do not know what words are inside."

"What words do you want?"

He stood up. "Maarenn," he said carefully, "you should not speak with such heat—it is not—"

"What words do you want?" she said again, and he saw tears in her eyes and turned away from them.

"I do not know. I know nothing of what I want or do not want." He felt the heat beginning in his own throat and did not wait to quell it or slow his words. "I am looking for a place and cannot find one. I think I am mad to stay here, where my people shun me, but I stay. Part of my looking is my staying. That is all I know, every day until now, but I think every day of change."

"And if she offers change? If she summons you to her great city in the sand?"

Nellyn breathed until the warmth within him was gone. "That great city is not my place. This I do know."

Maarenn matched her breath to his before she spoke again. "But if she says to live with her somewhere else?"

"No," he said, and again, "I do not know." He had struggled for answers before on this bank. He remembered how frustrated and amused Lanara had been, listening to his answers, or his silences.

"Do not open it," Maarenn said. "Or do—but stay. You say your people shun you, but I do not. Stay with me. This is our place."

He could not hear the ship now; he heard only the river flowing, and the silver leaves hissing when the wind rose. He laid his fingertips on the back of Maarenn's right hand and she turned it up. The lines of her palm were so deep, so distinct, like the markings of a writing stick on parchment. "I know how I change in her world," he said, "and now how I change in mine. These changes are like a river that cannot flow. There is no river for me, Maarenn, anywhere that I see."

She pulled her hand away from his. She said his name once, again, and then she ran from him. He could not watch her go. He sat down and unfolded the parchment.

Galha is dead and I am Queen in Luhr. I cannot love you now. Perhaps this no longer matters to you. I am sorry, if it does—but my sense of duty must be stronger than regret or indeed any other emotion.

When he had finished reading, he rose. The parchment fell from his fingers as he walked back to his hut. He lay down inside, rolled onto his belly and bent his arms over his head. He slept after a time, as the wind shifted his curtain and carried the last of the sunlight in to warm him.

~

Six months passed. Nellyn measured them as he had not measured the ones before Queen Lanara's ship came. He counted the first few with a dull, aching interest, a feeling of dipping one foot back into Queensfolk time. Then the interest turned to need and he began to mark full moons on the wall of his hut with lynanyn juice. When the sixth circle had been daubed, he sat back on his heels and stared at it, sucking the juice from his fingertip. Six moons—but he had no idea what season it was. *It is important to me,* he thought. *I must know what colour the leaves are in that town on the plain. I must know if Nissa is walking yet. This is my desire now.*

That night he slunk around the huddle of shonyn houses while the wise ones spoke their words of unchange and the flatboats lapped across the water. He walked quickly up the sand ridge, his head tucked against his chest as if he were not already invisible. He stopped in front of the Queensfolk living tent, which was dark. There had been a light within until about midnight; Nellyn had waited another hour just to be certain that the Queensmen would be asleep. The teaching tent had been dark since dusk, when the small ones had filed out and down, to words they understood. Nellyn stood awhile with his hand on the flap of the teaching tent. The canvas was sand-roughened and cool, and it made him remember so much that he had not thought about in such a long time. *Memories come from objects,* he thought, a*nd objects become memories.* He closed his eyes. *Once I would have thought "or" instead of "and." A Queensfolk dividing: or, and, yes, no, must be, must not. These words used to pain me.* He took a breath, then lifted the door flap and slipped inside.

The two Queensmen were sloppy; Nellyn saw this even before his eyes could tell him exactly what he was seeing. Leaning shadows rose from the ground and from the table: the writing trays, which he had expected, but also stacks of parchment, slippery with rolled ends, and long, thin boxes that had not been here before. The carpet was the same; the weak light from the open tent flap showed him this. He walked over the carpet, which was very smooth in the middle where so many small ones had sat upon it. He opened the bound sheaf of parchment that lay on the table, beside the writing trays. Lanara had sent for the binding materials from Luhr; she had been disgusted by the disarray of the papers that had been left for her, and determined to set them in order. He angled the book so that he could read the first few words on the upper page.

Queenswrit Eve in Luhr and other civilized parts of the realm. All has been the same as ever here, since the copper trader found us three weeks ago.

Nellyn set the book flat again. The copper trader had arrived with clamour and jests that Nellyn had heard from his hut. Three weeks ago, yes—that much he could calculate. And now Queenswrit Eve, which Lanara had told him came late-winter. *Snow is hissing against the shutters of the inn, and of the tower,* he thought. *The grass on the plain is bent and buried. The moss handprint is yellow-brown on the cliff. The sea is white on top and black beneath. The icemounts are singing.*

He turned from the parchment book to the stack of writing trays. It was a tall stack, and he had to reach to pluck the top one down. Its sand was dry and smooth, as was that in the next tray. He took them down one by one and looked at the sand in each of them, but there were no words there. He stared at the last tray for a long time. He drew his finger through the sand: a circle, then a spiral, then nothing as his palm swept the shapes away. He traced the letters of his name, so deeply that they half filled with sand as soon as he lifted his finger.

No wind tonight. The river's current is strong, as if there is a wind beneath the water. The moon is dark, but the sky is thick with stars.

There was no room to write all this, of course, even though he longed to do so. He wanted more than sand: a broad, curling sheet of parchment, and a black writing stick that would smudge his fingers but not the page. He had never written much in the tower log, but he would write now, lines and lines that would be all his days and nights since Fane. Since Lanara had first rowed to his shore. Since he had walked to his teacher Soral's tent, in sunlight, across the jewelled sand. And when these things were written, he would make words for the days and nights that would come to him. Not as many as the ones for before; not nearly as many.

He stood by the last tray, with all the others piled behind him, and again he touched his finger to sand. He made the letters carefully—Queensfolk letters, since the shonyn had none. When he had finished, he stood still. Then he spun, and the pile of trays behind him clattered to the ground.

When Rilhen ran into the tent, Nellyn had not moved from the table. "What—" Rilhen said. Nellyn wondered where the other one was. "—are you ..." He was speaking more slowly now, as Queensfolk always did when they spoke to shonyn. His hands were grasping his sleeping tunic into tight bunches.

"I am sorry," Nellyn said, and the man's hands stopped working even as his eyes widened. "I used to come here when I was a child. I wanted to see the place again. These trays." He gestured, and the man stepped forward, looked down.

"'Next,'" he said hoarsely. "Did you write this? You came up here before, during the rains. You're shonyn, but you speak as if you understand ... What is this 'next'? What does it mean?"

Nellyn smiled. "I understand." He took a step toward the open tent flap and the man held up a hand.

"Wait. I recognize you now—you're Nellyn, the one the Queen wrote to. The one she wrote about when she lived here. I've read all her entries. Stay with me awhile—I have so many things to ask you. And the Queen will be so pleased when she knows I've talked to you."

Nellyn shook his head, though he was still smiling. "No. I am sorry." He paused with his hand on the canvas. "But thank you, Rilhen."

The man called after him once more as Nellyn walked down the slope. There was a light in the other tent; perhaps the second man would come out, drawn by voices. Nellyn did not look back.

~

Four days. A precise count: four days after his visit to the teaching tent; four days in winter. Four days closer to spring.

The tunic Nellyn had worn from Fane was spread out on a flat rock by the river. The cloth was nearly black when wet; just light brown, dry. He had not worn it since the first week of his return journey, had worn his old, thin blue one instead, thinking its weight against his skin might bring the quiet back to him. Now he looked at the water-darkened cloth as if his gaze would hasten its drying. He knew it would not, so he turned and pulled himself up the bank, where he would bundle some of the lynanyn slices Maarenn continued to leave for him into his threadbare sack. He had not seen her since the day the letter had come, though he had almost gone to her many times. It would have been easy to touch her, to take her warmth and think himself shonyn again—but this would not have been true. It would also have been easy to go to her and command her to stop leaving lynanyn by his hut. *No,* he thought, *these things would bring change to her too*—and so he kept himself away as he did now, so close to leaving.

He glanced up at the sun, which was dazzling, hanging directly behind the tents on the ridge. He wondered again which way he would go. He had considered striking out across the river then continuing past the lynanyn trees, northward; or angling southwest, into the deeper desert. These were paths he had never taken, and their beginnings looked very stark to him in the sun's light—but he would choose one somehow, when his tunic was dry and his lynanyn slices wrapped. He blinked at the ridge. There were people shadows between the tent ones. Two tall forms, likely the Queensmen, and another nearly as tall, with the bulge of a pack at its back. Perhaps two packs, one behind, one to the side, though Nellyn could make out even less of this second shape. He saw one of the Queensmen point down the ridge. Down—finger and arm angled unmistakably past the houses of the village, so silent now, just before dusk.

A new Queensman or woman, Nellyn thought. Panic clutched at him. He was so close; he had finally decided, and was nearly away. But no: someone had come to ask him questions. Someone from Luhr, perhaps—maybe even from Lanara? *No. Be calm. No one from Luhr would travel through the desert, and there have been no boats since the copper trader came.*

The third figure was walking, that much was certain. It moved into deeper shadow as it descended the ridge. Nellyn considered retreating to his hut, but knew the person would have seen him standing here, motionless against the eastern sky that was no longer bright. He remained where he was for the space of four breaths. Then the figure stepped from shade into slanting light, and he saw strands of dark hair curling from beneath a white kerchief, red cloth straps tied over brown shoulders. And a child—a girl with long black hair, her arms and legs wrapped tight around her mother.

Nellyn walked. No waiting, though there would be a time for this again. He took one step and another. The child was down now, her arms wide and weaving, her legs buckling, quickly steady. He laughed as he watched her, laughed as he looked up and into Alea's eyes. He ran, and the river sang him home.

FIFTY-FOUR

Sannesh glared at the stone. It was white and very smooth, except where carved shapes rose from it. The smoothest patch was directly in front of him; he had chosen it because of this. He had imagined he would fashion something spectacular out of this very white, very empty place—but once he had sat down, with hammer and chisel beside him, he had had no idea what to do. This was his tenth day sitting here with the sea at his back, tempting him with waves. His tenth. Some of his friends had *finished* their carvings in seven.

"Nothing yet, hmm?" Sannesh started and knocked the chisel with his foot. Nannia always crept up on him so silently, and he was always surprised, even now that he was twelve and should be more composed. He shifted his glare from the stone to her knees, which were lined with salt and scratches.

"Go away," he said—but his sister did not. She squatted down beside him and pretended to study his piece of the stone wall. He bit his lip to keep himself from saying something she would laugh at.

"A big thing," she said, tapping her own lip with a forefinger. "Yes: something extremely large that won't require much skill. Perhaps a rock. That's it! You could carve a rock in the stone, and—"

"Go away," he said again, loudly enough that his voice did not tremble. This time she did go—not because he had told her to but because someone was calling her from the shore.

He looked at her carving as her running footsteps faded behind him. He attempted not to look at it ever, but this time he could not help himself. It was to his right, at the top of the wall. Their father had told them that this wall used to stand on its end in a pool of water. Sannesh could not picture this. It was a wall, very long and a bit taller than him—and Nannia had carved a vine in its upper right corner. So high, such a prominent location—he shivered at the boldness that had made her choose it. She was always certain of herself and her skills. She had carved her vine, with its one loop and its single flower, in six days when she was ten. The adults still talked about it, especially about how brilliantly she had managed to shape it around the tree that her uncle had carved, right after the pillar had toppled and become a wall. The tree trunk was broad and its branches wound halfway along the length of the stone. Nannia and Sannesh's father had carved some of the leaves. Anyone who couldn't think of something original simply added more leaves or blossoms. Sannesh was determined that he would not need to resort to this.

At least Mother's shell is ugly, he thought, reaching up to trace its rough swirls. He could see where she had gouged at the stone then drawn the chisel back and begun again. "It doesn't need to be ambitious, Sann," she had said to him many times, particularly in the last ten days. "It doesn't even have to be pretty—after all, look what I did. Just carve something that seems true, to you."

That, he decided as he trudged back to the houses two useless hours later, was exactly the problem. There was nothing "true" about tree trunks and leaves and flowers. Shells he had seen, washed up on the shore—but none with a living thing within, like the clawed creature his mother had tried to carve. But she had seen a creature like this, in the other Nasranesh; and Nannia had heard vines singing, from an island to the southwest, and had formed hers from the colours and textures she had heard. He heard no singing. This was not uncommon: many of the other children, and some of the adults, could not hear the songs of other places. His parents had told him that most of the selkesh who had crossed the ocean had lost this ability, quickly or slowly, after their return to Nasranesh. His uncle had been one of these, Sannesh knew. But his mother still heard the songs, and so did his sister—and his father heard them more clearly than anybody else, though he hardly ever spoke of it.

Sannesh was silent at the evening meal. A group of young selkesh had swum out to the living ocean and brought their spears back bristling with fish. This did not happen often, since the trip was very long and dangerous. People ate the fish, and praised the young ones who had got it. Sannesh listened to them, from his family's fire, and was too sullen to say, "I'll swim that far someday," or, "I'll take the boat that Aldron of the Flames left, or I'll build my own, and I'll bring fruit back from an island." He was usually sure of such statements—but if he could not manage even a small carving, what was the likelihood he would be able to succeed at more challenging things?

"You're very quiet tonight," his mother said. He shrugged, relieved that Nannia was not at their fire to offer her opinion on the matter. He was grateful too for the shadows of nightfall and dust that hid his face, and for the food that had made his mother too content to press him.

Later that night, though, his father lingered by Sannesh's pallet after his mother had left. Nannia was still off somewhere, swimming or running with her countless friends; she might not come back to the house she and Sannesh shared until the moon had set. It was just Sannesh now, lying beneath his fur blanket—and his father, kneeling, looking down at him. Sannesh could feel this gaze even though his face was turned to the rock.

"It's difficult," his father said at last. "The carving."

Sannesh shifted on the pallet as if he were merely trying to arrange his body more comfortably. He did not answer; perhaps his father would think he was too tired to speak. But he waited there beside the pallet. Sannesh's uncle Mallesh had been a silent man, from what Sannesh could recall of him. He had had a puckered scar on his throat and hardly ever talked. He had seemed always to be somewhere outside of words. Sannesh's father was like that a bit too, when he was not laughing with his children or telling stories. *He was a captive,* Sannesh thought, *and he suffered, and so he is sometimes quiet.* This thought made him squirm with shame, as it always did.

"My leaves took two weeks to carve," his father finally said, and Sannesh turned his head a little. "Two weeks! And they're crude things, even so. Though not," his father added after a pause, "as terrible as your mother's horn-shell crab."

Sannesh could not laugh—not quite. "But you knew what it was you were carving. You'd *seen* leaves, and Nannia heard something that helped her do her vine, but I have nothing to help me."

His father's hand was cool against Sannesh's forehead; so cool, so comforting that he did not even try to flinch away from it. "You don't have to carve now. You can wait until things are clearer for you."

"No"—shaking his head so that his father's hand fell away—"almost all my friends have already carved, and I know it's important to you ..." He bit his lower lip, hard.

"When we were boys," his father said, as Sannesh touched one of the amber pieces that lined these inner walls, "Mallesh always wanted more, and I always wanted less. So what's important to me is that you be content. Truly, this is what I want. If you're distressed by the carving, don't do it."

The amber piece closest to Sannesh's right ear was very bumpy. He knew without looking what was within: one tiny, transparent wing. From a starmoth, his parents had told them—beautiful creatures that had winked like points of fire above the pools that had lain within walls of earth. This one's wing had been torn from its body, so Sannesh would never know what the whole moth had been. But the wing was so familiar to him now that he could see it in the dark: curves and a point, white speckled with a darker colour, maybe green.

"I want to do one," he said, expecting his father to nod and smile and say good night. Instead he waited, quiet again, and Sannesh looked up into his face. "I need to," he said, groping for words but safe as long as his father was meeting his gaze, "because of my friends, and because it's important to you. And because I can't hear land or water singing, and carving something would make me feel more like a real selkesh." He paused. The sea was high tonight; he heard the waves pounding the rock of the shore. "Because," he said slowly, "you tell us so many stories about how things were. If I could carve something, I'd be part of the story, even though I'm not really. Or ..." He lifted his fists and ground them against his closed eyes.

"Sann, you *are* the story. It's yours, whether or not you carve or hear singing." Sannesh felt hands on his hair, lips brushing his forehead. He heard his father rise and part the fur hanging. The waves were louder as he stood there in the opening. Then the hanging fell.

Sannesh did not sleep in the new silence. His father's words often made him feel restless, larger than his own body. Now he was more than that: he was huge. Part of him wanted to get up and run into the waves, to swim and breathe where the water was calm—but he did not move. He lay on his side with his fingertips touching amber, thinking about a starmoth and the lines he might cut in stone to complete it.

When Nannia slipped in just before dawn, Sannesh was still awake. She groaned as she stretched out on her pallet. After that she made no noise for so long that he thought she had fallen asleep.

"Carve a big clod of earth," she said suddenly. "That'd be easy, even for you."

"Be quiet," he said, smiling, filling the rock house and all the night beyond like a thousand glowing wings.

~

Leish walked among the houses and the black pools that bubbled and spat. Some selkesh spoke his name as he passed; others simply held up their hands. The fossil stones that formed the outsides of the houses shone in the guttering light of the fires. The air still smelled of blackened fish. Leish breathed it in and thought again, as always, of Mallesh. Eight years ago he had set off swimming in search of fish. So he had said, in his almost wordless way, to Leish. He had never swum back again. There had been others through the years who had disappeared into the sea. Weak-bodied or weak-spirited, some selkesh said—but Leish imagined Mallesh going deeper and deeper into silence, and was not so sure.

The waves were very high, and Leish felt spray on his face and limbs long before he reached the shore. He stood where the water could find him, washing up and over his feet then back again to leave them cool and stinging. The shackle scar on his ankle ached in salt water even now. He lifted the foot and turned it gently round until it ached less.

"Is he asleep?" As she spoke, Dallia rubbed her palm across Leish's back, over his other scars.

"No. Not yet."

"And Nannia, is she back?"

Leish drew Dallia forward to stand beside him. She leaned into his arms. "Not yet," he said, and chuckled as he felt her sigh.

After a time she said, "All the singing's faint for me tonight, even the islands'. Can you still hear everything?"

He pressed his lips against her hair. "Yes. All the same songs. Silences too—old and new ones."

She straightened and stretched. Her own scar was white, no longer purple. It was mostly hidden by her hair, except when she shook it back as she was doing now. When she turned to him and said, "Let's swim this dust away before we check on the children," he smiled and took her hand.

They walked against the waves until their feet found the rock shelf that divided shallow sea from deep. They stood up and balanced, their fingers and webs spread wide, nearly touching. The light from moon and water turned their skin to scales, to shell, to shades of moss and earth. A wave rolled past them. Dallia teetered and slipped away beneath. Leish waited. He heard laughter far behind him, tasted salt and wind and ash. Then the ocean rose to meet him, and he swam.

Epilogue

"Choose among the deeds of every queen," my own Queen commanded me, "and craft for me one tome in which these will be documented. Do not linger overlong on any single queen, for the greatness of the line must be seen to have been shared equally."

I have read tablets and scrolls and books. I have read every word chiselled or written about every queen of this realm since its beginning. My own parchment lies thick on the desk before me—and yet I cannot fulfill the task set me by my Queen. The queens' deeds have not been equal in wisdom or majesty. I will never hold up my own time as a mirror to bygone eras. Such assertions would be untrue; and, even worse, deception.

Sarhenna was the First, and Galha was the Last: this I now know. Galha was the Last, and this realm has been sunk in the shadow of inconsequence ever since. She was a warrior queen, a ruler of passion and prowess. She was a learned queen, whose reign produced an unprecedented number of scribes and writings, both historical and contemporary. And after her? The ancient bloodline of the queens was broken. There were no more mindpowers, and no more resounding triumphs. The Queensrealm lost its hold on its northern and western borders. There were no more consort-scribes; the throne behind the queens' now belongs to the princes, who neither record nor instruct. The Scribestower is nearly empty, for there are, in my time, but eight students (and only three of these show any promise). Some in the realm insist that the queen whose reign I have long attempted to document is as wise, in her way, as any of her predecessors. Some say that Luhr's fountains and trees shine as brightly as they did in Galha's time. I know this is not so. The children who sail their parchment boats in these fountains know this is not so. How, then, can I complete the book my Queen has demanded of me?

I will think more on this tomorrow. Tonight I will imagine myself a child again, listening to tales in the gentle place before sleep—for stories told in darkness are the only ones that shine.